DARK TIMES FOR THE CLARKS FACTORY GIRLS

MAY ELLIS

Boldwood

First published in Great Britain in 2025 by Boldwood Books Ltd.

Copyright © May Ellis, 2025

Cover Design by Colin Thomas

Cover Images: Colin Thomas

A CIP catalogue record for this book is available from the British Library.

Paperback ISBN 978-1-83533-039-5

Large Print ISBN 978-1-83533-040-1

Hardback ISBN 978-1-83533-038-8

Ebook ISBN 978-1-83533-041-8

Kindle ISBN 978-1-83533-042-5

Audio CD ISBN 978-1-83533-033-3

MP3 CD ISBN 978-1-83533-034-0

Digital audio download ISBN 978-1-83533-035-7

This book is printed on certified sustainable paper. Boldwood Books is dedicated to putting sustainability at the heart of our business. For more information please visit https://www.boldwoodbooks.com/about-us/sustainability/

Boldwood Books Ltd, 23 Bowerdean Street, London, SW6 3TN

www.boldwoodbooks.com

This story is dedicated to all those who fought for our freedom in the 1914–1918 war and those who fought their own battles for the freedom to live by their pacifist principles. Each followed their hearts and did what they believed to be right.

PROLOGUE
JANUARY 1916, BRISTOL

'No!' he screamed. 'Don't go that way! Tell them to stop!'

Someone gripped his arm, shaking it. 'Gerald! Wake up, son.'

'Mother?' He looked around, peering through the smoke, his fear increasing ten-fold. 'You shouldn't be here. It's not safe.'

'It's all right, my darling. It's just a dream.' She touched his cheek, which was clammy with sweat and tears. 'Come on now, Gerald. Open your eyes. Look at me, that's it. Wake up. You're home. You're safe.'

Her voice finally penetrated the panic that had paralysed him and he opened his eyes. His vision was filled with the loving face of his mother. She smiled at him through her own tears, wiping away the sights and sounds of the nightmare that had gripped him. He shook his head, trying to shake off the fear and the noise, his hands reaching for the sanctuary of his mother's arms.

'I'm sorry,' he said. 'I didn't mean to wake you.'

She stroked his hair, her touch soothing him as his racing heart began to slow a little. 'And I'm sorry that it still haunts you. But I confess, I'd rather this than have you still serving in France.

At least now I know you're safe, although it breaks my heart to see how it still grieves you so.'

He sat up, feeling the damp of his sweat-soaked pyjama top against his back. 'I think what bothers me so much is the fact that, no matter what I did, I couldn't save enough of them,' he said. 'I probably should have stayed, but...'

'No, son. You shouldn't have. You volunteered right from the start, and lord knows what you witnessed out there. But a soul can only take so much and I fear yours has reached its limit. Anyway, you're still doing your bit for the nation here with your hard work at the market garden. With the German blockades, we need to grow as much food as we can.'

Gerald sighed and scrubbed at his face with his hands. 'I know. I've enjoyed working with the soil these past months.' It was a long way from the work he'd done as a solicitor's clerk before he'd volunteered to join an ambulance unit when war had been declared. He had chosen that path because, as a Quaker and a pacifist, he could not bring himself to take up arms against his fellow men. Instead, he had decided to serve as a stretcher-bearer and first aider, doing his best to save lives rather than end them. But, after so many months in France where he'd witnessed so much death and destruction, he had needed to come home and work on the land, to find solace in nature.

His mother was silent for a while, soothing him with her gentle touch. When he felt calm enough, he turned and gave her a weary smile. 'I'm all right now,' he said. 'You should go back to bed and get some rest.'

When she finally left him alone, Gerald knew he wouldn't be able to get back to sleep again. He got up and stripped off his sweat-sodden pyjamas and pulled on a fresh pair and his dressing gown, knotting the belt against the pre-dawn chill before he slipped his feet into the sheepskin slippers Mother had given him at Christmas. As quietly as he could, he left his room and went downstairs to the kitchen. There, he lit a lamp and stoked the range. While he waited for the kettle to boil, he went into the parlour and cleaned out the grate, laying fresh coal and kindling ready to light later. By the time he'd wrapped last night's ashes in an old newspaper and taken them out to the dustbin, the water had boiled. He made himself a cup of Horlicks and sat by the range to drink it.

The after-effects of his nightmare left him feeling nauseous and anxious. When he'd first come home in October, he'd had them every night but over the weeks, they had become less frequent. This week, however, following the government's approval of the conscription bill, they had returned more vivid than ever. He had said nothing to Mother, for fear of worrying her. But he knew that he would now be expected to take up arms like every other able-bodied man aged between eighteen and forty-one.

If his life-long pacifist beliefs hadn't been enough to deter him, his experiences as a volunteer with the ambulance unit would have persuaded him that fighting wasn't the answer. He was determined he wouldn't answer the call, but would instead seek an exemption certificate from one of the tribunals being set up around the country. He hoped that his time spent in France and current employment at the market garden would help his case. After all, food production was work of national importance.

But whatever happened, he would never take up arms. He would rather die than take another man's life.

1

MAY 1916

'What are you thinking, Louisa? You can't wear that for church. Go and put your Sunday dress on,' her mother ordered.

Louisa paused at the bottom of the stairs and looked down at her outfit. She was wearing a blouse and skirt with her walking shoes. It was much the same as she wore every other day of the week to go to work at the Clarks shoe factory.

'I'm not going to church,' she said. 'I thought I'd go for a walk as it's fine.'

Her mother huffed. 'Not this again. You've been home for weeks now. We can't keep making excuses for you. Now get ready. You're coming to church with us.'

Louisa closed her eyes for a moment, her stomach churning and her heart hurting. In her mind's eye, she saw everything she'd lost. Going to church with her parents wouldn't help. She'd tried it once last month when she'd arrived back in Street and she knew she wouldn't go again. It wouldn't change anything. Unable to bear it, she opened her eyes again and looked at her mother, outwardly calm.

'No,' she said, her voice firm. 'I'm not.'

Her father came into the hall to stand by her mother. 'What's this?' he asked.

'She says she won't go,' his wife told him.

'Nonsense. We've indulged you enough, Louisa. Get changed.'

Louisa sighed and shook her head. 'I won't, Pa. I told you. I'm done with it. I'll have nothing to do with a church that encourages this rotten war.'

'Don't talk rubbish, lass,' her father grumbled.

'It's not rubbish,' she replied. 'I heard a young lad at Walton church got thrown out the choir because he didn't want to sing the national anthem after his brother was killed in France.'

'Surely not,' said her mother. 'People spread such nonsense these days.'

'It's true. His sister told me. The poor lad is grieving and can't bear all the patriotic fervour, but instead of understanding and trying to help him, they threw him out as though he's the one in the wrong. Not very Christian of them, is it?'

Her father sighed. 'That's another parish, not ours.'

Louisa shrugged. She knew full well she'd be treated even worse than that poor lad if anyone at the church knew her secret. 'I'm still not going.'

'You must,' her mother insisted. 'People are asking where you are. They know you're back at work, so we can't keep saying you're not well.'

Louisa almost smiled at that. Her parents were so bothered by appearances that they were prepared to lie to protect their reputation. It was laughable and infuriating at the same time. 'Then tell them the truth. Maybe it would be better out in the open.'

Her mother looked horrified. 'Never! No one must know, Louisa, do you hear me? If you want any kind of decent life in this village, you'll stop being so silly and start behaving, young lady.'

She fought the urge to laugh, not that any of this was in any way funny. It simply amused her that her mother was so determined to act as though going to church and pretending nothing had happened would somehow miraculously make everything better.

'We all know it's too late for that, Ma. What you're really saying is you expect me to go into God's house and lie through my teeth. Well, I shan't.'

Her mother looked at Louisa's father in despair. He scowled.

'If you won't go to church, we'll have to get the reverend to come and talk some sense into you.'

Louisa felt her ever-present grief tighten around her heart as a now-familiar rage began to rise in her throat like bile. 'Fine,' she said. 'But bear in mind, I won't lie to a clergyman. If I have to talk to the reverend, I'll be sure to confess *all* my sins. I doubt he'll want me to taint his church after that.'

Her mother covered her mouth with her hands, her distress evident. 'Why are you being like this?' she cried. 'We only want what's best for you!'

There used to be a time, before she'd fallen in love with Mattie – and before she'd lost him and their future together – when her mother's tears would have moved her.

'No, Ma,' she said, her voice as ice cold as her anger. 'You want what looks best for you and Pa. What you think will increase your standing in the village, *not* what's best for me, because you stopped listening to me long ago. If you truly wanted it, you would've let me marry Mattie when he asked.'

Her father waved a hand in front of his face. 'You were too young to know what was for the best,' he said. 'And it wouldn't have stopped him from dying, would it?'

Louisa regarded him coolly. She could have argued the point with him, considering she was still convinced, despite his denials, that it was pressure from her Anglican father that had forced

Mattie, a Quaker and pacifist, to enlist. If he'd accepted Mattie's sincere beliefs and not pushed him to fight, he would still be alive today. But she saw no point in continuing the argument. It wouldn't bring Mattie back. Nothing would.

'Maybe not,' she said instead. 'But it would've meant I'd bear Mattie's name and could've kept our son.' As it was, she'd had to flee her home and throw herself on the mercy of Mattie's brother and sister-in-law, who were now bringing up her child as their own. She turned away, picking up her bag containing her art supplies and preparing to leave the house.

'Be reasonable, Louisa.' Her father's voice was gruff with impatience. 'What kind of a life would it have been for you, eh? Or the child?'

She blinked, her ice-cold rage giving way briefly to the red-hot pain of grief and loss that was never very far away. 'I don't know, Pa,' she replied, tamping it down and taking refuge in the cold again as she opened the door. 'All I know is that you gave me no choice and robbed me of something so precious, I'm not sure I can ever forgive you.' She stepped outside. 'I doubt I'll be back for luncheon,' she told them as she closed the door behind her and walked away.

2

'Thank you, Friends,' said the elder in charge of this morning's worship session at the Quaker Meeting House. After an hour of silent contemplation punctuated only by the occasional cough, the congregation began to move and greet each other, the noise level rising as their consciousness moved from inward reflection to outward communion with their neighbours.

Kate shifted on the wooden bench where she sat with her friend Jeannie. Her bottom had gone numb after sitting still for so long. She wasn't used to it yet, having grown up attending services at Holy Trinity Church with her late mother. Although services there were about the same length of time – or longer when the reverend got a bee in his bonnet and decided to expand on his sermon – the services there were punctuated by the ritual of standing to sing hymns, kneeling for prayers and approaching the altar to receive communion. Although she was happy with her decision to join the Quakers, she did miss the music at Holy Trinity. She liked it and it seemed strange to sit here at the Friends' Meeting House in silence instead of singing hymns of praise. Still, she wasn't about to complain. Without her dear ma, it just didn't feel right at Holy Trinity any more, especially once her brute of a pa had moved his fancy woman into the family home. Kate had felt ashamed and hated the pitying looks she'd received every time she attended the church, because no one there had lifted a finger to help her. It had got worse when her sweetheart, Ted Jackson, announced he was enlisting and had broken up with her. She still didn't understand why he'd gone so cold in the end. She had been sure they were getting along fine.

'Are you all right, Katie?' asked Jeannie as they stood up.

Dismissing her thoughts and resisting the urge to rub her bottom in an effort to get some feeling back, she nodded. 'I just don't know if I'm doing this right,' she confessed in a whisper, not wanting anyone else to overhear. 'I mean, I try to look within myself and think about the light, like you told me. But I find my mind wanders. Then, when I realise, I feel guilty and try to focus on God and all that, but I'm beginning to think that He's given up on me and I'll never see the light like I'm supposed to.'

Jeannie slipped her arm through Kate's. 'I'm sure He hasn't,' she assured her softly as they made their way out of the Meeting House. 'I find it difficult sometimes and I was born to this. Don't be so hard on yourself.'

Kate loved her friend for being so kind and patient. But she couldn't help feeling a little guilty that instead of thinking about God and trying to work out what He wanted her to do with her life, she had spent the last hour thinking about her ma and how much she missed her and how much she hated her pa for the awful way he'd treated her. Not very Christian of her, she knew, but she couldn't get those thoughts out of her head.

And whenever she'd managed to push them aside, memories of Ted had invaded her mind, which wasn't much better. He'd been her sweetheart for months and they'd grown especially close after her ma had died and his oldest brother had been killed in the trenches, their grief drawing them together. Then he'd suddenly upped and enlisted and told her before he left that he wanted to make a complete break because even if he survived the war, he had no intention of coming back to Street. It had been such a shock. It wasn't as though they'd had a great love affair like Louisa and Mattie had, but she'd thought they were close, and she could imagine a future with him. But he'd been gone for months now and she'd not heard a word from him. She didn't know why she was suddenly thinking about him again.

She couldn't help feeling that there was more to Ted's sudden decision to cut his ties with her than he'd been willing to let on. It hadn't made sense. But he'd been true to his word. No one had heard from him since he'd left on the troop train. Kate wasn't even sure whether he wrote to his parents. If he did, they certainly weren't telling her.

It made her sad to think about Ted, then she'd get angry. He wasn't worth thinking about. He'd been the one to turn his back on her, leaving her alone again at the mercy of her drunken pa. If it hadn't been for her siblings and friends, she'd never have escaped. She thanked God every day that she had found sanctuary in the form of lodgings with Mrs Searle – or Auntie Betty as she preferred to be called. She had lost her son Mattie in the trenches, and then Betty's other son Will had moved to Lincolnshire with his wife, Kate's sister Peg, to work in a tank factory. So the widow had been happy to take Kate in, providing her with the love and support that Ted had withdrawn so suddenly and without any explanation, and that her pa and his floozy had denied her.

Kate followed Jeannie out of the Meeting House, nodding politely to the elders as they went. Outside, they spotted Jeannie's brother Lucas talking to Tom, one of the engineers from the factory. Kate smiled as Jeannie's cheeks filled with warmth at the

sight of him. Even though Jeannie swore she had no feelings for
Tom and that she wasn't interested in finding another sweetheart
after being cheated on by Douglas Baker a few months back, it
was obvious to Kate that her friend was warming to Tom.

When Kate would have gone over to say hello to the lads,
Jeannie grabbed her arm and pulled her in the other direction,
towards the road.

'Don't you want to say hello?' said Kate.

Jeannie shook her head. 'No,' she said.

Kate frowned, looking between where Lucas and Tom were
chatting and Jeannie, whose cheeks were getting pinker. 'I was
only going to say hello. Has something happened?'

Again, Jeannie shook her head, her lips thinning. 'Not a
blesséd thing.'

'Ah,' she said with a small smile. 'Don't give up, love. I've seen
the way he looks at you, even if he's taking his time getting round
to declaring himself.'

She knew that Jeannie had a soft spot for Tom. But she was
wary of him. At first, Kate thought it was because she'd been
embarrassed about the incident with Sid Lambert, who had made
a grab for Jeannie one night outside the Street Inn. Tom had come
across them after she'd kneed Sid in the privates to get away from
him and had restrained the drunken lout while Jeannie got away.
But she confessed it wasn't just the embarrassment of that that
made her wary. Jeannie had thought that Tom was a drinker
because she had seen him coming out of the inn. But then she'd
found out that he'd been lodging there before moving into a room
at the home of a local temperance couple, so she'd realised he
wasn't a drinker. They wouldn't have had him in their house if
he was.

She had continued to avoid him, though, using the excuse
that he wasn't a Quaker and she'd decided she'd only consider

someone of her own faith as a potential sweetheart. But then Tom had started coming to Friends' meetings and had befriended her brothers and Kate had thought that Jeannie was finally softening towards him.

Jeannie shook her head. 'I don't think he's going to make any declarations where I'm concerned,' she said. 'He's friendly enough, but he pays more attention to my brothers than to me. I'm sure he doesn't think of me as anything other than their sister.'

Kate linked arms with Jeannie and leaned in closer. 'Nonsense! He doesn't look at you like you're someone's sister, believe me. At least, not when he thinks no one's watching. D'you think Lucas has warned him off?'

Jeannie shrugged. 'I don't know. But I'm not going to ask him, that's for sure.'

'I thought you liked him.'

Jeannie sighed. 'I think I do. But... I don't know.' She looked around to make sure no one else was listening. 'You know when he rescued me after Sid grabbed me outside the Street Inn six months back?'

Kate nodded.

'Well, he scared me a bit.'

Kate frowned and moved closer, feeling fierce. 'Why? What did he do to you?'

She shook her head. 'Nothing to me. But, well, he got really riled up at Sid. I can't explain it, but it was as though he was burning with rage. He looked at me with so much passion in his eyes, I was sure he wanted me to tell him to set about Sid. I was convinced he could've killed him if I'd just given him the nod, and he'd have taken great satisfaction in doing it.' She sighed. 'It scared the living daylights out of me to be honest, just as much as Sid's attack did, and that's why I ran all the way home.'

'But Tom's a gentle soul,' Kate protested. 'I'm not saying you were wrong, Jeannie, love. But every time I've seen him, he's been kind and polite. He doesn't get annoyed when he's called back to the Machine Room time and again to repair the machines when the girls mess them up. I swear some of them do it deliberately, hoping he'll be sent up. He's got the patience of a saint.'

'I know,' said Jeannie. 'And the more I see of him, the more I like him. But... I just can't get that look of his out of my mind. He's got hidden depths, Kate. What if he's got a temper that he's hiding from everyone?'

Kate thought about it for a few moments. 'You know what I think?' she asked.

'No. What?'

'It seems to me that he came across Sid attacking you and it enraged him that a drunken lout should treat a decent girl like that. I'm sure any of our brothers and any other decent lad in the village would have reacted in the same way. We all know Sid's a bully and most people give him a wide berth, but there's not many lads who would let him get away with what he did to you, I'm sure.'

'I don't know.' Jeannie looked sceptical. 'Sid's a big fellow.'

Kate shrugged. 'That doesn't matter. You bested him on your own, didn't you? Even if Tom hadn't arrived, you'd have got away from him. You'd already kneed him in the privates and had the big oaf on the floor, writhing in pain.' She grinned. 'Much as I wish it hadn't happened to you, I do regret missing that spectacle.'

Jeannie released grudging laugh. 'He did scream.'

'Yeah, and people still haven't let him forget he was beaten by a girl,' giggled Kate. 'You know he's gone now, don't you? The recruiting officers escorted him to the train after he spent weeks trying to give them the slip.'

Jeannie nodded. Her former sweetheart Douglas had thought

that pretending to be a Friend would mean he could get exemption from fighting when conscription came in. He'd gone off for basic training now, unable to get out of enlisting because the whole village knew he'd been lying to Jeannie about wanting to be a Quaker. The irony was that his deception had been exposed when she'd caught him kissing Sid's sister Doris at a dance. Now both lads were gone to fight and, much as Jeannie was against war, Kate knew she was glad they were both gone from Street.

Since conscription had come into effect in March, more and more unmarried men had enlisted. And now the government had announced that married men aged eighteen to forty-one had to enlist, which meant that Kate's brothers were now likely to be sent to fight.

'Do you know when your brothers have got to go?' Jeannie asked her.

Kate shook her head. 'No,' she sighed. 'They've filled in their forms and been told to expect a call-up soon.' She grimaced. 'I hope they don't have to go, but it's not looking good, is it? I think George's father-in-law is trying to get him an exemption on account of him being needed in his haulage business. But I doubt if that'll help. My sister-in-law Ada is talking about leaving the kiddies with her ma and taking George's place on the lorries.'

Jeannie looked shocked. 'Really? I wouldn't want to try and control one of those big vehicles. And how will she manage, hauling the goods off the lorry when she makes a delivery?'

'I have no idea. I think she's going to rely on the people where she delivers to help her. If there's no able-bodied men around, it'll be down to lasses, old fellows and young lads to do the lifting and carrying.'

'Can she even drive?'

'She says so. I've never seen her behind the wheel, although she grew up helping her pa, so I expect she knows what to do. I wouldn't want to try it. Those lorries George drives are great lumbering beasts. I doubt I'd have the strength to turn the steering wheel, let alone drag the goods on and off the back.'

Neither of them were aware of Lucas approaching until he spoke.

'What are you two yakking about?' he asked. 'I thought you'd be half-way home by now.'

Kate turned to him with raised eyebrows. 'You're a fine one to talk about yakking, Lucas Musgrove. You and Tom were chatting up a storm. Care to share your gossip with us?'

He chuckled. 'I couldn't compete with you girls. But if it makes you feel any better about all that hot air you've been sharing with my sister, Tom has offered to build me a splint for my arm. He reckons he can make something with leather and metal to hold it firm at the wrist so I've got more chance of using my weak hand.'

Jeannie looked around. Tom was nowhere to be seen.

'He's gone,' Lucas told her when he saw her looking. 'Said he can get on with designing it straight away. I'm going to pop round to his lodgings later so he can take some measurements.'

'That's kind of him,' said Kate, giving Jeannie a significant look. 'Anyway, I'd best be off. I can see Auntie Betty is saying her goodbyes. I'll see you at work tomorrow, Jeannie.'

The girls hugged and Kate joined Betty Searle, turning left out of the gate in the direction of their home in The Mead.

* * *

'So what do you think?' Lucas asked Jeannie as they turned in the opposite direction and headed along the High Street towards their cottage in West End at the other end of the village. 'Tom thinks with a firm splint my wrist will be less likely to twist like it has been.'

'It's worth a try, isn't it?' she replied, adjusting her shorter stride to try and keep up with his longer legs. 'Are you still getting pins and needles in your fingers?'

When he'd come home from the war, his injured right hand had been completely numb. But thanks to the hand massages Louisa had started doing for him – and had taught Jeannie to do for her brother as well – Lucas had begun to get some sensation back.

He nodded. 'I am. It's damned painful and irritating sometimes. But then I remember how awful it was when I couldn't feel anything and I'm grateful for the discomfort.' He held out his hand. It looked smaller than his left hand somehow. It seemed that his injury had caused it to wither. He frowned at it, as though willing his strength back into it and all five of his fingers twitched. He smiled and glanced at her. 'I couldn't do that a month ago,' he reminded her. 'It's still nowhere near good enough for me to go back to leather cutting by hand, but I'll get there one day, you see if I don't.'

He'd been a skilled clicker – the name given to leather cutters at Clarks on account of the clicking noise of their shears – but his injury to his dominant right hand had meant that he was put on operating a pressing machine when he returned. It was less skilled and frustrated him, but it was better than some of the returning injured soldiers could manage.

Jeannie nodded. 'You will, I'm sure. I pray about it every day. Just...' She hesitated, not sure if she should say anything.

'Just what?' he asked.

'I just worry that if you get better, they might send you back to fight again,' she confessed.

He scowled. 'I'll not go again,' he said. He took a deep breath, clearly looking within at the memories he refused to share with his family. 'But it's not likely. I couldn't use a gun while I'm like this and I don't expect any progress I make to be swift. It's taken months to get to this point and the doctors said I'm not likely to ever be fit for combat because of the damage the shrapnel did. Even if I do get all the feeling and strength back, it could take years. Please God, the war won't go on much longer. Let's face it, sis, both sides will run out of men if they carry on losing them at the rate they've been doing.' Again, that now-familiar shadow crossed his expression and Jeannie felt her heart squeeze at the thought of what he and so many other young men had gone through.

'What if the Germans win, Lucas?' she asked.

He glanced at her. 'You mustn't fret over that,' he said, his voice firm. 'No point in getting het up about something that might not happen. Our lads are doing their best. The Hun are losing as many men as we are, if not more. We have to believe we're going to win. Thinking we're going to lose is like admitting defeat and waving a white flag. We can't do that.'

He was right, of course. She nodded but she couldn't shake the dread that filled her blood at the very thought of being defeated. 'You're right,' she said. 'We have to think positive.' She only hoped the war ended soon, because if their twin brothers Peter and John were called up when they reached eighteen, she doubted Ma would survive it. Jeannie had worried that Ma was going to waste away and die when Lucas had gone off to fight and she was still barely recovered even now he was home safe. She hadn't come to the Meeting today because she was still so weak.

'Right, let's get a move on. I'm ready for my dinner, and I told Tom I wouldn't be long.'

Jeannie was out of breath from trying to keep up with her much taller brother by the time they reached the cottage in West

End. She tried not to think about how Tom was becoming a friend to her brothers and a regular visitor to the Musgrove home. She'd meant what she said to Kate. Much as she liked him and would like to get to know him better, there was something about how he was that night outside the Street Inn that worried her – a darkness within him that he kept well hidden, but which he had been hard put to conceal when he had his hands on Sid. Even though she'd seen no evidence of it in the months since then, it had made such an impression on her that she doubted she could ever forget it.

3

Jeannie, Kate and Louisa were walking to the Clarks factory canteen at dinner time a few days later, having decided to celebrate payday with a cooked meal, when they encountered Louisa's father. He glanced at them briefly before he turned away, completely ignoring his daughter and carrying on an animated conversation with the men accompanying him. Louisa sighed and carried on, her head held high, although Kate noticed that her shoulders slumped slightly.

'Are you feeling all right, Lou?' she asked as she and Jeannie linked arms with her.

'Yes,' she said, her voice firm. She didn't say anything else until they were inside the canteen and her father was out of sight. 'We had another row yesterday. Since I took myself off for another walk rather than accompany my parents to church on Sunday, they've barely spoken to me.'

'Oh my.' Jeannie's eyes widened. 'What did they say?'

'Threatened to bring the vicar round *to talk some sense into me*,' she said with a humourless laugh. 'I said I'd welcome the opportunity to have a frank discussion with him about how Pa had stopped me from marrying Mattie because he was a Quaker.'

'You didn't!' said Kate, her eyes wide as she realised that Louisa must have threatened to have a *frank discussion* that would entail a full confession to the clergyman about the real reason why she'd left Street after Mattie's death. She couldn't help but admire her friend's strength, but it also worried her that things were going to get worse for her if she defied her parents like this.

Louisa shrugged as they moved along the queue for food. 'He didn't like that, so now we've got a stalemate – I won't go to church and they're more worried about what folk will say than how I feel.' She kept her voice quiet, her face turned away from others so that they weren't overheard over the chatter and scraping of forks on plates around them.

'Oh, Lou, that's awful. But maybe having a chat with the vicar might help?' Jeannie suggested. 'You know, with your grief.'

Kate wanted to roll her eyes at Jeannie's naivety. She meant well, but of course, she didn't know the real reason behind the problems between Louisa and her parents. Only Kate knew about their friend's baby and how her parents' insistence that she give him up had multiplied her grief over Mattie's death ten-fold.

Louisa shook her head. 'I don't think the reverend will help me, Jeannie.'

'Me neither,' said Kate. 'He's not the kindest of men.'

'But surely,' Jeannie protested. 'He's a man of the cloth. He should be doing what he can to help anyone in his congregation who's suffering.'

'Like when Ma was dying?' said Kate, eyebrows raised. 'He wouldn't come and give her the sacrament until Ted's ma and pa shamed him into it, just because our Peg married a Quaker.' She shook her head. 'No, you can't expect any sympathy from him.'

'That's… Why, that's just cruel. Surely folk should be able to

expect support from their clergy in times of need? To deny it is...
well, it's unchristian. And folk say the Friends aren't true
Christians!'

Kate smiled. It took a lot to annoy Jeannie. She usually turned
the other cheek. She was definitely one of the most Christian
people Kate knew, along with Auntie Betty, her Quaker landlady.
Where Jeannie and Betty differed from the stuffed shirts like the
vicar and Mr Clements (who, to be fair, could be found across all
denominations) was that they lived their faith – praying daily and
serving others in any way they could. Jeannie didn't need to be
seen to be doing that, or to raise her voice singing praises. Her
faith was quiet and humble. Kate was coming to the conclusion
that she wanted to be more like Jeannie, but she had a feeling that
with her temperament, it would be an uphill climb to achieve
Jeannie's level of serenity.

'Thank you, love.' Lou touched Jeannie's arm. 'If anything, I'd
say you're more Christian than anyone I know. You don't judge.'

Kate nodded. She'd been telling Louisa this all along. Did this
mean she'd decided she could trust Jeannie with her secret at
long last? She hoped so. It was killing her, keeping it from her. But
it was Lou's choice, not hers.

Jeannie frowned. 'It's not our job to judge, but rather to serve.
Why would we judge someone when we're all just weak human
beings?' She tilted her head to one side. 'What I don't understand
is why they're judging you for grieving your loss. Is it really
because Mattie was a Friend and not an Anglican?'

Kate held her breath as Louisa blinked, her expression frozen
for a moment before she blinked again and gave a little nod. Kate
blew her breath out. She'd been suddenly afraid that Louisa was
going to confess to Jeannie right here that it wasn't just Mattie she
was grieving. But this wasn't the time nor the place. Kate shook

her head slightly, her eyes widening as she looked around at the women and girls surrounding them. Lou gave her a confused look before she turned back to Jeannie.

'I heard Pa say it with my own ears,' she said. 'He said he wished he'd never let Mattie near me as he'd had no intention of allowing his daughter to marry outside our own church.'

'So why did he let him court you?' asked Kate, glad that the conversation had moved on. Yes, she wanted her to tell Jeannie, but no one else needed to overhear.

Lou shrugged. 'I'm sure I don't know. I asked Ma. She said he thought I'd grow tired of Mattie – that I was too young to know my own heart and mind – and that she and Pa intended to make sure the next lad who courted me would be from their own congregation.' She gave a humourless laugh. 'But they're in for more disappointment now, because I'll never marry. Especially not a lad chosen by them.'

They collected and paid for their food and found an empty table. As soon as they sat down, Kate opened her mouth to speak, but paused as Jeannie lowered her head and closed her eyes. Her friends waited while she said a silent prayer of thanks for their meal, then Kate spoke up.

'Well, I'm going to the Meeting House with Auntie Betty and Jeannie now, so if you want to come as well, Lou, you won't be the only new one there.'

'Thanks, Kate,' she said. 'I'll think about it. I know if I did decide to attend meetings, I won't feel like I'm a complete stranger.' She nodded, looking determined. 'But regardless, I'm done with Holy Trinity and trying to please Ma and Pa.'

'Are you sure?' said Jeannie. 'I would hate for it to make things worse at home.'

Louisa shrugged. 'It can't get much worse,' she said. 'But, do you know, I'm beyond caring about it. I went to church with them the day after I got back and I knew straight away I couldn't bear it again.'

'Good for you,' said Kate. It might concern Jeannie, who wanted everyone to get along. But Kate knew Louisa's secret and Jeannie didn't. She knew that the chances of Louisa getting back to a loving relationship with her parents was unlikely for as long as they insisted they had done the right thing by her.

A movement in the corner of her eye caught Kate's attention before she could say any more. She turned to see her pa scowling at her. Her breath caught in her throat, the familiar fear and resentment gripping her heart.

'Look at you,' he sneered. 'Using *my* money to stuff your face.'

'It's my money, Pa. I earned it.'

'No, *I* did – by siring you, and giving you a roof over your head and food in your belly for all these years.'

The girls were quiet as Kate stared back at him. She knew it was pointless trying to reason with him, even if he was sober. Reggie Davis had long ago decided that his children owed him and he'd taken their wages for as long as he could get away with it. For her older siblings, escape had come through marriage. But for Kate, she'd been trapped and treated like a slave by her own father, especially after her ma had died and he'd moved his floozy and their illegitimate children into the family home. It had taken an intervention by her siblings and the involvement of Mr Roger Clark and Miss Alice Clark, directors of the company, to enable Kate to claim her own wages and to leave home to live with Auntie Betty.

Kate would forever be grateful to her friends for alerting her siblings to her plight and for Auntie Betty for taking her in. But her father had not forgiven any of them and wasn't above causing a scene whenever he saw Kate.

'Well, I'm not costing you anything nowadays, Pa,' she said. 'Maybe you should send Beryl out to work.'

He scowled at her. 'Leave her out of this. Anyway, she can't work. She's expecting again.'

Kate felt sick. She wasn't surprised, though. The Floozy, as she referred to her father's mistress, had already borne Reggie two children while Kate's ma had still been alive. She had passed them off as her husband's children, fooling the poor man into sending her his wages while he worked away in the merchant navy, even after she'd upped and moved into the Davis home before Kate's ma was barely cold in the ground. He'd come home to surprise her a few months ago, only to find her living at her lover's house. One look had shown him that the children weren't his either – they were the spitting image of Reggie Davis. An awful fight had ensued before he'd gone back to sea. So now, no money arrived for the Floozy and with Kate gone, they had to get by on just Reggie's day rate wages. It gave Kate a measure of satisfaction that, with yet another mouth to feed, there'd be little money for her pa to spend on cider.

'Congratulations,' she said, trying not to let her sarcasm get the better of her. 'But if she can't go out to work, maybe she can take in washing or something.'

Pa's scowl grew deeper. She knew she was taking a risk, goading him like this. They both knew that the Floozy never lifted a finger around the house. Kate didn't want to think about what a mess the place would be in since she'd left. Her ma had been so proud of her home and Kate had done her best to maintain her standards, even when she'd been working all day and looking after her sick ma at night. It had been harder when Pa's other family had moved in. They'd treated her like a slave and she was sure she would be dead now if she hadn't been rescued.

'You're just like your bloody mother,' he spat. 'Holier than thou. I should've beaten you more often.'

Jeannie gasped and Louisa stood up, the legs of her chair scraping loudly on the floor, reminding Kate that her friends as well as everyone in the canteen were witnessing this. She closed her eyes briefly, knowing she had to do something to defuse the situation, otherwise he'd explode and cause a scene that would leave her humiliated for months to come.

'That's uncalled for Mr Davis and you know it,' said Louisa.

'Mind your business,' snapped Pa.

'It's all right, Lou,' said Kate softly, rising to stand next to her and put a hand on her arm.

'No, it's not,' she began, only to be interrupted by another voice.

'Watch your mouth, old man.' It was Fred, Kate's oldest brother, speaking low as he came to stand at his father's side. 'Mr Clements has just walked in and he don't look happy that you're berating his daughter and her friends.'

Reggie Davis turned to glare at his son, even as he took a step back. Kate breathed a quiet sigh of relief at her brother's intervention.

'It's a bad day when a man can't even talk to his own daughter without being criticised,' her pa snapped.

'We know full well you're not being friendly. Leave her alone,' said Fred.

The older man snarled. 'Don't worry, I'm going. Bloody girl's given me indigestion.' Then, without even looking at Kate, he turned and walked out of the canteen.

'You all right, Katie, love?' asked her brother.

She nodded. 'Yeah. Thanks, Fred. I didn't see him until it was too late to avoid him.'

He nodded. 'I'll keep an eye out, make sure he stays away from you.'

As he took his leave, Kate wondered what she'd do if Fred had to go off and fight. Without her brothers to protect her, who knew what Pa was capable of?

4

The hooter sounded the end of the working day and Jeannie sighed with relief. Her fingers ached as she finished the shoe lining she was working on and pulled it off her machine, shutting it down and sitting back. The rumble of machinery ceased as she stretched her aching back, to be replaced by the chatter of three hundred women and girls as they quickly tidied up their work areas, shed their aprons and prepared to the leave the Machine Room.

Jeannie took her time, flexing her fingers and rubbing her sore wrists. She wondered how long it would be before she began suffering with her joints like her ma did after years of working at the factory. Thinking of Ma reminded her to get moving. Although she had been better since Lucas had come home from the war, their widowed mother was far from well and she often needed help from Jeannie to get the supper on the table when the four Musgrove siblings got home from the factory. While she could cajole her brothers into helping with the clear up afterwards, they wouldn't do any of the cooking, so it would be up to Jeannie if Ma was too poorly.

'Come on, slow coaches,' said Kate. 'Let's get out of here.'

Jeannie heard Louisa sigh before she stood up. She looked at her friend, concerned that even all these months since her sweetheart Mattie had been killed, she was still so sad all the time. Not that Jeannie would dream of trying to persuade her to cheer up. Grief was a very personal thing and she'd seen how her own ma was still lost, over a decade since Pa had died. The love that had burned between Mattie and Louisa had been something powerful – almost blinding everyone around them – so Jeannie could understand why it was still so hard for her.

'I don't want to go home,' said Louisa. 'It's not as though we have anything to say to each other.' She looked at Jeannie. 'Maybe I could walk out to West End with you, Jeannie? I wanted to see how Lucas is getting on with that new splint Tom made him.'

It had only taken Tom a few days to put together a splint from leather and metal. Jeannie had been amazed at the workmanship and it really seemed to be helping Lucas overcome the weakness in his arm and hand.

She frowned. 'You're always welcome,' she said, her tone tentative. 'But won't your ma have your supper ready?'

Louisa shrugged. 'I'm not hungry.'

'But won't she worry if you don't come home?' Jeannie persisted. 'I'm not saying don't come to ours, but, well, I'd feel better if you at least popped home and told her where you were going.'

Kate put an arm around both their shoulders. 'She's right, Lou,' she said. 'We know things are bad, but won't it make it worse if you start going off without telling them? I know your ma always insists you eat together as a family and she'll fret if you don't show your face. If she keeps your pa waiting for his meal, it'll only make him grumpier, won't it?'

Jeannie nodded, relieved that Kate was backing her up. 'Why

don't you run home and tell them, then come over? I'd come with you, but I need to get back to make sure Ma's been able to cook. If she's had a bad day, I'll have to start supper.'

Louisa sighed again and nodded. 'You're right. I'll go and tell them. Then I can come and help you.'

Jeannie nodded, thinking she needed to do some extra potatoes so that she could offer Louisa some food if she decided she was hungry after all. There was never a lot of spare food in the pantry because her three lanky brothers had stomachs resembling bottomless pits. Even though there were four of them earning now, they needed to watch their pennies to make sure there was enough food on the table to satisfy the boys' appetites.

Kate seemed to read her thoughts and gave her shoulder a squeeze. 'I'll walk with you, Lou. Maybe it would help keep the peace if you had your supper before you went to Jeannie's. You don't want to be around when the twins start in on their meal – I've never seen lads scoffing their faces like they do. No wonder they're as tall as Lucas already. I reckon they've got hollow legs.'

Jeannie laughed. 'You're not wrong,' she said. 'They're pigs. And now they're so much taller than me I've got no chance of telling them off. Thank God Lucas is home to keep 'em in line.'

Peter and John had been beasts while Lucas had been away in the army. He'd made the mistake of telling them they were the men of the house. They'd taken that as licence to ignore their sister and do nothing to help Jeannie and their ma. They'd even started drinking cider and smoking. She'd been at her wits' end until Louisa had written and told Lucas, and he'd got Kate's brothers to sort the twins out. They'd told them if they wanted to be on the football team, they couldn't be drinking and smoking. That had dealt with that problem, although they still hadn't done much to help Jeannie. But now that Lucas was home, things were much better. Jeannie could leave it to her older brother to maintain discipline in the house and make sure they all shared the chores.

Louisa pulled a face. 'Sorry, Jeannie, I didn't think. It was rude of me to assume I could come round when you'll be busy with your supper. But I really would like to come round later, if that's all right?'

She nodded and smiled. 'You're always welcome, Lou, you know that.'

Louisa kissed her cheek. 'Thanks, Jeannie. I'll see you then.'

At home, Jeannie was relieved to see that Ma had had a good day and a meat pie was cooling while potatoes, carrots and peas were boiling in saucepans. She kissed Ma and set about laying the table as the boys talked about football and work.

'It's not fair they've stopped our schooling,' complained Peter as they sat down to eat. Lessons at the day continuation school for fourteen- to sixteen-year-old workers at Clarks had been suspended as lads were needed to work all hours.

'There's too many gone to fight,' said Lucas. 'They need all hands working so we can keep production going.'

'But what about my apprenticeship chances?' said Peter. 'I've got to get my mathematics and science up to scratch or I'll miss out.'

John scoffed. 'Why d'you want to tie yourself to years of learning on an apprenticeship? You'll be no better than slave labour. You won't catch me signing up for that.'

'There's nothing wrong with having plans for the future,' Peter told him. 'I'd rather a few years of hard graft for little money and then earn a good wage than being stuck making cartons for the rest of my days.'

John shrugged. 'Do what you like. But I won't be missing the book work. I've been thinking I won't be at Clarks much longer. There's better things to do than being stuck in a factory all my life.'

That got everyone's attention. 'What are you talking about?' asked Lucas.

'I've been talking to George Davis. He works for his father-in-law.'

'We know that,' said Jeannie. 'What's that got to do with anything?'

'He's not stuck in a factory. He drives his lorry all over the place. I reckon I want to do that.'

'Not much of a future in it,' said Lucas. 'Unless you marry a lass whose pa owns the business. At least then you've got a chance of being the boss one day.'

'But if I worked for them for a bit – learned to drive and such – I could save up and buy my own lorry. I'd be my own boss.'

Peter laughed. 'You'd be working longer than my apprenticeship to save up for a lorry, you idiot. It's not like you're good with money, is it? And I doubt you'd earn much more in haulage than you would at Clarks.'

'Why would you want to leave Clarks?' asked Ma. 'They're good people. They look after their workers.'

John scowled. 'I hate it,' he said. 'It's like being in prison, working there.'

'So ask for a transfer,' said Lucas. 'There's plenty of other departments to try out before you can say there's nothing there to suit you.'

Ma nodded, looking worried. 'I don't want you to be unhappy,

John, love. But you need to think about your future. One day, you'll have a wife and family to support, and Clarks is your best chance for a steady job around here.'

'I'm sick of being beholden to the Clarks,' he grumbled.

'Even George's father-in-law depends on Clarks for a good portion of his business,' Jeannie pointed out. 'So it won't be much different.'

'Yes it will,' John insisted. 'I'll be out and about, not stuck in the factory.'

No one said anything until Ma got up to fetch the sponge and custard she'd made for pudding. Then Peter leaned forward, keeping his voice low so that she didn't hear.

'There's no point in fretting about the factory,' he said. 'We'll be eighteen soon enough and we'll be called up. I don't reckon anyone will give us exemption – they're turning down a lot of Friends who apply. We'll be sent to the trenches and then you'll get all the fresh air you want. You'll be damned glad to get back to the factory after that, eh, Lucas?'

Jeannie shivered at the thought. 'Hush now,' she hissed as Lucas glared at him. 'You're only fifteen. The war will be over long before you get to eighteen.' At least, she hoped and prayed it would.

Lucas pointed a finger at the twins. Keeping his voice low so Ma wouldn't hear, he said, 'And don't even think about lying about your age to get in early.'

Ma came back and began dishing up the pudding. She didn't seem to notice the tension around the table.

'This looks lovely, Ma.' Jeannie smiled at her as she accepted her bowl.

'I know it's getting a little warm for custard, but there was plenty of milk and I thought, why not?'

'I love custard,' said Lucas.

She chuckled. 'I know, son. You'd eat it even if it was a blazing summer's day, wouldn't you?'

He grinned at her and Jeannie felt her heart swell at the glimpse of the Lucas of old. He was much changed by his war service and his injury, so it was good to see his carefree expression as he enjoyed his pudding.

'John,' said Ma after everyone was served and she joined them to eat. 'I know you're restless, son. But I'd prefer it if you followed Lucas's advice and looked at what else Clarks has to offer before you decide to give up your job there. Will you do that for me?'

John looked rebellious. He flinched as one of his brothers kicked him under the table, glaring at both of them, who glared back.

'It can't hurt, can it?' Jeannie asked, keeping her tone mild.

She was treated to her own glare before he rolled his eyes and sighed. 'All right. But I'm not giving up on the idea. If there's nothing I like at Clarks, I'll be asking George to put in a word for me with his father-in-law.'

* * *

The twins were bickering over the washing up when Louisa arrived. Jeannie ushered her into the parlour where Ma was reading a book.

'Sorry I took so long,' she said softly, so as not to disturb Mrs Musgrove. 'I thought about what you said and decided it would be better to at least eat with them.'

'How was it?' Jeannie asked.

Louisa pulled a face. 'Uncomfortable. I don't know what to say to them these days. If I try to have a normal conversation, it always comes round to someone's son they want to pair me up with. I've told them time and again that I'm not interested, but Ma just won't give up.'

'That must be difficult for you,' Jeannie sympathised. She glanced at her ma, who was engrossed in her novel. She was glad she hadn't started encouraging Jeannie to walk out with any other lads after the fiasco with Douglas Baker.

Ma turned a page and looked up. 'Oh, hello, Louisa, love. How are you?'

'I'm very well, thank you, Mrs Musgrove. And you?'

Ma smiled and nodded. 'I'm fine, my dear. Thank you for asking. I wanted to say how grateful I am that you showed our Jeannie how to do those hand massages you started doing for Lucas.'

'I'm glad to help.'

'Oh, you have indeed. Not only is she helping Lucas; she's been doing them on my gnarled old fingers and it's given me some relief from my arthritis, I can tell you.'

Jeannie nodded. 'It's true,' she confirmed. 'Ma was able to get the dinner cooked and on the table by the time we got home this evening.'

'I'm so pleased it's helping, Mrs Musgrove,' said Louisa. 'My ma swears by it. Her grandpa and his pa were outworkers, hand-sewing sheepskin slippers in their cottages for Clarks back when they started all those years ago. Her grandma taught her how to massage their hands to help keep them supple. They both worked to a good age and never suffered too badly with their joints.'

'Well then,' said a voice from the door. 'We're both mighty thankful for your ma's grandma, aren't we, Ma?'

Louisa turned around to see Lucas smiling at her. She smiled back. Jeannie found her own lips turning up. It was good to see Lou in good spirits.

'Lou wanted to see the splint Tom made you,' said Jeannie.

He held up his right hand and pulled up the sleeve of his shirt to reveal the leather and metal contraption strapped to his wrist with buckles.

Louisa stepped closer to have a better look at it. 'Ooh, it looks like a gauntlet but without the fingers.'

He moved his hand around, examining the splint. 'I suppose it does.'

'Is it helping?'

He nodded. 'My arm aches less when I've got it on.' He twitched his fingers. 'And it seems to make it easier to move my hand. I'm still having trouble gripping anything for more than a moment or two, but I couldn't even do that before.' He stroked the fingers of his left hand across his right hand. 'And I can feel that now. It was completely numb before.'

'I remember,' she said softly.

Jeannie knew that when Louisa had visited Lucas at the military hospital after he'd been brought back to England, she'd held his injured hand and he hadn't even realised that she was touching him. That was when she'd begun massaging it. She'd told Jeannie she'd hoped it might help in some way but she hadn't been sure it would. Jeannie was just grateful that Louisa had thought to try it, because, along with Tom's splint, it *was* making a difference. Lucas was hopeful that one day, he'd have full use of his hand again.

'Tell the twins to put the kettle on, Lucas, lad,' said Ma. 'We haven't even offered our guest a cuppa.'

'I'll do it,' he said. 'They've just finished their chores and gone for a kickabout.'

'Let me help,' said Louisa, following him into the kitchen.

Jeannie watched her go and turned to look at Ma. 'I'd better go as well,' she said.

Ma held up a hand. 'Let them do it, love. You stay here with me.'

Jeannie frowned, not sure what Ma meant. Her mother smiled. 'It's good to see them getting on, isn't it?' she said quietly. 'Lucas could do well with a lass like her at his side.'

'Ma!' She was shocked. 'Tell me you're not match-making.'

She smiled and shook her head. 'Not at all. But they've got a bond since young Mattie died. I know Louisa's letters helped him a lot when he was away and she's a good friend to both of you. I'll not try and push them together, but you can't blame a mother for hoping, can you?'

Jeannie shook her head. 'Don't get your hopes up, Ma. Louisa's already told us she won't marry now Mattie's gone. It's driving a wedge between her and her ma and pa.'

Ma sighed. 'It's such a tragedy, this awful war. No doubt there'll be a lot of young women like Louisa, left to live their lives without the love of a husband.'

Jeannie sat beside Ma on the sofa and rested her head on her shoulder. 'It's going to be harder than ever to find a decent man with so many of them being killed, isn't it? I'll probably be a spinster all my life as well.'

Ma patted her cheek. 'We mustn't fret over it, love. The Lord has plans for all of us, I'm sure. I pray to Him every day that He rewards your faithfulness and kindness with the love of a good man. That boy Douglas wasn't right for you, and he was caught out in his lies, wasn't he? I'm sure that was God's hand, keeping you safe from harm.'

'I don't know about that,' she sighed. 'But at this rate, there won't be enough lads left to go round, so I'm thinking I should be more like Louisa and Kate. Neither of them want to marry and they're thinking about their futures without relying on a man.'

'There's nothing wrong in doing that,' agreed Ma. 'But don't shut yourself off from the possibility of love. I'm sure there's someone out there for you, Jeannie, and he'll be the luckiest man on God's earth to have you for his wife.'

* * *

In the kitchen, Lucas made a pot of tea.

'How are you getting along?' he asked Louisa.

'I'm fine, thank you,' she said as she set out cups and saucers. 'It's good to be back at work. Less time to think.'

'I know what you mean. Even though I can't do my old job, I'm keeping busy. I felt useless all those weeks in the hospital. At least now I'm earning a living again.'

She looked at him. 'Do you miss clicking?'

'Yeah, I do. It was skilled work and it took a long time to learn. I'm angry with myself that I threw away all those years of learning. I should've stayed home and then I might not have lost so much.'

'You'll get it back one day, I'm sure. Look how far you've come in just a few weeks. You just need to be patient.' She fiddled with the teaspoons, looking away from him. 'That's what I keep telling myself.'

She had confessed her secret to him when she'd visited him in the hospital. She hadn't intended to, but then he'd suggested he wouldn't go home and she'd told him, letting him know that running away from problems didn't solve anything – you just took them with you wherever you went.

He regarded her for a moment, but she didn't look up. 'And is it helping?'

She looked up then and shook her head. 'Of course it isn't,' she said. 'But we're talking about your hand, not my heart.'

He nodded. 'Are things any better with your parents?' he asked.

She rolled her eyes. 'If anything, they're getting worse. I swear my ma is panicking that with all the lads being conscripted, there'll be no one left to marry me off to.'

Lucas grinned. 'None left but Quaker lads and damaged goods like me and Tom. No wonder she's fretting.'

She giggled. It did his heart good to hear it. 'I know,' she said. 'And I've made things worse by saying if they insist I go to church, I'll be going to the Friends' Meeting for worship on Sunday with Jeannie and Kate.'

'Oh my word, I don't suppose your pa took very kindly to that.'

She sobered, looking away again. 'No.' She took a deep breath. 'But I'm afraid I find it difficult to care what he thinks these days.' Her blue gaze caught his, holding him still. 'Does that make me a wicked person?'

He wanted to reach out and touch her cheek, to try to wipe the sadness and grief from her expression. But he held back, simply shaking his head. 'No, Louisa. You're not wicked. You're just someone who's lost more than she should have. I'm sorry it's so difficult at home. But you know you can always come and talk to me and Jeannie, don't you?'

She nodded. 'And Kate, although it's hard going to her home now that she lodges with Mattie's ma. I'm always so afraid I'll blurt out the truth in front of her and break Mrs Searle's heart all over again. That's part of the reason why I'm thinking about going to the Friends' meetings – I hope that seeing her more often will make it easier for me to deal with how I feel when I see her.'

Lucas picked up the pot and started to pour the tea. 'That's a good idea,' he said. 'The Meeting House is a neutral space as well. You never went there with Mattie so you won't be plagued by memories of him there.'

Louisa put a hand on his arm as he rested the teapot on the trivet. 'Whereas you must see him in every corner of the place,' she said, her voice gentle with sympathy.

He swallowed down against the lump forming in his throat. 'Everywhere I go around here is like that,' he confessed. 'I think that's why I enlisted: to get away from it. But now I find I get more comfort from my memories than from escaping them.' He took a deep breath. 'Anyway, can you fetch the milk jug? Ma will be wondering where her cuppa has got to.'

5

Kate was boiling the kettle when Betty Searle arrived home from the factory one evening the following week.

'There's a letter for you, Auntie,' she said. 'Sit down and read it while I pour you a cup.'

'Ah, bless you, love.' She picked up the envelope from the table. 'It's from my cousin in Bristol.'

Kate put a cup of tea beside the older woman. 'Do you want me to make a start on peeling some potatoes?' she asked as she joined her at the table. 'I can shell some of those peas you picked from the garden as well.' She took a sip of her own drink before looking up, realising that Auntie Betty hadn't answered her. 'Is everything all right?' she asked when she noticed her landlady's pale face.

Betty shook her head and sighed. 'No lass, it's not. Oh my lord, it's too cruel.'

'What?' She hoped it wasn't news of another death or maiming due to this horrible war.

She put the letter down on the table. 'My cousin's son, Gerald

– he's been turned down for exemption from fighting by his local tribunal.'

'Oh. I'm sorry. I'd heard they've been turning down a lot of Quakers. Can't he appeal? I mean, if he's a born Friend...'

'It's not just that,' she said. 'That lad already volunteered. He went off with an ambulance unit back in 1914. Spent more than a year out there, he did, saving lives and never once picking up a gun. But it all got too much for him and he came home. Now they're saying he's not a true pacifist and must go and fight.' Her eyes filled with tears. 'How can they say that? Hasn't he done enough?'

Kate took Auntie Betty's hands in her own. 'I'm so sorry. It's mighty unfair. It sounds like he's already done his bit. Isn't there anything else he can do?'

She shook her head. 'I don't know. He took himself off to work in a market garden, reasoning that producing food was essential work. But they won't have it. My cousin says they're going to arrest him and hand him over to the army. If they take him to France and he refuses to fight, she says he could face a firing squad.'

Kate caught her breath. 'No! They can't do that! There must be something we can do.' She didn't even know this young man, but she couldn't bear the thought of anyone being treated so.

'I don't know, lass. But I'm going to try my best to find out.' She gathered up the letter and stood up. 'I heard Mr and Mrs Clothier are looking into the plight of conscientious objectors. I'll take this round to them. If anyone can help, it'll be young Esther and her family.'

Mrs Esther Clothier was a Clark by birth – sister to Miss Alice and Mr Roger. Kate knew her and her husband and son by sight. They were regular worshippers at the Friends' Meeting House, so Auntie Betty knew them well.

'I hope they can help,' said Kate. 'Do you want me to cook the supper while you're out?'

She shook her head. 'I find I've lost my appetite, Katie love. You go ahead and eat without me.' She frowned. 'I just hope I don't interrupt the Clothiers' meal. But I can't wait around doing nothing. I'll feel better if I can talk to them, see what can be done.'

Kate nodded. 'Do you want me to come with you? I'd like to help, if I can. Not that anyone would take any notice of someone like me... but, well, like you, I can't bear the thought of all this. If there's anything I can do to make a difference, I'll do it, I swear.'

Betty touched Kate's cheek as she gave her a sad smile. 'Bless your heart. By all means, come with me if you want, although I don't expect you to.'

'I want to,' she said. Like Betty, she had lost her appetite anyway. She'd rather walk to the Clothiers' house to burn off some of the indignation churning up her gut at the unfairness of all this.

Betty nodded. 'Right then. Let's be off.'

'This is outrageous,' said Mrs Clothier as she read the letter that Auntie Betty had shown them. She passed it to her husband. 'We must be able to do something.'

Mr Clothier skimmed it, frowning. 'It does seem particularly harsh, given that this young man has already spent over a year with an ambulance unit. It's clear evidence of his adherence to his Quaker roots. The tribunal should have granted him exemption. We must take action on his behalf.'

'But it says they're going to arrest him tomorrow, sir,' said Auntie Betty, looking worried. 'What if they put him straight on a troop ship and rush him off to the trenches?'

He shook his head. 'Don't distress yourself, Mrs Searle. Despite his experience of the trenches as a volunteer medical orderly, he would still be required to undertake basic training in this country before being posted overseas as a conscript. We have time.'

Even though they had interrupted their supper, the Clothiers were gracious and patient as they talked with Auntie Betty about other cases that had been brought to their attention.

'We are building up a movement of support for these young men,' said Mrs Clothier. 'My husband and other Friends have already attended some hearings to speak on their behalf. We've had some success.' She gave Betty a gentle smile.

'Although not in every case,' Mr Clothier tempered his wife's reassurance. 'But we've been successful in ensuring that they're not shipped off to France. However, if we can't overturn the tribunal's decision, and they continue to refuse to take up arms, it could mean a prison sentence.'

'So they won't shoot him?' asked Kate. She'd been silent up until now, a little intimidated to be in the home of one of the Clark family. But Auntie Betty's distress over this lad's fate had filled Kate with a nervous energy, a desire to put things right for her landlady's relative, just as the older woman had put Kate's life right when she'd believed there was no hope.

Mr Clothier shook his head. 'There's no guarantee, of course. But we're starting to understand how the military are working – they tend to attempt to persuade them into accepting the King's shilling. The conscription regulations state that a man is deemed to have enlisted and is therefore required to fight. If they can get them to a barracks, simply using army cutlery is regarded to be an acceptance of fact of enlistment. We're warning the young men about that, telling them to make sure they take their own personal items with them if they're forced to go and to stand firm in their refusal to take up arms by not using any of the King's equipment. If they hold steady, I understand that the next level of intimidation is being forced into uniform and transported to the front. If they continue to refuse to take up arms when they arrive, that is when they could face execution.'

Betty covered her eyes. 'I can't bear it,' she cried. 'How could they be so cruel? Is there nothing to be done to save him?'

Mrs Clothier patted Betty's shoulder. Kate wished someone would comfort her too. She felt sick with the injustice of it all, even though she didn't even know this young man. She realised that Mattie and Lucas might have faced this if they'd refused to fight. Betty was probably thinking the same thing and sending up a prayer of gratitude that Mattie's brother, Will, was safe from being called up as he had gone to work in a tank factory. As he was in an occupation of national defensive importance, he was confirmed as exempt.

Kate's nausea got worse as she thought about her own brothers. They weren't Quakers. They had no choice but to go and fight if they were called up. Not for the first time, she felt her whole body clench with fear at the thought of what they might face. It had been hard enough when Ted's brother Albert had been killed, then his other brother, Stan, had lost his mind in the trenches – the poor lad was unlikely to ever leave the asylum where he now resided. Mattie had died and Lucas had been injured, and then Ted had gone off to fight. Not for the first time, she wondered whether he was still alive.

She hated this war, but felt so helpless to stop it. *How many more lads will be killed or maimed before the powers that be finally come to their senses and stop it all?* she thought.

She hadn't realised she'd spoken that thought out loud until Mr Clothier turned to her.

'Our thoughts exactly, young lady. We must pray every day for peace and do what we can to protect those whose faith prevents them from fighting.'

Kate felt her cheeks warm and she nodded. 'Yes, sir. I hope you can help Mrs Searle's relative.'

'We'll certainly do our best,' said Mrs Clothier. 'But, as my husband has said, if we cannot obtain exemption for them, the best we can hope for is that they receive a prison sentence.'

'I want to help,' she blurted out. 'I don't know what I can do. I'm just a factory lass. But if there's anything I can do...'

Mrs Clothier smiled at her and Betty nodded her approval. 'Thank you. I'm sure we can find something for you to do. Our campaign is relatively new, but we receive news like this every day. The more hands we have on board, the lighter the task.'

Mr Clothier nodded. 'We face a growing mission to help these young men. Now, Mrs Searle, I suggest you pen a note to your cousin and I shall ensure that someone delivers it this evening. I intend to travel to Bristol in the morning to see what I can do on the ground to prevent this injustice.'

'Thank you, Friend, and God bless you.'

* * *

Back at their cottage in The Mead, Kate and Auntie Betty still had no appetite for any supper, so they got out their knitting and sat in the parlour.

'I hope he manages to save the lad, Auntie,' said Kate. 'I hadn't realised how hard it was for Quaker men.'

Betty sighed. 'I know. I dread to think what it would do to the poor dear boy if they sent him back there. I'm sure he'd prefer prison to that.'

Kate nodded, her stomach churning as she thought about

Mattie going off to fight and never coming back. She had never understood why he'd chosen to go even before they brought in conscription. But no one would ever know now.

'I confess I was upset when Will got that job in the tank factory and moved all the way to Lincolnshire,' the older woman went on, her eyes on her knitting. 'But, much as I hate the thought of the destruction those machines can wreak, I'm thankful now that he's in a reserved occupation and won't face what his cousin is going through. I don't want any mother to go through what I have, losing a son. I thank God every day that He found a way to spare my William. At least he'll be around to see his son grow up.'

Kate couldn't hold in the sob that escaped her, causing Betty to look up.

'Oh, Katie, love. Don't cry, child. I'm not complaining, really I'm not. I'm counting my blessings. I know that some mothers have faced even more pain than I have – look at Mrs Jackson. That poor woman has sacrificed three sons.'

'Yet she bullies other women into doing the same,' said Kate. 'Why couldn't she hold onto Ted, at least, instead of pushing him into a uniform? No wonder he said he would never come back, even if he survives the trenches.'

Betty shook her head. 'I don't know what went on in that household,' she said. 'All I know is that the woman is afraid and truly believes she's doing the right thing. All we can do is pray for her and for young Ted on foreign shores and his brother in Heaven and the other in his own personal hell in the asylum.'

Kate blinked away her tears, taking a deep breath and looking up at the ceiling. 'Mr Jackson deserves our prayers as well. That poor man has to live with her without his sons.'

'He does,' she agreed.

They fell into silence again, the only sounds the soft clicking of their knitting needles and the ticking of the clock on the mantel. They were making socks for soldiers. Lucas had told them that, when it rained, the trenches became mud baths and a lot of lads who didn't have enough pairs of socks were getting rotten feet when their boots leaked. The women had decided to make sure that they sent out plenty of pairs so that the lads could try to keep their feet dry and free from rot.

As she worked, Kate felt the churning in her stomach calm a little but not completely. It hadn't been the thought of Mrs Jackson that had made her cry. It had been Betty's comment about Will seeing his son grow up. Sometimes, it was hard to remember that her landlady had no idea that her grandson was actually the child of Mattie and Louisa, and not Will and Peg's natural son. It hurt to know that secret and all the pain that went with it. For Louisa, it was a double grief, having lost her lover and her son. For Peg and Will, as well as having lost Mattie, they had to face the fact that Peg wasn't able to bear a child of her own. Louisa had run away to Lincolnshire with them when her ma had been determined to give the child to strangers and they had cared for her through her pregnancy and confinement. But leaving baby Mattie behind had just about broken Louisa, even though she knew she was doing the right thing for her child.

Kate knew that Peg and Will loved little Mattie as their own, even though they were really his aunt and uncle, and would give him a happy, loving home. But she also knew that their love was tinged by the guilt they felt because Mattie and Louisa would never be able to hold and acknowledge the baby borne of their love. But she could never tell Betty any of this. She had promised Louisa, Peg and Will. Sometimes, like now, it was so hard, but it wasn't her secret to reveal.

'I do hate this war so,' she whispered. 'And now my brothers are going to have to go and who knows whether they'll ever see their wives and children again?'

Betty didn't answer. She just shook her head, her sadness settling around her shoulders like a shawl.

6

On a warm Saturday afternoon in late June, Louisa had been on a solitary walk through Walton and beyond to Ashcott, the villages to the west of Street. She decided to call in on Jeannie on her way home. Louisa was spending a lot of her free time at the Musgrove cottage in West End. While she still presented herself at her own family table for most meals to placate her mother and still slept in the room she'd grown up in, she found it hard to talk to her parents and the atmosphere at home was tense and unhappy.

Sometimes, she wished it could be different and that they could get back to the loving relationship they'd shared before she'd fallen in love with Mattie. She would try to make conversation and act as though the past year or so had never happened. But then, quick as you like, her mother would assume that the old Louisa had returned and she would start her scheming to match her with someone's son or nephew and everything would descend into acrimony again when her daughter refused to countenance such a thing. These conversations would remind Louisa of all the pain she had been through and of everything she had lost as a result of her parents' prejudices and she would revert to the cold, distant young woman she had become in their presence.

So she took refuge in long walks with her sketch pad. She had long ago filled the one that Mattie had given her for her birthday just before he was killed. Drawing and painting soothed her. She drew landscapes, flowers, birds and even her friends. When she wasn't losing herself in her art, she would visit Jeannie's house, where she received a warm welcome. She still couldn't bring herself to go to see Kate at the Searle family home – it held too many memories, not least of the last time she had been there alone with Mattie, when their son had been conceived. She hoped that Mrs Searle wasn't offended by Louisa's failure to visit her there. She didn't seem to be, always greeting her with a kind smile and gentle words when they met.

It was the thought of seeing Mattie's ma away from anywhere that Louisa had memories of visiting with Mattie that had made Louisa consider attending the Friends' Meeting House. She felt sure that, if she did, Mrs Searle would be pleased to see her and make her feel welcome. This was in contrast to her own parents' reactions to her idea. She had had to endure her mother's tears and her father's icy silences, heavy with parental disappointment, but she remained stoic. She still hadn't been to a meeting, but she thought that she might find a measure of comfort and strength there that she couldn't get at her parents' church.

Lucas opened the door when she knocked. He nodded and stood back for her to enter. He never commented on her visits, for he knew better than anyone why she felt the need to escape her parents.

'Been walking again?' he asked.

'Yes, I went as far as Ashcott,' she said, pulling her sketch book out of her bag and showing him. 'I sat on the side of the road and tried to capture a view of the gates to Lockhill Hall. It's not very good, though.'

He looked at the drawing. 'It is good. I recognise it.'

She laughed. 'It could be any other wall and pair of gates in the country. But thank you for your kindness.' She looked around. 'Where's Jeannie?'

'In the garden, shelling peas. Go on out to her. I'll bring you a cold drink. Ma just opened a bottle of elderflower cordial. You're lucky the twins are out playing football, otherwise there'd be none left.'

Jeannie greeted her with a smile. 'D'you mind if I carry on with this?' she asked, indicating the two buckets at her side. One held a pile of pea pods, the other, the empty shells, while the fresh peas were collected in a large bowl. 'Only we've had a better early crop than we expected and if we don't get on and shell and bottle what we don't eat now, they'll be wasted. Ma's suffering with her joints today, so she's gone to bed. She says if we get any more from the plants, we'll hang up the pods in the shed and dry them, but we're going to try preserving some of these in jars first. There's only so much you can eat fresh before the twins complain they're bored with us serving them up at every meal.'

'Of course I don't mind,' she said, sitting beside her on the garden bench. 'Give me some and I'll help. Lucas said he's bringing out some cold cordial for us.'

'Oh, that will be nice.' Jeannie nudged her shoulder. 'You realise he wouldn't have thought of it if I was out here on my own, don't you? I think my brother has a soft spot for you, Louisa Clements.'

Louisa frowned and stared at her. 'I...' She shook her head and laughed a little nervously. 'Don't be daft,' she said. 'We're friends, that's all. Just like you and me. On account of Mattie, that's all.'

Jeannie's expression softened. 'I know you both miss him something awful. I expect Lucas made a promise to look out for you when Mattie went away.'

Louisa sighed. 'I'd hope he's my friend on his own account. I should hate for Lucas to feel obliged when he didn't want to.'

'When I didn't want to what?' asked Lucas as he came through the door with three beakers of cordial on a tray balanced on his good hand.

She took the tray and put it on the bench between her and Jeannie. 'Thank you, Lucas. I was saying I hope that you're not being my friend out of a sense of duty,' she said. 'I don't want to be seen as Mattie's grieving sweetheart, but rather as someone you share a bond of friendship with on our own account.'

Lucas picked up his drink from the tray and then sank onto the grass in front of the girls. Jeannie took her own, tucking the tray under the bench as they all took a sip of the cool, sweet cordial. He looked up at Louisa, his expression thoughtful.

'I confess, it's a mixture of the two,' he said. 'At the start, you were Mattie's girl and Jeannie's friend and I didn't know much about you. But then, through our letters while we were both away and our conversations since we came home, we've got to know each other better and now you're my friend as well. You can rest assured, I don't spend time with you out of a sense of duty.'

Jeannie smiled at his words. Louisa felt some of her tension release and she nodded. 'Thank you,' she said. 'It's good to know... and it's the same for me.'

The three of them drank their cordial and enjoyed the afternoon sunshine, then the girls returned to shelling the peas. Lucas lay back on the path and Louisa thought he'd dozed off. She concentrated on the task in hand, but couldn't resist glancing at him now and again. He was taller than Mattie had been, his hair a light, mousy brown like Jeannie's rather than Mattie's rich, dark-brown locks. His time in the army and subsequent injury had hardened him in mind and body and he seemed older than his years. Louisa thought he was looking better than he had when he'd come home in the spring, but she doubted he'd ever lose the lingering sadness that surrounded him, any more than she expected to lose her own.

After a few minutes, he stretched and sat up. 'Here, let me have some,' he said, reaching for a handful of peapods. He opened one, albeit a little clumsily with one hand, emptying the raw peas into his mouth and eating them.

Louisa laughed as Jeannie scolded him. 'You're supposed to help, not eat the lot,' his sister said.

He shrugged and shucked the next lot into the bowl on the bench. 'I was peckish,' he said. 'And you can't beat peas fresh out of the pod for a quick snack.'

'Well we'd better get these done before the twins get home and follow your example, or we'll never have enough to preserve for the winter.'

Louisa looked down the long, narrow garden. 'You seem to have a good crop of vegetables this year,' she said.

'I know,' said Jeannie, pride brightening her pretty face. 'Ma was fretting that we might not be able to get fresh produce with the war dragging on so. Mr Baker, the old chap next door agreed to give us some advice as we didn't have a clue. We've been working hard to keep it productive.'

Lucas chuckled. 'What Jeannie means, Louisa, is that she has been breaking her back doing most of it, with a bit of help from me and Ma and a lot of hindrance from the twins.'

The girls laughed. Louisa's heart swelled at the gentle, affectionate teasing between brother and sister and the loving atmosphere in their home. *This is what I want. Not status and ambition, nor the recriminations that come because of my lack of regard for either. I could've had this with Mattie. But now I'll have to try and find a way to get it on my own, for I can't go on as I am at home.*

She saw Lucas frown slightly, sending her a questioning glance. She smiled again, realising he'd seen the shadow pass over her face. She didn't want this happy time to be tainted by her sadness.

The peas were soon all shelled. Lucas picked up the bucket of empty pods and took it down the garden to the compost heap. Some folk would keep the pods and eat them as well, but Jeannie explained that none of them had a fondness for them. The girls watched him, neither inclined to move. They were enjoying the sunshine too much.

'You're good for him,' said Jeannie. 'I know you don't think of each other in a romantic way, but it's good to see you together. You both seem happier when the other is around.'

Louisa turned to look at her, confused. 'I'm happier when you and Kate are around as well.'

'I know,' she replied. 'But... I don't know... it's as though you and Lucas are calmer in each other's company. You have a special bond. As though you feel safe when the other is there.' She shrugged. 'I can't explain it. It just seems right when you're together.'

Inside the house, a door slammed, followed by the sound of the twins laughing.

Jeannie let out a breath. 'Here comes trouble. Our peace is about to be disrupted.'

Louisa didn't say anything, relieved that the twins' arrival had distracted Jeannie. She was trying to process what her friend had said. *Surely she doesn't think that Lucas and me...?*

The twins burst out into the garden, bringing a wave of energy that crackled and spun around the girls.

'Where's Lucas?' asked John. 'We've got to tell him.'

'He's down the garden. Tell him what?'

'You'll never guess,' said Peter as John took off down the path towards Lucas. 'Not in a million years.' Then he was gone, racing after his brother.

The girls looked at each other, bemused by the boy's excitement. 'What on earth could that be about?' said Jeannie.

'I don't know. But it can't be bad, can it? They're delighted about something.'

The boys were talking nineteen to the dozen as Lucas listened. At first he frowned, then his expression changed and he looked astonished and began questioning them.

'Well, whatever it is, let's go and find out,' said Louisa, standing up. 'The suspense is killing me.'

But before she could follow them, there was a firm knock at the cottage door.

'I'd better see who that is before they disturb Ma,' said Jeannie.

Louisa wanted to know what had got the boys excited, but realised it would be rude to leave Jeannie to her own devices. 'I'll come with you.'

Tom was standing at the front door when Jeannie opened it. He looked out of breath and a bit flustered, as though he'd been running.

'Hello,' said Jeannie, giving him a shy smile. 'The boys are in the garden if you're looking for them.'

He looked relieved. 'They came straight home then. Good.' He seemed to be talking to himself.

'Have they been up to mischief?' Jeannie looked worried.

He shook his head. 'No, they aren't in trouble, it's just...' He blew out a breath and ran a hand through his hair. 'Look, can I have a quick sit down, Jeannie? I ran here to catch up with them and I'm starting to regret it.' He grimaced in pain.

'Oh! Of course, come in, come in.' She ushered him towards the settee in the parlour but he shook his head and limped into the kitchen where he pulled out a chair from the table and sat down.

'Ah, that's better,' he said as he took the weight off his bad leg. 'Sorry about that, but if I sat on a settee right now, I'd likely not be able to get out of it again any time soon. I'm better in an upright chair.'

Jeannie nodded and went and got him a beaker of elderflower cordial. 'Here,' she said, putting it on the table in front of him. 'Have that before the twins come in and drink it all.'

He sent her a grateful smile as he raised it to his lips and drank deeply.

Louisa could see the Musgrove brothers, still gossiping at the end of the garden, while Jeannie watched Tom. She noticed that her friend's cheeks had taken on that becoming pink hue that they always did when he was around. Normally, Tom would be looking at her with an equally besotted look, but today he was agitated.

'What on earth has happened, Tom?' Louisa asked. 'The boys are acting mighty odd and what are you thinking of, running on that poor leg of yours if they haven't been up to mischief?'

Whereas Lucas had injured his hand, Tom had come back from the war with a permanent limp. He always walked in a steady, measured manner. It wasn't like him to be dashing anywhere.

He sighed as he put the beaker down and looked up at the girls. 'They didn't tell you?'

They shook their heads. 'But whatever it is, I think they're spilling the beans to Lucas right now,' Louisa said, pointing out of the window.

He sighed again and looked out through the window above

the sink to see the twins gesturing and talking over each other while Lucas listened intently. Louisa could see one of the boys pretending to kick a ball and the other waving an arm in a long arc. She was still trying to work out what it was all about when Tom began to laugh. It started as a low chuckle in his chest as he covered his face with a hand. Then it exploded from him as a full-blown guffaw. The girls looked at him, not knowing what to make of it.

'What?' asked Jeannie.

He threw his head back and laughed. 'You should've seen their faces,' he spluttered.

'You've got to tell us now,' said Louisa, a smile tugging at her lips. His mirth was a joy to see. He was usually so serious. 'Come on, the suspense is killing us. It must be something astonishing. Look at how shocked Lucas is.' She pointed out of the window. Then she turned back and nodded towards Jeannie. 'And now Jeannie's worried. So come on, Tom. What's happened?'

He wiped the tears of mirth from his eyes before replying. 'Sorry, girls. Didn't mean to worry you. It's just that I passed the twins playing football and when they saw me, they kicked the ball over to me. I forgot myself and went to kick it back.' He huffed again, as though the memory was too funny.

Louisa frowned, confused. 'That's it? You kicked a ball? I don't understand what all the fuss is about. I'm sorry, Tom, but that's not even funny.'

He blew out a breath and shook his head. 'I know. But I've no business trying to kick a ball or anything and I forgot that and did it anyway. And, well, my foot flew off and shot further than the blasted ball did.'

Jeannie gasped and put a hand to her chest while Louisa gaped at him. She squeezed her eyes shut and shook her head. 'I must have some wax in my ears,' she said, opening her eyes to stare at him. 'Did you really just say your foot flew off? How is that possible?'

Tom pulled a face, looking at Jeannie with what seemed to Louisa like regret before he turned back to her. 'Sorry to shock you both. But you didn't hear me wrong. What nobody round here knows – or at least, they didn't until that stupid kick – is that the reason I limp is because the Hun managed to blow off my foot. I've got a false one for walking, but it's not fit for doing things like playing football, no matter how keen I am to do it.' His glance slid back to Jeannie, watching her reaction. When she didn't say anything, he went on. 'So I kicked out with the wrong foot and it went flying through the air and I'm left with the ball on the ground in front of me and my boot heading towards the twins.'

The picture he painted with his words created such a vivid image in Louisa's mind that she couldn't stop the giggle that escaped her mouth. 'Oh, my word,' she said. 'I'm so sorry, Tom. It's no laughing matter.'

'Don't fret,' he said, waving away her apology. 'I'd rather you laughed than showed pity.' A shadow crossed his face. 'That's why I don't tell anyone. I'd rather they thought I was just left with a gammy leg than none at all. I'm still the same man, even if I'm not whole any more.'

Jeannie nodded, putting a hand over his across the table. 'I'm sorry about your foot, Tom. But it's clear you're not a self-pitying man and you're doing fine as you are. As you say, you're still the same lad we know, so it shouldn't make any difference.'

'Except when you kick your foot at the twins instead of the ball,' said Louisa, giggling again. 'I wish I'd seen their faces.'

Tom chuckled. 'It was a sight to see. I was as shocked as they were when it happened, which is why I came after them when they headed home. They got a head start on me as I had to put my foot back on. But now I think on it...' He laughed again and shook his head. 'Anyway, I came to ask them to keep it quiet. I don't want the whole village knowing and treating me different on account of it.'

Jeannie stood up. 'I'm going to go and get them to come in and apologise to you. I can't believe they were so ill-mannered as to run off and leave you like that. However did you manage?'

'Don't fret, Jeannie,' he said. 'They did pick up my boot and bring it back to me. But, well, I was a bit put out at the time and yelled at them. That's when they ran off. I think I scared 'em.'

She frowned. 'Well, it seems to me you had a right to be cross. That's no excuse for them, though.'

With that, she turned and ran out of the kitchen door. Tom sighed and rested his elbows on the table and his chin on his hands. He glanced sideways at Louisa, who studied him with interest.

'What?' he asked. 'Come on, I can see you want to say something. Spit it out.'

'All right, I will,' she said. 'Is your lack of a foot the reason you haven't asked Jeannie to be your sweetheart?'

He blinked and stilled, his face going blank. 'I don't know what you're talking about. She's my friend's sister.'

She pressed her lips together and glared at him. Part of her was astonished that she'd challenged two lads in the same hour, but she wouldn't be deterred. Maybe if she'd challenged Ma and Pa more in the past... She brought her thoughts back to the matter in hand. 'That she is,' she replied. 'But that's not how you look at her when you think no one's looking. Don't deny it. And you know full well she blushes every time you're around. So are you going to answer my question?'

He looked away. 'You're right, yes. It's part of it. But that's all I'm saying.'

'But—'

Before she could go on, one of the twins burst through the door.

'Tom! Are you all right? I'm s-so sorry, we sh-shouldn't have left you. Lucas said he'll box our ears and burst our ball if... if we do it again.' Peter stood in the doorway, his face bright red as he stammered over the words.

'And so will I,' said Jeannie, coming in the door and pushing him out of the way. 'I've never been so ashamed of the pair of you in my life,' she declared as she glared at Peter fiercely before turning to John, who was trying to slide in through the doorway unnoticed. 'What have you got to say to Tom, John Musgrove? And no mumbling, mind. I want to hear a clear and sincere apology from you right now, young man.'

Lucas appeared behind him and gave him a shove towards the table. 'So do I.' He looked at Tom with concern. 'Are you really all right? I was about to come and find you.'

Tom held up a hand. 'I'm fine.' He looked at the three brothers. 'Though, my secret's out, that's for sure. It was daft of me to forget myself and try kicking that ball. You left it behind, by the way, lads. I dropped it by your front door.'

John immediately moved to retrieve it, but Jeannie stood in his path, hands on hips, glaring at him.

'What have you got to say for yourself?' she demanded.

He glared back at her for a moment, until Lucas's quiet voice saying his name brought him to his senses. His face flushing, he turned away from his sister but didn't look Tom in the eye. 'Sorry,' he said. 'We shouldn't have run off like that. Didn't mean no harm.'

Louisa noticed Tom's lips twitched a little but he kept his expression grave as he nodded. She hid her smile as she realised he was remembering the twins' reaction and finding the recollection of it amusing.

When Tom didn't berate him, John got a bit braver and pointed at Tom's feet. 'Will you show us?' he asked.

Jeannie gasped and boxed his ear, making him yelp. 'John Musgrove, don't you dare try and turn him into some kind of circus sideshow. Show some respect!'

'She's right,' said Lucas, scowling at his brother. 'It's no one's business but Tom's.'

'That's right,' said Jeannie. 'So we'd better not hear you're going around the village telling all and sundry.'

Louisa watched as Tom glanced at Jeannie, his admiration for her shining in his regard. Then he caught her watching and he wiped his expression clear, but not before she saw the sincere regret he tried to hide. She frowned. It didn't make sense. It was obvious to all of them that Jeannie wasn't thinking any the less of him now that she knew he was an amputee. What was really holding Tom back from declaring his feelings for her?

He cleared his throat. 'That's why I came straight here,' he said. 'I would prefer it if people took me as they find me, and not look at me and see a cripple. So I'd appreciate it if you lads were to keep my secret. I've worked hard to learn to live with things I can't change. The last thing I want is pity. There's plenty of others who deserve that more than I do. I just want to be left alone to get on with the rest of my life in peace.'

The twins looked shame-faced and nodded their heads. Tom took pity on them and went on. 'There's nothing worth seeing, believe me. They took away my foot and part of my lower leg. There's just a stump below the knee. The false foot fits onto it. That's what makes me limp. I've been working on making myself a better one – maybe with a hinge of some kind to make it act more like a real foot and ankle.'

'Like the splint you made Lucas?' said Peter, his expression thoughtful. 'It helps him hold his hand in a more natural manner. That's a good idea, fitting a hinge, you being an engineer and all.'

Tom nodded. 'I reckon I've got the skills to help myself. There's too many men out there needing help from the government. I can't keep going back and complaining that I don't appreciate having a limp. They'll tell me I'm lucky I'm alive and there's plenty of men a lot worse off than I am, which is true.'

Lucas nodded. 'Well I'm grateful for the help you've given me, so if there's anything I can do to help you with your new foot, let me know.' He held up his splinted hand. 'Although I'm not likely to be able to do any detailed work for you. But I can sand some wood blocks or maybe talk through your ideas if that helps.'

'I want to help as well,' said Peter.

John tilted his head to one side. 'You know, maybe there's money to be made with this – making false legs and the like.' Jeannie went to box his ear again but he ducked out of her reach. 'What? I'm only saying.'

She poked at his skinny chest. 'Your brothers want to help because it's the right thing to do. But you, you little beggar, are thinking what profit you can make from it. That's rude, selfish and I'm ashamed of you. Now get on out of here before I slap you again!'

Louisa wanted to cheer. It wasn't often that Jeannie got riled up, but when she did, she was magnificent, something Tom couldn't fail to notice.

John muttered and grumbled but left the room, his ears bright red. Peter followed after him, stuttering his apologies again as he went. A moment later, the front door slammed.

The girls flinched and Jeannie huffed. 'And now they'll have woken Ma. I'd better put the kettle on. She'll be down in a moment, wondering what all the noise was about.' She turned to Tom. 'I'm so sorry. They're idiots.'

He chuckled, his eyes glowing with admiration as he looked at her. 'Don't worry, Jeannie. It's not how I wanted people to find out, but I have to confess, once I'd got over the shock, their reactions gave me the best laugh I've had in a long time.'

Lucas sat at the table. 'From the way they were rambling on when they got home, I can imagine their faces were a picture. Peter thought you'd kicked the ball so hard, you'd torn your own foot off.'

By the time Mrs Musgrove came into the room, the four of them were sitting around the kitchen table, crying with laughter.

7

Kate, Louisa and Jeannie were enjoying their dinner break on the grass outside the factory. There were plenty of others around them, enjoying the summer sunshine, but the friends took no notice of anyone else.

'Look,' said Kate. 'I know something's going on. What is it?'

Louisa frowned. 'What makes you say that?'

She narrowed her eyes and looked at Jeannie, who flushed and looked away. 'Jeannie's acting strange.' She held up a hand. 'Don't deny it. She can barely look me in the eye yet she looks fit to bursting about something.'

Louisa sighed as Jeannie began to bluster. 'It's all right, Jeannie,' she said, putting a hand on her shoulder. 'I did ask, and he said we can tell Kate. But no one else, remember. So for goodness' sake, try and keep it under your hat a bit better.'

Kate smirked. 'Jeannie can't keep a secret to save her life.' She shared a significant look with Louisa. She'd said the same thing to her all those months ago when Lou had discovered she was carrying Mattie's child. Jeannie was so honest that it was impossible for her to lie or even pretend about something. That was why they had decided not to tell their friend about Louisa's plans to escape her parents and make her own arrangements for her beloved baby's future. Jeannie had been upset when she'd found out that Kate knew where Louisa was, but she still didn't know about the child and it seemed as though she never would. Lou nodded, a shadow crossing her pretty face before she rallied and beckoned Kate closer with the crook of her finger. She leaned in, as did Jeannie, so that the three girls' heads touched.

'You mustn't tell anyone,' said Louisa, her voice low so that no one else could hear. 'But we found out that Tom is an amputee.'

Kate lifted her head to look at them, shock widening her eyes. 'No! Really?'

Jeannie nodded, hooking a hand around Kate's neck and pulling her back into their huddle, explaining quietly what had happened on Saturday afternoon.

Kate shrieked with laughter, drawing smiles and curious glances from the people around them. She covered her mouth with her hand as her friends hissed at her to keep quiet, but she couldn't stop the mirth that overtook her.

'I... I'm sorry,' she gasped. 'But I can just imagine the twins' faces.'

The other two joined in her giggles. 'We all wished we'd seen that,' said Jeannie. 'Even Tom had a good belly laugh about it when he'd calmed down a bit. He said they were a picture. Anyway, he's been designing and making different false legs in an effort to find one that lets him walk with less of a limp,' said Jeannie. 'Lucas is going to assist him, seeing as how Tom helped him by fashioning that splint for his wrist. He says it's helping him no end, so the least he can do is work with Tom in his endeavours.'

'Ah,' said Kate. 'I thought he was walking easier lately than when he first got here. I thought it was just his leg healing.' For a moment, she felt a wave of sadness for Tom and Lucas, and Stan

Jackson who was condemned to life in an asylum on account of his shell shock. So many young men forever changed by the war, and just as many cut down and never to return like Mattie or Albert Jackson. She didn't let herself think about Ted's fate. She wondered if she'd ever know whether he survived the war – whole or otherwise. 'I wonder if that's why he came to Street. I mean, he could've gone back to his job at the boot factory in Northampton, couldn't he? Why move right across the country? I suppose if he didn't want pity, it was easier to make a fresh start away from people who knew him before.'

Jeannie tilted her head to one side, her expression thoughtful. 'He never mentions his family,' she said. 'I don't even know whether he has any brothers or sisters. All I know is he came from Northampton and that he used to be a Methodist.'

'I thought he was a Friend,' said Louisa, looking confused.

Jeannie shook her head. 'He is now, of course. But he told me he was a Methodist before he enlisted. It was what he saw on the battlefield that made him re-evaluate his beliefs.'

'I didn't realise,' said Louisa. 'But at least you can be sure he's not another Douglas, trying to fool everyone.' She frowned. 'Doesn't mean he hasn't got other secrets though, does it?'

'I know,' said Jeannie.

Kate stared at her. 'Why would you say that? I mean, I know he makes you nervous, but it's not like you to be so distrustful.'

Jeannie blushed and she looked away. 'I don't mean to be judgemental,' she said. 'But... I don't know. Even after he confessed about his foot, I still felt like he was holding something back. I can't explain it...'

'You're right,' agreed Louisa. 'He's definitely hiding more than just his missing foot.'

Kate turned to Louisa. 'What do you mean?'

Louisa shrugged. 'I don't know. It's nothing I can put my finger on. It might just be that he's not inclined to share his business, but...' The back-to-work hooter sounded and she looked relieved as she jumped to her feet. 'Time's up. Come on.' She took off across the grass, leaving Kate staring after her, baffled.

'We'd better go,' said Jeannie, getting up and wiping down her skirt. 'Don't pay any mind to us. Like Lou says, he's probably just private, not wanting anyone to know his business. But, after being made a fool of by Douglas – with him pretending he wanted to become a Friend because he was in love with me, when he was just fooling everyone so that he could claim exemption from fighting when conscription came in – I'm inclined to stay well away from anyone who I can't be sure is completely honest.'

'I can understand that. But hiding his war injury is understandable, isn't it? As for anything else, wouldn't it be better to just ask him?'

'What?' she asked, looking confused. 'I can hardly ask him what he's hiding, can I?'

Kate looped arms with Jeannie as they climbed up the stone steps to the Machine Room. Louisa was well ahead of them in the centre of the crowd of women and girls heading in the same direction. 'Of course not, silly. But there's no harm in having a conversation with him, is there? You could ask him about his family – does he have brothers and sisters, are his ma and pa still in Northampton, that sort of thing. Even the most private of people can't object to those sort of questions, can they?'

'I suppose so,' she said. 'But I'm not sure it would make much difference. I'm sure he's not interested in me other than as Lucas's sister.'

Kate laughed. 'You can ask the same questions of a friend, you know. If you're not interested in him as a sweetheart, then stop thinking about him as anything other than a pal. What I don't understand, why didn't you tell me about Tom's foot when we were at the Meeting House yesterday?'

'I couldn't. Tom was there, and he'd asked us not to tell anyone. I didn't know Louisa had asked him about you. And anyway, you were busy with Auntie Betty, talking to Mrs Clothier, remember?'

Kate nodded, her mood dipping a little. 'Mr Clothier has been trying to help Auntie's cousin's lad, Gerald. The tribunal won't give him exemption, so he's been arrested. We think he's going to be sent to prison, even though he's a life-long Friend and had been over to France volunteering as a stretcher-bearer for over a year before he had to come home again.'

'That's horrible,' said Jeannie.

'I know,' Kate sighed. 'I've offered to help their campaign. I'm going to be writing to Betty's relative – you know, to offer him some support and friendship so that he doesn't feel so alone in prison. I might write to some others as well. The Clothiers are hearing about more and more lads being arrested because the tribunals refuse to grant them exemptions on religious grounds.'

Jeannie squeezed her arm as they reached the Machine Room. 'Maybe I could write some letters as well. I should have thought about it myself. You're such a good person, Kate, and an inspiration. I'm sure they'll all appreciate hearing from you.'

She nudged her friend's shoulder. 'Go on with you. I'm nothing special. I just hate it when people aren't treated fair.'

* * *

Jeannie set about the afternoon's work with a lighter heart. She would do as Kate suggested and think of Tom as a pal. It was no good mooning over him if he wasn't going to ask her out, but she would like to be his friend. She'd ask him questions as well, get to know him better.

In the meantime, she'd write to some of the pacifists who were being arrested, offer them some moral support. It must be so hard for them to stand up against the strength of the war mongers like Mrs Jackson and the government and so many people who were pushing young men to go and fight. Yes, she would write to them and befriend them, to let them know they weren't alone in their struggles to do what they believed was right. And who knew? Maybe she'd find a sweetheart amongst them when this awful war was over.

She felt a little better once she'd decided that. But it didn't stop her heart aching a little to think that her growing feelings for Tom were not reciprocated. Despite what her friends said about the way he looked at her, he had never treated her with anything but polite friendship, so she was sure he didn't think as highly of her as she did of him.

* * *

After work, Kate and Louisa waved goodbye to Jeannie and headed in the opposite direction down the High Street towards The Cross, where the two of them would go their separate ways.

'What did you mean earlier?' asked Kate as they walked along arm in arm. 'You know, when you said you thought Tom was holding something back?'

Louisa pulled a face. 'I don't know. It's probably nothing. Don't tell Jeannie, but I asked him straight whether it was being an amputee that was holding him back from asking Jeannie to be his sweetheart.'

'You never did!' exclaimed Kate, her eyes wide. 'Oh my, Lou. What did he say?'

She recounted the conversation. 'But just as he admitted it was only part of it, Jeannie marched the twins into the kitchen to apologise to Tom and I didn't get the chance to ask him what he meant.'

'Ooh, so he does like her?'

She nodded. 'I think so. But, like Jeannie said, he seems to be holding something back. Something else that's stopping him from declaring himself.'

'Maybe he's not as fond of her as we think?'

She shook her head. 'No, he's sweet on her. I'm sure of it. You've seen how he looks at her. I've seen Lucas watching them. I'm sure even he's noticed.'

'Do you think he's warned him off? Some big brothers are protective like that.'

Louisa frowned, thinking about it. 'I don't think that's it. They're getting on fine as pals. I'm sure Lucas would rather Jeannie was courting Tom than any other lad.'

'I don't know,' said Kate. 'He's a little older than all of us, isn't he? Maybe he thinks Jeannie's too young for him.'

Louisa scoffed. 'He's maybe in his mid-twenties, but what does that matter? My pa's ten years older than Ma. And Jeannie's not some silly girl. She's more grown up than a lot of lasses around here.'

Kate squeezed Lou's arm. 'I think all three of us are after this past couple of years.'

She sighed. 'I know. Maybe that's why I don't see Tom as being that old, even though he's been through more than any man of his age should have. God, I hate this damned war!'

Kate nodded, trying not to think of everything that had happened since the war began. She felt older than her years, that was for sure; had done for a while now. 'So, if it's not her age, and it's not his foot – or lack of one – what's holding him back?'

'That's what we've got to find out,' said Louisa. 'Because Jeannie deserves some happiness, and if Tom's not willing to offer it to her, we need to help her look elsewhere. It's not right to leave her hanging like this with his puppy-dog eyes.'

Kate burst out laughing. 'Puppy-dog eyes? What are you on about?'

Louisa huffed. 'You know what I mean. He gives her these longing looks that make Jeannie blush and hope and then he does nothing about it. He's got to make up his mind and stop leading her on.'

'So what can we do?'

She frowned. 'Probably nothing. But I think we should get Lucas to have a talk with him and find out what he's playing at. It's not fair on Jeannie.'

As they approached The Cross and the Street Inn, Kate looked around, checking that her pa wasn't on his way to the pub. The last thing she wanted was to be caught unawares by him again. She breathed a little easier when she saw that he was nowhere to be seen.

'All right,' she said. 'But careful you don't get Lucas all riled up and righteous on Jeannie's behalf and turn them against each other. Tom's been good company for him, what with him making that splint for his arm.'

Louisa sighed. 'I know. It's not escaped my notice that Tom is proving to be a good friend for Lucas. It's been hard for him since we lost Mattie and he was injured. Tom understands better than anyone what it's like.'

Kate studied her, wondering. 'Does it bother you? That he's taking Mattie's place?'

She shook her head. 'No. Lucas and Mattie were friends all their life. No matter how much Tom understands about going to war, he can't compete with all those years and memories. Whatever their friendship might be like, it'll never be the same as Lucas's relationship with Mattie. Nothing will.'

'Fair enough. I can see that the two lads might have a unique understanding of each other after they've both fought and been injured, don't you?'

Louisa tilted her head to one side, considering it. 'Do you think that's Tom's problem... that he's still suffering from what he saw on the battlefield? They say some men will never get over what they've been through. Perhaps he's worried he shouldn't get involved with a gentle soul like Jeannie. You know, in case his memories get the better of him.'

'I don't know,' Kate said, and she honestly didn't. She couldn't imagine what went on in a man's head after being at war. She thought about poor Stan Jackson, driven mad by witnessing his brother Albert's death, unable to banish the horror of it from his mind so that in the end, he didn't know what was real and what wasn't. 'I hope not.'

'I think Lucas still has nightmares,' she said quietly, as though whispering it would take away the power of her words.

Kate wanted to weep for their friend. 'I'm not surprised,' she said. 'This damned horrible war is the stuff of nightmares and lord knows when it will all end.' She sent up a silent prayer that it would be over before her own brothers got caught up in it.

8

Jeannie was standing at the kitchen window, reading a letter from Michael, one of the conscientious objectors she had started writing to.

'Oh my lord,' she muttered to herself as she read it.

I am mighty grateful to dear Mr and Mrs Clothier for their advice. If not for them, I might now be in uniform and facing a firing squad for refusing to fight.

Jeannie put a hand to her chest, horrified by the thought of someone being shot for holding fast to their faith.

As it was, they stripped me of my clothes and took them away, leaving me with only army-issue apparel to wear. When I refused to put it on (for that would be tantamount to accepting the King's shilling), they shoved me out into the guardroom courtyard and left me there, naked, in the rain overnight.

I apologise if it is inappropriate for me to tell you such things, but I thank God for it because the experience brought on a chill, which quickly turned to pneumonia and I had to be transferred to the hospital. News of how I came to be so ill reached a general's wife (who happens to have a brother who is a Member of Parliament) when she visited a sick relative in the ward. She immediately protested to her husband and brother and urged them to investigate. Thanks to that dear lady, I was transferred to this civilian prison and have been assured that no other man will face the same treatment that I did.

Jeannie closed her eyes and sent up a silent prayer of thanks to the woman who had showed such Christian kindness to Michael. He seemed like a good man and she hoped he would be better treated where he was.

She glanced through the window as she folded the letter and put it in her pocket. She noticed a strange young man standing in their neighbour Mr Baker's garden. At first, she thought it was her cheating old sweetheart, Douglas, who was the old man's great nephew. But then she remembered that he was gone – off to basic training now that he couldn't pretend to be a Friend to claim exemption from conscription – and anyway, this lad looked a little shorter and leaner than Douglas.

She wondered whether he was a vagrant with his eye on Mr Baker's vegetables. He certainly seemed to be studying the neat beds as though wondering what to pick first, but he was too smartly dressed in a tweed suit to be needy enough to contemplate stealing from an old man. She moved from the kitchen window to the back door and stood in the open doorway, watching him just in case, ready to make a fuss if he started scrumping the old man's crops.

She was about to challenge him when she saw Mr Baker come

out of his door and hand the lad a mug of tea. As he turned, the old man spotted Jeannie watching them.

'Evening, young Jeannie,' he called out, more cheerful than usual. 'This here's my grandson, Cyril.' He pointed at the lad, who turned, confused to see Jeannie. He clearly hadn't noticed her at all.

'Evening, Mr B. Hello, Cyril. Nice to meet you. Come to visit your grandpa, have you?'

The lad nodded and raised his tea in greeting. 'How do.' He gave her a shy smile. Now that she could see him face on, he didn't look much like Douglas at all. His face was thinner, his skin paler, as though he didn't see much sun. He had nice eyes though and his smile seemed quite pleasant, so she found herself smiling back at him.

'He's a bright lad,' said Mr Baker, patting him on the shoulder. The old man's big hands, gnarled from years of factory work and gardening, nudged his arm, nearly causing him to spill his tea.

Jeannie held back a giggle as Cyril went red. She'd always thought of Mr Baker as being old and frail, but compared to his pale grandson, her elderly neighbour seemed robust and in the best of health.

'He'll be teaching at the board school come September,' he went on. 'Got all the brains, has our Cyril. Knows his number work and the proper grammar.' He nodded. 'Not like his old Grampy, barely able to write me name, eh?' He laughed, a hearty sound that made Jeannie smile.

'You're as sharp as a tack, Mr Baker,' she said. 'You can teach all of us a thing or two.'

Cyril nodded, his expression earnest. 'That's what I keep telling him,' he told her. 'I've just been lucky that my teachers noticed I had potential and persuaded my pa to let me stay at school.' He seemed embarrassed to see Jeannie was watching him, interested in what he was saying, because he glanced away, his cheeks warming again. "Course, I wasn't much use for factory work anyway on account of my asthma.' He cleared his throat before taking another sip of his tea.

'Ah, not everyone's built for factory work, lad,' said his grandfather. 'Someone's got to teach the new generation what they need to know. With all these new machines and what have you, they need more learning.' He shook his head. 'When I started at Clarks as a lad, I never dreamt of steam engines and electric lights. Now look at us with all them machines at the factory!' He shook his head in wonder. 'If we can just keep the Hun at bay, you youngsters are in for a grand future, you mark my words.'

Jeannie didn't know what to say to that. She hated to think about the war, knowing that if it didn't end soon, more and more lads would be sent to fight and perish. She glanced at Cyril and noticed he looked uncomfortable as well.

'So, you're a teacher?' she asked. She'd never met a teacher outside of her own classrooms when she'd been at school. He seemed awfully young, but must be older than he looked. Maybe he looked so youthful because he was so thin and pale. *That would be the asthma,* she thought. She remembered a girl who had it in primary school who couldn't join in with their games in the playground and would be sent into fits of coughing at the slightest exertion. She frowned, recalling that the girl had died young after catching a chill in the winter that had turned to pneumonia.

He gave another cough and nodded. 'I will be in September. I'm to specialise in mathematics,' he said. 'The army won't have me on account of my chest.'

Jeannie gave him a sympathetic smile, not sure whether he was relieved he couldn't enlist or frustrated. She knew that under the conscription regulations, teachers were eligible for exemption from fighting unless they chose to enlist, although she hadn't heard of any in Street who had applied for the certificate. But with a weak chest, he wouldn't need to worry about that. It also occurred to her that the pneumonia that Michael suffered might have left him with sufficient damage to his lungs that the army might now reject him anyway. She decided to mention it when she wrote back to him.

'Anyways, he'll be lodging with me come the new school term,' said Mr Baker. 'His ma and pa live over at Taunton, where they've got a butcher's shop. Young Cyril don't know many folks around these parts, so he'll be needing to make new friends.' He gave Jeannie a hopeful look.

'That's nice,' she said. She could see that Cyril wasn't the type to work as a butcher any more than he'd manage factory work. He didn't look fit enough to be a butcher's dog, let alone the owner's son. She wondered what kind of friends he had back in Taunton. She suspected they'd be other lads like him – pale and bookish, more interested in learning than playing football or cricket. As he coughed again and tried to catch his breath, she couldn't imagine him joining her and her friends for a walk up Collard Hill or Glastonbury Tor on a summer's afternoon. She wondered how he'd cope with a class full of lively children. 'Well, I'd better get on,' she said. 'Nice to meet you, Cyril. When you move in, I'll introduce you to my brothers.'

She waved and went inside before Mr Baker could suggest she show his grandson around the village and introduce him to people. She didn't think she'd have anything in common with him and she doubted a teacher would be interested in a factory girl like her anyway.

Peter and John were standing in the kitchen as she came through the door.

'Got a new sweetheart?' asked John with a smirk. 'He's a bit of a weed, ain't he?'

'Oh, get on with you. He's Mr Baker's grandson visiting from Taunton. He'll be moving here to teach at the board school in September.'

'Huh, got himself a teaching job to stop from fighting, has he?'

Jeannie glared at him as Peter nudged him and shook his head, muttering at his twin to shut up.

'For your information, he volunteered, but got rejected on account of having asthma,' she told him. Outside, they could hear him coughing again. 'He's very good at mathematics, apparently.' She glanced at Peter, ignoring the snort from John. 'He might be able to help you get your engineering apprenticeship – if you haven't changed your mind about it.'

He glanced out of the window. 'I haven't. Tom's putting in a good word for me.'

'You're a mug,' sneered John. 'You won't catch me working for peanuts for years, stuck in that factory.'

'You're the mug,' said Peter. 'There's more to life than football. I'll be earning a good living while you'll end up too old to kick a ball and stuck in a dead-end job doing what? Driving lorries?'

John scowled at him. 'I'll do all right, you wait and see. I'll be my own boss, see if I'm not.'

Jeannie rolled her eyes. The twins seemed to argue more than they agreed these days. 'I wish you two would agree to disagree. Just because what the other wants doesn't suit you, doesn't make it foolish or wrong. You have to find your own paths.'

John turned his scowl onto Jeannie even as Peter nodded in agreement with her. 'What would you know about it? You're stuck in that Machine Room with all them other silly girls until you find some fool daft enough to marry you and keep you. Going after the teacher, are you?' He tilted his head towards the two men still chatting in the garden. 'He's probably the best you can hope for. Better get in quick. He sounds like he's heading for an early grave.'

Jeannie saw red. John had been a beast when Lucas had been away but he'd watched his tongue since he'd come home. But today, he'd overstepped the mark. She reached up and grabbed his ear and twisted, causing him to yelp.

'Don't you dare talk to me like that, John Musgrove! You show me some respect or I'll show you *daft*.' She twisted further, pulling his head down until he was bent nearly double. He yelped again and grabbed her wrist, trying to prise her off his ear. 'You know better than to be so rude to anyone, so don't you go thinking you can treat me so ill,' she went on, her indignation giving her the strength to keep him captive. 'Why, if it weren't for me helping Ma, you'd not have food on the table nor clean clothes nor a fresh bed to sleep in. So you think on that next time you sneer at me, you rotten so-and-so!'

'All right, all right,' he hissed. 'Let go, for God's sake! You're a flipping mad woman!'

She boxed his other ear for good measure before she pushed him away. John stumbled back and had to grab onto the kitchen table to stop himself from falling on his backside. As he righted himself, he took a step towards her, his eyes blazing. Jeannie glared back at him, daring him to touch her. She'd brought Sid Lambert down with a knee to his privates and she was mad enough to do the same if John thought he had the right to attack her.

'John!' Lucas's sharp voice halted him. 'What the heck do you think you're doing?' he demanded as he stood in the door from the parlour.

Jeannie wondered how long he'd been there. She'd been so angry that she hadn't taken any notice. Peter sniggered as John began to complain about her treatment of him. She huffed and crossed her arms over her chest, letting him have his say. Not that the stupid boy made any sense.

'Are you done?' asked Lucas when John eventually ran out of steam. 'Because it seems to me that Jeannie was fully justified in putting you in your place.'

'No! I just— She wasn't—' he protested.

Lucas held up a hand. 'Yes she was. I heard the whole thing and you were damned rude. If you'd have talked to me like that, I've had put you on your backside, that's for sure.' He pointed a finger at him. 'I'm still of a mind to do it. I'm ashamed of you, talking to our sister like that. Jeannie's right. You were rude and disrespectful and I won't have it in this family. We pull together and treat each other right, d'you hear? You want to give Ma a heart attack?'

'She started it,' he said, glaring at Jeannie.

Lucas rolled his eyes. 'For God's sake, grow up! If you want to be treated like a man, start acting like one instead of a stupid boy with less sense than a donkey.'

Peter sniggered again, earning him glares from all of his siblings. He went red and stared at the floor. 'Sorry,' he mumbled.

They were all silent for a moment. Jeannie was glad Lucas had been on her side, but she'd held her own against her younger but taller brother. His nasty comments had put a spark to her temper like she'd never known before. She was sure he'd think twice about talking to her like that again. He'd better not. She worked damned hard for the family and John's attitude toward her both hurt and infuriated her.

A movement behind Lucas caught her eye. Ma stood there, looking unutterably sad. When Lucas noticed Jeannie's gaze, he turned. Ma put a hand on his arm and walked into the kitchen.

'Oh John,' she sighed. 'Why must you always fight so? Your sister doesn't deserve such treatment.'

'You heard us?' said Jeannie, feeling shame wash over her. 'I'm sorry, Ma. He just set me off.'

John snarled. 'She attacked me, Ma. It was her fault.'

Lucas took a step towards him as Peter took one back to get out of the line of fire. Ma put out a hand to stop them. 'No, Lucas. Leave him.' She looked at John, who was staring defiantly at his older brother. 'Look at me, John,' she said quietly.

He did as he was bid, his demeanour softening a little under her gentle gaze. 'What?' he said, still sullen enough that he clearly wasn't going to apologise willingly.

Jeannie wanted to box his ears again, but Ma's presence held her back.

'Now, John, son, I know you're keen to grow up and find your way in the world. But one of the measures of a man is how he treats others, especially the weaker sex.'

Jeannie bristled at her mother's words. She didn't feel weak at the moment. She felt full of fire and strength. Even though all of her brothers were a good foot taller than her, she knew she was as bright and hard-working and resourceful as they were – if not more so in John's case. She'd proved she wasn't weak by putting John firmly in his place.

Peter giggled. 'Nothing weak about our Jeannie,' he said, clearly agreeing with her.

'Shush!' she said, not looking at him as she hid a smile.

'No, there certainly isn't, Peter,' said Ma. 'For which I'm proud and thankful. But that doesn't mean she shouldn't be treated with love and respect, especially by her brothers.' She paused and blew out a long breath. 'It breaks my heart, hearing you talk to your sister like that, John. Promise me you'll think on what you said and that you won't do it again. Jeannie does so much for all of us and I can't bear it if you mistreat her.'

When John said nothing, Lucas stepped forward again. 'Well? What have you got to say for yourself?' he demanded.

John finally had the decency to look shame-faced. 'Sorry,' he muttered, not looking at any of them. 'But she didn't need to attack me like that, did she? Is she going to apologise for that?'

She opened her mouth but had no idea what to say. She *should* apologise for being so violent and angry. But she found she couldn't bring herself to want to. John had been a difficult boy for more months than she cared to remember – especially since Lucas had gone off to the army – and her reaction to him today had been a culmination of all of that.

'I'm sure she's sorry,' said Ma.

'But she's taken more from you than she should have,' said Lucas. 'Truth be told, you deserved it, John, and I for one don't think she needs to apologise for it.'

'He's right,' said Peter, earning a glare from his twin. 'She was only being polite to that lad. If it had been us outside, we'd have been the same so as not to shame Ma. You didn't need to be so nasty to Jeannie about him.'

John frowned. 'How was I nasty? You saw him. He's pale and sickly. It's not nasty to state a fact, is it?'

'You didn't have to imply I was going to start walking out with him as though I was so desperate and couldn't get anyone else,' snapped Jeannie.

He laughed. 'Aren't you? I mean, who's asked you out since you chucked your dandelion and burdock all over Douglas Baker and Doris Lambert, eh? And let's not forget how you kneed Sid in the—'

'That's enough,' said Ma, her voice firmer than Jeannie had heard in a long time. 'Now, I came down for a cuppa when all this ruckus was going on. Put the kettle on, Peter. You and John can make me and Jeannie a cup of tea and bring it through to the parlour when it's brewed. Lucas, love, will you keep an eye on them and make sure they don't make a mess? Come on Jeannie, my angel. Let's have a sit down on the settee and you can tell me about Mr Baker's visitor.'

Jeannie followed Ma into the parlour and sank down onto the settee with a sigh. 'I really am sorry, Ma. He just made me so angry.'

'I know, lass. He's vexing everyone lately. I'm sure he doesn't mean anything by it. He's just confused and getting himself in a tizzy over what he wants to do with his life. We need to be patient with him. He'll find his way soon, I'm sure.'

'I hope so. Because I'm heartily sick of him speaking to me as though I'm of no account. I just saw red, and once I'd grabbed his ear, I wasn't inclined to let go, even though I knew I was hurting him and violence is never the answer.'

Ma smiled and stroked her hair. 'I know, my love. And I know you're not the sort of person who usually solves problems with aggression. But please, try not to do it again, eh? I do so hate to see my children fighting.'

She sighed. 'I'll try, Ma. But John needs to watch his tongue.' She shook her head. 'I've never been so cross – not even when I caught Douglas canoodling with Doris.' Even though she'd been mad enough to throw their drinks over them, she'd acted on instinct, more out of shock rather than anger. But even that had been out of character. 'I... I just hated that he was laughing at me and saying no one wanted me.' She felt tears well and dashed them away, getting angry all over again that his words had upset her so. 'Truth be told,' she said, her voice dropping to almost a whisper. 'I think I got so mad because he said what I've been wondering. I mean, I know there's a lot of lads gone to fight, but there must be someone out there to suit me, mustn't there?' She turned to Ma for reassurance, knowing full well that she couldn't give it.

'Hush now, don't fret, lass. There's a good man out there for you.' Ma kissed her temple. 'I did wonder about Lucas's friend Tom. He seems to like you well enough.'

Jeannie shrugged. 'So everyone says. But he hasn't asked me out, so he's probably just being polite.'

Lucas came in with the tea tray, balancing it on the flat of his left hand and holding it steady with his injured right one. Jeannie thought she ought to jump up and relieve him of it, but she noticed that with his new splint on, he had more control over it so she stayed where she was. He put it on the sideboard and handed her and Ma their cups before retrieving his own and sitting in the armchair facing them.

'Are you all right, Jeannie?' he asked.

She nodded, but more tears welled and she sniffed and wiped her eyes.

'He's enough to drive us all to violence,' he said. 'Well done for not letting him get away with it.'

'Where is he?' Ma asked.

'John wanted to go and play football, but I told him he had to stay home and do chores. I threatened to puncture his ball if he defied me. I sent them both down the garden to check the vegetable beds. There should be some new potatoes and broad beans ready. There's a good crop of gooseberries as well. Maybe we can have a crumble?'

Ma nodded. 'If you like, son.'

'So long as he doesn't crush them all as he picks them,' said Jeannie. 'You know how he sulks. Maybe you should've let him go.'

He shook his head. 'No. He's got to learn that his actions have consequences. Letting him go out for a kickabout after what he said to you would be like rewarding him for bad behaviour. We've got to be tougher with him. God forbid, if he ends up having to enlist, he'll soon get himself into trouble if he doesn't do as he's told.'

Ma closed her eyes and covered her mouth. 'Please God, let this terrible war be long over by the time they get to eighteen.'

Jeannie patted Ma's shoulder, glaring at Lucas. He should know better than to say things like that. 'I'm sure it will be, Ma,' she said, hoping with all her heart that it would prove true.

Lucas grimaced, his way of apologising to his sister for his comment. 'Jeannie's right, Ma. I just think we need to be a bit tougher on them now they're growing up. Like I said to John, if he wants to be treated like a man, he has to start acting like one. We've been too soft on both of them. But don't worry. I'll sort them out.' He nodded, determination lighting his eyes.

'Don't be too hard on them, son,' said Ma. 'They're good boys really.'

Jeannie and Lucas shared a look before they both reassured her.

'Anyway,' said Lucas, turning to his sister. 'Enough about those idiots. Who is it you're wanting to ask you out? I didn't know you were sweet on anyone.'

Jeannie felt her cheeks warm. She sighed. This day couldn't get much worse, could it?

'No one. I'm not.'

He raised his eyebrows and waited.

'It doesn't matter. He's not interested anyway.' She looked away. 'I'm going to be an old maid.'

Lucas chuckled. She felt her hackles rise. Why did everyone find it so funny?

'Don't be daft. You're what, eighteen? You've plenty of time to find a husband.'

'Not if they all rush off and leave Street,' she grumbled. 'But anyway, like I said, it doesn't matter.'

He frowned. 'So who is it?'

'Mind your own business,' she snapped. She put her cup aside and stood up. 'If you're not going to check on the twins, I'd better do it.'

She left the room, not wanting to hear Ma tell him that she was pining over his friend. It had been bad enough that she'd carried a torch for Mattie for years, only to see him fall head over heels in love with Louisa the moment he met her properly. But at least no one had known about that. Maybe she should look for a sweetheart who wasn't one of her brother's friends? It would save her a lot of heartache and embarrassment.

9

Kate signed her name at the bottom of the third letter she'd written this weekend and waited for the ink to dry before folding the sheet and putting it into the envelope. With Mrs Clothier's encouragement, she was corresponding with three young men who had been arrested when they refused their call-up for military service, including Auntie Betty's cousin's son, Gerald. Much to everyone's relief, the War Office had issued an order in June, relegating conscientious objectors to the custody of the civil authorities rather than military prisons. Gerald had been sent from the military barracks where he'd been held to Exeter Prison to serve his time. It was now late July and he was over half-way through the three month sentence he'd received. They said he'd been put to hard labour – no doubt a ploy to try to persuade him that fighting in the trenches was preferable, although Kate doubted it would make any difference to a life-long Quaker and pacifist who had already seen the horrors of the battlefield as an ambulance volunteer.

She'd had some replies from Gerald and the others already.

She supposed the poor fellows didn't have much else to do but write letters when they were locked up in their cells. They were all written in pencil as they weren't allowed pens and ink. All of them expressed their gratitude for her letters, saying that news from the outside world was much welcome. Each of them seemed resigned to serving their sentences and didn't whine or complain. Instead, they gave thanks for little things, like the kindness of some prison guards or a glimpse of sunshine beyond the walls of their cells. It made Kate feel humble and determined to find things in her own life to be grateful for. She tried to make her letters happy and encouraging.

'All done, lass?' asked Auntie Betty.

'Yes, Auntie. I'll drop them in the post box on my way to work in the morning.' She sighed. 'I wish I could do more for them. One of them mentioned having visitors. But it's too far to go. I'm still saving for Ma's headstone, so I don't have any money to spare for a train fare. And anyway, I can't afford to take time off work, even if Clarks let me.'

'I'm sure they appreciate your letters, but I'm not sure visiting a prison is something a young woman should be doing,' said Betty, looking doubtful. 'They're not nice places, lass.'

Kate pulled a face. 'I don't suppose they are. But these lads are innocent of any real crime, aren't they? I should like to visit them to show solidarity with them. But we're close to having enough to pay for Ma's headstone at last, so I'm putting all my spare money towards that. We wanted to get it done before George and Fred have to go off to fight.'

'Do you think Peg will come for a visit to see it when it's erected?' she asked, looking hopeful. 'I do miss her and my Will so, and I'm desperate to set eyes on that beautiful baby of theirs.'

They both glanced at the pencil drawing that Louisa had

given her of the newborn child. Betty had had it framed and looked at it often. Kate tended to avoid studying it, recognising it for the accurate representation of the little boy she'd seen when she'd gone to Lincolnshire with George to bring Louisa home. It was drawn with so much love by the woman who had given him birth, it always made her feel sad to look at it, knowing the pain that Louisa was still feeling after having to give up her baby. Kate was torn every time she saw it, thinking of the joy that little Matthew brought her sister Peg and brother-in-law Will in contrast to Louisa's grief.

'If not,' Auntie Betty went on, 'I'm thinking I might try and make the journey to Lincolnshire for a few days when the factory closes for the summer break in August. I'm long overdue a grandmother's first embrace of little Mattie.'

Kate smiled. She'd forgotten about the factory closure. 'You should, Auntie. Have yourself a proper holiday.' It would certainly be easier for Louisa if Betty went to visit Peg and Will rather than the other way around. Kate wasn't sure how Louisa might react if they came home to Street with the baby so soon. She had the feeling that Lou was trying to prepare herself for after the war ended and Will no longer had to work away at the tank factory. He would bring his family home to Street. It would be so hard for Louisa, but by then little Matthew would be older and she might have had time to come to terms with the fact that the boy was growing up as someone else's son.

Betty nodded. 'I might just do that.' She smiled. 'I'll write to them and see what they think.'

Kate left her landlady to her letter writing and went out into the garden, enjoying the summer evening sunshine. She wondered how Betty would manage the journey to Lincolnshire. George might be able to take her in his lorry, but who knew whether he might have been called up by then?

The familiar dread tied a knot in her stomach as she thought about her brothers being sent to war. It had been hard enough when her beloved Ma had died after months of illness. The prospect of never seeing either of her brothers, or God forbid, both of them, again was too much to bear. But, if the worst did happen, she knew that she'd have to bear it. She would have to do what she could to support her sisters-in-law, Ada and Vi, and their children. They had all helped her when Ma had been ill, and stepped in when Pa had moved his floozy and illegitimate children into the family home. So, while her brothers were doing their duty for king and country, she would do what she could to make life easier for their families. And she would pray every day that they came home safe to them at the end of the war.

At work the next day, the talk was of the battle that had been raging in the Somme since the start of July. While some folk insisted it would be the campaign that would bring victory for the Allies, others shared rumours of terrible casualties, gas attacks and retreats.

'How do we know what's true and what's propaganda?' asked Kate as they sat on the grass in the sunshine and ate their food. 'For all we know, German spies could be spreading lies to frighten and demoralise us.'

'I hate all this,' said Jeannie. 'So many lads gone. Did you hear that one of Mrs Howard's sons was killed? Him and most of his regiment, if the postman is to be believed. He said he was delivering death notices all last week. At this rate, there'll be no one left.' She scrubbed at her eyes. 'I can't bear it. Are they set on killing all our menfolk? What's to become of us if they don't come back? They should put a stop to all this.'

Louisa touched her arm. 'I know, Jeannie. But don't you see? They can't give up now or we'll lose the war and then we'll all be for it.' She shared a glance with Kate. 'The longer this war goes on, the more I think Ted's ma is right to be afraid, even if she is so fierce about pushing lads to enlist.'

Kate scowled. Mrs Jackson had encouraged all three of her sons to enlist and for all they knew, she had lost all three of them by now. Albert would never return, Stan would never be the same again. As for Ted... He'd told her he had offered himself for service to prevent poor Stan from facing a firing squad for desertion. Yet no one they knew had seen him at basic training, so she had no idea where he'd gone.

Yet, despite Mrs Jackson's losses, the woman was still a prominent member of the White Feather Movement, chasing down any man who didn't enlist, handing them white feathers and denouncing them as cowards, regardless of their religious beliefs. It was as though she wanted every other mother to suffer as she had.

'She is afraid,' agreed Jeannie.

Louisa's lips thinned. 'I know, yet aren't we all? She's not the only one who's lost someone, had their whole future destroyed by this bloody war.' Her tone was bitter. 'I know you said the same when she turned on you that time – remember, when we were helping with costumes at the Operatic Society?'

All three girls were quiet for a moment, remembering how Louisa and Mattie had persuaded Jeannie and Lucas to help out – the girls on the costumes and the lads on making scenery – so that Lou and Mattie could steal some time together without her ma and pa knowing. Mrs Jackson had been there and got into an argument with another woman and then turned on Jeannie when she had tried to offer them the pacifist point of view. It had shaken Jeannie; she was a peace-maker, but she hadn't blamed

Mrs Jackson. Instead, she'd pointed out that the older woman was frightened of what might happen if the Hun were victorious and invaded the country.

'I know you wouldn't judge her then, and I respect you for that,' Louisa went on. 'And, now... after everyone and everything we've lost so far and with no sign of it being over... well, I confess I'm starting to be as scared as she is.'

Kate frowned. 'You think we'll lose?'

She shrugged and looked away. 'I hope not. But for me, we've already lost. My life will never be the same. Mattie's gone. Everything's different and I don't expect to ever be happy again.' She shook herself and took a deep breath, as though trying to pull herself out of the slough of despair the conversation had dragged her into. 'But that doesn't mean I want us to lose the war or for us to have to learn German. We have to trust that our lads will triumph. They have to. If not, my Mattie's sacrifice and what Lucas and Tom and poor Stan are still suffering would all be for nothing, wouldn't it? That's why we have to fight on.' She sent a sympathetic glance at her friends. 'I'm sorry. I know I shouldn't be saying things like this and I hate it. But I can't see a way out of this. If our men don't carry on fighting, we'll all be lost, won't we?'

Kate felt a chill, despite the hot sun on her back. 'We've got to keep praying,' she said. 'We can't give up hope.'

Again, Louisa looked away. Jeannie's gentle gaze caught and held Kate's, though. Jeannie understood them both – Lou's despair and grief (even though she didn't know the half of it) and Kate's fear for her brothers. She'd felt all of those emotions when Mattie and then Lucas had gone off to war, and now she saw how hard it was for her brother to live with his injury and the loss of his best friend, as well as the awful things he'd seen on the battlefield.

Kate closed her eyes and lowered her head. 'We can't give up hope,' she repeated. 'We have to go on.'

As though in response to her words, the hooter sounded across the factory grounds, calling everyone back to work.

10

Lucas caught up with Jeannie and Louisa as they left the factory at the end of her shift on Saturday. 'Where's Kate?' he asked.

'She's gone to the Trimmings Department to see Auntie Betty. They're off to get some groceries,' said Jeannie. 'Are we getting ours on the way home, or waiting until later?'

Lucas frowned. 'Kate needs to see Fred,' he said, ignoring her question.

'Why?' she asked.

Louisa put her hands to her chest. 'Oh no. He's got his call-up, hasn't he?'

He nodded. 'He's got to report for training on the first of the month.'

'What about his brother?' asked Jeannie.

He shrugged. 'Don't know. It seems like they're calling men in age groups. There's a couple of years between them, so George might not be in this cohort.'

'But Fred's Vi is having another baby. They can't expect him to leave her now.'

Lucas shook his head. 'Doesn't make any difference. If he's got a call-up, he's got to go or be arrested.'

'Do you want me to find Kate and tell her?' said Louisa. 'I expect she'll want to go round to Fred's.'

Lucas nodded. 'Would you? I expect George will know by now if he's not out on the road.' Kate's brothers lived on the same road and the wives were good friends. 'Fred wanted to let Kate know before she heard it from somewhere else and got upset that he hadn't told her. Tell her he's looking for her will you, Louisa?'

She nodded. 'I will. She's going to be upset anyway. But I'll stay with her as long as she needs me.'

It occurred to Jeannie that Louisa always welcomed an excuse not to go straight home. She wondered whether her friend would ever reconcile with her parents and it made her feel sad that the Clements family seemed to have broken down into a household of strangers when before the war, they had had a close, loving relationship. Then she felt mean for thinking Louisa was using Kate as an excuse to not go home when in truth, she was clearly thinking of their friend rather than her own situation.

'Do you want me to come with you, Lou?' asked Jeannie.

Louisa shook her head. 'You've got your groceries to buy. I'll tell her you wanted to come and you're thinking of her.'

Jeannie opened her mouth to protest that she wanted to do more, but Louisa hurried away. Lucas put a hand on her arm. 'Let her go, sis. You'll see Kate at the Meeting House tomorrow.'

She sighed. 'I suppose so.' She noticed Lou's pa coming out of the main gate. 'Let me just let Mr Clements know where Louisa's gone so he doesn't worry if she doesn't get home right away.'

Lucas snorted but didn't stop her as she ran over and explained the situation to the foreman.

'Thank you for taking the time to tell me,' he said, before he strode off in the direction of his home in Somerton Road.

She watched him go, thinking he didn't look very happy about it. But then again, Mr Clements looked older these days and always seemed grumpy. She couldn't remember the last time she'd seen him smile. Not that Louisa seemed much happier.

'Come on,' said Lucas. 'There's the twins. They can come and help carry.' Despite the improvement his new splint had made, he still couldn't rely on his right hand when it came to gripping and carrying anything heavy. He beckoned them over before Jeannie realised that Tom was with them.

Jeannie felt her cheeks warm when he caught her eye and smiled. 'Lovely day to have the afternoon off,' he said.

'I don't know about an afternoon off,' she said. 'We've got shopping to do.'

'Ready lads?' Lucas asked the twins. 'There'll be plenty to carry.'

'But we've got a match,' said Peter. 'Got to be at the pitch by two.'

'Yeah,' said John. 'So we're off for our dinner now so we're fighting fit for it. Ma said she'd have it ready.'

'It won't take long,' said Jeannie. 'You'll still make kick-off.'

'But—' both twins started to protest.

'If you want to eat, you have to carry the shopping,' said Jeannie. 'And the longer you argue, the longer it will take.'

'She's right,' said Lucas. 'It's got to be done and with the amount you two eat these days, we can't manage it all.'

Peter sighed and his shoulders slumped. 'Come on then. Let's get it over with.'

John glared at his siblings. 'You knew we had a match,' he complained.

'And you know we've all got to do our bit for the family,' said Lucas, his tone mild but firm. He took some money out of his pocket and handed it to him. 'Take this and get down to the mill.

Ma wants a new sack of flour and some fresh yeast for bread. Get that home and you can get on with your dinner.' He turned to Peter. 'Can we trust you to get eggs, milk, butter and cheese from the dairy while me and Jeannie go to the butcher and greengrocer?'

Peter nodded, took the money and ran off.

'Don't run and break the eggs,' Jeannie called after him.

He raised a hand and carried on running while John huffed and walked away muttering about flour and smelly yeast and why couldn't Ma buy bread from the bakers.

Jeannie laughed. 'Be grateful Ma's feeling well enough to make bread,' she told him as he left. 'It saves us a pretty penny which means more of everything else to fill your bellies.'

Tom smiled at her amusement. 'I'm glad your ma's feeling better,' he said.

'Thanks,' said Lucas. 'She's always better in the warmer weather. And she makes the best bread I've ever tasted, so we make the most of it when she's got a mind to bake it.'

'We'd better get on,' said Jeannie. 'There'll be queues.'

She expected Tom to take his leave of them, but instead he said, 'Can I help? I've nothing better to do, so I can carry some bags for you.'

Before Jeannie could refuse, Lucas nodded. 'That'll be grand. Thanks. So, how's life in the mechanics' shop?'

Jeannie trailed after them as they headed up the High Street towards the greengrocers, wondering whether Lucas needed her at all if he had his friend to help. She didn't say anything though as she was too busy trying to keep up with their long gaits and admiring Tom's broad shoulders.

'Good,' he said in answer to her brother's question. 'Plenty to do all over the factory, so no time to get bored. I haven't said anything to Peter yet, but it looks like they might give him a trial after the summer break.'

Lucas nodded. 'That's good news. He's dead keen.'

'It is,' agreed Jeannie. 'Thank you for helping him. It's a shame John's not so keen. I swear that boy hates to do anything he's told.'

'Unless he's getting orders from the football coach,' said Lucas with a grin.

'But that's not going to put food on his table, is it?' she said. 'I wish we could find someone like Tom who might inspire him as much.'

Tom looked a little startled as he glanced over his shoulder at her. 'I'm hardly inspiring,' he said.

'You are,' she said, trying not to smile or blush. 'It was talking to you about being an engineer that encouraged Peter to want to follow that path. We're mighty grateful for your influence on him.'

He chuckled. 'Don't thank me until he's got his papers. He might find he hates it when he's covered in machine oil. I expect you'll be cursing me when you're trying to get it out of his overalls.'

Her heart sank at the thought that she might still be doing the family's laundry when Peter was a fully qualified engineer, which would be years in the future. But she refused to contemplate it. 'With any luck, he'll have a wife to deal with that for him before long.'

Lucas frowned at her. 'Don't be daft,' said Lucas. 'He's still a kid.'

She blushed, feeling foolish for speaking her thought. 'I'm not talking about now,' she said. 'But when he qualifies. He'll be a good catch.'

Lucas grinned at Tom. 'Does that mean you're a good catch?' he asked him.

Tom frowned and shook his head, not looking at Jeannie. 'No, I'm not. Hardly worth bothering with.'

She didn't dare say anything. She assumed he meant because of his missing foot – and maybe his war experiences. It seemed as though men coming home injured had to deal with the mental anguish they brought home with them as well and that was hard on their womenfolk. Jeannie wanted to reassure him that he had nothing to be ashamed of and that he *was* a good catch, but she didn't want to embarrass him or herself any more.

They reached the greengrocers. Jeannie turned to Lucas. 'Why don't you get the fruit and veg, and I'll see what's left at the butchers?'

'It might be easier if we do it the other way around,' he said. 'Then Tom can help you carry the bags back. I'll only need one hand for the meat, but we need more bags of veg.'

She didn't see why Tom couldn't help Lucas, but she supposed it would be less awkward for a girl to have someone carrying bags for her than for a lad. With a sigh, she got one of her string shopping bags out of her work bag and handed it to him. 'Go on then.'

He handed over some of the housekeeping money, nodded to them both and wandered off.

'Right,' said Tom, rubbing his hands together. 'What do you need?'

Despite their efforts in the garden, they still needed cabbage, carrots and salad stuff as well as fruit for pies and crumbles. Their potato crop was barely enough for the odd meal so far, so they needed more of those.

'I thought we would be growing all this by now,' she said as she selected some onions and added them to her purchases. 'Even with old Mr Baker giving us tips, we're none of us very good at growing produce – apart from peas, that is. We've got more than we know what to do with of those.'

He smiled. 'I like a nice fresh pea. And my ma made the best pea soup from dried ones in the winter.'

She stilled, glancing at him.

'What?' he asked when she saw her expression.

'That's the first time I've ever heard you mention your family. Is your ma still with you?'

He sighed. 'Yes, she is. So's my pa.'

'You must miss them.'

'I do,' he said. But he didn't elaborate. 'What else do you need?'

She looked around. 'Some beetroot, radishes, watercress. Oh, and those marrows look like they're a good price. We can stuff those.' She busied herself paying for them and packing the bags she'd brought with her. She was about to tell him she could probably carry everything herself when he stepped forward to pick up the shopping, leaving her with just her work bag.

'Thank you,' she said as she followed him out of the shop. 'I'm sure you've got better things to do on a Saturday afternoon.'

He shrugged and smiled. 'Not really. I've no one to take care of but myself and my landlady offers meals and laundry, so all I have to do is keep myself and my room tidy and let her know when I want feeding.'

'Ah, that must be so nice,' she sighed.

He chuckled but she immediately felt ashamed. 'It's not that I don't love my family, I do, and I'm happy to serve them,' she said. 'But...' She fell silent and looked away.

'But everyone deserves a break,' he said softly. 'I know you work hard at home and at the factory.'

She looked down at her hands gripping her work bag. 'I'm no busier than anyone else. Lots of lasses have to help at home. And lots of wives have had to go back to work at the factory while their menfolk are away and still keep their homes and children in order. That doesn't mean I'm ungrateful. I do appreciate you helping me today.'

He nodded. She noticed that he'd adjusted his stride to match hers so she didn't have to rush to keep up with him now. She wondered if it was easier for him, considering his false foot. It must be hard for him to match the strides of the other lads all the time. She hoped it didn't hurt him. He didn't seem uncomfortable – he walked with just a slight limp these days. Hardly noticeable at all. Or maybe it was because she'd got used to seeing it? Whatever it was, it didn't mean she'd forgotten about his injury.

They walked along in silence for a bit. She knew that she'd be stopping every few yards by now, adjusting the handles of the string bags, trying to ease the ache in her fingers caused by the heavy loads if Tom hadn't taken the burden from her.

'Will you go home to Northampton for the August break?' she asked.

He paused and glanced at her, his face blank. 'I hadn't thought of it. It's not an easy journey.'

'But it would be nice to see your ma and pa, wouldn't it?'

'It might,' he said. 'But I'm not planning on it. We get by with letters.'

'Oh. I'd hate it if I couldn't see my ma and feel my arms around her when I need to. I don't remember much of my pa, of course, because he passed when I was little. But...' She fell silent. The smiling man of a few minutes ago was gone, replaced by this stranger whose expression she couldn't read. 'I... I'm sorry. Not everyone is close to their parents. Lord knows my friends have enough problems with theirs. I should mind my own business.' She turned and started walking a little faster.

She heard Tom sigh behind her, then his steady tread as he followed her. 'Jeannie, wait,' he said.

She stopped, ashamed again as she realised she was being

ungrateful and rude by rushing ahead when he was being so kind.

'I'm sorry,' she said again, holding out a hand. 'Do you want me to take one of those bags? Or all of them? I expect you're regretting helping me now, with me being so nosy.'

He held onto the bags and shook his head. 'It's all right,' he said, his expression softening. 'I'm sorry I'm such a miserable beggar. I'm just not used to talking about myself.'

She frowned. 'Why not?' she asked, before she remembered herself and slapped a hand over her mouth. 'Forget I said that,' she mumbled behind her fingers. 'It's none of my business.'

He laughed softly. 'Jeannie, you're the least nosy lass I know. In fact, I'm surprised you've not asked a lot of questions before now. Plenty of people have tried.' He tilted his head towards the end of the High Street and the start of West End, where the Musgrove cottage was. 'Let's get on. Your ma will be wondering where you are. Ask your questions. If I don't want to answer them, I'll tell you.'

They started walking again, Jeannie's mind awhirl. 'Now you've said that, I can't think of a single thing to ask,' she said. 'I really don't want to pry. I... I'd just like to get to know you a bit better, is all. I mean, you've become a good friend of my brothers and I don't even know if you've got any brothers or sisters of your own.'

'Well, that's easy to answer. I'm the youngest, with four sisters.' He gave her a sideways glance. 'So you and your friends in the Machine Room hold no fear for me, Miss Musgrove. If I can survive the lasses in my family, no woman frightens me.'

She giggled. '*Four* older sisters? Oh my. I'll bet you were spoilt rotten being the only lad.'

He raised an eyebrow. 'You think so? Not at all. They made my life a misery,' he said. 'Now they're doing the same for their husbands.'

'Any nieces and nephews?'

'So many I've lost count,' he said.

Jeannie gave him a sympathetic look. 'You must miss them all a lot.' She knew she would if her family was too far away to visit, no matter how annoying her brothers could be.

He shrugged, his focus on the road ahead as they approached her home. 'Not really. I'm enjoying the quiet life.'

Lucas was coming out of the front door as they reached it. 'There you are,' he said. 'Thanks for helping her, Tom. I've just got to pop to the grocers now as Ma wants some tinned goods.'

'Then take a wicker basket rather than a string bag,' said Jeannie, nodding at the bag in his hands. 'You can hook the handle over your arm easier.'

Lucas looked at it and frowned. 'All right,' he said, turning back into the cottage to get one.

'Want me to come with you?' Tom called after him. 'I'm enjoying having something to do out in the sunshine.'

'If you like,' said Lucas.

'Right. Let's get this lot inside,' he told Jeannie. 'Then I'll do escort duty for your brother.' He followed her inside. Ma sat at the table while the twins gobbled down their dinners as though afraid someone would snatch them away if they slowed down.

'Please excuse my brothers' horrible manners, Tom,' said Jeannie.

'Wha'?' asked John with a mouth full of food.

'We've got a match,' said Peter as he put his knife and fork down and pushed his plate away. 'Got to go.' He stood up as John shoved the last mouthful in and followed suit.

'Boys,' said Ma. 'Slow down. You'll give yourselves a belly ache.'

'No time, Ma,' said John. 'Grab our boots, Pete.'

'Good luck, lads,' said Tom.

They both grunted in that way of all lads when their focus is elsewhere, but Tom didn't seem to mind. Instead he lifted the bags he was carrying onto the kitchen table as Jeannie cleared the boys' plates. Lucas came out of the pantry with a basket.

'Ready?' he asked Tom. Within moments, all four lads had gone, leaving Ma and Jeannie and a welcome peace. That Jeannie felt a bit let down that Lucas had dragged Tom away so quickly, she wouldn't admit to anyone.

'He's a nice lad, that Tom,' said Ma. 'Helping you and Lucas like that.'

'Yes, Ma,' she said as she began unpacking the vegetables. She'd noticed that he was keen to rush off with Lucas just when she thought they were getting on quite well. But she supposed he was her brother's friend more than hers, so she shouldn't complain. The news that he wasn't planning on seeing his family over the summer holiday bothered her. He was on good money, so he should be able to afford to go home to Northampton if he wanted. Yet she had a feeling there was more to it than he was willing to tell her. Had they had a falling out? Why wouldn't anyone want to see their kin when they could? Unless they were like Kate's pa, of course. Just because Tom was nice didn't mean his family were. But if he didn't want to talk about it, she would never know, so she should just forget about it.

'I got a couple of decent marrows.' She held them up to show Ma. 'I thought we could stuff them.'

They talked about the meals they could prepare with the provisions they had as they put them away in the pantry. By the time they'd done that and made a fresh pot of tea, Lucas was back.

'Where's your friend?' asked Ma when he came in alone.

'He decided to go and watch the match.'

'You could've offered him some dinner,' she said. 'To thank him for his help.'

'I did,' he said. 'But he wasn't hungry.'

That told Jeannie all she needed to know. Watching the twins play football was more interesting to Tom than spending time with her.

Ma shook her head. 'Really, Lucas. The least we could do is feed him after using the poor lad as a pack horse.' She looked stern, but her eyes were twinkling with mirth. Jeannie smiled, happy to see Ma in such good spirits. 'Well, sit yourselves down both of you. You'll be ready for some dinner now. There's shepherd's pie in the oven. I saved mine so I could eat with you both.'

Jeannie sank into her chair, relieved to sit at last. She was mighty grateful to Tom for carrying her load for her today. Her back and shoulders were aching from a long week bent over her machine at the factory. As Ma put a plate in front of her, she bowed her head in thanks that she didn't have to cook this meal and that she might get an hour to relax in an armchair before she had to get on with any more chores.

'So what were you and Tom chatting about while you were shopping?' asked Lucas as she took her first bite.

She chewed the food and swallowed before she answered. 'This is lovely, Ma,' she said before turning to her brother. 'We were just chatting, nothing important. Did you know he's got four older sisters?'

Lucas looked startled. 'Really? Poor so-and-so. One's enough for me.'

'Oh, you,' Ma chuckled. 'You don't mean that.'

Lucas raised his eyebrows but didn't say anything.

Jeannie huffed and rolled her eyes.

'Count yourself lucky there's only one of me,' she told him.

'Do you think that's why he moved all this way – to get away from his sisters?'

'Probably. I would.'

Jeannie laughed and shook her head. 'You're lucky to have me, you ungrateful wretch.'

'Says you,' he teased. They carried on eating in silence. When he had cleared his plate, he sighed and sat back. 'That was grand, Ma.'

Ma smiled but said nothing. Lucas turned to Jeannie, his expression thoughtful. 'So how did you find out about Tom's sisters?' he asked her.

She shrugged and concentrated on her food, hoping he'd turn his attention elsewhere. But he waited and she sighed. Ma was watching her with interest as well. 'I was interested, is all. I asked if he was going to see his family in the factory summer break.'

'And is he?'

She shook her head. 'Apparently not. He didn't say why, apart from his sisters making his life a misery when he was younger.' She frowned. 'I think he was joking about that, but...'

'Probably not,' said Lucas. 'That's far too many women in one house.'

She tutted at him. 'They're all married now. He's the youngest.'

He raised his eyebrows and stared at her. 'You had quite the conversation, didn't you? He's never talked about his family to me.'

'Well, he didn't talk about them with me until I actually asked him,' she pointed out. 'Have you ever bothered to find out? Or do you just talk about football and work?'

This time, it was Lucas who shrugged. 'We're lads. What else are we going to talk about?'

Ma smiled and tilted her head to one side. 'It would be nice if you talked about taking some nice lasses to the Crispin Hall dance,' she said. 'I'm sure there's lots of young ladies who would love to walk out with you.'

Lucas frowned. 'I'm not looking to walk out with anyone,' he said. 'And anyway, they're not exactly queuing up, Ma. Not with my useless hand.'

Ma reached across and patted his arm where it rested on the table. Jeannie wondered whether he could feel it. He gave no indication. 'You're not useless, son,' said Ma. 'You're still a good, hard-working man, and as handsome as your pa. Any girl would be proud to be seen on your arm. And with all those lads going off to fight, you'll have your pick of the pretty lasses.'

Lucas sent Jeannie a look, silently asking for help. She was tempted to ignore it, but realised that Ma would be turning her attention on her soon enough if they didn't distract her.

'I thought you promised to take Louisa when she's ready?' she said.

For a moment, he looked appalled at the idea, although Ma didn't notice as she'd stood up to take their empty plates to the sink. He glared at Jeannie and she raised her eyebrows in a parody of how he'd looked at her just now then crossed her eyes. He sighed and shook his head, no doubt convinced she was going doolally.

'Leave those, Ma,' she said, trying not to laugh. 'I'll do them in a minute.'

'Thanks, love.' She sighed and sat down again. She winced as she adjusted her bottom, trying to get comfortable. 'My back's that stiff and sore today, I'm not sure I can stand at the sink for too long.'

The two of them frowned as they regarded their mother. 'Maybe you should go and have a rest, Ma,' said Jeannie.

'Do you need to see a doctor, Ma?' said Lucas.

'Oh no, son, don't you worry. It's just my old bones. We don't need to be spending money on a doctor.' She put her hands on the table and pushed herself upright. 'I think I'll take Jeannie's advice and go and have a lie down.'

They watched with concern as she made her way out of the kitchen. Jeannie turned to Lucas. 'Should I go with her?' she whispered. 'Make sure she gets up the stairs without falling?'

'I'll do it,' he said, standing up and leaving the room.

She heard him talking softly to Ma as they made their way upstairs. With a sigh, she got up and did the dishes, all the time worrying. She knew Ma suffered with her joints in her hands and shoulders, and sometimes her neck bothered her. But she'd never complained of back pain before. Of course, she'd had weeks when she'd taken to her bed when Lucas was away, so perhaps it had left her with a weakness? Jeannie had hoped that she would get better now he was home and safe, but she seemed so frail. Ma was getting old before her time.

11

By the end of July, both of Kate's brothers had been called up and were off to basic training. Louisa and Jeannie offered to go with Kate to see them off, but she'd said it wasn't necessary.

'I'm not going to the station. Auntie Betty is coming with me to see them tonight and there'll be my sisters-in-law, the kiddies and all my brothers' in-laws with them to wave them off tomorrow,' she told them as they turned off their machines after the dinner hooter had sounded. 'But even if I was going to wave them off, I know how hard it is for both of you. You've done your turns of seeing menfolk off to war what with Mattie and Lucas, so I wouldn't ask it of you. But I appreciate that you were prepared to.'

Louisa didn't want to point out how hard it would be for Kate, saying goodbye to her brothers, whether it be at their homes or on the station platform. Instead, she asked, 'Will your pa be there, do you think?'

Kate gave a snort of laugher. 'Huh. Not likely. If he's not sleeping off his cider, he'll be drinking more. Anyway, none of the family want to see him so I doubt if they've even told him. Who'd want a run-in with that drunken oaf the last time you saw your family before going to war?'

'I know what you mean,' she said. 'I was just worried that he might turn up. That's why I was prepared to be there – to help keep him away from you.'

'Me too.' Jeannie nodded.

Kate smiled as she studied their earnest faces. 'Aw, you're both so good to me.' She opened her arms and the three girls hugged. 'But you don't need to worry. I'll be saying my goodbyes in private. As for tomorrow, he won't be there, I'm sure. Anyway, with luck, they'll be home again for a few days once they finish their training, before they ship them out. So it's not the last goodbye, is it?'

Louisa squeezed her eyes tight shut against the wave of grief that engulfed her as she remembered the magical few days she had had with Mattie between the end of his training and his deployment to France. They had wanted to use the time to marry, but her parents had refused to countenance it. So she had slipped away from the factory on Mattie's last day at home and they had sneaked into his mother's cottage and had declared their love in his bed – an act that she would never, ever regret, but which had had consequences that had broken her heart all over again nine months later.

As though aware of her thoughts, Kate tightened her arm around her and she kissed Louisa's temple. The simple, loving gesture soothed her and she was able to take a calming breath and step back without breaking down. She was learning to cope with her grief now, to hold it at bay.

'Girls,' she said, her tone hesitant. 'I wanted to tell you... George has asked me if I'd go to church with Ada while he's away, to help her with the little ones.'

'You're going back to Holy Trinity?' Louisa and Jeannie said at the same time.

She nodded. 'I talked to Auntie Betty about it first. I didn't want her to think I was rejecting the Friends. I still think their faith is a good thing. But... as I told her... Ada needs me, and, to be honest, I've been missing the familiarity of the Anglican services. Don't get me wrong, I'll still not enjoy the long sermons the reverend likes so much, but... I think I'll be content with the rest of it, even without Ma there. And Auntie said it didn't matter where I worshipped, so long as I served God and welcomed Him into my life. I think I'll still go to the Meeting House sometimes when Ada's not going to church. Auntie said that it was up to me.' She paused. 'I thought I'd let you know, Lou, in case you wanted to go and sit with me and Ada.'

Louisa sighed and shook her head. 'I can understand why you're going back, Kate. But it's not for me.' *Not now. Maybe never.*

'I understand.' She nodded. 'I just thought I'd mention it.'

They joined the throng of women and girls leaving the Machine Room. Louisa was in no rush. She had no appetite these days. It was worse at the end of a shift, when she dreaded going home. At least with her friends, she felt a little hope that things would eventually get better. At home, it was as though she was drowning in despair.

'What's the matter, Lou?' asked Jeannie, linking arms with her as they followed Kate down the worn, stone stairs.

Louisa glanced at her and smiled. 'I'm fine, love. Just feeling sorry for Kate having to see her brothers off. I wish they didn't have to go.'

'I know what you mean. I pray night and day that peace will be declared soon.'

Louisa squeezed her arm. 'God's more likely to listen to you than to me,' she said. 'But I pray for that too.'

'I'm sure He hears all of us,' she said. 'And why wouldn't He listen you just as much as He does me?'

Louisa shrugged. Jeannie had no idea of the sins she had committed in the eyes of the church and her parents, nor the price she would continue to pay for them for the rest of her life. 'Your faith is stronger than mine.'

They reached the bottom of the stairs and walked out into the sunshine. Kate was waiting for them. Louisa raised her face towards the sky and felt the warmth on her skin. 'The weather's glorious, isn't it? I hope it stays like this for the factory holiday.'

'Have you got any plans?' asked Kate.

She shook her head. 'To be honest, I'm dreading it.'

'Why?' asked Jeannie as Kate nodded her understanding.

She sighed. 'My parents are talking about us going somewhere, maybe Lyme Regis. But I don't want to go.'

'I'd love to go to Lyme Regis,' said Jeannie, looking wistful. 'I'd like to see the places Jane Austen describes in *Persuasion*. It would be so romantic, walking in the steps of Anne Elliot and Captain Wentworth.'

Kate rolled her eyes. 'Rather you than me, although a paddle in the sea might be nice.'

'I doubt I'd do either with my parents,' said Louisa. 'Ma will want to go shopping and to visit tea shops while Pa will find an armchair in the boarding house and read the paper or snooze all day.' She pulled a face. 'That's all he seems to do these days if he's not at work.'

Jeannie frowned. 'He did look tired the last time I saw him. Is he poorly?'

'Not really,' she said, blowing out a breath. 'I don't think he's ill or anything. It's more that he's in a permanent sulk because he's so disappointed in me.'

'But surely he's coming round by now?' she asked, looking upset. 'That's not fair. All you did was love Mattie.'

Louisa couldn't say anything, because Jeannie didn't know the half of it. She wanted to drop her head to her chest and shut out the world, but instead she lifted her head to the sun again, trying to dispel the chill she felt at the thought of having to spend a whole week in her parents' company. 'He might have come round eventually, if Ma wasn't being so difficult. She's suggesting we go with a couple of other families from church, which will make it even worse.'

'Who?' asked Kate.

Louisa's smile didn't reach her eyes. 'Guess.'

'Mmm, let's think.' She put her index finger to her chin. 'Someone with a son, no doubt, and as most of them have been called up, it must be one who got rejected. Maybe someone with bad eyesight, a weak chest or pigeon-toes? Those seem to be the only reason they turn them away these days.'

'Our neighbour's grandson, Cyril, got turned down on account of his asthma,' said Jeannie. 'He's going to be teaching at the board school next term.'

Both girls looked at her and she blushed at their attention. 'What? He's going to lodge with his grandpa and I met him a few weeks back, is all.'

'Is he handsome?' asked Kate with a smirk. 'Is that why you didn't mention meeting him?'

'No,' she denied, looking horrified. 'I forgot all about it until just now. He's too pale and skinny. And shy. Painfully so. I'm not sure he'll cope in front of a class.'

'Shame,' said Kate. 'I thought you might have found a new sweetheart, seeing as how Tom's dragging his feet – or foot.' She giggled and covered her mouth with her hand, looking round to make sure no one else heard her. But no one was paying them any attention. 'Sorry,' she said.

Louisa smiled, glad that their focus had turned to Jeannie.

'I'm not looking for a sweetheart,' declared Jeannie. 'I can't see the point.'

'Whyever not?' asked Louisa. Of the three of them, Jeannie was the one who was most suited to the role of wife and mother. Louisa's chance had died with Mattie, and Kate had gone right off men after her father's abuse and Ted's unexpected desertion of her. But Jeannie had always dreamed of finding a good man and settling down.

'After being fooled by Douglas, I doubt I can trust anyone. Not that anyone would ask me out now, you know, after I kneed Sid and soaked Douglas.'

Kate laughed. 'You were defending yourself against Sid when he was in his cups and Douglas needed someone to cool him down after he tried to swallow Doris whole in full view of everyone when he was supposed to be at the dance with you. In both cases, it was entirely their fault, not yours.'

Jeannie shrugged, looking unhappy. 'Doesn't matter. If they're not laughing at me, lads are giving me a wide berth. And anyway, Cyril is Douglas's cousin.'

'Ah,' said Kate. 'Not a good prospect then.'

'But Tom likes you,' said Louisa, frowning. 'I don't understand why he's not asked you out yet.'

'He does,' agreed Kate. 'But, I don't know, maybe he's struggling with his pride on account of his injury? You know how daft lads are, even the more mature ones. Just because he's got a false foot, he probably thinks he's not worthy of a lass as sweet as you.'

'He's worth more than most of the lads round here,' said Jeannie, her expression fierce. She blinked and looked around like Kate had, but no one was taking any notice of the three of them. Then her face fell and she looked down at her feet. 'But that's beside the point. No matter what you both say, he's not given me any sign that he likes me like that, so I think you're wrong.' She looked up and her gaze caught Louisa's. 'Anyway, we got off track. Who is it your Ma's wanting to go on holiday with?'

Louisa groaned and covered her eyes for a moment. 'Remember Horace?'

'The spotty lad from the office? Laughs like a donkey?' said Kate. 'I thought you put your ma straight about him.'

'I did. And then she tried to foist his equally awful cousin on me and we had another battle. Well, it turns out they've yet another cousin, a bit older than them, who's been studying Theology and is coming to Holy Trinity as the new curate. He's going to Lyme Regis with his relatives before he starts.'

Kate groaned. 'Oh no. That won't suit you at all. You don't even go to the church any more.'

'I know,' sighed Louisa. 'I think Ma's hoping I'll take a shine to him and decide to go back. I haven't even met him, but if he's anything like his cousins, there's not a chance in hell that I'll want anything to do with him. I keep telling Ma I'm not interested, that I'm not intending to marry anyone now anyway, but she just won't listen. Truth be told, it's exhausting.'

'What are you going to do?' asked Jeannie.

Louisa wished she knew the answer to that, but she didn't. If her mother wouldn't listen and Pa continued to act as though she was such a disappointment to him, she couldn't see any solution that would suit all of them. It occurred to her that, even if they did become more reasonable, she wasn't sure if she could ever forgive them for stopping her from marrying Mattie. 'I think I need to leave home and make my own way in the world,' she said. 'But I know they'll object and make it impossible for me to do anything until I'm twenty-one. So I suppose we'll just have to muddle along until then. In the meantime, I'm saving hard so that I have a nest egg to see me through. And I'm not going to Lyme Regis with them, no matter what they say.'

Jeannie looked worried. 'You won't run away again, will you?'

Louisa swallowed against a lump in her throat, remembering that Jeannie had no idea of the real reason *why* she'd had to run away before. She blinked to prevent the tears she felt welling and shook her head. 'I'll not,' she said, not adding the words in her mind – *unless they give me no choice*. 'But I will fight tooth and nail to stay home for the holiday. I will not be manipulated again, thank you very much.'

Her words were delivered with a determination that she could see shocked Jeannie. Kate wasn't so bothered. She was busy eating the cheese and pickle sandwich she'd brought for her dinner. It was good to see her enjoying decent food after months of near starvation at the hands of her rotten pa and the Floozy.

'Well, me and Jeannie aren't going away either,' said Kate after swallowing her food and before Jeannie could say anything else. 'So we can do some things together, can't we? Maybe we could get the train to Weston for the day and paddle in the sea there?'

Jeannie shivered. 'I'm not keen on the train. Not after that derailment a few years back.'

A train to the seaside filled with Clarks workers and their families had come off the rails, stranding the passengers at the side of the track for hours. Thankfully, there hadn't been any serious injuries, just a few bumps and bruises. But it had frightened Jeannie and she claimed it put her off train travel. But Louisa suspected it was more a case that she worried about spending money on a day trip and leaving her ma alone all day. She knew Mrs Musgrove would be delighted for Jeannie to have an outing with her friends, but Jeannie's sense of responsibility was strong.

Kate waved a hand at her. 'Don't be daft. It's never happened again, has it? And no one was hurt. It just meant everyone had to sit by the side of the track until another train could be sent down the line to get them.'

'I don't know,' said Jeannie. 'If the tide's out when we get there, all we'll see is mud for miles. Not much fun trying to paddle then.'

'Oh, you're such a killjoy,' Kate scolded her. 'Live a little! Even if the tide is out, we'll be somewhere different and enjoying the sea air. You never know, you might meet the man of your dreams on a day out.'

'No thank you,' said Jeannie, looking all prim and proper. 'Anyway, I couldn't leave Ma.'

Louisa nudged her shoulder. She wasn't going to let her use that excuse. 'But you leave her alone all day while you're at work. I'm sure she'd be happy for you to have a nice day out.'

Jeannie didn't look convinced. Louisa resolved to speak to Lucas about it. Jeannie deserved a treat and a day at the seaside would be perfect. But she was having none of it.

'I'll come out for walks and a picnic round hereabouts maybe. But I don't fancy the train. Now, I need to use the privy before we go back to work. I'll see you back upstairs.' She packed up her half-eaten food and dashed off up the stone steps towards the Machine Room.

'We've got to get her on the train,' said Kate, watching her go. 'Or at the very least a charabanc. A day out of Street will do her good.'

'We do,' Louisa agreed. 'I'll speak to Lucas.'

'And while you're at it, make sure he's not warned Tom off, will you? Maybe he's the reason why he's taking his time.'

12

Kate spotted her pa in the crowd leaving the factory a couple of weeks later. Everyone was in good spirits as they contemplated the prospect of a whole week off work and were laughing and joking like children at the end of the school term.

Reggie Davis didn't look happy, though. He looked downright furious and he was heading in her direction. She froze, overwhelmed by memories of his meaty hands walloping her, of his floozy's violence and their savage children treating her like a slave. As he came close, she closed her eyes, bracing herself for a blow. But it never came. She knew the moment he brushed past her, recognised his cider-soaked, sweaty odour as his shoulder pushed her out of the way. She stumbled, but managed to stay upright, opening her eyes in shock and relief as he continued on, oblivious to the fact that his own daughter had been standing there.

The object of his fury stood just outside the factory gate – the Floozy's lad waited for him.

'What do you want?' Pa yelled at him. 'Can't a man have any peace even at work?'

Kate watched as people around Pa moved out of his way. Some laughed while others frowned with disapproval. Not that Pa cared. Even sober, he was a brute and had no respect for manners or what was decent, a fact proved as he grabbed the boy by the scruff of his neck, careless of the fact that people were stopping to watch the spectacle.

'Well?' he demanded. 'What's she after now? Bloody woman only bothers when she wants something.'

The boy wriggled a bit, but he didn't let go of him. 'She says you need more cider and some tobacco.'

'Why can't she get 'em herself, the lazy mare?'

'She says you never left her any money and anyway, her ankles are swollen so she's got to keep her feet up.'

Pa growled and released him, shoving him out of his way. 'You tell that lazy cow there'll be no more money from me if she can't get off her fat arse and make me a decent dinner, you hear? If I'm to starve, so will all you parasites.'

Some of the onlookers laughed. 'What's the matter, Reggie? You told us you'd found the perfect woman,' one called out. 'Sounds like she's playing you for a fool.'

Kate shrank back into the doorway as her Pa glanced around and told his tormentor to shut up. She didn't think he knew she was there, he'd been too intent on her half-brother to notice her, but she didn't want to take the chance that he would. When Kate had lived at her pa's house, the Floozy had forced her to do all the housework and cooking. It sounded like she was still refusing to do anything and Kate could imagine Pa's rage at that. The last thing she wanted was for him to grab her and drag her back to wait on them hand and foot again. It had been hard enough to escape them with her brothers' help. Now that they were both away in the army, she'd have no one to protect her and she was aware of her vulnerability.

She knew Auntie Betty would try to rescue her if it came to it, but she wouldn't put it past Pa or the Floozy to attack her and Kate would never forgive herself if that happened. So she cowered in the doorway, hating herself for being a coward but knowing she couldn't win against her pa.

Her pa's voice echoed across yard. 'Now get out of my sight, you little runt. Tell her to get her own cider and tobacco. I'm off to the inn.'

'But she ain't got no money, Pa,' he whined.

Kate peeked out in time to see Pa cuff the lad, sending him flying. 'Don't you "Pa" me. The law says you belong to that other fool she fleeced, and don't you forget it. If she wants money, tell her she's going to have to work for it like everyone else.'

'She says she can't on account of the baby.'

Pa growled and the boy ducked to avoid another blow. 'I'll bet she ain't even expecting. She's just a fat, lazy cow. Well, I've had enough. Get yourself home and you tell her from me, my house better at least be tidy when I get home or you'll all be out on your ears, you hear me?'

'You're a mean old sod!' screamed the boy, running out of Pa's reach when he went to hit him again. 'I hate you! My other pa was a lot better than you!'

The crowd cheered, highly entertained by it all, causing Kate's pa to go red with anger and shake his fists at them as the child ran off. Kate stayed well back as he swore and muttered before stalking off in the direction of the Street Inn. She waited until the crowd dispersed, not wanting to draw attention to herself as the people who had witnessed the scene laughed and gossiped about what a mess Reggie Davis had made of his life thanks to his lust for cider and the Floozy. She was glad her friends hadn't been around to see it all. She was ashamed enough as it was about what people were saying, she didn't want Jeannie and Louisa to hear it too. Though no doubt word would spread round the village like wildfire and everyone would know before long.

Eventually, most of them had gone and she felt safe to emerge from the shadows. She hurried along the High Street, keeping an eye out for her pa. If she bumped into him now, she'd be for it for sure. He was in a foul mood. She wouldn't be surprised if he got into a fight at the inn.

'If only someone would knock some sense into him,' she muttered to herself as she hurried home to Auntie Betty's.

* * *

Kate got to the cottage in The Mead without incident and closed the front door with a sigh of relief. The postman had delivered some letters, including one from Gerald and another from her sister Peg.

It was warm in the small kitchen, but she still stoked up the fire in the range so that she could boil the kettle for a cup of tea. While she waited for the water to heat, she opened the back door and sat on the bench outside, relaxing for the first time since she'd set eyes on her pa. She opened her letter from Peg and began to read, giggling at her sister's stories of little Matthew, now a bonny babe of five months. He was sitting up on his own, blowing raspberries to entertain his parents and showing off four baby teeth. She wished she could go and see them with Auntie Betty, but she was still nervous of spending money on anything other than essentials and her landlady was going all the way to Lincolnshire by train – a long journey that Kate simply couldn't afford if she was going to pay her share towards her late ma's headstone. That was another reason to resent her pa. He had refused to pay for a stone, spending his money on drink instead. He had preferred to buy cider rather than pay for medicines that might have made Ma's last days more bearable as well, and for that, Kate could never forgive him.

She took a deep breath, trying to dispel the gut-churning feeling she had every time she thought about him. Betty had said they should try and "hold him in the light" and to pray that God would show him the error of his ways. But Kate thought he was beyond redemption. She would rather hold Auntie Betty and her brothers and sister and her friends in the light and pray for good things to happen for them.

She turned back to her sister's letter. Peg asked after Louisa, although she worded her enquiry carefully so that Kate could show the letter to Auntie Betty without causing any suspicion. Louisa had asked that Peg and Will would claim little Matthew as their own and that they wouldn't tell Betty that her grandson was really Louisa and Mattie's child. Kate wasn't sure whether it was the right thing to do because she was sure that she wouldn't judge, but Louisa was terrified that Mattie's ma would disapprove like her own parents had. Her friend couldn't bear the thought of the older woman turning against her and had made Kate, Peg and Will swear they would never tell her the truth of it.

She put her letter down and got up to make the tea when she heard Betty arrive home.

'Are you there, lass?' she called.

'I am,' she replied. 'Just got the tea in the pot.'

'Ah, bless you. I'm ready for a cup, that's for sure.' She put her bags onto the table. 'I've gone and bought another rattle for little Mattie and a nice scarf for our Peg, and now I'm wondering whether I can fit everything into my case.'

Kate chuckled. 'Oh, Auntie, they won't be wanting presents. Just seeing you will be enough. I've had a letter from Peg and she's that excited about your visit.' She put a cup and saucer in front of Betty. 'There you go. I was going to ask if you could take my reply to Peg, but now I'm thinking even a sheet of paper might be more than you can manage along with everything else.' She giggled.

Betty shook her head and laughed. 'Oh you, stop teasing me. I'll manage. I might look like a pack horse with everything I want to take, but nothing's going to stop me.' She took a sip of her tea. 'Ah, that's lovely. Now, are you sure you're going to be all right here on your own?'

'I am.' She nodded. 'Me and Jeannie and Louisa are going on walks and on a picnic, and if we can persuade Jeannie, we might even have a day trip to Burnham-on-Sea or Weston-super-Mare on the train.'

'That'll be nice. You girls all deserve some nice days out.' She drank some more, looking thoughtful. 'Has Louisa said anything about her pa?'

Kate frowned. 'No more than usual. Why?'

She shrugged. 'I'm not sure. It's just that I saw him on the way home and the man looked proper poorly to me.'

'Oh. Maybe he's just coming down with something? Lou hasn't mentioned that he's been ill.'

'Mmm. I wouldn't be surprised. He's a conscientious man, a bit of a stickler who believes in working harder than everyone else to set an example for everyone to follow. I've seen others like him work themselves into an early grave. Let's hope the factory holiday will do him good, give him a chance to rest and recuperate.'

Kate nodded but didn't say anything. Jeannie had said something about Mr Clements seeming tired as well. But relations between Louisa and her parents had never recovered since Mattie's death, so apart from complaining about her ma's attempts to get Lou married off, and both parents' anger about her refusing to go to Holy Trinity on a Sunday, she rarely talked about things at home. She wondered whether her friend was even aware that her pa might be ill. If she were honest, she'd thought he looked older when she'd seen him across the factory yard, but she'd just assumed the man was unhappy because of the situation with his daughter. But maybe he really was poorly.

Their tea drunk, the two of them worked together to put supper of chops and potatoes on the table and once they'd eaten and cleared up, Kate remembered she had a second letter to read.

Gerald, the conscientious objector she was writing to in prison, was in good spirits. 'Aw, bless him,' she said as she read his letter. 'Listen to this, Auntie. Gerald got a posy of flowers that little Peter Clothier picked. He asked his mother to send them. Gerald said there were enough flowers to split them into three bunches and share them with two other chaps in adjoining cells. He says: *I've written to young Master Clothier to tell him that his gift brought some of the sun's warmth into our bleak cells. With high windows and even higher walls surrounding us, we rarely see the sun and never see the beauty of the natural world from our prison. That little boy cannot have any notion of what joy his kindness has brought to us.*' She wiped a tear from her eye. 'What a sweet boy he is.'

Betty smiled. 'That he is. He's a credit to his ma and pa.' She reached over and patted Kate's arm. 'As you are a credit to your dear ma, Kate. Gerald's ma and I appreciate the friendship you've offered him, and I'm sure he appreciates your letters as much as those flowers. Thank you, lass.'

That made Kate blink away more moisture from her eyes and shake her head. 'No more than I appreciate his letters. He's so brave and humble even while he's suffering for his faith. It makes me see that there are good men in this world.' She sighed. 'Not like Pa. He caused a right ruckus outside the factory today.'

She explained what had happened, her heart beating with the shame of it. 'I hid, Auntie,' she said. 'I couldn't bear it with everyone jeering at him and that boy screaming his mother's words at him, letting everyone know their business.'

Betty touched her cheek. 'Don't fret, lass. Keeping out of it is the best thing you can do. Reggie Davis has made his bed and he's got to lie on it, but it doesn't mean you need get involved. You're safe now.' She frowned. 'Just don't let him in if he comes round here.' Her frown deepened as Kate's eyes widened at the thought of her pa hammering on Auntie Betty's door. 'Maybe you should come with me after all. I don't like the idea of you being here alone.'

Kate didn't like the idea either, but she couldn't afford it and it wouldn't be right to let Betty pay for her. So she shook her head and lifted her chin. 'Nonsense. I'll be fine. I'll lock the doors and pretend I'm not here if he comes round. But I doubt he will. He probably doesn't even know you're going away.'

'Well, if you're sure?'

'I am,' she said, her voice firm as she tried to convince herself as much as her landlady. 'And I've got all sorts of plans for the holiday with Jeannie and Louisa. I can't let them down, can I?' She kissed her cheek. 'Now, why don't you see if you can fit those last bits you bought into your bag while I write back to Peg and Gerald?'

With a sigh, she agreed. 'All right, lass. But promise me you'll be careful while I'm away?'

'I will, Auntie. I'll not put myself in Pa's path ever again, don't you worry.'

13

Louisa took a deep breath before she opened the front door of her parents' house. She didn't think of it as home any more. It was a place she was expected to live in, but a *home* was supposed to be a place of shelter and security. This building didn't feel like that. Rather, it was a prison, somewhere she longed to escape from.

'There you are,' said Ma as she entered. 'I need you to pack your bag. We're catching the charabanc to Lyme Regis straight after church tomorrow.'

Louisa turned away to shut the door. With her hand on it, she closed her eyes and sighed. 'No.'

'I beg your pardon?' Ma bristled. 'You'll do as you're told.'

She opened her eyes and turned to face her. She could see Ma's temper sparking from her eyes, but Louisa felt nothing. 'I said no. I'm not going.'

'Oh yes you are, young lady.'

She shook her head. 'What are you going to do, Ma? Drag me kicking and screaming? Because that's what it will take for you to get me on that charabanc. What will your church friends have to say about that?'

Her mother advanced on her, grabbing her by the shoulders. 'Now you listen to me, Louisa. I've had just about enough of your petulance and I won't have it any more, do you hear me?' Her voice rose and she was shaking with fury. She shook Louisa, who stared back at her, numb. 'Do you?' she shrieked. 'You will act like a normal, decent girl and stop this nonsense.'

Louisa wasn't even shocked by her ma's loss of reason. Ever since she had rounded on her almost a year ago and slapped her when she'd revealed she was carrying Mattie's baby, Louisa had been waiting for something like this to happen. It was as though her previously placid and kind mother had become a monster that she didn't recognise. She had loved her other ma. But this woman did not care about what Louisa was suffering, while fretting constantly about what other people might think if they knew the truth.

She stared at her mother, saying nothing. What was the point? They'd had the same argument almost daily since she had come back to Street from Lincolnshire. Ma had assumed that she would settle back into life and act as though nothing had happened. But how could she do that? It was impossible. She wasn't the same girl any more and never would be. She had lost the love of her life and then been forced to give up the child borne of that love, all because of her father's prejudice and her mother's snobbery.

Her mother opened her mouth to berate her again, only to be stopped by her father opening the front door. He found it blocked by Louisa, who had stepped back against it when Ma had grabbed her.

'What's this? Barricading me out of my own house, are you?' he said, his tone jovial.

Ma turned away, her hands dropping to her sides, allowing Louisa to step sideways to avoid her and to make room for Pa to open the door and enter the house.

His rare smile dropped and he frowned when he saw their faces. 'What's going on?' he asked.

Louisa said nothing, staring at the wall opposite. But Ma had plenty to say.

'This girl is being difficult and she's a disgrace. She's still refusing to do as she's told. I've told her she must come to Lyme Regis with us and she says she won't. I'm sick and tired of her defiance and ingratitude. I won't have it!' Her voice rose, as did the colour on her cheeks. 'Tell her. Tell her she must stop it and act like a dutiful daughter should.'

Louisa didn't know whether to laugh or to weep at her words. 'I'm sorry,' she said, her voice calm and clear, in direct contrast to her mother's hysterics. 'But when I acted like a dutiful daughter, it cost me my fiancé and my child.'

Ma scowled. 'You were never engaged to him. We wouldn't have allowed it. He knew that. It was only you, you stupid girl, who thought otherwise.'

'Oh, I knew, Ma,' she said, feeling unutterably sad that Ma had focused on Mattie and again ignored her baby. 'But if he hadn't been forced to enlist in order to prove himself' – she spared a glance at her father; he looked grey in contrast to her mother's high colour – 'then we would have carried on courting until I was twenty-one and then you couldn't have stopped us getting married.'

Ma huffed and looked away. 'Oh, you're such an obstinate child. You were too young to know what you wanted and you'd have soon lost interest in him, mark my words.'

'So why send him away?' she asked. 'If you were so sure, why send him to his death?' She was surprised that she was able to maintain a calm tone, when she was weeping inside. Mattie's death was so pointless, so cruel. And her parents' part in it was something she could never, ever forgive.

Pa sighed and rubbed at his chest. 'I told you, Louisa, I didn't force him to go. I was as surprised as anyone.' His tone was weary. No doubt he was tired of this endless argument between Louisa and Ma. 'Now, can a man have a cup of tea after a week's work?'

Ma huffed again. 'Of course, dear. I'll get it while you talk some sense into this girl.' She turned and stalked into the kitchen.

Louisa looked down at her hands, waiting for Pa to take up the baton that Ma had passed. But instead of berating her, he took off his jacket and hung it on the coat stand before walking into the parlour and lowering himself into his armchair with a sigh.

She followed him, curious as to why he was so quiet. He had rested his head back and closed his eyes. In days gone by, she would have asked him if he was all right. But neither of her parents asked that question of Louisa these days and she'd decided that if they didn't care enough for her well-being, then she wasn't interested in theirs. After a moment, she felt ashamed. She realised how petty her attitude was and she didn't like herself very much. He really didn't look right.

'Are you all right, Pa?' she asked eventually.

He opened his eyes and looked at her briefly before looking away. It had become a habit for him to do that, as though he couldn't bear to look at her. She immediately regretted asking.

'I'm fine, lass. Just tired, that's all. Looking forward to a holiday. Some quiet time by the sea will be nice.'

'Not if Ma is set on match-making again,' she said, sitting down on the settee. 'You know I won't put up with it.'

'Can you not just be polite to folks for a few days?' he asked softly. 'For the sake of family harmony?'

Louisa sighed. 'I'm sorry, Pa, but no. You know she'll push and push and I can't bear it. I hated it before Mattie, but now... I just can't. It's better if I stay home.'

'I don't like it, lass.'

'I know. But you'd like it even less if I were there. I'll only embarrass you.' Personally, she thought it was Ma who would cause the embarrassment, but if she said that, she'd cause another row.

He rubbed at his chest again as he thought about what she said.

'Are you sure you're all right?' she asked quietly as Ma came in with the tea tray.

He dropped his hand. 'Of course I am. Just a touch of indigestion is all. I just need a cup of tea and ten minutes to rest and I'll be right as rain.'

Ma frowned. 'Do you need some Milk of Magnesia?' she asked.

He shook his head. 'It doesn't work,' he grumbled. 'I just need a cup of tea and a bit of peace.'

Ma handed him his drink and slanted a glance at Louisa. 'Of course you do. So, is Louisa going to pack ready for our trip?'

Pa took a sip of his drink before he replied. Both Louisa and Ma braced themselves. One of them was going to be sorely disappointed and both were ready to argue their point of view.

'Leave it, woman. You know she won't come. You're just working yourself up into a lather and for what?'

Ma glared at Louisa as though it was her fault. Lou blinked, keeping her face carefully blank. She was as surprised as Ma was by his words.

'She's got to learn. She can't just throw her life away sulking,' Ma snapped. 'What are we going to tell people if we leave her behind?'

Louisa couldn't stop herself from rolling her eyes. 'That I'm not a child and I'm perfectly capable of looking after myself,' she said.

'Don't you talk to me like that, young lady. You know what I mean. First you take yourself off for months, then you refuse to go to church and now you're turning your back on our friends. I'm tired of making excuses for you.'

'Then don't,' she said, getting up. 'Tell them it's none of their business and that I've better things to do than try and be polite to their sons and nephews.'

Ma rounded on Pa. 'Are you going to let her talk to me like that?'

Pa put his cup down and scrubbed at his face. 'I said leave it,' he said. 'I'm tired of this incessant bickering every time I come home.' He looked at his wife. 'I'm bone weary and need a holiday and I don't want it spoilt by the same ill-feeling there is in this house. She can stay here. We can all have a break from this blooming sniping and snapping.' He raised a finger and pointed it at Ma. 'That's the end of it. We go to Lyme Regis. She stays here. We all have a week of peace and quiet and, please God, we come back together rested and happier and try to get along like civilised people.' His irritated gaze went from her to Louisa and back. 'Is that clear, both of you?'

Louisa nodded, relieved beyond measure. Ma stood frozen for a long moment, staring at her husband until she lowered her eyes and nodded too. She turned away.

'I've got things to do,' she said as she left the room.

For a moment, Louisa felt sorry for her. Her shoulders had slumped and her head was down as she had turned away. Lou knew all too well what it felt like to be defeated and unable to do anything about it. But then she remembered how her mother had been responsible for much of that helplessness she'd experienced and she hardened her heart.

* * *

After an uncomfortable, silent meal, Louisa excused herself and walked the length of the village to visit Jeannie and Lucas. She was surprised to find Tom there when Mrs Musgrove sent her through the house to the back garden. The three of them were picking strawberries in the late-afternoon sunshine.

'Louisa!' Jeannie greeted her. 'We're picking these before the twins and the birds eat them all. Ma and me are going to make jam.'

She grinned as she spotted Lucas having a sneaky bite of a luscious berry behind his sister's back. He winked at her, knowing she wouldn't tell on him. But he didn't reckon on Tom, who nudged Jeannie and pointed at him.

'Lucas Musgrove, you strawberry thief!' she exclaimed. 'Get off with you. There'll not be enough for all the jars Ma's got at this rate.'

Louisa and Tom both laughed as Lucas finished the fruit in his hand and jumped out of Jeannie's reach when she swiped at him.

'I deserve a treat for all the picking I'm doing.' He nodded towards the large bowl at his feet. 'Just because you can resist them, don't mean we should, eh, Tom?'

Tom shrugged but didn't say anything. Louisa giggled when she realised he'd kept silent because his mouth was full. He smiled and tried to look innocent, but a dribble of strawberry juice escaped his lips. Jeannie gasped when she spotted it.

'Not you as well!' She put her hands on her hips. 'Honestly. I thought I could trust you, Tom.'

He tilted his head to one side as he swallowed. His tongue came out to chase the juice. 'Sorry, Jeannie. But Lucas said if I helped, I could eat what I fancied. They're hard to resist. You should've said earlier.'

'I think you lads had better scarper,' said Louisa. 'I'll help Jeannie finish off.'

'Yeah,' said Jeannie. 'Be off with the pair of you.'

Lucas grabbed a handful of big berries, handing one to his friend as they headed up the path towards the house. He winked at Louisa again as he passed, slipping one into her hand. She laughed and shook her head at him as she realised what he was doing. When they disappeared, she opened her fingers and offered the lush fruit back to Jeannie.

She shook her head, laughing despite herself. 'You have it,' she said. 'What they don't know is Ma and me had a nice bowl of them with some sugar before they turned up. I was just teasing 'em.'

The girls giggled and Louisa took a bite, enjoying the sun-warmed sweetness on her tongue. 'Ooh, that's good. I can understand why they were tempted.'

The girls set to, checking the remaining plants for ripe fruit. 'So,' said Louisa. 'Tom's still coming round?'

'Mmm,' said Jeannie, bending over and checking under the leaves of another plant. She dropped a couple of fruit into her bowl and moved to the next plant. 'To see Lucas, not me.'

Louisa smiled, noting her peevish tone. 'And he's hanging around Street during the factory shut down?'

'Mmm,' she repeated, her cheeks reddening, not looking at Louisa.

'Maybe you should tell Lucas that we're going on walks and picnics. He could ask Tom if he wanted to come along as well.'

Jeannie straightened up and looked at her, frowning. 'I didn't ask Lucas. I thought it was just us girls. I didn't think you or Kate would want lads along.'

Louisa shrugged. She knew why she might think that. The first time she had met Mattie properly had been when Jeannie had asked Lucas to bring some of his friends along on a walk to Collard Hill for a picnic. It was the first time Ted had set his cap at Kate as well. Now both lads were gone and Lucas was forever changed by his experiences in the trenches. The girls were changed as well, and neither Louisa nor Kate wanted to give their hearts to a lad again. But Jeannie *did* want a sweetheart and she had her heart set on Tom, even though she would deny it. Both Kate and Lou thought the two of them were a good match, so they'd agreed they should get Lucas to bring Tom along to help the two of them to finally get together.

'They can carry the picnic baskets,' she said.

'None of the lads did last time,' Jeannie grumbled.

Louisa didn't want to remember that long ago day when life had been perfect. Well, she did, but not now when Jeannie was watching her. Those memories were for the times when she was on her own and she could remember her love and pretend for a moment that she was back there with him. It was all she had left.

'Well, we'll make sure they do this time,' she said. 'You said Tom was good at carrying things,' she teased.

Jeannie blushed. 'It was only the once. I think he learned his lesson and keeps well away from us when he knows it's a shopping day.' She picked up her bowl and the one that Tom had filled. 'I think we've got all the ripe berries for now. There's still a few green ones. I can't believe we've done so well with them. I'm looking forward to strawberry jam on a nice slice of crusty bread.'

Louisa carried Lucas's bowl as she followed Jeannie into the house.

'Oh, well done, girls,' said Mrs Musgrove. 'Here, tip them into the bigger bowl by the sink and I'll wash them and pull the stalks off. Then I'll cover them and hide them in the pantry so the twins don't come home and eat them all.'

'Are they off playing football again?' asked Louisa. 'I thought they'd have switched to cricket by now.'

Jeannie rolled her eyes. 'Aren't they always? They're not keen on cricket. If they can't kick or head a ball, they're not interested.'

'Ah, it keeps them out of trouble,' said her ma. 'I'd rather they were out, running in the fresh air than getting under our feet here, wouldn't you?'

'I suppose. But it would be better if they actually did some chores before they disappeared,' she grumbled.

'What can I do to help?' asked Louisa.

'Nothing, lass,' said Mrs Musgrove. 'You and Jeannie go and relax. You've both been working at the factory all week. I can manage to clean some fruit.'

Jeannie tilted her head towards the back door. Louisa followed her out and they wandered down past the vegetable beds to the end of the long garden. Beyond it was one of the many orchards in and around Street, the trees heavy with cider apples. It was peaceful here, with only the twittering of birds and the buzz of insects around them. The friends sat, looking towards the house.

'Your ma looks well today,' said Louisa. She picked a couple of daisies and twirled them in her fingers.

'She is. She's always better in the warmer months. She gets tired easy though, so we have to make sure she doesn't overdo it.'

Louisa nodded. 'I think my pa's overdoing it,' she said. 'Between trying to keep the Clicking Room going despite the labour and material shortages on account of the war, and then me and Ma always bickering at home, he's reaching his limit, I think.'

'I thought he looked tired when I saw him the other day,' she said.

Louisa looked up at the clear blue sky, aware that the warmth of the sun would soon be waning a little as it began its slow descent into the evening. The nights were drawing in slowly now. Before they knew it, it would be her birthday, then autumn would arrive and there'd be no more lazy sunny days like this.

'He says he needs some peace and quiet this holiday, especially as the factory's only shut for a week instead of a fortnight, like it did before the war, so he agreed I can stay home when him and Ma go to Lyme Regis tomorrow. Not that I was intending to go anyway, but Ma was in a right tizzy when he got home today and I thought he was going to force me to go just to shut her up.' She blew out a breath. 'But, thank God, her tantrum had the opposite effect and he told her to stop fussing and that he'd rather I stayed home so he could relax and enjoy his holiday than have to put up with us arguing all the time.'

Jeannie frowned. 'I can't imagine your ma having a tantrum. She's always so controlled.'

'Well she wasn't today. She was almost hysterical. I thought she was going to burst a blood vessel, she was getting that worked up.'

'I'm sorry you're not getting along with her. It must be miserable. Don't you think it might make things easier if you agreed to go with them like she wanted?'

Louisa shook her head. 'No. Definitely not. She wants me to be that silly little girl who did what she was told and never questioned her. But, well, I'm not that girl any more. Not since my Mattie.' She swallowed against the lump in her throat, wanting to acknowledge *both* of her Matties – to tell Jeannie everything behind the rift between her and her parents – but she knew she couldn't. It wouldn't be fair on Kate, Peg and Will if she did. They had lied to Auntie Betty to protect her and her son, and she couldn't break their faith now. She loved Jeannie, but she was so sweet and honest that she didn't think she'd be able to keep the secret.

Jeannie reached over and patted Louisa's shoulder. 'I hope she'll come to understand that so that you can learn to get on better one day. Maybe a week away from each other will help you both.'

'I hope so,' said Louisa. 'Because Pa's not the only one who's tired of it all.'

14

The Quaker Meeting House wasn't as full as it usually was for a Sunday meeting. It seemed as though half the population of Street were taking advantage of the factory's summer closure and the good weather, and had gone away. Those who could afford it were off for a few days while others took day trips on the train to Weston-super-Mare or Burnham-on-Sea, or like Auntie Betty, made journeys further afield to visit family that they might otherwise not see from one year to the next. The better-off families like the Clements could afford a holiday in Lyme Regis.

Jeannie was still surprised that Tom had decided not to visit his family in Northampton. After all, if Auntie Betty could get herself to Lincolnshire and back, then surely it was possible for Tom to make the journey to see his kin. Northampton wasn't as far as Lincoln, was it? But he'd reacted so strangely when she'd mentioned it that she wouldn't mention it again for fear of offending him.

She could see him on the other side of the big room where the Friends were gathered around in a circle for silent worship. She tried not to notice him but rather to focus on spiritual matters.

She closed her eyes to contemplate the light within herself. Her daily prayers for the last two years had been for peace, safety for Lucas and the other lads sent to fight, and better health for Ma. She often asked for God to give the twins a nudge, so that they might be less silly and selfish. At other times, she asked for Him to comfort Louisa in her grief and thanked Him for rescuing Kate from her pa and the Floozy. After thinking of those she loved, she felt she could ask for Him to send her a sweetheart – a good lad who she could love and would love her and want to marry her. But she didn't hold out much hope for that – after her horrible encounter with Sid Lambert and then her disastrous relationship with Douglas Baker last year and the very public end to that, she doubted there was any lad in Street or thereabouts that would take her seriously. She had had high hopes that Tom might be interested in her. He seemed to like her and was always very nice. But he had never asked her out or shown any sign that he might, despite what Kate and Louisa kept saying.

Unable to resist, she opened her eyes to look at him. She blinked in surprise to see that his gaze was on her. His lips turned up briefly when he saw her looking and she felt her cheeks go hot under his warm regard. But then he lowered his head and closed his eyes, breaking the connection. She sighed and closed her own eyes. It was always the same. He would look at her with such warmth and she would blush, then he'd cut her off. Jeannie was sure she'd detected regret in his gaze before he looked away. She couldn't understand it and it made her feel like crying.

He really was a handsome lad – well, a man really as he was about six or seven years older than she was. Maybe he thought she was too young for him? She didn't think she was, but she couldn't tell what was going on in his head. She knew he set all the girls in the Machine Room twittering whenever he appeared. She wouldn't be surprised if some of the more brazen lasses were deliberately sabotaging their machines in the hope that he'd be sent to fix them. But he never seemed to take any notice of their flirting and teasing. She supposed it was because he had so many sisters that he didn't get flustered by all the female attention.

But that didn't explain the looks he gave her, nor why he never seemed to take things any further than that.

A cough from Ma reminded Jeannie that she shouldn't be thinking about Tom but rather she should be trying to connect with the light, to try and understand what God wanted from her and how she could serve Him. She felt a rush of shame that she'd been so easily distracted.

After the meeting, Ma cheerfully went off along the High Street with another of the ladies, after telling Jeannie not to rush. 'I'm feeling fine today. I'll get the dinner on. You enjoy some time with your friends. Sort out that picnic you're going to have this week.'

Jeannie felt a rush of love for Ma. She kissed her cheek. 'I will,' she said. 'If you're sure?'

Ma patted her cheek. 'I am, lass. I'll have the food on the table at about one. If you see the boys, tell them not to be late.'

Seeing Ma so bright and walking without too much pain today made Jeannie thank God. It felt as though a great weight had been lifted from her shoulders. Knowing she had some time to spend with her friends and that Ma was well enough for her to be able to leave her and enjoy her time off made her want to dance with joy. She hadn't realised how much Ma's poor health had been weighing her down.

'You're looking cheerful,' said Kate, as she arrived from the direction of Holy Trinity, where she had started worshipping again with her sister-in-law since her brothers had enlisted. She linked arms with Jeannie and whispered in her ear, 'Is it anything to do with the meaningful looks I'll bet you and Tom were sharing in the meeting?'

'Stop it!' she hissed, blushing scarlet. 'We didn't!'

'Didn't what?' asked Louisa as she joined them. She had arranged to join them outside the Meeting House today after her walk. 'It must be something to do with Tom if you're blushing like that.'

Jeannie covered her cheeks with her hands. 'Please, stop, both of you,' she begged.

Her friends laughed but took pity on her. 'Have you got to rush off?' asked Kate.

'No. Ma says I can stay out until dinner time.'

'Good,' she said. 'So we're all fancy-free. Auntie Betty went off first thing this morning, and Lou's ma and pa are on their way to Lyme Regis as soon as their service is over, so none of us has got anyone to answer to for a couple of hours at least. Why don't we go to The Mead for a nice cuppa and a good gossip?'

Louisa stilled. 'I don't know,' she said.

Jeannie could see that she was still reluctant to go into Auntie Betty's house. The last time Louisa had been there, Mattie had been alive. She could understand that it might be hard for her. 'Maybe it will be easier while Auntie's not there,' she said gently.

'That's what I thought,' said Kate. 'If it's too much for you, we can always go in the garden, or go somewhere else. I know it will be difficult for you. But maybe you'll feel better if you can walk in there again while Auntie's away, and once you've got that over with, then you'll be able to come and visit her when she gets home. She'd love that. She misses you and she knows you miss Mattie as much as she does.'

Lou's eyes filled with tears. 'I don't know if I can. It's the last place I was happy with him.'

Kate pulled Louisa into a hug. 'I know, love. But you can try to remember the good times you had with him there, rather than all the horrible stuff that happened after. They say the deeper the grief you feel, the stronger the love you experienced. Grief is a monster that suffocates us with pain, I know. But... as painful as it is to know I'll never see my ma again in this lifetime, I'm comforted when I let myself remember her sweet smile and how she cared for me. It helps me to remember the good times and I'm grateful for the memories I have of her. Come to the cottage, Lou. Think about the good times you had with Mattie there.'

Louisa sniffed and nodded. 'I know what you mean. As awful as things are without Mattie, I don't regret knowing him. I'll never love anyone as much as I loved him. I just don't know if I'm ready to go into his house without him.'

The girls had been standing in a huddle outside the Meeting House. Friends had walked around them, and now the yard was almost empty. Jeannie saw that Lucas and Tom were standing across the road. Lucas was frowning as he watched the girls. When he saw her looking their way, he raised his eyebrows as if to ask what was going on.

She shrugged and tilted her head to one side, because she wasn't sure. Clearly Louisa *wasn't* all right. Lucas said something to Tom and began walking back towards them. Tom raised his chin and gave Jeannie a little wave before he turned and walked away. She sighed, wishing he'd stayed. But then again, she wouldn't have known what to say to him and Louisa was upset and needed her support, so it was probably for the best that he'd gone.

Lucas went straight to Louisa. 'What's the matter?' he asked, his tone as gentle as Jeannie's and Kate's had been.

She nodded, blinking away her tears. 'Kate thinks I should go to Mattie's house, just for a cuppa. She thinks it might be easier to be there while his ma's away.'

'You don't have to if you don't want to,' he said. 'But she might be right. You've been fretting about going there, haven't you?'

Jeannie was surprised by her brother's tone and how understanding he was of Lou's feelings. She knew that they had become friends since Mattie's passing, but it was only now she was realising just how close they were.

Louisa nodded, looking miserable. 'I don't know what to do,' she said.

'Do you want me to come with you?' he asked. 'Or would you rather just go home?'

She shook her head. 'No. Ma and Pa are supposed to get the charabanc to Lyme Regis after church, but they might not have gone yet. If the reverend's sermon went on, they might still have to pick up their suitcases. I don't want to see them when I'm feeling like this.'

Kate hugged Louisa to her side. 'You're right, he had plenty to say this morning. So why don't we go down to The Mead and see how you feel when we get there? If you don't want to come in, we'll walk on to the riverbank and sit there for a while.'

'That's a good idea,' said Jeannie. 'It'll be up to you, Lou.'

'Yeah,' said Lucas. 'You don't ever have to do anything you don't want to,' he repeated.

The look that Louisa gave Lucas puzzled Jeannie. That he grimaced and muttered a soft apology confused her even more. It was as though the two of them had a secret language. She glanced at Kate and on seeing her expression, Jeannie's heart sank. It was clear that the three of them were thinking of the same thing – yet Jeannie couldn't for the life of her understand what it was and what it meant and she felt excluded. She wondered whether they were thinking about when Lou's parents had tried to make her go and live with her aunt in Exeter after Mattie's death. They'd said it would help her get over him if she had a fresh start somewhere else. But Louisa had been dead set against it, so much so that she'd run away to Lincolnshire to live with Peg and Will. She'd only come home after their baby, little Matthew, had been born.

Louisa nodded, straightening her spine and taking a deep breath. 'You're right,' she said. 'It's better I do it while Mattie's ma is away, and I can always turn around and leave if it gets too much.'

Lucas nodded and held out his arm. She linked hers with his and let him lead her out of the Meeting House yard.

They turned left out of the gate and walked towards The Cross at the end of the High Street. Kate and Jeannie followed behind the two of them. All of them were silent at first, aware of the tension in Louisa's shoulders and the stiffness of her back. They crossed the junction into Glastonbury Road and turned right at Turnpike Cottage into The Mead. Just a little way along sat Betty Searle's cottage, facing the fields that went down to the River Brue and Pomparles Bridge.

'Are you sure this is a good idea?' Jeannie whispered to Kate.

'I don't know,' she replied, keeping her voice low so that Louisa didn't hear her. 'But better to do it now than when Auntie's there, especially if she breaks down.'

Ahead of them, Lucas was talking quietly to Louisa, but Jeannie couldn't hear what he was saying. She was surprised by the gentleness her brother was showing her friend, but then again, maybe she shouldn't be. Mattie had been Lucas's friend all his life and he'd felt his loss so much that he'd gone against his own pacifist principles and enlisted. When he'd first come home, he'd felt he owed it to Mattie to look out for Louisa, but now they were good friends. He certainly understood her grief.

Before long, they were all standing in front of the Searle cottage. Kate nudged Jeannie and indicated she should follow her inside, leaving Louisa and Lucas by the garden gate.

'We'll get the kettle on,' she told them.

Jeannie remembered the first time she had been here – when she'd brought Kate here after her brothers had challenged their pa in the factory yard and attracted the attention of Mr Roger Clark. He had persuaded Reggie Davis to hand over his daughter's pay packet and to let her leave home, where his floozy and her children had been abusing Kate. Jeannie had been with Kate when Miss Alice Clark had listened to their story and kept her safe while Mr Roger Clark had spoken to Reggie and his sons to get their testimonies. Once it had been resolved, Jeannie had been charged with escorting Kate to Betty Searle's cottage, as the older woman had offered Kate sanctuary there. The Davis brothers had marched their pa home and packed up Kate's things so that she didn't have to ever go back to her old home again. Jeannie remembered the feeling of relief at Mrs Searle's warm welcome and the knowledge that her friend was safe at last.

As she entered, she glanced back and saw that Lucas was standing beside Louisa, looking at the cottage. He didn't speak or pressure her, he just waited. Knowing that her friend was in good hands, she turned and followed Kate into the kitchen. Together, they set out cups and saucers and Kate opened the biscuit barrel and put some treats on a plate.

'It's such a warm day, I thought I'd just have a ploughman's lunch for me and Lou today,' she said. 'I can't see the point of cooking.'

Jeannie nodded, her mind on the two outside. She half expected Louisa to turn tail and leave without coming in, she seemed that strung up about it. But just as Kate poured the tea, she heard the latch. Through the open kitchen door, she saw Louisa enter with Lucas right behind her. As he closed the front door behind them, Louisa looked around the parlour. She must have spotted something as she gasped and moved out of Jeannie's

line of sight. By the time Kate had picked up the tea tray and the
two of them moved into the room, Louisa was standing in front of
the mantlepiece, her gaze fixed on two picture frames there.

Lucas stood beside her, a hand on her shoulder. They were
both staring at the pictures. The first was a photograph of Mattie,
looking serious and handsome in his uniform. Next to it in a
matching frame was a pencil drawing of a baby. Jeannie realised it
must be Peg and Will's child. She recognised Louisa's style in the
lines. She must have drawn this before she left Lincolnshire and
given it to Auntie Betty.

'Aw, that's a lovely picture of the babe, Lou,' she said, coming
to stand on the other side of her and touching the picture frame.
'I can see the likeness to Will. Auntie Betty must have been so
happy that you drew it for her. And now she's gone to meet the
little man for the first time. I'll bet she can't wait for her first
cuddle.'

She didn't expect the reaction from all three of them. Kate and
Lucas turned on her with equally fierce expressions while Louisa
put a hand to her mouth, too late to hold back the sob that
escaped as tears flowed down her cheeks.

'Oh, my, Lou,' she said, moving closer. 'I'm sorry. I didn't mean
to upset you.' She'd thought that focusing on the drawing of the
baby would distract Louisa from the photograph of Mattie, but it
didn't seem to have worked at all.

Louisa shook her head and turned away. Lucas gathered her
into his arms and Kate rushed over, pushing Jeannie out of the
way to rub Louisa's back, leaving Jeannie stunned and feeling as
though she'd done something very wrong. But she couldn't for
the life of her understand why the two of them were glaring at her
like that while Louisa sobbed as though her heart would never
recover.

Jeannie felt her own tears well, unable to bear her friend's heartbreak. 'I'm sorry, I'm so sorry. I didn't mean to upset you,' she said again.

Lucas shook his head, mouthing to her to shut up as he stroked Louisa's hair while she sobbed against his chest. Jeannie covered her mouth with her hand, hurt that he looked so angry and that Kate had pushed her out of the way. She hadn't meant any harm. She'd wanted to make Louisa feel better. She hadn't realised she would react so strongly to her words.

'Please don't cry, Lou.' She stood frozen to the spot, feeling awful that the others were able to comfort her while Jeannie couldn't. She was so confused.

When neither Louisa nor the others responded, she sank down onto an armchair, at a loss to know what to do. She had a feeling that if she tried to touch Louisa, both Lucas and Kate would fight her off. Jeannie was crying silently and shaking as she watched them comforting Louisa, leaving her feeling as though she was on the outside of their little circle. That hurt as well. She'd been friends with Louisa since the day they'd started school together at age five. Yet at this moment, it felt as though she was separated from her, Kate and her own brother by some invisible barrier. She didn't understand what was happening and why her innocent words should cause such distress. All she knew was that Louisa was sobbing and trembling as though her heart was breaking all over again and that she, Jeannie, was responsible.

It seemed like hours before Louisa started to calm down, although it was probably only minutes. She eventually rested quiet in Lucas's arms, her face buried against his chest, her breath jerky as her trembles slowly subsided, but she didn't raise her head. Jeannie didn't dare move or say anything as the other two comforted their friend, murmuring gently and stroking her back and hair. She couldn't help thinking that his shirt must be damp, but he didn't seem to notice or care and she felt ashamed all over again as she realised how ridiculous her thoughts were. What did it matter if he was wet from her tears? What really mattered was that Louisa was in pain and it was all Jeannie's fault.

When her sobs had died away, Lucas touched Louisa's cheek. 'All right?' he asked softly.

Still hiding her face, Louisa nodded.

'How about a nice cup of tea?' asked Kate, her tone gentle, like she'd been with her ma when she'd been ill.

For a moment, Jeannie felt a spike of fear that Louisa was ill too. She hadn't been the same since Mattie's passing and even all those months in Lincolnshire didn't seem to help. She'd come home at Easter looking like a shadow of the girl she'd been before Mattie had enlisted.

'Let me do it,' she said, jumping up, wanting to do *something*.

'Thanks, Jeannie,' said Kate. She nodded her head towards the tray on the sideboard. 'That lot's probably cold now. There should be some hot water still in the kettle on the range. Could you make a fresh pot?'

Feeling as though she'd been dismissed, Jeannie nodded and picked up the tray of now-tepid teacups and went into the kitchen. As she busied herself pouring away the tea and rinsing out the pot to make fresh, she could hear the others talking quietly in the parlour and her feeling of isolation increased. It upset her as much as being responsible for Louisa's distress did and she dashed away more tears.

She spooned tea leaves into the pot and poured hot water over them, then rinsed and dried the cups while it brewed, all the while hearing the low murmur of voices from the other room. When it was ready, she took the tea tray back into the parlour, aware that the three of them had stopped speaking as soon as she'd walked into the room. She couldn't look at them, she felt so awful. She wished she hadn't said anything. She handed out the cups of tea in the silence. Instead of picking up her own, she left it on the tray and took a deep breath before she finally looked at Louisa.

'Look, I'm really sorry, Lou. I never meant to upset you. I hope you'll forgive me. But in the meantime, I'll go.' She turned towards the front door before Louisa spoke.

'Don't go,' she said, her voice scratchy after all that crying. 'I'm sorry, too. It's not your fault, Jeannie. Please, sit down. I've got something to tell you. I should've told you months ago, but I couldn't bear to. You might hate me when you know, but I have to share my secret with you, then maybe you'll understand. I don't want you to think it's you in the wrong when it's me.'

Confused, Jeannie sat down. 'I don't know what you mean,' she said.

'No, you don't,' said Lucas, his expression fierce. 'But when you do, you have to promise never to tell anyone about this, you hear?'

15

Jeannie walked up the High Street towards home, her mind in a whirl. *The baby was Louisa and Mattie's!* How had she not realised? When Louisa had told her, everything had become clear – her friend's flight to Lincolnshire, the breakdown of her relationship with her parents, her reluctance to visit Auntie Betty, all of it. While Jeannie had been relieved that Louisa's distress today hadn't entirely been her fault, her heart ached for the pain that her friend continued to feel after having lost her sweetheart and then having to give up their child. She also understood why Kate knew – she had been the one to suggest to Lou that Peg and Will would be better to bring up little Matthew than the strangers her parents were suggesting. Jeannie could see the logic in that – after all, they were kin to the babe and it meant that Auntie Betty would see her grandson grow up.

She was so caught up in her thoughts that she didn't even see Tom until she bumped into him hard. She yelped as he grunted, his arms coming round her to prevent either of them from falling onto their backsides.

'Oh! Tom! I'm so sorry,' she gasped. 'I didn't see you.'

He frowned down at her. 'Why are you crying? What's the matter?'

She brought a hand up to her face and swiped at her cheek. She hadn't even realised she'd been weeping as she walked along. She took a deep breath, wishing she could tell him, but knowing she couldn't. She shook her head.

'I'm all right. It's nothing...' But it *wasn't*. 'No, it's... I'm sorry I can't tell you. I promised, you see and... oh lord.' She sniffed and blinked hard against fresh tears. 'I found something out today and...' She shook her head. 'I mustn't say any more. I promised I wouldn't.'

He didn't let her go as he looked down at her with concern. It occurred to Jeannie that she'd never been this close to him and hadn't realised before just how tall he was. But he was the same height as Lucas, and she knew how tall he was, so why hadn't it occurred to her before? She clamped her lips together and shook her head. She had to stop all this nonsense rambling in her head or she'd go doolally for sure. The thought brought fresh tears.

'Aw,' Tom said as he pulled her against his chest. 'Let it out, love. Tears are always best shed. Come on, you're safe with me. I'll see you home.'

'N... No. Not yet. I can't let Ma see me like this. Not when I can't tell her...'

She was vaguely aware that he had guided her away from the centre of the pavement and now they stood together in the doorway of a closed shop. She was grateful for his thoughtfulness while at the same time she was mortified that he was seeing her like this. She wasn't one of those girls who was able to cry prettily. She would be red in the face and her eyes would be bloodshot and puffy.

'Don't worry,' he soothed her. 'We can stay here as long as you like. I won't leave you when you're so upset.'

'But I promised Ma I'd be back for dinner, and Lucas has stayed behind, so she'll be fretting if neither of us turn up.'

Tom took her face in his hands, his warm fingers soothing her and making her look up into his eyes. That made her already pounding heart stutter at the concern in his gaze. 'Jeannie, it's all right, lass. Take a deep breath now, that's it, nice and slow. And again.'

She did as he bid and realised that it was helping her to calm a little. Then, as she continued to stare at him, taking strength from his calm presence, he leaned forward, closing the gap between them and kissing her gently on the lips.

'Feeling better?' he asked.

She nodded, shocked and thrilled. His brief kiss had been the sort of kiss she'd always dreamed of. 'Yes. I'm sorry. I've just had a shock is all. But please don't ask me what it's about, because I can't tell you.'

She expected him to question her further. Her brothers all would have done, demanding to know what was wrong. But Tom simply nodded, making her like him even more. 'Fair enough,' he said. 'You don't have to tell me anything. It's none of my business. I'm just bothered by the fact that you're so upset. Where's Lucas? I thought you were with him.'

'I was, but he said he'd be home later, so I left him.'

'It's not your brother who's upset you, is it?' He frowned.

'No,' she denied. 'No. It's... it's about someone who's no longer here. He was killed in France and...' She closed her mouth, squeezing her lips together. 'I'm sorry, that's all I can tell you. It's not my secret to tell.' She took another deep breath, wishing this simple act could take away the sick feeling of helplessness that returned and threatened to bring on more tears. 'It's just so unfair.'

She had barely noticed that she was still standing in Tom's

arms, her hands on his broad chest until he pulled her closer and her cheek came into contact with the damp patch she'd left on his shirt by crying all over him. An image of Louisa crying in Lucas's arms and her inappropriate thoughts about how she was making her brother's shirt wet flashed through her mind.

'I've made you damp,' she said, putting her palm against the patch. 'Sorry.' She wished he'd kiss her again.

He shook his head. 'Don't worry. It'll soon dry. Look, I'm sorry for your loss. It never gets any easier, especially when it's a young lad. Was he your sweetheart?'

She realised he had misunderstood her, but she couldn't explain. 'No. Nothing like that. But I knew him all my life and now his...' She couldn't go on without giving away Louisa's secret, so she closed her eyes and rested her cheek on his chest again, ignoring the damp and instead focusing on the strong beat of his heart. She never expected to be in this position and she found she liked it. She wished she could stay here forever.

But then she realised that she barely knew him and anyone walking past would say they were canoodling and Tom might think she was a bit of a floozy, clinging to him like this and she became embarrassed. She went to step back, but he kept his arm around her and soothed her with his free hand on her hair.

'I've got you, Jeannie. Just relax. You can't go home to your ma in a state, now, can you? Your brother would expect me to look after you.'

'I don't need another brother!' she snapped, unable to stop herself. Why bring up Lucas at all? Why didn't he just kiss her again?

He sighed. 'I know. I'm sorry if that's what you think I meant. I just want to take care of you. You're in no fit state to be wandering through the village on your own.'

She knew she should step back, separate herself from him,

especially after her outburst. The last thing she wanted was for him to act out of pity. *Why can't he see me for who I am rather than as my brothers' sister?* But she felt so out of sorts by the revelations of the past hour and his brief kiss had unsettled her so that she couldn't bring herself to do the sensible thing and walk away from him. Instead, she sighed too and relaxed against him, taking comfort from his warm, solid presence and sliding her arms around his waist.

'I hate secrets,' she whispered. 'I wish I didn't know this one. But what hurts the most is they didn't tell me because they didn't think I'd be able to keep it.'

He lowered his head so that his lips were close to her ear. 'I hate secrets as well,' he said. 'But sometimes, we have no choice but to have them. If you knew mine...'

She raised her head to look at him. 'You have a secret?'

He nodded.

She frowned. 'I already know about your foot.'

He shook his head. 'I know. It's not that.' He grimaced. 'No, it's something much worse. One that means I really shouldn't have kissed you. I know I should apologise, and I will if you want me to, but I'm not sorry. I can't regret it. But because I did it, I've a feeling I need to confess my secret to you, because I'm becoming far too fond of you, Jeannie Musgrove, and I shouldn't. It's not fair on you.'

She felt her cheeks warm and hope fill her heart at his words. 'You're fond of me?'

He nodded.

The joy she felt at those simple words wiped away her misery for a moment. 'I'm fond of you, too,' she confessed with a shy smile. But then his solemn gaze filled her with dread. He looked so regretful. 'What is it? Can you tell me?'

He blew out a breath and rested his forehead against hers. 'I'm sorry, Jeannie. I don't mean to lead you on, and you've already been upset enough today. I want to tell you, but when I do, I reckon you'll want nothing to do with me. I'm selfish enough to want to put off the inevitable.'

'No,' she whispered, wishing he would move his head and kiss her again. It felt so intimate, standing in the doorway, their arms around each other and their foreheads touching. 'No secrets,' she said. 'Please.' She couldn't imagine anything that would be so terrible that it would put her off him.

He was silent for a long moment and her mind conjured up all sorts of things he might be keeping secret. Had his injury affected more than just his leg? Had he been left less than a man? Was that why? She was too shy to ask something so private. But then he spoke. 'I wish I was free to court you, Jeannie. You're a fine girl and I'd be proud to be your sweetheart. But... the truth is, I have a wife back in Northampton.'

She gasped and this time when she stepped back, he dropped his arms and let her go. 'You're married?'

He nodded, misery making his shoulders slump. 'I am. Although she has no respect for the vows we took and while I was in the trenches, she took up with my cousin. They're back in Northampton, living as husband and wife. She doesn't even have to change her surname.'

Jeannie wanted to weep at the unfairness of it all but she was too shocked to cry. 'How did you find out?'

'My ma came to see me in the hospital when I got back to Blighty. She told me. Said my missus was expecting, six months along, while I'd been away a full year. It caused a right old row in the family, with my pa and his brother coming to blows.'

She covered her mouth with her hands. 'That's why you didn't want to go home.'

'It is. The lovers told people I'd died. I said Ma should let it lie.

I'll never go back. Even if he deserts her, I'll never have her back. I just couldn't. That kind of betrayal, it cuts deep, you know? Me and my cousin were like brothers. For him to do that to me with her...' He shook her head, looking away. 'I'd divorce her if I could. But it's not easy, not for folks like us. It costs a lot of money and takes a long time. One day, I might be able to afford it, but not right now. I'm trying to start again, building a new life well away from them.' He looked back at her, his gaze full of regret. 'That's why I haven't asked you out, Jeannie. I'm not free; I couldn't do that to you. I know other men would just ignore the fact they were married and would simply take up with another woman, but I'll not be a bigamist or expect someone to live with me in sin. You're a sweet girl; you need someone who can do the right thing by you.'

She nodded, wondering whether this day could get any worse. She took another calming breath, blinking hard against even more tears. 'Thank you for telling me,' she said. 'I wish...'

He touched her cheek. 'So do I. I'm so sorry. But I can see that it's important to be honest to you, especially if your friends have been keeping secrets from you. Like I said, I shouldn't have kissed you, but I can't bring myself to regret it.' He dropped his hand. 'You're the only girl I'd want to court if I could. I've thought that from the day I met you. You were so fierce and brave. But I can't, so you should forget about me and find yourself a nice lad who'll be able to marry you and give you the life you deserve.'

'We can still be friends, though, can't we?' she asked, her heart breaking all over again. She had a feeling that no other lad would quite live up to Tom.

He nodded, though his smile was rueful. 'I'd like that, although it will be hard when you're walking out with someone else.'

She shrugged. 'Not much chance of that these days,' she

muttered before she turned away. 'I must get home to Ma. She'll be wondering where I am.' She wiped at her face, making sure there were no more stray tears. She hoped her eyes weren't too red and puffy.

'You look beautiful,' he said softly, as though he'd read her thoughts. 'Come on, I'll walk with you.' He held out his arm. 'The fresh air will clear your cheeks.'

For a moment, she thought she ought to refuse and leave him to go on his own way. He was *married!* He had vowed to love and cherish another woman, to love her until death parted them. But it wasn't his fault that his bride had broken those vows and betrayed him in the worst possible way with his own cousin. She couldn't imagine why any lass would prefer someone else over Tom. He was handsome and kind and brave and didn't deserve to be treated so ill. So she slipped her arm in his and they walked slowly up the High Street towards West End.

'I won't tell anyone,' she said. 'It's no one else's business.'

He shrugged. 'Thank you, but I don't mind if you tell your family and friends. I'm starting to think I've nothing to be ashamed of. It's only that I can't declare myself for you that really upsets me. If there was anything I could do to put that right, Jeannie, I promise you I'd do it. But I can't expect you to wait on a miracle that might never happen.'

He left her at her front door. He didn't kiss her again, although she could see in his eyes that he wanted to. She went inside and closed the door, leaning against it for a moment to catch her breath and collect her thoughts. The past couple of hours had been one shock after another and she was feeling emotional.

'Is that you, Jeannie? Are the boys with you?' Ma called from the kitchen. 'Can one of you help me get this roasting tin out of the oven? My hands are stiff and I don't want to drop potatoes all over the floor.'

Jeannie took a deep breath. 'Don't worry, Ma, I'll do it,' she said as she pushed away from the door. She would help get dinner on the table before the twins arrived, tell Ma that Lucas would be along after a while and wanted them to leave him a plate, and then later – much later – she'd think about all the secrets that had been revealed today.

16

Kate and Louisa stood outside the Musgrove's cottage in West End the next day.

'What if she doesn't want to see me?' asked Louisa. 'She probably hates me now she knows the truth.'

Kate put a hand on her arm, stopping her from turning away. 'Don't be daft,' she said briskly. 'Jeannie's not like that. It was just a shock for her yesterday, that's all.'

'I didn't mean to upset her. But I was in such a state, I couldn't bear to lie to her any more.'

Kate nodded. Truth be told, she was relieved that Jeannie knew it all now. It had been so hard all this time to keep her in the dark, even though it hadn't been her secret to share and she understood the reasons for it. But it had been impossible for Louisa to deny her child yesterday when confronted by her own drawing of him. It worried Kate that it would be a hundred times harder for Lou when Peg and Will came back to Street, as they planned to do once the war ended. How would she bear it, seeing little Matthew with his adoptive parents?

'You did the right thing, telling her,' she said.

'I know,' she sighed. 'I couldn't let her think it was something she'd said that had upset me. She was being so sweet. But now I'm standing here, I'm frightened she'll have thought about it and found me wanting.'

'I told you, don't be daft. Jeannie's not like that. She'll be hurting for you. Come on, let's go in and get it over with before you get in any more of a tizzy over this.'

When Lou nodded, Kate knocked at the door. One of the twins answered, holding a broom. Kate was pretty sure it was Peter. He was more likely to get on with his chores than John was. He still didn't look happy about it. He opened the door wide to let them in, tilting his head towards the kitchen. 'She's doing the washing,' he mumbled, then went back to his sweeping.

Kate shared a smile with Louisa and they left him to it.

Jeannie was at the deep sink, using a washboard and scrubbing brush on her brothers' trousers. Her face was red in the steam and her hair was escaping her bun. She was so intent on her task that she didn't hear them come in until they were standing on either side of her.

'What can we do to help?' said Kate.

Jeannie yelped and dropped the brush, causing the hot, soapy water to splash up her front as she put her wet hands to her chest. 'Oh my, you startled me!' she gasped.

Kate chuckled. 'Sorry, love. Now you're all wet.' She pointed at the damp patches down her apron. 'Do you want to go and change that while me and Lou carry on?'

Jeannie looked round at Louisa, who gave her a nervous smile.

'Hello, Jeannie?' she said. 'I... I wanted to make sure you're not angry with me.'

Jeannie closed her eyes briefly and her shoulders dropped. It looked to Kate as though she was giving thanks. She was probably relieved that Louisa had made the first move after the drama of yesterday.

'I'm not angry with you,' she said softly as she opened her eyes. 'I'm just sorry I couldn't have been of more help to you when you needed it. And I'm more sorry than I can say that you had to do what you did, Lou. It's so unfair.'

Lou swallowed hard. 'Thank you.' She looked down before whispering, 'I'm only grateful that Peg and Will are able to give him a loving home with his father's family.'

Jeannie looked like she was going to burst into tears. 'I want to give you a hug, but I'm soaked and we'll all end up blubbing, won't we?'

'Right, and this won't get the washing done,' said Kate, nudging Jeannie with her hip. 'Do you want to get out of your wet clothes?'

Jeannie looked down at herself and laughed. 'No, don't worry. It's mainly my apron that's wet. I'll just change that.' She undid the ties and pulled it off, hanging it over the back of a kitchen chair.

'We can help,' said Louisa. 'Many hands make light work.'

'You don't have to do that,' she said. 'I'm nearly done. I'm just trying to get the mud and grass stains off the twins' trousers. They're such a messy pair. Kate, could you make us a cuppa while I finish them? You know where everything is. Lou, sit down, love. You can help me with the mangle outside in a minute.'

She took a clean apron out of the dresser drawer and put it on before returning to the sink.

'Are your ma and Lucas around?' asked Kate as she poured hot water into the tea pot. 'Will they want a cup?'

'I do,' Peter called from the parlour.

Louisa looked startled. 'Did he hear us?'

Kate went to the doorway. 'Peter Musgrove, are you ear-wigging on us from in there?'

'No,' came the gruff reply. 'I just heard someone say cup and I've got a thirst on.'

'Is that right? Because if I ever catch you listening in on us, I'll box your ears,' said Kate. 'I don't care how tall you're getting, I'll stand on a chair to reach if I have to.'

'I'm not interested in what you lasses have got to say. I just want a drink. With two sugars.'

Jeannie rolled her eyes. 'You'll have one sugar,' she responded. 'We told you, there's shortages and you'll still want jam and cakes, so don't go sneaking an extra spoon.' She turned to Kate. 'Lucas is down the garden, weeding with John, and Ma's having a rest. She overdid it a bit yesterday, so she's suffering today.'

Kate nodded. 'I'll make everyone a cup. Sounds like you could all do with one.'

Louisa jumped up and helped her gather cups and saucers from the dresser while Jeannie finished off the last of the washing. By the time she poured the tea, Jeannie had rinsed it and dropped it into the tin bath by the back door, ready to be carried out to the mangle. Kate sent Peter upstairs to deliver a cuppa to his ma and Louisa delivered drinks to Lucas and John outside.

Jeannie sank onto a kitchen chair and accepted a cup and saucer with a sigh. 'Thanks, love,' she said. 'I'm ready for this.'

Kate studied her friend, feeling concerned. 'Are you really all right?' she asked. 'We've been worried about you. You rushed off yesterday. Are you angry at us?'

Jeannie frowned. 'No. Not angry. Upset for Lou. Hurt, maybe, that you didn't tell me before. But once I'd had a chance to calm down and think about it, I can see why you didn't. I can still barely believe that Mr and Mrs Clements were so set on giving away their own grandchild.'

Kate scowled. It made her angry and frustrated every time she thought about it. 'If they'd let Lou and Mattie marry when he asked, none of this would've been necessary. But maybe now you'll understand why she can't forgive them.'

Jeannie sighed and nodded. 'I suppose. Only... well, I learned something else yesterday after I left you and that's made me think folks shouldn't rush into getting wed.'

'What d'you mean?' she asked as Louisa came back into the kitchen and joined them at the table.

Jeannie craned her neck to look into the parlour. 'Is Peter still upstairs?' she asked. 'Only I don't want him to hear this.'

'Yes, I can hear him speaking to your ma,' said Kate.

'What it is?' asked Louisa. 'What have I missed?'

Jeannie looked at the two of them. 'I was just saying to Kate I learned another secret yesterday on my way home. Like yours, it explained a lot.'

Louisa went a little pale, but didn't say anything. Kate wasn't so patient.

'So come on. What is it?'

Louisa put a hand on Kate's arm. 'Kate, don't. It's a secret. We can't expect Jeannie to keep mine if we insist she tells us everyone else's.'

'It's all right,' said Jeannie. 'He said I could tell you. I've already told Lucas and I'll probably tell Ma because she keeps dropping hints about how nice Tom is, but I'll not be discussing it with anyone else.'

Louisa leaned forward. 'So it's about Tom? Has he asked to be your sweetheart at long last?'

Kate frowned. 'Hang on, Lou. Think about what she just said. What's he done to you, Jeannie?'

Jeannie shook her head and looked away, but she couldn't

hide the flush that warmed her cheeks. 'He's done nothing to me... well... at least...'

'Spit it out, Jeannie,' said Kate.

Louisa regarded her with narrowed eyes. 'Did he kiss you?' she asked.

Kate blinked. It hadn't occurred to her that he might have actually kissed Jeannie, but judging by her blush, he must have done. She grinned. 'He did, didn't he? And about time too.'

Jeannie looked up at the ceiling, looking far from happy about it. 'Yes, he kissed me. Just a little peck. It was lovely and he said he was fond of me. But it doesn't matter, because nothing can come of it.' She blew out a breath and looked back at them. 'Before he went to war, he got married to his sweetheart in Northampton.'

'He's married?' Kate squeaked, covering her mouth with her hand. She hadn't expected that. 'So what's he doing here on his own?'

Jeannie sighed again, looking miserable. She told them what Tom had told her.

'Oh my lord, that's awful,' said Kate. 'So he was stuck in hospital, minus his foot and suffering lord knows what after fighting for king and country, and that strumpet ran off with his cousin?'

Jeannie nodded. 'His pa and his uncle came to blows apparently. It's torn the family apart.'

Lou put a hand on Jeannie's shoulder. 'Oh, love. So that's why he's not asked you out?'

'Seems so,' she agreed. 'He's stuck, legally wed to her, even though she's had another man's child. He said he won't lead me on because he doesn't know if or when he'll ever be free and that I should look for someone else.'

Neither of the girls knew what to say to that. Kate sipped her tea and thought about what rotten luck the three of them had had with lads. First Louisa had lost Mattie, then Ted had upped and left her without so much as a glance back. Now poor Jeannie was pining for someone who was stuck, unable to act on his feelings for her. 'At least he was honest and told you,' she said. 'Someone else might have just gone ahead and led you on.'

'She's right,' said Louisa. 'Can you imagine if he'd said he'd marry you, then his wife turned up just as the vicar was about to declare you man and wife?'

'Then he'd be a bigamist,' Kate pointed out. 'He'd be thrown in jail.'

Jeannie put her elbows on the table and covered her face with her hands. 'Please, stop,' she groaned.

'Sorry,' said Kate.

'So what happens now?' asked Louisa.

Jeannie shrugged, dropping her hands. 'Nothing. We're going to be friends, that's all.'

Kate and Louisa pulled identical faces but didn't say anything else. Kate felt so sorry for both of her friends. She was glad she'd sworn off love after Ted's sudden departure from her life. She was content to write her letters to the conscientious objectors she heard about through Mrs Clothier and Auntie Betty. They seemed to be nice lads – sincere and honest and truly brave to be keeping faith with their beliefs in the face of opposition from all sides. But she wasn't interested in anything else.

'That's a shame,' she said. 'But better to know now, isn't it?'

'I suppose,' she said. 'It looks like all three of us are going to end up old maids, doesn't it?'

'Suits me,' said Kate with no hesitation.

Louisa shrugged. 'Me too. I'll not settle for second best, no matter what my ma and pa think.'

Jeannie sighed. 'I prayed really hard last night that your parents would have a nice week away and realise that all the pressure they're putting on you is unfair. I really, really hope they'll come home from their holiday and tell you they love you and won't force you into a loveless marriage.'

Kate bit back a scoff. She couldn't imagine that happening. It seemed from Louisa's expression that she didn't either.

'Thank you, Jeannie,' she said. 'I appreciate it. But I doubt that will happen. If anything, Ma's getting angrier and angrier.' She drained her cup and put it down on the saucer. 'But I don't have to worry about her for a few days, so come on, let's sort out that washing and get it mangled and up on the line while the sun's still shining.'

The friends worked well together and soon all the washing was dealt with. John and Peter had done a few chores before rushing off for a kickabout with their chums. Lucas put the gardening tools away and sat in the sunshine. Kate noticed he was watching Louisa and his sister, as though he was waiting for one or the other of them to burst into tears again. She walked over to him and sank down onto the grass beside him while the others inspected the vegetable garden.

'Sounds like Jeannie had plenty of surprises yesterday,' she said as she watched them. 'Did you know about Tom's wife?'

He shook his head. 'Not a clue. But then again, I didn't know he had sisters until he told Jeannie a while back. He's very private.'

She nodded. 'It's a shame though. Jeannie really likes him.'

Lucas frowned. 'She never said.'

She rolled her eyes. 'She wouldn't, would she? But anyone who cared to look could see. It's obvious he likes her too. Me and Lou couldn't understand why he hadn't asked Jeannie out. We thought you'd warned him off your sister.'

He shrugged. 'I might have done if I'd thought he was going to hurt her. She's too soft-hearted.'

'You say it like that's a bad thing. But it's what her friends love about her.'

He didn't say anything for a while. He closed his eyes and raised his face to the sun. Kate could see that he had a much healthier colour these days. When he'd come home from the hospital, he'd been pale and looked old for his years. There was still an air of sadness about him that hadn't been there before Mattie had been killed. Louisa had it too and Kate could understand why the two of them got along so well. Their shared grief for Mattie brought them closer. Kate was glad of that. Louisa needed all of her friends now, more than ever.

'So,' she said after a while. 'Are you going to warn him off now?'

He opened one eye and glanced at her sideways. 'No. Why? He's been honest. Jeannie knows he can't be more than a friend.'

'Like you and Louisa, you mean?' She didn't know why she was pushing, but she couldn't help herself. It had occurred to her yesterday, when he'd comforted Lou in all the upset with the baby's drawing and Mattie's photograph and Jeannie's unintentionally cruel words, that Lucas and Louisa were good for each other. Perhaps when the sharp pain of grief had dulled, one day, the two of them might find more than friendship together. She knew they wouldn't thank her for suggesting it. But it didn't stop her wondering what the future might hold for them.

Lucas closed his eye again and resumed his sun worship. 'For a lass who hates lads, you seem mighty interested in pairing everyone else off, Kate Davis,' he muttered. 'I'd appreciate it if you accepted that sometimes friendship is all folk want.'

She lay back with a sigh and closed her eyes. 'Fair enough. It's all I want or need, that's for sure. Looks like we'll all still be single when we're old and grey. Will you push me in my bath chair? I rather fancy sitting there while someone wheels me from one place to the next.'

'Rather you than me,' he said.

Now she felt bad, remembering Lou telling them about how he'd hated being pushed around the hospital grounds in a bath chair.

Jeannie and Louisa came over with their drinks and sank onto the ground next to Lucas and Kate.

'Oh, it's good to stop for a minute,' said Jeannie with a sigh. 'It doesn't feel like we're on holiday. I don't think I've had a moment's rest so far.'

'All the more reason we should have a day out,' said Kate. 'Did you think any more about a trip to Weston-super-Mare? I fancy a picnic on the beach and a paddle in the sea.'

Lucas snorted. 'More mud than sand round there, and if the tide's out, you'd be walking for miles to chase a quick paddle.'

Louisa chuckled. 'You're such a killjoy, Lucas,' she said.

'I think he's right,' said Jeannie, looking earnest. 'And you'd have to be careful of that mud if you go out too far. I've heard people have got stuck in it and drowned when the tide rushed back in.' She shuddered. 'I'd rather have a paddle in the River Brue.'

Kate tutted. 'We can do that any time. It's our one week off in the summer. We've got to have an adventure.'

'To be honest,' said Louisa, 'I'm rather enjoying the peace and quiet in Street now that so many folk have gone away. If we go to Weston, chances are we'll find most of them there. It won't be much of an adventure if we're surrounded by people we know, will it?'

'She's got a point,' said Lucas. 'I'm content to stay right here.'

Kate gave him a sideways glance before glaring at Louisa.

'Well, at least you two managed to escape from here for a bit, while me and Jeannie have been stuck here all the time.'

'Kate!' Jeannie gasped. 'It was hardly like they were... I mean... neither of them were on holiday.'

Kate felt ashamed as she realised what she'd said. 'Sorry,' she mumbled. 'I didn't mean anything by it. I'm just feeling like I want to spread my wings and get away from here for a bit.'

'Why didn't you go with Auntie Betty?' asked Louisa, her kind expression letting Kate know she hadn't taken offence. 'You could've had a nice time with her and your sister.'

Kate sighed. 'I know. But I thought it best to let Auntie meet her grandson without me. I was sure I'd mess up and say the wrong thing and she'd realise the truth.'

Louisa reached over and touched her cheek. 'You gave up the chance of a proper holiday to protect me?' she asked softly. 'Thank you.'

'This is all so difficult, isn't it?' said Jeannie. 'I just hope I don't give the game away.' She looked at the others, a worried frown creasing her brow. 'Once I'd calmed down and thought about it, I realised why you didn't tell me. I'd have given your secret away for sure. Your pa is pretty scary, Lou. I doubt if I'd have been able to lie to him.'

Louisa smiled sadly. 'I am sorry we didn't tell you, though, Jeannie. I just couldn't risk him finding me.'

'I can see that now,' she agreed.

They were all silent for a few minutes, sipping their drinks and basking in the sunshine. Around them, they could hear the chirp of birds, the occasional bark of a dog, the buzz of insects around the garden.

'This is so nice,' said Kate.

'So you're not sulking because no one wants to go to Weston?' asked Lucas with a smirk.

'I don't sulk,' she said. 'I was just annoyed and frustrated. But I can see why you're all reluctant.' She sighed. 'But I might have a little trip out on my own if I can manage it.'

'Not to Weston,' said Jeannie, looking horrified. 'You could get stuck in the mud and none of us would be there to save you.'

Kate laughed. 'It's good to know you care,' she teased. 'But no, don't worry, I've gone off that idea. I might just see if I can get a bus somewhere for a day.'

'Check the timetables,' Jeannie advised. 'You don't want to get stuck somewhere if you miss the last bus.'

'You're such a worrywart,' said Lucas.

'She's right, though,' said Kate, not wanting Jeannie to feel bad for worrying about her. 'I'll make sure I know the time and be waiting for the bus home in plenty of time.'

'We can at least have a walk and a picnic, can't we?' asked Jeannie. 'We can leave Ma for a couple of hours, I'm sure.'

'So long as it's not up Collard Hill,' said Lucas under his breath.

Louisa heard him and nodded. 'I'd rather not go there again. Not without Mattie.'

'Me neither,' said Lucas.

They discussed and dismissed several ideas. It had to be somewhere they could walk or get to by bus.

'It's a shame we don't all have bicycles,' said Louisa. 'I've got my old one in the shed. I was thinking of getting it out so I could venture further afield for my sketching.'

Lucas frowned. 'If you haven't ridden it for a while, you'd better let me have a look at it. It might need some maintenance.'

She beamed at him. 'Would you? I'd be ever so grateful. I've been thinking about it for a while but, what with all the aggravation at home, I haven't liked to ask Pa to check it for me.'

He nodded. 'I can do that for you. I'll get my own bone-rattler out as well. So long as the twins haven't wrecked it, it should be serviceable.'

Kate sighed. 'Shame you can't get all of us on two bicycles, eh?'

'Don't you know anyone you could borrow one from?' asked Lucas.

She looked thoughtful for a moment. 'I think George and Ada had some before the children arrived. I remember them peddling off on a Sunday afternoon when the weather was fine. Ada showed me how to ride hers.'

'Well,' said Louisa. 'If she's still got it, maybe she'll be happy to lend it to you.'

Kate smiled, feeling hopeful. 'I'll pop round there later and ask her.' She turned to Jeannie. 'We just need to find one for you, now. Shall I see if George's one will suit you?'

Jeannie looked uncertain. 'Won't I have to wear breeches like a lad if I rode his bike? It'll have a high bar in the middle like Lucas's bike.'

'I made myself a couple of pairs of breeches that look like a skirt for riding my bicycle,' said Louisa. 'It looks like you're wearing a long skirt when you're walking along, but they're split into wide legs so you can mount a bicycle without compromising your modesty. Ma found an old pattern in a ladies' magazine. Apparently they were all the rage in Victorian times when women first started riding.'

Lucas chuckled. 'Compromising your modesty,' he repeated. He sobered and looked a bit bashful when all three girls glared at him. 'Sorry. I just thought it sounded funny. I thought you were all modern young women who can do anything a man can. I didn't reckon modesty came into it.'

'Yes, well, we can,' said Louisa. 'But that doesn't mean we want to flash our legs at you lads at every turn.' She turned to Jeannie.

'If you can get hold of a bicycle, you can borrow one of my breeches skirts,' she said. 'What about you, Kate?'

She shrugged. 'I'll see if Ada's got something I can borrow. If you like, Jeannie, you can use her machine and I'll ride George's. I wouldn't even care if I had to wear boy's breeches. I always thought they looked more comfortable to wear than skirts and petticoats.'

Jeannie looked shocked. 'Oh no, Kate. You can't pretend to be a lad.'

Kate laughed. 'I won't. I'm a lass but I don't see why I should risk breaking my neck by trying to cycle in a long skirt when a pair of lad's breeches will get the job done without the chance of me catching my clothes in the chain and flying over the handlebars.' In fact, the thought of being able to dress like a lad appealed to her. It had to be more comfortable and liberating than boring skirts and dresses.

'You're not making it sound very safe,' Jeannie complained.

'Well if you'd agree to getting on a train, we wouldn't need to find another form of transport to get us out of the village, would we?' she challenged.

Jeannie sighed and lay back on the grass, staring up at the blue sky above. They could hear the swallows high up, chirping to each other as they ate their fill of the flying insects that were plentiful above the surrounding farmland and orchards.

'At least give it a try, Jeannie,' said Lucas. 'You used to have a go on my bicycle when I first got it. Remember?'

'I do,' she said. 'I used to love it.'

'Well, there you are,' said Louisa. 'We'll gather up enough machines, sort out suitable outfits and we'll be off on an adventure. Agreed?' She looked around at them, her face glowing with anticipation.

'But what about Tom?' Lucas asked.

'What about him?' asked Kate, not sure what he meant.

'I'm not spending an entire day with you lot without bringing another lad along for moral support,' he grumbled. 'But I'm not sure he'll be able to cycle given his injury.'

Kate laughed. 'Coward,' she teased him. 'Although I reckon if Tom wants to ride a bicycle, he'll find a way. He's not let the loss of a foot hold him back thus far, has he?'

Lucas nodded. 'You're right. I'll ask him. In the meantime, we'll gather up what machines we can find and see if we can get them roadworthy. I'll start with mine.' He got up and disappeared into the shed, where the girls could hear him moving things and grumbling about the mess and spiderwebs.

'Do you mind that, Jeannie?' Louisa asked her softly.

Jeannie sighed. 'I suppose. But I think Tom might not want to come.'

Kate felt so sorry for poor Jeannie. And for Tom. It was rotten luck that he'd been snapped up by a lass back in Northampton, only for her to betray him like that and leave the poor lad trapped in a horrible situation where he couldn't get on with his life with someone decent like Jeannie while the strumpet enjoyed marital relations with another man. She shuddered as she imagined her to be a younger version of the Floozy who had got her claws into Pa, despite having her own husband, and Pa having a good and faithful wife.

'I'm sure he will,' she said. 'You agreed to be friends, didn't you? What can be more innocent and friendly than a bicycle ride with a crowd of us?'

17

When Lucas went round to Wilfred Road and asked Tom about riding a bicycle, he laughed.

'Funny you should mention it now. I bought myself one just last week.'

'Are you getting on with it?' asked Lucas, not wanting to mention his disability.

Tom nodded. 'I am now. I've rigged up some straps to hold my false foot on the pedal and I'm getting the hang of it.' He pointed at Lucas's injured arm. 'How will you manage?'

Lucas shrugged. 'I should be grand, thanks to the splint you made me. I can use my good hand for braking. I used to be able to ride in a straight line without using either of my hands, so I don't think I'll have too much trouble.'

'Good. I've been round the village a couple of times and across to Glastonbury. I'm ready to try exploring further afield now. I'd be glad to go on some rides with you. You can show me the area.' He gave him a rueful smile. 'And pick me up and help me find my way back if I fall off.'

'Has it happened a lot?'

'A couple of times in the last week. I keep forgetting to put my good foot down on the road when I stop, so while I'm trying to get my false one loose of the straps, I land in the dirt.'

'Why'd you get a bike then, if you weren't sure you could ride it?' asked Lucas.

Tom looked wistful. 'I'm hoping I'll get the hang of it again soon. I used to ride a lot. Me and my cousin would go off all day, peddling maybe forty or fifty miles at a time.'

Lucas gave him a narrow-eyed look. 'Would that be the cousin who's carrying on with your missus?'

Tom stilled, his face blank. Then he sighed and nodded. 'She told you, then.'

'She did. She said you didn't mind me and her friends knowing. We won't tell anyone else. I'm sorry it's happened to you. It's not a situation I'd want to find myself in. You don't deserve that. Not from the people you trust the most.'

Tom ran a hand through his hair. 'It's a damned mess. I try not to get angry about it because it will just leave me all bitter and twisted. But how could they do that? It's like, the moment I went off to fight, she decided I was dead to her and took up with him. Now I'm left with nothing and can't even offer anything to a decent girl like your sister.'

Lucas frowned. 'So you do like our Jeannie? I wasn't sure, but Louisa and Kate were sure you did.'

He nodded. 'I'll not lie to you. I think Jeannie's a fine lass and if I was free, I'd be proud to court her. But I can't lead her on and pretend I can wed her, because I can't. That's why I told her. She needs to find someone who's free to give her the life she deserves.'

Lucas nodded. 'I appreciate your honesty. If you'd led her on, I'd have had to sort you out.' He felt a corner of his mouth turn up as he tried not to grin. 'Not that I think I'd have won against you in a fist fight, but you know... we've got to protect our sisters, haven't we?'

Tom threw back his head and laughed. 'I'm glad we'll have no reason to find out,' he said. 'You've become a good friend. Don't worry. I'll not dishonour your sister, Lucas. As for my sisters, they're all older than me. I heard a couple of them had a right go at my missus in the street, although they didn't resort to physical violence on account of her expecting.' He pulled a face. 'I'd rather they hadn't. Knowing them, half of Northampton will have heard my business because of it. That's why I prefer not to go back there.'

Lucas felt sorry for him. He knew what it was like with everyone knowing your business – first when Pa had died at the factory years ago; next when Jeannie clashed with Sid Lambert and Douglas Baker last year. Now, everyone knew about his useless hand and he was tired of the looks of pity he got whenever someone caught him struggling. He understood why Tom didn't tell many people about his foot. No one wanted to be treated like a freak. No wonder he didn't want word getting out about his faithless wife.

'Would you have your wife back if she came to you?' he asked.

Tom shook his head, his expression set. 'Not a chance in hell. I could never trust her again. Any affection I felt for her died when I learned how she betrayed me.'

'I can understand that. Once trust is gone... especially when she went off with your own cousin. Is there no way you can be rid of her? Won't the church annul a marriage if she had no intention of being faithful to her vows?'

Tom shrugged. 'Unfortunately not, as we were wed for over a year before I enlisted. Someone with money might be able to get a legal divorce, but that needs a court hearing and lawyers. As there's no guarantee of it being granted, I can't afford to throw that kind of money away, even though I'm earning a decent wage.' He sighed, looking miserable. 'So, short of her leaving him and finding a rich man who'll pay for her freedom... or her dying – which is unlikely as she's as healthy as a horse – I'm stuck. Not that I'd wish anyone dead. I've seen enough of that to never want to have to face it again.'

'I know what you mean,' muttered Lucas, looking away. He still had nightmares about his experiences in the trenches. He dreamed of Mattie as well – reliving memories from when they were young and carefree before the war changed everything. When that happened, he felt indescribably happy. But then he'd wake up and realise Mattie was gone and he'd sink into the depths of guilt and despair again.

The two of them were silent for a while, each lost in their own thoughts. Then Lucas straightened his shoulders.

'Look, it's a rotten situation, and this damned war isn't helping anyone but the arms manufacturers to get rich, but we have to make the best of it, don't we? So, are we going for a cycle ride or two while the factory's shut?'

'We are,' Tom agreed. 'I've a fancy to see Cheddar Gorge. That's not too far from here, is it?'

'About a dozen miles. I'm not sure the lasses will want to go that far, though.'

Tom raised his eyebrows. 'Oh. They want to come as well, do they?'

'Yeah. They're talking about having a picnic somewhere and I need to go with them to make sure they're all right if they get a puncture or one of them falls off their bike. I want you to come so I've someone to talk to and I'm not nagged to death by them all. But I reckon we should take them somewhere closer so we don't have to put up with their moaning when their bottoms get sore and their legs ache.'

Tom laughed. 'Which they will do, no doubt.'

Lucas chuckled. 'Of course they will. So why don't we aim for a short ride and picnic with them, then a longer ride for the two of us out to Cheddar on another day?'

'Sounds like a good plan.'

* * *

Kate managed to acquire the loan of bicycles for her and Jeannie, although it took Lucas and Tom a day to work on all the machines to make sure they were roadworthy. Deciding where they were going for their adventure took just as long. Routes that Lucas suggested were turned down by his sister and her friends on account of some long and steep hill climbs.

'But then we'll be able to enjoy the views,' he argued. But they had no intention of arriving at their picnic all hot and sweaty.

'There must be somewhere on a flatter route,' said Jeannie. 'It's supposed to be a fun excursion, not an endurance race.'

'All right. Fenny Castle. That's my final offer. If you don't want to do that, me and Tom'll go out on our own. We're not scared of a few little hills like you lasses.'

The ruins of the ancient motte and bailey castle was north of Glastonbury on the way to Wells, a distance of just over six miles by his calculations. Tom, being an engineer, had arrived with a saddle bag filled with a puncture repair kit, a tin of grease for bicycle chains and a pump attached to the frame of his machine. In the girl's front baskets they had stuffed bottles of cordial and apple juice, bread, cheese and slabs of cake. Lucas wore a ruck-sack containing picnic blankets.

He grinned. 'At least if I fall off, I'll have a soft landing.'

'So long as you don't land flat on your face,' said Kate.

'I hope none of us fall off,' said Jeannie. She'd had a little practice up and down West End the day before and was getting better at cycling, but she was still nervous. 'What will we do if one of us gets hurt miles from home?'

'We'll all be fine,' said Tom, his gaze gentle on her worried face. 'There's no rush. Just take your time.'

Lucas watched as his sister's cheeks bloomed pink under Tom's regard. He looked away, feeling unutterably sad. He knew what it was like to love someone and not be able to do anything about it. He didn't want that kind of misery for Jeannie.

'Come on, then,' said Louisa, her eyes bright with anticipation. 'Let's go!'

Louisa had forgotten the joy of feeling the wind on your face as you cycle through the lanes. She was soon pedalling along, enjoying the sunshine and the freedom of leaving the village behind her for a few hours. She and Kate were rushing along side by side, laughing with pure happiness. Behind them, Lucas and Tom were keeping their pace slower as they rode on either side of Jeannie.

'Woooh! Isn't this marvellous?' cried Kate.

'It is. We must do this more often. Will Ada let you keep her bicycles for a while? We could have some Sunday-afternoon rides while the weather holds.'

'Now she's got the children, she's got no call to use hers, so she said I could keep it.' Jeannie was riding that one. Kate was on her brother's bike, wearing a pair of Louisa's wide breeches. 'I can hang onto George's one as well, so long as I don't wreck it in case he wants it back when he gets home.'

Louisa nodded, feeling a shiver of dread run down her spine. She hoped and prayed that both of Kate's brothers would come home unharmed, but after what had happened to Mattie, Lucas and Tom, as well as countless other lads they knew who had been maimed or killed in this awful war, she was afraid to even hope.

'So,' Kate went on, 'you, me and Jeannie can have as many adventures as we like.' She grinned as she glanced over her shoulder. 'Although she's going to have to learn to speed up a bit or we'll never get anywhere.'

Louisa stopped peddling for a moment and looked back at the others as she coasted along. She chuckled as she saw Jeannie's earnest face, going red with exertion, while Lucas looked like he'd like nothing more than to leave his sister in the dust and race off without her. Tom seemed more content, smiling encouragement at Jeannie, although she barely noticed as her concentration was on the road ahead.

'Maybe we should drop back and ride with Jeannie for a bit to let the lads burn off some energy. Lucas looks fit to burst at their slow pace.'

Kate smirked. 'I think Tom's enjoying himself, though.'

Louisa pulled a face. 'I know. But it's a bit cruel, isn't it? No matter how much he likes her and Jeannie returns his regard, they can't do anything about it, can they? It might be better not to encourage them.'

Kate sobered. 'I suppose so. I'd forgotten about that. It's such a shame, isn't it?'

'It is,' Louisa sighed. 'But what can you do?' She knew all about being in impossible situations and she felt sad for Jeannie.

'Nothing, I suppose. But maybe we can ride with her so she's not stuck with Tom and her brother?'

With a nod, the two lasses slowed so that the others caught up with them.

'We're nearly there, Jeannie,' said Kate. 'Look, that's Coxley up ahead.'

'We need to take the next left, before we get into the village,' said Lucas.

'Right-o,' said Louisa. 'Why don't you and Tom ride ahead?'

Lucas grinned at her. 'Getting tired after your mad dash to be in front?'

She returned his smile. 'No. We just thought Jeannie might prefer some better company than you two.'

Tom laughed. 'I think we've just been insulted. What's wrong with our company?'

'Not a thing,' she said.

'But ours is better,' said Kate. 'So go on, stretch your legs and get there ahead of us. We'll expect the blankets spread out somewhere pretty when we arrive. Chop chop. If you don't hurry up, we'll end up overtaking you again.'

The lads couldn't resist the challenge. Lucas sped off, although Tom cast a regretful glance at Jeannie before he took off after him. 'See you there,' he called over his shoulder.

'Be careful!' Jeannie shouted after them.

Tom raised a hand in acknowledgement but didn't slow down.

'How are you getting on, Jeannie?' asked Kate.

She nodded. 'My bottom's getting a bit sore from this hard saddle. I hope we get there soon.'

'Mine too,' said Louisa. 'But we're nearly there. We can have a nice sit down on a blanket.'

They peddled along, side by side until they came to the turning on the left where the lads had disappeared. Kate led the way, narrowly missing an old man with a hand-cart coming out of a gate.

'Watch where you're going!' he shouted, shaking a fist at her.

Kate swerved to get out of his way as the other lasses squeezed their brakes and came to a halt inches from him.

'Sorry, sir!' called Kate. 'We didn't see you from the road. Maybe whistle next time and we'll be warned.'

The old farmer grumbled something about youngsters and no respect. He glared at the other girls as they went round him, sending him apologetic smiles.

'Goodness,' gasped Jeannie as she caught up with Kate. 'I thought you were going to crash into him for sure. I nearly screamed. But when I opened my mouth, I couldn't make a sound.'

Kate laughed. 'I swear my life flashed in front of my eyes,' she said, blowing out a breath.

'Let's take it nice and slow now,' said Louisa. 'You gave us both a fright.'

Ten minutes later, they saw the lads near the mound of Fenny Castle rising out of the landscape. They'd left their bicycles on the ground and had laid out the blankets. Tom was standing with his back to them, hands on hips, looking up at the ruins of the motte and bailey castle, while Lucas was lounging on the ground, resting on an elbow.

'Come on, you slowcoaches,' he called. 'I'm hungry.'

'You're lucky we're here at all,' said Jeannie. 'Kate nearly got knocked off her bicycle by a farmer with a hand-cart.'

Tom turned around, frowning. 'Are you all right?'

Kate waved away his concern. 'Of course. I missed him and here I am.' She left her bicycle next to the others and sank onto one of the blankets. 'Gave me a heck of a fright, though.'

'Maybe we should make sure we all ride together on the way back,' said Lucas.

'Good idea,' said Kate. 'But let's eat first. I'm starving.'

They spent an hour or so enjoying the summer sunshine and their picnic. Louisa noticed that Jeannie stayed far enough away from Tom so that they couldn't have a private conversation, and neither of them glanced in the other's direction. It made her feel sad. They were being prevented from exploring what might be between them through no fault of their own. She cursed Tom's faithless wife for denying her friend the chance of happiness with a decent lad.

They were lying on the blankets, half dozing in the sun when a motor car pulled up on the lane. A well-heeled gentleman and his wife got out and made their way towards them. Louisa sat up, curious as to what they wanted.

'D'you think they're lost?' she wondered.

'You there,' called the man, pointing at them.

The others sat up.

'Yes, sir?' said Lucas. 'Are we trespassing? Sorry, we didn't mean to. We're just having a little picnic. We'll not cause any damage.' It was pasture, so they weren't spoiling any crops.

The man frowned. 'I'm more concerned about what two healthy young men are doing idling here when your country needs you in the trenches.'

'You should be ashamed of yourselves,' said his wife, glaring at the lads. 'While you're frittering away your time here like cowards, our sons are fighting for our liberty.'

Before either of them could say anything, Louisa leapt to her feet. She couldn't remain silent.

'They have nothing to be ashamed of, and they're no cowards,' she told the couple, her glare as fierce as their own. 'Both of them enlisted before conscription and both have paid the price. Why, Tom here came home with only half a leg and Lucas's right arm will never be the same again. The army gave them both honourable medical discharges. They've done their bit, so we don't appreciate you denigrating them so.'

The woman gasped at Louisa's outburst, clutching at her chest.

'She's right, ma'am,' said Jeannie, her tone a little more conciliatory. 'I'm sure if you ask him, Tom will show you his false leg and explain how he has to strap his foot to his bicycle so that he can ride it.'

'And Lucas has a special splint so that he can hold his arm right,' said Kate. 'But his wounds mean his grip is too weak now to hold a weapon.'

Lucas shook his head at the girls, looking unutterably sad. 'I'm sorry, sir, ma'am. But the girls are right. Both my friend and I have been in the trenches and the army says we're done. I hope your lads have better luck than we did.'

The couple stared at them. 'You both look in the best of health,' said the gentleman.

With a sigh, Tom rolled up his trouser leg to reveal the hard shell of his false limb. 'D'you want me to take it off, or is this proof enough?' he asked as he knocked on it with his knuckles. The woman flinched, covering her mouth with her hand.

All three girls glared at her, each equally outraged that she couldn't hide her revulsion. Tom ignored them all, rolling his trouser leg down again before he looked at Lucas with raised eyebrows.

With an exaggerated sigh, Lucas pulled up his sleeve and began unbuckling the splint on his arm. Jeannie moved towards him, batting his hand away.

'You don't need to prove anything to them,' she whispered.

'I know,' he said. 'But I'm going to anyway. So are you going to help me or not?'

She set to work, her deft fingers doing the job twice as fast. When the splint slipped off his wrist, he held out his arm, revealing the network of scars on his skin.

The gentleman coughed as his wife looked away. 'I see. I apologise. We live in difficult times and there seem far too many young men who should be fighting still loitering around these parts.'

'I think you'll find, sir, that the ones who haven't gone yet have either been rejected by the recruitment officers or are working in essential industries,' said Tom, his tone mild. 'We still need the farmers hereabouts to keep the nation and the army fed.'

'Or,' said Jeannie, 'they might look the age to fight, but are actually too young. We've got two brothers who are only fifteen, but they're already taller than Lucas and people keep giving them white feathers. Begging your pardon, sir and ma'am, but you shouldn't be so quick to judge.'

The woman turned on Jeannie. 'My sons are fighting for you, young lady!'

Jeannie nodded. 'And I'm grateful to them for their service and I pray every day that all our young men will come home safe and whole. But my brother and our friend here have served, too. Now they're home and working hard to help overcome the shortage of labour caused by this awful war. But this week is the factory's summer break, so we've come out to enjoy the sunshine in God's creation. I think they've earned that right, don't you?'

Louisa wanted to cheer and applaud Jeannie. She might be timid by nature, but she could be as fierce as anyone else when she was faced with injustice. She was glad her friend had spoken up. If she had opened her mouth again, Louisa was sure she'd have been sarcastic and quite rude to the couple who had interrupted their innocent excursion so abruptly. She glanced across at Kate, who kept her head down. She could see the smirk that the lass was trying to hide. No doubt, if the couple didn't leave soon, she would laugh in their faces.

They were strangers – probably from nearby Wells. They had no idea who she and her friends were, so who were they to judge?

With a huff, the woman said, 'If you have a genuine injury,

you must apply to your regiment to receive a Services Rendered badge,' she told the lads. 'Wearing it would prevent misunderstandings.'

Lucas nodded. 'I read about that in the newspaper,' he said. 'Maybe we should apply. Thank you for reminding us.'

She turned around and walked back to the motor car. The gentleman had the grace to look embarrassed and muttered an apology before going after his wife.

The friends watched in silence until he started the vehicle and drove away, then they turned and looked at each other.

'Well, I say,' said Kate. 'How rude! I'm glad you spoke up, Jeannie. I'd have said the same thing, only not so polite.'

'Louisa spoke up first,' she pointed out, her cheeks flushing pink.

'She did,' said Kate. 'But you put them firmly in their place. Well done, love.' She turned to the others. 'She was magnificent, wasn't she?'

'She was,' said Tom. His gentle smile was offset by the sadness in his eyes.

'Yeah. Well done, sis,' said Lucas, struggling to put his splint back on. Again, Jeannie batted his hand away and refastened it.

'You said just the right thing, Jeannie,' said Louisa. 'I was losing my patience with them.' She chuckled. 'It didn't help that I could see Kate was rolling her eyes and pulling faces behind their backs.'

'I'm impressed you restrained yourself, Kate,' said Lucas. 'We don't know who those folks are. They might have been important – acquaintances of the Clarks, perhaps. If you'd laughed in their faces, things might have been awkward.'

Kate rolled her eyes at that. 'I know when to hold my tongue, Lucas Musgrove, don't you fret.'

Louisa nodded. She knew that Kate had learned that the hard

way, knowing when to stay silent rather than take a beating from her pa or his fancy woman.

'I'm surprised they didn't just hand over white feathers,' said Lucas, gazing down the lane where the motorcar had disappeared. Louisa had a feeling he wasn't looking at the view, but instead remembering things he'd rather not.

'Wouldn't be the first,' agreed Tom. He too looked preoccupied. 'Won't be the last. I've not wanted to get one of those badges, but I'm starting to think it's a good idea.'

Jeannie frowned. 'But everyone knows you've both been wounded. Well, not that couple, seeing as how they're strangers to us. But surely not in Street?'

Tom shrugged. 'You heard what they said. We look young and healthy. Plenty of folks think we should be heading back to the trenches.'

She sighed and sank down onto the blanket next to him. The others said nothing as Jeannie touched Tom's arm. 'Maybe you need to be honest with people about the extent of your injury,' she said softly. 'Then they'd understand.'

'I don't want pity,' he said, looking grim.

'I know,' she replied. 'But you're doing such a good job of walking on your prosthetic that unless you tell people, no one will realise the truth of it.'

'And why would they pity you?' Kate challenged him. 'You're fit and well and holding down a good job. And you're a hero – a man who answered the call to arms and did your bit long before the likes of some of the lads we know.'

The side of Tom's mouth lifted in a half-smile. 'Like that Sid Lambert, you mean?'

Jeannie covered her cheeks with her hands. 'Do we have to think about that beast? We were having such a nice afternoon.'

Tom looked apologetic.

'Not much of a beast,' said Lucas, his eyes shining with mirth. 'More like a mangy dog who got a kick in the privates for his trouble, isn't he?'

Jeannie glared at him as the others laughed. Tom nodded.

'He was pathetic, that's for sure. Our Jeannie showed him what for. I've never seen a man whimpering like that before.'

All four of them stared at him. Louisa saw he hadn't realised he'd called her 'our' Jeannie. If he realised it after they all gaped at him, he chose not to draw further attention to it. Instead, he rolled onto his knees and carefully stood up.

'Anyway, I reckon it's time we packed up and headed back, don't you? No point in sitting here waiting for someone else to roll up with a bunch of white feathers, is there?'

18

The rest of the week rushed by and before they had time to catch their breath, it was Monday and they were all back at work at the factory.

'I swear there are more stairs up to the Machine Room since our last shift,' complained Kate. 'Or have we grown lazy after just a few days off?'

'I don't know about lazy,' said Louisa. 'My legs are still aching from our bicycle ride.'

'My legs were fine,' said Jeannie. 'It was my bottom that suffered. That saddle was *hard*. I swear it left me bruised. I daren't look.'

'I know what you mean,' sighed Kate.

'I wanted to write to Michael about it – you know, the young man in gaol? But then I thought it might be upsetting to hear about what fun we've had.'

'I don't know,' said Kate. 'Gerald tells me he enjoys hearing about what I get up to – it takes his mind off things and helps him to imagine life going on outside the prison walls. I think you should tell him. Maybe not about your sore bottom, though.' She grinned.

'Oh, you!' she laughed. 'All right, I will.'

'It was nice having a week off,' said Louisa. 'But it's so much harder coming back, isn't it?'

'Well if none of us get wed, it's all we've got to look forward to until we're old and grey,' said Jeannie, pulling a face.

Kate laughed out loud. 'Oh, bless you, Jeannie, love. You'll be wed, I'm sure. You've just got to be patient and wait for the right man to come along.'

Louisa looked thoughtful as she watched Jeannie. It had occurred to her on their picnic that her friend's feelings for Tom were stronger than she was admitting. If that was the case, then the poor lass was probably trying to come to terms with never marrying unless she was prepared to settle for less. It made her feel sad because she knew how hard that was. But, once you find *the one*, you can't imagine anyone else tempting you into marriage. She shook her head, trying to shake away the wave of grief that hit her at the thought.

'Anyway, we had a nice week and now it's over,' said Kate, pulling on her apron. 'It's back to work for us today, so let's get at it before Mr Briars starts to grumble.'

The Machine Room was soon buzzing with the whine and rumble of the sewing machines, overlaid with the loud, high-pitched voices of women and girls as they caught up with each other after the holiday. So long as they worked while they chatted, Mr Briars let them be for once, although he frowned at some of the girls who were giggling over something.

'I forgot to ask, Louisa, did your ma and pa have a nice holiday?' Jeannie asked.

She nodded but didn't say anything. They had returned home

on Sunday afternoon, both looking more rested after their break. Louisa had made the effort to bake a cake to welcome them back. Pa had appreciated it, although Ma had sniffed and said she'd eaten far too much in Lyme Regis and needed to watch her waist-line now she was home. That simple response had told Louisa that she wasn't forgiven, so she'd gone to her room on the excuse of getting ready for work in the morning. She'd noticed that Pa hadn't looked happy when she'd left the room, but what could she do? While she missed the easy affection she'd enjoyed with her parents before Mattie had come into her life, she couldn't see any way in which it could ever be restored if Ma wasn't willing to compromise.

The girls worked steadily through the day, eating outside on the grass at dinnertime to make the most of the August sunshine. It would be autumn soon enough. They didn't hang around, though, because there was a lot of work on.

Half-way through the afternoon, a lad ran into the Machine Room and delivered a note to Mr Briars. The foreman immediately came over to the bench where the girls were working.

'Miss Clements,' he said. 'Can you turn off your machine, please?'

Louisa finished her line of stitching before she looked up. 'Turn it off?' she asked, puzzled.

He nodded and waited for her to do as he asked. 'Come with me, lass.' He turned and walked towards the main door. Kate and Jeannie paused, frowning.

'What's going on?' asked Kate.

'He wants me to go with him,' Louisa said, standing up. 'I don't understand. Am I in trouble?'

Jeannie nudged her. 'Of course not. But you'd better get after him. Look, he's waiting for you.'

Louisa went to join Mr Briars where he waited by the door. He put out a hand, indicating she should follow him out of the Machine Room.

'Have I done something wrong, Mr Briars?' she asked, worried she was about to be sacked. She couldn't think of a single thing she'd done that would justify the foreman escorting her out of the Machine Room, but judging by his grim expression, it was something serious.

'No, lass. Don't fret. You're a good worker.' He paused and looked at the note in his hand. 'No, it's your pa, Louisa. He's collapsed in the Clicking Room. They've carried him to see the first-aid nurse in the ambulance room and you're to go there immediately.'

Shock held her motionless for a moment. 'What's wrong with him?'

He shook his head. 'I don't know. But if they're carrying him, it sounds serious. Off you go, now. Go to him. Find out from the nurse what's what, then hurry home and tell your ma.'

Louisa nodded, looking down at her hands. They began to shake as she was suddenly overwhelmed by the memory of Pa carrying her to the ambulance room after she'd fainted and banged her head. It was an off-hand comment by the nurse about her monthlies that had made her realise that she might be expecting. Now she had to go back into that room where her nightmare had started, only this time it was her pa who was being taken there.

She blinked, trying to gather her wild thoughts. 'Can you ask Kate to bring my bag and jacket to my house after the shift ends? I'd better not waste time going back for them.'

'I will. Now off you go, lass. I hope your pa will be all right. Give him and your ma my best wishes, and don't worry about your numbers today. We'll work something out.'

She dashed down the stairs and across the yard. She arrived at the ambulance room out of breath. She stood outside the closed door, trying to calm herself. She could hear voices inside, but she didn't recognise any of them as Pa's.

She remembered how, when she'd come round from her faint and found herself in Pa's arms, he had kissed her hair and she had felt his love and concern wrapping around her heart. It hadn't lasted, of course. Once he knew she was with child, his disappointment and anger had wiped away all those feelings, leaving her with no choice but to run away to save her child from being given away to strangers who could never love him as much as Mattie's family did.

But he was still her pa, and she couldn't help but be worried. No matter what memories stepping inside that room would stir, she had to do it for his sake.

Taking a deep breath, she stepped closer and knocked on the door.

It opened almost immediately. A man she didn't recognise stood there, blocking her view of the other occupants. She got the impression of several people, but she couldn't be sure.

'Yes? Is it an emergency, lass? Only we've got a serious case to deal with right now.'

She thought for a moment he was going to shut the door on her face, so she raised her hand to stop him. 'I'm Louisa Clements, sir,' she said. 'I was told my pa's here. Can I see him?'

He frowned and turned to say something to someone. A moment later, the nurse appeared and beckoned her in.

'Come in, lass. He's conscious but a bit groggy. Go around to the other side of the bed, that's it. You can hold his hand. Try and keep him calm. We've sent for the doctor. I think it's his heart.'

She followed her directions and stood at Pa's side. His eyes were closed as she picked up his hand. It felt cold and his lips looked blue in his pale face. Louisa squeezed his hand, afraid he had expired. He was so still. But then his chest rose and he took a long breath as he opened his eyes.

'Louisa?' He frowned. 'What's going on?'

She stroked his forehead. His skin felt cold and clammy. 'Hush, Pa. You collapsed and they brought you to the nurse.' She put a hand on his shoulder when he tried to sit up. 'No, Pa. You must stay still. Rest and get your breath back. They're fetching the doctor to check you over.'

'I've work to do,' he grumbled but lay back and closed his eyes. 'And so do you. We're neither of us paid to lollop around.'

'Now, now, Mr Clements,' said the nurse. 'Mr Roger Clark himself said you're to stay here until the doctor arrives and sent someone to get your daughter, so make the most of it and try to relax. Are you in any pain?'

He shook his head, but then he winced. 'Not much. I seem to have permanent indigestion these days.'

'Had a big dinner, did you?' the woman asked, watching him carefully as she checked his pulse.

He shook his head. 'I wasn't hungry, so I stayed in the Clicking Room and got on with my paperwork while it was quiet.'

'Mmm. That might explain why you fainted dead away.' She tutted. 'You should know better than to miss a meal when you're working.'

That Pa didn't argue with the nurse told Louisa more than his words. She felt a tremor in his fingers as he sighed. 'I'll be all right,' he said, although his voice was thin and reedy – not at all like his usual deep, assured tone. 'Just give me a minute and I'll get back to work.'

'We'll let the doctor decide that,' came the brisk response. 'You'll not be going back to work until he says so. I'm thinking it

will take more than a missed dinner to fell a man of your consti-
tution, so you rest up now.' She made a note of something on her
notepad before she looked at Louisa and tilted her head towards
the other side of the room.

Louisa kissed Pa's cheek and tucked his hand under the
blanket that had been laid across him before following the nurse.
They stood by the window a few feet from the bed.

'How has he been lately?' the woman asked, keeping her voice
low and her eyes on the patient. 'Has he collapsed before?'

'No, never,' whispered Louisa. 'Although he's been tired a lot
lately and complaining of indigestion.'

'How was he last week?'

Louisa frowned. 'I'm not sure. Him and Ma went to Lyme
Regis for a few days. He seemed fine when they got back
yesterday.'

The nurse nodded. 'And he threw himself back into work the
minute the factory gates opened again this morning, no doubt.'
She shook her head. 'I've seen it often enough with men of his
age. They forget they're not getting any younger and now with so
many lads off fighting, they're trying to keep things going while
neglecting their health.'

'Is he really going to be all right?' she asked, struck by how
frail Pa looked as he lay on the bed with his eyes closed.

The nurse patted her shoulder. 'I don't know, lass. But Mr
Clark came when he saw them carrying him over here and he's
summoned the doctor. He'll make sure he gets the best care, you
mark my words. They look after their workers do the Clarks.'

Louisa nodded, aware of the irony that her pa sometimes
talked as though he hated the Clarks, denigrating their religion
while tugging his forelock in supplication to them when he felt he
had to. Yet it seemed that, if he really was seriously ill, he would
need the Clark family's care and generosity even more.

The door opened, making her jump. Mr Roger Clark and another man came in. The nurse moved toward them to report on the patient and to assist the doctor while Louisa stayed where she was, unwilling to get in the way and at the same time afraid that if they noticed her, they would send her out.

It seemed to take just a few minutes for the doctor to examine Pa and to declare that it was his heart and that he needed specialist care.

'There's a chap in Bristol I'd recommend,' he told Mr Clark. 'I can telephone him to see whether he can attend.'

'You can use my office telephone,' he said.

The doctor nodded. 'In the meantime, this man needs full bed rest at home.'

'But—' Pa began to protest. Louisa could see the concern in his eyes. She knew he always worried about being unable to work. He'd grown up poor with a pa who struggled with his health and often had periods when he couldn't earn.

'No buts, man,' said Mr Clark. 'We'll see that you get the best care, but you must do your part by listening to the experts. If the doctor says you need bed rest, that's what you'll have. Now, I'll escort the doctor to my office to make his call, and when I get back, we'll get you into my motor car and I'll drive you home.' He turned to Louisa, shocking her when she realised he'd been aware of her presence the whole time. 'Miss Clements, I think it best if you run home to your mother and let her know what has happened. It will give her a chance to prepare herself before we arrive on her doorstep with the patient. Assure her that your father is as well as can be expected that we're doing everything to ensure that he will make a swift return to his usual robust health.'

Louisa glanced at Pa, her eyes filling with tears as she took in his pale countenance, pain marring his features.

'Can you do that, my dear?' asked Mr Clark, his tone gentle as he noted her distress.

Louisa blinked rapidly and nodded, squaring her shoulders and looking away from Pa. He was right. It was better for Louisa to warn Ma than for her to open the door to the company secretary with the news that Pa was seriously ill. 'Yes, Mr Clark,' she said.

He nodded his approval and she leaned over and kissed Pa's cheek, whispering that she loved him, before she left the ambulance room and ran like the wind.

* * *

When Mr Briars returned to the Machine Room without Louisa, Kate and Jeannie paused in their work and watched him approach with worried expressions.

'Kate,' he said. 'Louisa's pa has been taken poorly and she's not likely to be coming back before the end of the shift. She said can you take her bag and jacket round to her house?'

'Oh my,' said Jeannie, putting a hand to her chest. 'Is he all right? He hasn't had an accident, has he?'

Kate put an arm around Jeannie and hugged her quickly before she turned to Mr Briars, who was shaking his head.

'I'm not privy to the circumstances,' he said. 'But I don't want to hear about either of you gossiping about this.'

Kate spoke up as Jeannie began to tremble. 'We wouldn't gossip, Mr Briars, you know we're not like that,' she told him. 'But Jeannie lost her pa in an accident here in the factory, remember? It's only natural she's worried when you say something's happened to Louisa's pa.'

'Ah.' The foreman nodded. 'I forgot. Sorry, lass. But as far as I know, he just took poorly and needs checking over. Don't fret yourself.'

Jeannie nodded. 'Thank you, Mr Briars. It scared me, thinking something awful had happened like it did to my pa. Are you sure he's not dead?'

He raised his hands. 'I honestly don't know. All I know is they took him to the ambulance room and someone sent a note asking for Louisa to go there. If Kate takes her things round after work, she'll be able to find out, won't she? Now' – he glanced at the clock on the wall – 'there's another hour before the shift ends and I'm a worker down, so I need you lasses to get back to those machines. We've got orders to complete.'

* * *

The girls had barely reached the bottom of the stairs into the yard at the end of the shift when Lucas ran up to them.

'Where's Louisa?' he asked. 'Does she know about her pa?'

Jeannie nodded. 'She was sent to the ambulance room to see him and didn't come back. Kate's taking her things round to her. What happened?'

Lucas shook his head. 'I'm not sure. He was fine one minute, then he just grabbed his chest and collapsed. They picked him up and rushed him to the nurse. Someone came back and said he's alive and Mr Roger and the doctor were taking him home. D'you think Louisa's all right?'

'We don't know,' said Kate. 'But I'm going right round there to find out. Do you two want to come with me?'

They both nodded. 'Best that we find out,' said Jeannie. 'I'll only fret all night otherwise.'

'And Ma will get in a state if we can't tell her the man's alive,' said Lucas.

'I know,' said Jeannie. 'I nearly fainted dead away when Mr

Briars told us why he'd sent Louisa off. I thought about Pa and was so scared.'

Lucas closed his eyes. 'Yeah. Well, let's go and see what's going on, then we can see if Louisa needs anything as well as be able to reassure Ma, can't we?'

'Come on, then,' said Kate, praying as they walked down the High Street towards Somerton Road that things weren't as bad as they feared when they got there.

19

It took two men – Mr Clark being one of them, along with his driver – to help Pa up the stairs to his bedroom. Ma went with them, asking Louisa to make a pot of tea and to bring a tray up. She had been shocked when Louisa had arrived home early and horrified to hear of Pa's collapse. But the moment the car had drawn up outside, and Ma had seen Pa emerge, albeit with a lot of help, she had calmed. Louisa supposed she was satisfied that he was alive and her focus was now on making sure he was comfortable.

Louisa was just loading the tea tray when the driver came into the kitchen. 'I can carry that up for you, miss,' he said. 'Although I'll have mine down here, if you don't mind? Mr Clark is speaking to your parents. Apparently, the consultant from Bristol should be here first thing tomorrow to examine the patient.'

She nodded and poured two cups and removed them from the tray. 'Thank you. I'll stay here as well.' She desperately wanted to go upstairs to find out what Mr Clark had to say, but she had a feeling she ought to wait and not get in the way.

She sat at the kitchen table and sipped her tea, aware of the low murmur of voices upstairs. She assumed Ma would be helping Pa into bed, given what the doctor had said about him needing complete rest. She didn't think he'd be very happy about that, especially with his big boss standing there, but he could hardly tell the man to go, could he? If Pa was seriously ill and needed medical treatment, that was going to cost a lot. She knew her parents were careful with their money, but if Pa couldn't work for a while, their savings would soon disappear.

She frowned. Her plan had been to save as much of her wages as she could after paying Ma her usual housekeeping so that she could build a nest egg to allow her to move out of the family home as soon as she could. But if Pa couldn't work, she couldn't in all conscience abandon them. She would have to stay and hand over more of her earnings to help keep food on the table.

The driver came back down after delivering the tray. She added sugar to his tea when he confirmed he liked it sweet and offered him a biscuit from the tin. She wondered whether she should have sent some of them upstairs with the tea, but realised they had better things to worry about than ginger biscuits. There was still a steady hum of conversation above her head, but she couldn't make out the words. Mr Clark seemed to be doing most of the talking, with occasional comments – questions perhaps? – from Ma. Pa was quiet, no doubt worn out by it all.

'Try not to worry, lass,' said the driver, his expression full of compassion. 'Mr Roger will make sure your pa gets the best possible care.'

She nodded, feeling tears well. 'Thank you. But it's hard not to worry. He's always been so strong.'

She couldn't help feeling as though everything that had happened over the past couple of years – her courting Mattie, then him getting killed and the discovery of her pregnancy and her escape to Lincolnshire – had all contributed to Pa's declining health. She'd noticed that he hadn't been himself since her return, but she'd not allowed herself to care about it. She'd been so wrapped up in her own grief and ready to blame Pa for much of it, she hadn't thought that the tension in the house might have been making him ill. She'd decided that her parents didn't care for her any more, that they simply expected her to fall in with their wishes for the sake of appearances. As a result, she'd gone about her business as though nothing else mattered.

Now, Pa was so ill that Mr Clark himself had called in a consultant all the way from Bristol. It occurred to Louisa that his condition must be far more serious than she had imagined when she'd heard the doctor say he needed bed rest. What if he died? Despite the pain and upset of recent months, Louisa realised she really did love Pa and wished with all her heart that things could go back to how they used to be.

Mr Clark came downstairs and his driver leapt to his feet and went out to start the motorcar.

'Miss Clements.' Mr Roger nodded in her direction. 'Your mother is helping your father settle. As you know, he's to have complete bed rest until he can be examined by the consultant tomorrow. Once he has concluded his examination, we will know whether he needs to be removed to a hospital for further treatment. I've assured your mother that Clarks will do all we can to assist you all at this difficult time. Should you wish to stay at home tomorrow to assist in the care of the patient, I shall inform Mr Briars that you are not to be penalised in the circumstances.'

'Thank you, sir,' said Louisa, touched by his consideration. 'I'll see what Ma says. Knowing Pa, he'll fret if I miss work. It's important to him that we do a good job to earn our pay. I wouldn't want to cause him upset.'

'Very admirable.' He nodded. 'Your father is a good and loyal employee, and I can see he has passed his values onto his daughter. However, my offer stands.'

'That's very kind of you, sir. I'll see how things are tomorrow.'

As she closed the door behind Mr Clark, Louisa leaned her head against the wood and sighed. She was full of conflicting emotions. This changed everything. It occurred to her that Ma might also insist that she went to work, not only because it would stop Pa fretting. She barely seemed to be able to tolerate Louisa's presence these days. She hoped that with Pa being ill, they might find a way to get along and help each other, but Louisa didn't dare raise her hopes.

* * *

Louisa was making some soup when Kate, Jeannie and Lucas knocked on the door.

'We've brought your things, love,' said Kate.

'Is your pa all right?' asked Lucas. 'One minute he was fine, then he dropped like a sack of spuds.'

Louisa shrugged, leading her friends into the kitchen. 'I don't know. There's someone coming from Bristol tomorrow to see him.' She told them what had happened after Mr Briars had sent her to the ambulance room.

'So Mr Roger Clark himself brought him home in his motor car?' asked Jeannie. 'Goodness. It must be serious.'

She nodded. 'Pa looks awful,' she said softly, not wanting to disturb her parents. No doubt Ma wouldn't appreciate having them all in her kitchen, but Louisa was glad of her friends right now. 'He's so grey and pale. Ma's so worried, she won't leave his side.' She looked up towards the ceiling. 'She's keeping vigil, even though he's sleeping peacefully now.' She took a deep breath. 'I think it's my fault. All the upset we've had since Mattie... What if he dies? I'll have killed my own pa.'

Kate pulled her into a hug as her tears began to fall. 'It's not your fault. You mustn't think like that. He's got a lot of responsibility at work and times are hard with so many men being away fighting. That's more likely to have put a strain on his heart. But, look, don't invite trouble, eh? Wait and see what this doctor from Bristol has to say. For all you know, your pa might be as right as rain after a few days' rest.'

'She's right,' said Lucas. 'He works hard, pushes himself more than any of the men. I think he's been overdoing it.'

'He was looking fine after his holiday in Lyme Regis,' she said through her sniffles. 'But he was back at work for one day and he had to be carried home.'

'Well, there you are,' he said. 'It's his job that's taking its toll.'

Louisa nodded, although she couldn't shake off the guilt she felt. Pa might well have worked too hard for a man of his age, but she was sure that the tension at home had contributed to his condition.

Jeannie looked around, seeing the vegetables that Louisa had been peeling and chopping. 'Now, what can we do? Lucas, I think you should get home and tell Ma what's been going on and I'll stay here and help get this food cooked. I expect Lou's ma will need a hearty meal to see her through while she's caring for him. I don't suppose Mr Clements will be the easiest of patients, will he?'

That brought a watery smile to Louisa's face. 'No, he won't be. In the ambulance room, he kept saying he just needed a minute, then he'd get back to work. The nurse had to practically hold him down to get him to stay on the bed.'

Kate grinned. 'The exact opposite of my pa. That old beggar

would loll around all day, given half the chance. Which is why yours is a foreman and mine is barely hanging on with day rates.'

'But you don't need to stay,' said Louisa. 'I can manage.'

'You and Lucas go, Jeannie,' said Kate, 'or your ma will worry. If you can pop round via The Mead and tell Auntie Betty where I am, I'll stay with Lou.'

Despite Louisa's quiet protest, the friends agreed, so in the end she gave in, grateful for the company while Ma kept her vigil upstairs.

After Jeannie and Lucas took their leave, Kate rolled up her sleeves and helped Louisa finish chopping vegetables for the soup. Louisa got out some pearl barley and some chunks of ham and added them to the pot. Once it was simmering, she turned to her friend.

'Thanks for coming round and bringing my things. I didn't dare stop to collect them.'

'Glad to help. You know me and Jeannie both will do anything we can, don't you? Lucas too. Just ask.'

She nodded, blinking away more tears. 'I thank God every day that you're my friends, all of you. I'm so blessed.'

'Us lasses are the Three Musketeers, remember? We'll always be here for each other. Lord knows, we've needed to be over the last couple of years, haven't we? Let's hope things will settle down again soon.'

Louisa sighed. 'Amen to that. Anyway, you'd better get on home to Auntie Betty. She'll be wondering where you are.'

'If you're sure?'

Louisa nodded. 'I'll take some soup up to Ma and Pa in a minute, then I'll work out what needs doing over the next couple of days. If I can do some of the cooking, Ma won't have to worry about it.'

'Will you come to work tomorrow?'

She shrugged. 'I don't know. I really want to be here to find out what the consultant says. But you know what Pa's like. He might well insist I go to work.'

20

Both Mrs Musgrove and Mrs Searle insisted on sending food and their good wishes to the Clements household over the next few days, as did several women from Holy Trinity. Louisa did stay home for the morning when the specialist arrived from Bristol and declared that Mr Clements was gravely ill and might need an operation. He left to consult with his colleagues and sent a message that the patient should continue bed rest until the following week, when an ambulance would be sent to take him to hospital in Bristol.

Kate and Jeannie did their best to try and keep Louisa's spirits up, but she remained quiet and worked hard, rushing home at dinner times and as soon as their shifts ended. Her friends offered what support they could, but there was little anyone could do. Louisa and her ma simply had to wait and hope that the operation would help Mr Clements get back his health.

'I'm so worried about Louisa,' said Jeannie as she sat with Kate in the canteen at dinner time on Friday. 'She looks like she's not sleeping.'

'I know,' agreed Kate. 'I don't suppose it's easy. Let's hope this operation will see Mr Clements right.'

Jeannie leaned a little closer, shielding her mouth with her hand so that no one could lip-read her words. 'Lucas walked her home after work yesterday so that he could see how she was. He says her ma is staying by her pa's side and barely talking to her. Poor Lou is trying to help as best she can, but Mrs Clements isn't letting her.'

Kate nodded. She thought that might be the case, although Louisa hadn't said anything. She wanted to feel sorry for the woman, what with her husband being so poorly. She wished she could do something to encourage Louisa and her ma to get along better, but she couldn't help but remember how horrible the woman had been to her own daughter over Mattie and the baby. Mrs Clements had gone from a loving mother to a monster who had forced her to make the hardest of all choices. Kate wondered whether she should feel guilty when she couldn't find it in her heart to feel any sympathy for Mrs Clements, especially now when Louisa was willing to put aside the hurt between them and make peace with her parents for the sake of her sick father. But Mrs Clements clearly wasn't prepared to do the same thing.

She sighed. 'Let's hope it all works out,' she said.

Auntie Betty came over to them as they prepared to go back to the Machine Room. 'Ah, Kate, lass, I'm glad I caught you. I got a message from Mrs Clothier. It seems young Gerald is due to be released from prison and Mr Clothier is going to collect him and bring him here.'

Kate brightened immediately. 'Oh that is good news. I'm so pleased he's getting his freedom at last.'

Auntie Betty nodded and smiled. 'My cousin is impatient to see him. She'll be coming down from Bristol on the bus. She'll stay with us overnight and be reunited with her boy when Mr

Clothier brings him to Street. That's what I wanted to tell you about – young Gerald has expressed a wish to meet you in person and thank you for your correspondence while he's been incarcerated, so we're invited to tea with the Clothiers on Sunday.'

Kate stared at her. 'Really? I'm invited to tea with the Clothiers?'

Betty smiled and touched her cheek. 'Yes, lass.'

She shook her head, suddenly feeling unsure. 'I don't know...'

'They're good people, Kate,' said Jeannie softly. 'You've met them before. They've no airs and graces, even though Mrs Clothier is a Clark. And it's to meet your friend, Gerald. You've been writing to him and fretting for him for months now. Don't you want to see for yourself that he's all right after his ordeal?'

She nodded, feeling equal parts excited and terrified. What if the Clothiers hadn't realised she was Reggie Davis's daughter? They might change their mind about inviting her into their home again if they knew. She looked at the two of them, both watching her with smiles on their faces, and she knew she couldn't bear to tell them what she was thinking. No, her shame concerning her pa was her own and she had no wish to share it. 'I should like to meet Gerald very much,' she said.

Auntie Betty's smile widened and she squeezed Kate's shoulder. 'Good. I'll let them know. Now, I'd better get back to work. Miss Bond wants to talk about next week's targets. With these labour shortages, we've lost a few women to other departments to fill men's jobs. I'm not sure I'd want to be doing that, but some of the lasses are dead keen. Mark my words, when this war is over and the men come back, they'll find their womenfolk won't be so happy to give up their jobs and go back to the housework.'

Kate grinned. 'While some will be glad to give it all up and go back to their kitchens, I'll wager.'

The two girls headed back into the Machine Room and were surprised to see that Louisa still wasn't back.

'Maybe her ma's finally started talking to her again,' said Kate. 'I mean, Lou's been rushing home and fetching and carrying so that her ma doesn't have to leave Mr Clements' side. It's about time she noticed and stopped treating her own daughter like a pariah.'

Jeannie sighed as she switched on her machine. 'I know. It's so sad. If only they'd let Louisa get married when Mattie asked...'

Kate scowled. 'There's no point in thinking about "if only." What's done is done, and I can't help feeling that Lou's ma should bear most of the blame. If only she'd not been such a snob, encouraging Mr Clements to put his foot down... Oh lord, I'm doing it as well, aren't I?'

'It's hard not to, isn't it?'

They settled down to work, all the while keeping an eye on the door for Louisa.

'If she's not here in a minute, she'll lose a quarter hour's pay,' said Kate.

'I hope nothing bad has happened.'

Mr Briars came over. 'Where is she?' he asked.

'We don't know, sir. She popped home at dinner time. Maybe her ma needed some help with Mr Clements.'

He nodded. 'It's not like her to be late. Let's hope she turns up soon.'

But she didn't.

* * *

'Your father wants to talk to you.'

Louisa looked round to see her ma in the kitchen doorway. 'I was just warming up some broth for him. And you, of course.

Shall I cut some bread as well?' Pa hadn't had much of an appetite, but Louisa hoped that he'd start feeling better soon.

Ma shook her head. 'Leave it. Go to him. He won't rest until he's spoken with you.'

Something in her mother's expression unnerved Louisa. 'Is he feeling better?'

Ma huffed. 'No, he is not. Did you expect some miracle to wipe out the way you broke his heart and continue to do so? Now it has taken its toll and the poor man is suffering. But if seeing you will ease his mind, then that's what he'll get.' She pointed a finger at Louisa. 'But if you upset him again, young lady, I will make you pay, so help me God. Now, get yourself up there and mind what you say and how you look at him. No matter what you think, he's still your father and a damned good man.'

Louisa hung her head. 'Yes, Ma,' she said and hurried out of the room.

Pa looked frail and even greyer than the last time she'd been in her parents' bedroom. He was propped up on several pillows, the blankets neat around his body, so neat in fact that she realised he was hardly moving. It was such a contrast to her usually vital father who barely stayed still, always on the go, that for a moment, she was frightened that he'd stopped breathing. But as she approached the bed, he opened his eyes and looked at her.

'Louisa, love. Come and sit.' He patted the mattress next to him.

Afraid to jostle him, she sat gingerly on the edge of the bed, her body twisted so that she faced him. He held out his hand and she took it in both of hers.

'How are you feeling, Pa?' she asked. 'There's some broth warming for your dinner.'

He shook his head. 'Not hungry,' he said before he winced. 'I need to talk to you.'

She nodded, stroking his hand. 'I'm here, Pa.'

'My time's coming, lass. I can feel it.' His voice rasped, barely above a whisper.

'Don't say that, Pa. Mr Clark says you'll get the best treatment there is. He thinks very highly of you and he's determined to see you better.'

He sighed. 'He's been a good boss, but he's not God. I've told your ma to get the vicar round. No... listen to me,' he said when she opened her mouth to argue. 'I'm not long for this world, lass, and there's things I need to say to you.'

She swallowed hard, trying to dislodge the lump in her throat. 'I'm listening.'

He took a moment to gather his thoughts. 'I've had time to ponder while I've been lying here, and I have to tell you, Louisa, I'm sorry for the mess I've made of things with you and young Matthew.' He took a deep breath, which made him cough. Louisa was frightened it would finish him off, but eventually he settled back against the pillows and sighed again. 'I let my feelings about losing my only child, who I love with all my heart, to another man – and a Quaker at that – blind me to the fact that he was a good lad and that you loved each other.'

Louisa couldn't hold back her tears at his words. It was far too late to make a difference, but somehow it did. That he should say them meant the world to her.

'He was a good lad,' she agreed softly, her heart aching. 'But what's done is done. We can't go back and change it now.'

'I know, lass, and I wish I could, for it breaks my heart to see you so unhappy.'

She shook her head. 'Don't fret, Pa, please. You need to rest and concentrate on getting better.'

He squeezed her hand. 'I love you, Louisa, and so does your ma.' He smiled, although it was so sad, it made Louisa gulp as she tried not to sob. 'I know she doesn't show it much these days, but be patient with her, lass. She had such high hopes and we've both disappointed her in our own ways.' He winced again.

'Are you in pain? Should I run for the doctor?'

'No point,' he said, his voice faint. 'Better to get the reverend. I need to beg forgiveness.'

'Don't say that!'

'Hush now. Go and get your ma, then run round to the rectory, there's a good lass. Tell him to hurry.'

Louisa shouted for her mother as she ran down the stairs.

'What is it?' she asked, coming out of the kitchen.

'He's in pain and says I need to get the vicar. Should I go for the doctor?'

Ma gasped and covered her mouth. 'Oh my lord. I must go to him.'

Louisa nodded as she reached the hall and got out of Ma's way so that she could rush up to the bedroom. 'Who should I fetch first?' she called after her.

'The doctor first. Go there, then run to the vicar. Hurry!'

Louisa ran like the wind. But it was to no avail. Her pa was dead before his wife reached his side.

21

Kate stood beside Auntie Betty outside Mr and Mrs Clothier's house on Sunday afternoon. She felt so out of sorts – equal parts nervous, excited and sad. The news that Louisa's pa had had a final, fatal heart attack on Friday afternoon had left everyone numb with shock. They'd been so sure he'd recover because Mr Roger Clark himself was arranging his treatment, but God had other plans for him. It left Kate feeling as though she needed to put her friend first.

'Maybe I should've gone round to Louisa's with Jeannie,' she said, hesitating at the gate. 'You don't need me here. I can meet Gerald another time.'

'I'm sorrier than I can say about Mr Clements,' said Auntie. 'But I've a feeling his wife will turn most people away today, especially her daughter's Quaker friends. Leave them to the Holy Trinity people on the Sabbath, lass. If Louisa doesn't come to work tomorrow, you can pop round and see how she is and what she needs. You must be sure to give her my love and let her know... if there's anything she needs...'

Kate sighed and nodded. It wouldn't surprise her to hear that

Mrs Clements had sent Jeannie away with a flea in her ear. Neither Louisa nor her ma had come to Holy Trinity this morning. She hoped with all her heart that the two of them would grow close again as they shared their grief over Mr Clements' passing. But she was worried that it might not be like that. Louisa's ma hadn't been the warmest of women before Mattie had entered her daughter's life. Since then, the relationship between mother and daughter had gone from bad to worse.

'But for now,' the older woman went on, 'our Gerald is keen to meet the young woman who brightened his dark days in prison and his ma would be mighty disappointed if you weren't to go in.'

Auntie's cousin had arrived in Street the day before and spent the night at the cottage in The Mead. Gerald's ma, Ethel, had been pleased to meet Kate and had thanked her for writing to her son. She had joined them at the Friends' Meeting for worship this morning, and then gone with Mrs Clothier to her home in order to wait for the arrival of her son.

Kate took a deep breath and turned to Betty. 'It's not just wanting to be with Louisa in her grief, Auntie. I've enjoyed exchanging letters with Gerald, but, well, it's not the same as meeting someone face to face, is it? I mean, he's obviously well-educated and a man of the world.' His father had won a scholarship to study at the Bristol Cathedral school as a boy and had worked as a clerk in a solicitor's office. This had meant that Gerald had been able to stay on at school and had been planning to study at university before his father had been struck down by tuberculosis. He'd gone to work for the same solicitor after his father had died. 'I'm just a factory girl – and Reg Davis's daughter at that. He's sure to be disappointed when he meets me.'

Auntie Betty crossed her arms and glowered at Kate. 'Well, I've never heard such a load of nonsense in my life. You are you, Kate. An intelligent, kind and fierce young woman that any man would be pleased to meet and call his friend. Forget being Reggie's daughter and remember that you're more like your blessèd ma than anyone and she was far too good for the likes of him.'

Kate closed her eyes and felt the familiar ache in her heart at the remembrance of her ma. She missed her so much. A soft touch on her cheek brought her eyes open to see Betty's gaze upon her, full of sympathy and understanding.

'It's a difficult time, lass,' she said. 'But we'll all get through it, God willing. Now, let's go inside and have a lovely afternoon with some good people, eh?'

* * *

Gerald was a surprise. He was tall and lean, not unlike Ted had been, but the likeness between the two lads ended there. Gerald had a shock of red hair and warm brown eyes. Despite his prison pallor, his smile lit up as he was introduced to Kate.

'Miss Davis,' he said, taking her hand in both of his and shaking it. 'I'm delighted to meet you. I feel I've come to know you through your letters, so it's wonderful to see you after all these months.'

Kate felt her cheeks warm at his enthusiastic greeting. 'Call me Kate, please. It's nice to meet you,' she said, giving him a shy smile. 'I'm so glad you're free.'

'Thank you,' he said. 'I can't regret it, but I confess I'm glad it's over.'

'Come and sit down, Kate,' said Mrs Clothier. 'Would you like milk or lemon with your tea?'

Kate had never heard of anyone having lemon in their tea and she wasn't sure she would like it. Weren't lemons sour? She hoped her ignorance wasn't showing as she sat in the seat indicated and replied. 'Milk please, Mrs Clothier.'

They had a pleasant hour, drinking tea and eating delicious little sandwiches and cakes. Little Peter Clothier was a delight, presenting Gerald with coloured drawings of the flowers, birds and insects found in his parents' gardens. 'You said you missed seeing nature from your prison cell,' he reminded Gerald. 'So I sketched some of it to remind you.'

Kate smiled, wanting to hug the little boy. 'What a lovely thing to do.'

'Indeed.' Gerald ruffled the lad's hair. 'Thank you, Peter. You're very kind.'

The little boy was so sweet. She remembered when Jeannie's brother Peter had been the same when he was younger. Now, of course, the Musgrove twins were almost men and could hardly be called sweet. She hoped that when Peter Musgrove finally matured, he'd be a good man like his older brother and not a miserable so-and-so like his twin was becoming.

Mr Clothier spoke with Gerald about his plans. It seemed that he still had the offer of a job at a market garden near his mother's home on the edge of Bristol, growing vegetables and soft fruits.

'That's good,' said Mr Clothier. 'That should earn you your exemption certificate, although there has been some confusion over whether such an occupation is covered by the rules regarding exemption for food production workers. I know of at least one young man who was denied his certificate and is serving a sentence, but I believe that the authorities have been persuaded to add market gardening to the list of reserved occupations. It hasn't been announced yet, but I'm sure it will be soon enough.'

The conversation turned to other things and Kate was content to sit and listen. As Auntie Betty and Ethel chatted with the Cloth-iers about shortages and harvests, Kate realised that Gerald was watching her. When he caught her eye, he smiled. 'Would you like a walk in the gardens?' he asked.

She nodded and Peter offered to show them, the boy rushing ahead. Out in the sunshine, Gerald sighed and lifted his face to the sun. 'I've missed this,' he said. 'I'll never take it for granted again.'

'I can imagine,' she said.

Peter called them over to inspect his rabbit hutch. They exclaimed over the pretty white bunnies, a little taken aback when the boy announced that although he loved stroking his pets' soft fur, he also liked eating rabbits. 'I have a mummy and a daddy bunny, and Papa says they might have babies. If they do, we'll have some for the pot, just like the chickens when we leave some of the eggs for them to hatch.'

Kate chuckled softly to herself as Peter ran off again, in the direction of the chicken coop.

'Funny little fellow, isn't he?' said Gerald, offering her his arm.

'He is, but sweet with it,' she said, accepting the gesture. She felt more comfortable with him now that they were outside and not under the keen scrutiny of the others. 'I'm just surprised he's so keen on the idea of butchering his pets. I suppose I thought that a family like this wouldn't need to do that.'

He shrugged. 'With the sea blockades, shortages of supplies are getting worse. It's only sensible for everyone to consider how they might feed their families.'

She nodded, frowning as her thoughts turned to Louisa again.

'Is that something that worries you?' he asked.

She shook her head. 'Not really. I... my needs aren't great and between Auntie Betty and the Clarks' factory canteen, I'm well fed.' She didn't want to talk about how she'd been half-starved by her pa and his mistress over several months. That was in the past. 'No, I'm sorry, I didn't mean to think of it now, but a dear friend of mine lost her pa quite suddenly this week and I can't help wondering how she and her ma will cope. He was a foreman, on good money. Now Louisa is the only earner in the family and it's a burden that's going to be hard for her to bear. She lost her sweetheart in the trenches last year, you see, so she's known nothing but grief for months now.'

He patted her arm as they strolled along. 'I'm sorry for your friend's losses. You're a good friend to be so concerned about her.'

'Thank you. I feel so helpless, though. I don't know what to do. I'd do anything I could to ease her pain.'

He smiled. 'Further evidence that you are indeed a good friend and one that I will always treasure. I can't express how grateful I am that you chose to write to me in my darkest days. Thank you, Kate.'

His words filled her with pleasure and she smiled back at him, not knowing what to say to that. He blinked, looking a little stunned before he turned to see where Peter was waiting for them by the chicken coop. They made their way over to him and the child proceeded to introduce them to the magnificent cockerel and each hen by name and their rates of egg production. The little boy's presence ensured that their conversation was light and focused on the flora and fauna in the gardens.

In the distance, they heard the church clock chime at five o'clock.

'Mr Clothier has kindly offered to take my mother and I home to Bristol,' said Gerald. 'But before we take our leave, I should very much like to ask you to continue our correspondence, Kate. Would that be possible? I know that you have been writing to others like me, so I will understand if you feel you need to devote your time to supporting others still incarcerated. But, the thing is, I have enjoyed your letters so much that I feel that we are true friends, especially now that we've met. What do you think?'

She looked at his earnest expression and nodded. 'Yes, I should like that,' she said.

They made their way back into the house to find his mother and Auntie Betty preparing to take their leave. Kate thanked Mr and Mrs Clothier for their hospitality, grateful that Auntie Betty had given her a talking-to before they knocked on the door. She had been right. Kate was her mother's daughter and nothing like her pa. Even if the Clothiers knew of him, they clearly didn't hold her relationship with him against her.

As they gathered at the front door to say goodbye, a small group of women came along the road. Kate recognised Ted's ma, Mrs Jackson, among them. When they halted by Mr Clothier's motor car, Kate felt a shiver of dread run down her spine.

Mr Clothier noticed them and approached. Kate couldn't hear what was being said, but clearly, Mrs Jackson had plenty to say.

'Oh no,' Kate breathed.

'What's wrong?' asked Gerald as Mrs Clothier and Auntie Betty frowned.

'The White Feather Movement,' said Kate, keeping her voice low. 'I'm so sorry.'

Auntie Betty tutted. 'They're relentless. As if we haven't lost enough of our lads, their own included.'

'I'm afraid you'll have to run the gauntlet,' Mrs Clothier told him quietly. 'Best not to engage with them.'

'They're frightened,' whispered Kate, echoing Jeannie's thoughts when Mrs Jackson had turned on her all those months ago. 'But they're not helping.'

Gerald watched as Mr Clothier spoke to the women for a moment before he sighed. 'It's all right,' he said. 'We must all keep faith with what we believe to be the way forward.'

Kate stood aside as he and his ma said their goodbyes. Auntie Betty escorted her cousin to the motor car and at a nod from Mr

Clothier helped her inside. While they were doing that, Gerald turned to Kate and took both of her hands in his.

'Thank you again, Kate. It's been a delight to meet you at last and I look forward to continuing our correspondence.' His smile was sad as he glanced at the people waiting for him by the vehicle. 'I'm sorry you have to witness this.'

'It's not your fault,' she said.

He shrugged. 'Nevertheless...' He dropped her hands and turned to say a few words to Mrs Clothier before he squared his shoulders and approached Mr Clothier, who opened the passenger door for him.

Before he reached it, Mrs Jackson stepped forward into his path, brandishing a large, white feather. 'You should be fighting. Your country needs you.'

When he didn't attempt to take the feather, Mrs Jackson grasped his jacket by the lapels and roughly shoved the feather into his breast pocket. 'You're a coward!' she cried. 'You should be ashamed.'

With a cry, Kate rushed towards them. 'Stop it! You're wrong! You have no idea what he's been through!'

Mrs Jackson turned on her. 'You! I might have guessed you'd be consorting with a coward. My Ted might have been taken in by you for a while, but he knew what he was about and dropped you like you deserve.' Kate flinched as the woman waved a hand towards Gerald, the back of her hand hitting his cheek. He didn't move, even as Mrs Jackson continued to glare at Kate. 'Now you're collaborating with cowards and dissenters like him while my boy is risking his life to keep the likes of you safe. You should be ashamed of yourself.'

Kate gasped. It was the first time his ma had actually made any reference to Ted being alive and fighting. Since he had gone away, she had refused to discuss him with anyone and Kate had

had no idea whether he was dead or alive. 'Ted. How is he?' she couldn't help but ask.

Mrs Jackson scowled at her. 'You're not fit to say his name, missy, and it's no business of yours. He's better off without you, that's for sure. You're a disgrace!'

Mrs Clothier and Auntie Betty stepped forward together, shielding Kate from the woman's venom.

'That's enough, madam,' said Mrs Clothier. 'You've made your point and you are, of course, entitled to your view. But I'll not have you abusing my guests outside my home. I'll thank you to leave.'

'Come on now, dear,' said Auntie Betty gently as she touched Mrs Jackson's arm. 'I pray for you and your boys every day. We've both known loss, haven't we? Let's not fall out.'

Mrs Jackson drew back as though burned by the other woman's touch. She glared at them all as Mr Clothier urged Gerald to move and get in the car. For a moment, Kate thought he would refuse to go, but a quiet word from Mr Clothier got him moving. He sent Kate an apologetic look, but she shook her head slightly then tilted her chin towards the car, silently urging him to get in. Moments later, Mr Clothier cranked the motor to start it before he got in and they drove away, leaving the women staring at each other, frozen in a tableau of fear and mistrust.

22

Hundreds of people turned out for Mr Clements' funeral the following week. He'd lived in Street all his life and was well-known at both the factory and the parish church. Louisa knew that he would be pleased and proud to see so many folk paying their respects to him, although she found it rather overwhelming to see the crowds lining the route from their home in Somerton Road to Holy Trinity.

'Chin up, Louisa,' said her mother under her breath as they followed the horse-drawn hearse. 'Don't let him down now.'

Louisa did as she was told, lifting her chin and pulling her shoulders back. She kept her gaze fixed on the coffin in front of them, blinking back her tears and breathing deep in an effort to remain calm, when all she wanted to do was weep. She didn't dare let herself think of anything but the quality of the wood that now protected her pa's body from prying eyes and the slow, steady pace set by the undertaker as he led the cortege on Pa's final journey. Once today was over, she could allow the thoughts of all she'd lost and the fears about the future to consume her again.

But Ma was right. She needed to do Pa proud today, while the whole world stopped to bid him farewell.

Entering the packed church behind the pall-bearers was as hard as she'd thought it would be. But when she hesitated, Ma gripped her arm and forced her forward. To everyone looking on, the grieving widow had simply reached for her daughter in her time of need. But Louisa knew it was more than that. It was an action intended to make sure Louisa didn't shame her by running out of the church again.

The service and the internment in the churchyard were an ordeal, but Louisa managed to keep her emotions under control. Anticipating the number of people who would attend, Mrs Clements had arranged for teas to be served at the Crispin Hall rather than try to deal with so many people in their house. Louisa tried to get busy by helping, but she was gently ushered away by the ladies from the church who assured her that everything was under control and she should look after her mother.

Louisa reluctantly walked back towards Ma, stopping to acknowledge greetings and condolences as she made her way through the crowd. It was hard. She didn't want to talk to these people. She didn't even want to be here.

When yet another hand touched her shoulder, she sighed and turned, hoping that she could remain polite and not let her mother down. To her relief, it was Jeannie. She pulled her friend towards her and gave her a heartfelt hug.

'Thank you so much for coming,' she said, meaning it for the first time that day. Over Jeannie's shoulder, she saw Lucas standing there, watching her with concern. 'Both of you.' She didn't know why they should bother. They'd called at the house as soon as they'd heard the news, but Ma had sent them away, barely polite as she told them the family needed to be with their own kind in their grief. Louisa had tried to make allowances for Ma's state of mind, but she had been ashamed of the hostile rudeness she had shown her friends. 'I'm really sorry about the other day.'

'Hush now,' said Jeannie as she stepped back. 'We didn't expect much. We just wanted to let you and your ma know that we were sorry and to offer any help.'

'I know, and I thank you for it.'

Lucas moved closer. 'Your pa was a fine man to work for,' he said. 'We'll all miss him. I'd say as much to your ma, but I don't suppose she wants to hear it from the likes of me.'

Louisa wanted to argue with him that it shouldn't matter who said it to Ma, she should take it with the grace and good will that it was offered, regardless. But she knew that now wasn't the time. She'd only get angry and upset all over again and there were too many pairs of eyes watching her today.

Kate joined them, giving her a hug, then standing back with her hands on Louisa's shoulders to study her face. 'Are you getting any rest at all? You look proper pasty.'

She shrugged. 'I try, but it's hard,' she said softly. Kate and Jeannie leaned in close, as they always did when the three of them wanted a private conversation away from the prying eyes of the lip-readers. 'If only Ma and I could talk... but she doesn't want to. She spent a lot of time alone with Pa once he was laid out and made it clear she didn't want me there.' His corpse had been prepared and placed in his coffin to lie in their parlour until the funeral. 'My aunt arrived two days ago and the ladies from the church have been in and out, so I've spent most of the time in my room. I wanted to go back to work, but Mr Clark sent a letter saying he was giving me a week's paid leave to look after Ma and help her arrange the funeral. I could hardly go back after that. I mean, what would he have thought if I told him I was the last person Ma wanted around her?' She'd had nothing to do with the arrangements for today, either. She'd simply done what she'd been told.

Lucas cleared his throat and the girls looked up to see a number of people watching them over their tea cups. Louisa raised her chin and turned back to her friends. 'Have you had a cup of tea? There are some cakes and biscuits as well.'

'We're all right, love,' said Jeannie. 'We're more concerned with how you are.'

She gave her a sad smile. 'I'm fine. Sad, but I know I'll survive. At least this time I got to have a funeral, didn't I?' She blinked rapidly, willing her tears away. 'Anyway, I should get back to Ma in case she needs me.'

Lucas looked over her head. 'Don't fret. Your aunt and the vicar's wife are there. They all seem to have plenty to say to each other.'

Louisa nodded, and relaxed a little. If Ma was occupied, she wouldn't notice what her daughter was doing or who she was speaking to. She glanced around. She'd spoken to most people in the hall, including the members of the Clark family who had come to pay their respects but had now left. She wondered what they'd think if they'd known of Pa's real feelings about his employers' Quaker faith.

'She blames me, you know,' she said softly. 'She's convinced that all the trouble I caused weakened his heart.' Truth be told, she was inclined to think the same thing. She was only grateful she'd had those final moments with Pa and felt that they'd made their peace. Ma didn't know that, though, and probably wouldn't believe it if Louisa tried to tell her.

Jeannie gasped. 'Oh, Lou. That's awful.'

'It is,' said Kate through clenched teeth. 'And not true. If anyone should look to their own conscience, it's your ma.'

'Kate.' Jeannie shook her head. 'I don't think we should...'

'No, we shouldn't,' said Lucas, giving Kate a cool look. 'Not here, not now.'

Kate sighed. 'I know. I'm sorry, Lou. I just get so cross when I think about what happened.'

Louisa nodded, touched that her friends seemed more concerned about her than her own mother was.

'Watch out,' said Lucas. 'The vicar's wife is coming this way. Do you want us to make ourselves scarce?'

'Only if you want to,' she said, hoping they would stay. She had nothing to say to the woman, but it seemed from her determined expression that she had plenty to say to Louisa. Thankfully, they chose to stay at her side.

'Louisa, my dear.' The vicar's wife gave her a sympathetic smile. 'You're bearing up remarkably well. Your father would be so proud of you, child.'

She swallowed on a lump in her throat and tried to smile. 'Thank you. It was such a shock.'

'I'm sure. Although...' She looked puzzled, then shook her head. 'I commented to my husband that Mr Clements was looking peaky these past months. Maybe if he'd seen a doctor earlier... But it doesn't pay to speculate now, though, does it? It was God's will.'

Louisa felt herself bristle at the woman's complacent tone, as though 'God's will' made it acceptable that her father had died far too soon. It reinforced her feelings that the type of God her parents believed in was a cruel being that she did not wish to worship. Before she could comment, however, the vicar's wife continued.

'Your mother is to be admired for her fortitude. I feel she's making the right decision, planning for a new life rather than wallowing in self-pity. It's so important to stay busy and this scheme that she and your aunt have decided upon is an excellent idea.'

Louisa remained silent. She had no idea what the woman was talking about.

'Anyway, my dear. You can be assured of the parish's support as you pack up the house and prepare for your move. You must be very excited about this wonderful opportunity in Exeter. I expect you'll be pleased to be going back to the city after your visit there last year.'

Aware that her friends were expressing surprise and dismay, Louisa glanced over at her mother to see that she was watching her. In that moment, she realised that it had been her intention – to send the vicar's wife to tell her this completely unexpected piece of news. Ma saw the moment that Louisa understood. Something in Louisa's expression must have disturbed her, because she looked away. In that moment, Louisa realised that the rift between her and her mother would never be healed. It made her feel heartsore because she had promised Pa she would do her best to mend fences and she had truly hoped that they could begin to understand each other. But if Ma could make plans like this – apparently to give up their home in Street that Pa had worked so hard to buy and to move them to Exeter, without so much as a passing mention of it to her daughter – then Louisa could see no possibility of a reconciliation.

She turned to face the vicar's wife again. 'You must have misunderstood,' she said. 'My mother might be moving the Exeter, but I have a job here. I'm staying in Street.'

The older woman looked shocked. 'Don't be ridiculous, child. It's not your decision to make. You must do as your mother says until such time as the responsibility for your protection is handed to your husband.'

Before she could reply, Lucas stepped forward and took her

hand in his. She noticed it was his injured hand, yet he managed to grasp her fingers in his warm grip. That small thing took her mind off the shock of the woman's words. It made her feel safe when moments earlier she had felt lost and afraid.

'Then it's just as well,' he said calmly, 'that Louisa has agreed to be my wife.'

23

After a moment of stunned silence, Lucas noticed Louisa take a deep breath and lift her chin as she squeezed his hand. He was sure she had stopped breathing when the woman had revealed her ma's plans, and her pleading glance as the vicar's wife had been speaking had left him no choice but to act. He only hoped he hadn't made things even worse for her. He had simply listened to the voice in his head and heart – one that sounded remarkably like Mattie – that told him he needed to claim Louisa in order to save her.

'That's right,' she said, her voice quiet but firm. 'I'm not going to Exeter because I'm getting married to Lucas. At the Friends' Meeting House,' she added, her expression challenging the woman to say anything. Everyone knew that if she objected in public, it would be an insult to the Clark family, the biggest bene-factors of the whole village. Lucas knew she wasn't that daft.

'We haven't said anything before now, on account of Louisa's pa being poorly,' said Lucas, trying to soothe things over. 'Nor have we had time to speak to Mrs Clements yet.'

'But she knows that Pa wanted me to be happy,' said Louisa,

her clear gaze challenging her. 'It was the last thing he said to me. He knew and respected Lucas.'

The vicar's wife gaped at them. Lucas felt a measure of satisfaction that they'd left her lost for words. But he also felt a shiver of apprehension rush down his spine. He'd meant what he'd said. He'd spoken on instinct, but it was true – he *would* marry her to help her escape the fate her ma had planned for her.

But that also meant he had to tell her about what had really happened between him and Mattie.

* * *

Lucas's declaration sent shock waves through the gathering at the Crispin Hall and Louisa could see that her ma was hard put to hold her fury in check. Yet Louisa couldn't bring herself to care. The calculated way in which Ma had excluded her from the plans for Pa's funeral and the shocking news that she was selling the family home and expected her daughter to follow her to Exeter, to leave behind everyone she cared about, was simply cruel. That she hadn't even bothered to tell her in private but had rather let the vicar's wife mention it as though she should already know about it had been the final straw for Louisa. So when Lucas had offered her an escape route, she had followed his lead.

She had a small measure of satisfaction to see Ma put in the same position she'd left Louisa in by sending the vicar's wife over to talk to her. Of course, Ma couldn't blow her top as Louisa was sure she wanted to because she would never let her true feelings show in public. So she'd simply ignored Louisa and Lucas and carried on playing the role of grieving widow.

'What the heck is going on?' Kate hissed in her ear.

Louisa glanced at Lucas before looking at her. 'It seems my ma is moving to Exeter and I'm staying and getting married to Lucas.'

The absurdity of the past few minutes caught up with her and she lifted a hand to cover her mouth as a giggle escaped.

'Really?' Jeannie squeaked. 'I thought you were teasing.'

Louisa shrugged. She wasn't sure whether Lucas had intended it to be a joke or not. But she had a feeling it was going to get out of hand very quickly now that the vicar's wife was speaking so earnestly to Ma.

'Lou...' Kate looked worried.

Lucas stepped forward. 'Can you give us a few minutes?' he asked her. 'I need to talk to Louisa.'

She nodded and took his arm, letting him escort her out of the hall. They didn't stop until they were outside the building. They walked a little up Leigh Road, away from prying eyes and ears. When they were completely alone, he turned and looked at her.

'I'm sorry,' he said. 'I made a proper mess of that, didn't I?'

She gazed up at him and shook her head. 'Don't worry about it. I know you meant well. And if it stops Ma from forcing me to move away with her, then I'm grateful for it.'

He pulled a face. 'It wasn't until I saw the woman's horror when I said it that I realised your ma will likely be dead set against the idea – like she was when Mattie asked your pa if he could wed you. I hope I haven't made things worse for you. That's the last thing I want to do.'

She sighed and looked away. 'I really do appreciate it,' she said, checking that they were still alone and not overheard. 'But you didn't really mean it, did you? I know you don't feel that way about me, and you know I'm set on never marrying now. We need to discuss how we get out of this situation so that Ma lets me stay here when she moves.'

She expected him to agree, but he surprised her again when he frowned and leaned closer.

'Louisa, listen. I admit this was completely unplanned. I saw in your eyes that you needed help and it was the first thing that came to mind. So I acted without thinking it through, and I'm sorry if that's put you in an awkward position. But... if it will help you, I am prepared to marry you.'

She gaped at him, shocked beyond words. She'd been convinced he hadn't meant it. Yet he looked so serious now, so sincere, that she knew he meant every word he was saying.

He saw her hesitation and raised a hand. 'Don't worry, I'm not expecting us to be really married... you know... to... I won't expect us to have marital relations. I know you're Mattie's girl.' He spoke quickly, his voice low and earnest. 'I just can't bear to see you being forced into something else you really don't want. You've put up with enough these past couple of years and I want to help.'

She blew out a breath. 'You've taken me by surprise, Lucas, I can't pretend otherwise. And I'm more grateful than you'll ever know. If I had to marry, I'm sure you'd be a fine husband. We get along well, don't we?'

He nodded.

'But I can't ask you to sacrifice your chance of meeting a nice lass and making a love match of it.'

He looked away, his expression troubled. This time, it was Lucas who checked that they weren't overheard before he moved closer. 'Look, Louisa, if that's all that's holding you back, then you've nothing to worry about. But... Look, I've got a secret that I'm going to share with you. And, like when you told me your secret, I'm praying you'll not change your good opinion of me when you know what it is, although I'll understand if you do. Will you hear me out?'

She felt her heart race as she nodded and waited for him to speak.

He took a deep breath and squared his shoulders. 'I know I'm not going to fall in love with some lass, Louisa, for the same reason I know that you'll be safe from any unwanted advances from me.' He ran his good hand down his face and sighed. 'Please don't hate me,' he said. 'But there's something inside me... I can't help it. I loved Mattie in the same way you did. Not as a friend. He was my everything.' He dropped his head to his chest. 'And I'm the reason he ran off to fight. I'm sure of it. I told him how I felt, you see. I shouldn't have and I'm more sorry that you'll ever know that my stupid, selfish act had such awful repercussions for you and him and your child.'

She stood there, gaping at him. Part of her was shocked rigid... and yet another part of her realised that of course it was true. Suddenly, it all made sense and her heart ached for him. He took another shaky breath, blinking rapidly. She had never seen him look so wretched and unhappy.

'I'll understand if you want nothing more to do with me,' he went on, looking up again. 'But, if you can find it in your heart to forgive me – which is something I will never do for myself – but, if you can, then let me help you now. Let me do something to protect the girl that Mattie loved more than anyone in the world. It's the least I can do after the mess I made of everything.' He paused and frowned. 'Unless... do you think you might find someone to love again?'

She shook her head. 'Not after Mattie,' she said, feeling unutterably sad. 'Oh, Lucas,' she sighed, reaching up and touching his cheek. 'How we've both suffered so, my friend. And all because we loved him with all our hearts.'

Searching her face, he covered her hand with his own, holding it against his cheek. 'But I should have kept quiet, like I'd done all the years I'd been feeling like this. I knew nothing could come of it. I knew he didn't feel the same and anyway, his heart was yours. But... it... it was like when a Friend feels compelled to share ministry in a meeting – I felt it shaking me to the core and I couldn't leave it unsaid. It was wrong of me; I knew it at the time. Now I feel as though my sin caused his death.'

She shook her head. 'Hush. Don't say that. He loved you too, I know it. And don't you ever talk about it being a sin to love someone. What kind of world is this if we can't love freely and without fear? I thought the Friends were more tolerant of these things. Anyway, no one made him go, I realise that now. Not you, not my pa. He was strong enough to stand up against anything. It was something inside him – maybe like that compulsion you felt to tell him your feelings – and I don't know whether that was his own mind or some higher power that took him over. But I've learned in recent days that blaming yourself is only going to do *you* harm, no one else.'

His eyes filled with tears. 'So you don't hate me?' he asked.

She shook her head.

He closed his eyes and a single teardrop slid down and blessed their mingled fingers against his cheek.

'Hush now,' she whispered, wishing she could ease his pain.

A movement behind him caught her attention. Ma was bearing down on them, looking furious.

'Oh my. Brace yourself,' she told him. 'Here comes your future mother-in-law.'

24

A couple of weeks later, Jeannie was so wrapped up in her thoughts as she walked along the High Street that she didn't notice Tom until he was standing in front of her, blocking her way. She gasped and pulled up short, a hand going to her heart as she looked up and realised who it was.

'Oh! Tom! You startled me,' she said.

'Sorry, Jeannie. I called out, but you didn't seem to hear me. Are you all right?'

'Of course,' she said with a smile that didn't feel natural. She hesitated before pulling a face. 'Actually, I'm not sure. There's lots going on at the moment.'

He nodded. 'I couldn't believe it when Lucas said he was getting married to Louisa. I wasn't expecting that. I wasn't sure it was true at first or if he was pulling my leg.'

'Oh, it's true,' she said. 'It's all been a bit of a shock, but when Louisa's ma announced they were moving away from Street, he stepped in and declared himself.'

'Did you even know he was sweet on her?' he asked. He looked as confused as she'd felt about it all.

Jeannie sighed. 'I knew they were friends,' she said carefully. 'But, well... has anyone told you about Mattie?'

'He was Louisa's sweetheart who didn't come back from France, wasn't he?'

She wanted to cringe at his gruff description – *he didn't come back*. She supposed it was better than saying the lad was dead. But when it was someone you'd known all your life, it still hurt to think about it, whichever way anyone described his fate.

'That's right. He was Lucas's best friend as well. After he...' She shrugged, still not comfortable saying the words. '...Lucas enlisted himself and Louisa's parents decided to send her away to get over Mattie.' She didn't tell him that Louisa ran away and chose her own path, no matter how much she wanted to. 'The two of them wrote to each other the whole time they were away and have become good friends.' She paused. 'I didn't realise it was a love match, though. Neither of them said.'

He studied her face. Jeannie felt her cheeks warm. It was as though he could see into her heart and soul. It had been two weeks since Mr Clements' funeral and Lucas's shocking announcement, and Jeannie still couldn't believe it.

'That's good news, though, isn't it? I mean, she's your good friend and now she'll be your sister-in-law. Only...' He regarded her thoughtfully. 'You don't seem very happy about it.'

She wanted to squirm. She was right. He *could* see into her heart. She looked around to make sure no one was listening in to their conversation. 'Don't get me wrong,' she said as she turned back to face him. 'I love Louisa, and I'm thrilled she's going to be my sister-in-law. But... well, like I said, she was Mattie's sweetheart and they adored each other. She's not like that with Lucas. Nor is he with her. Neither me nor Kate had any idea they were even thinking of anything like this. My brother always said he had too much on his plate to take on a wife, and Louisa said she would never marry now that Mattie was gone.' She shrugged. 'Can you see why I'm concerned? I've a feeling he stepped in to save Louisa from being forced to move to Exeter with her ma. We all know that leaving Street again is the last thing Louisa wants.'

'Mmm.' He shoved his hands in his pockets and stared off down the High Street. 'So you're worried he's jumped in as some sort of act of chivalry? Her very own knight in shining armour?'

She couldn't help chuckling at that image. 'He's hardly that,' she said. 'But yes, I suppose so.' She sobered. 'I confess, I've thought about the two of them getting together eventually and even prayed for it. But this... it's such a rush, as though neither of them have thought it through.'

'Marry in haste, repent at leisure?'

She glanced at his face and away again, feeling uncomfortable as she remembered Tom's own situation. He would know all about that kind of thing, given that his wife had betrayed him and was living with another man. She wished it wasn't so, because she liked Tom so much. It made her heart ache, thinking about it. 'Something like that,' she murmured.

'Do you know why they're rushing into this?' he asked. 'Maybe they're calling Mrs Clements' bluff and he's just trying to help Louisa gain some time to reason with her ma.'

She nodded. 'That's what I was hoping. But it sounds like Mrs Clements has dug her heels in and said if Louisa doesn't go with her when she leaves, then she'd better get wed as she'll be washing her hands of her. Louisa says she'll not leave Street – that she'd rather live in a ditch than move to Exeter. It... it's got bad memories for her from when we lost Mattie.' She didn't want to say any more than that, but she remembered how devastated Louisa had been when her parents had declared their intention to send her to Exeter to live with her aunt. At the time, they'd told everyone it was to help her get over Mattie's death, but now

Jeannie knew that it was actually to conceal the fact that she was expecting her sweetheart's child. 'Lucas might feel obliged to marry her rather than leave her destitute without her ma's protection,' she went on. 'He'd never leave her to cope on her own.'

Kate had also been shocked by the proposal and had insisted that Louisa didn't need to marry anyone. She'd reminded Lou she was always welcome at Betty Searle's cottage. They could share the room that Mattie and Will used to occupy. But poor Lou couldn't face it. She was sure she would give away her secret if she were to sleep in Mattie's childhood bed and to spend every day in Mattie's ma's company. Jeannie could see her point. It would be torture for her. But she couldn't tell Tom that. She had promised that she'd never breathe a word about it to anyone.

'And, of course,' she went on, feeling more and more despondent, 'as soon as Ma heard about it, she was so happy. It's all she can talk about. Her first-born getting wed. If they don't actually marry now, she'll be devastated.' She risked another glance at him and saw that he was still watching her with a thoughtful expression on his face. 'I'm worried Lucas suggested it on the spur of the moment and now he's going to end up getting wed whether he wants to or not.' She looked away again, resisting the urge to move closer to him. She would dearly love to rest her head against his broad chest and feel his arms around her. If she could do that, she would feel better about everything. But then she remembered why she couldn't do that and she felt even worse.

'I understand,' he said, making her glance at him again, wondering whether he was reading her mind. She thought she caught a glimpse of regret in his gaze, but it soon passed and she realised he was talking about Lucas's situation. 'But, well... maybe he's been carrying a torch for her all this time and he sees this as a chance to take their relationship further? We lads do daft things like that sometimes because it's hard to actually express our feelings.' He shrugged. 'Maybe if my cousin had declared himself before I wed, my wife might have chosen him then and saved me a whole mess of heartache.'

Jeannie frowned, thinking about Lucas and Louisa. She wouldn't let herself think about Tom and his absent wife. That hurt too much. 'You know, you might be right. I mean, Lucas has never been one for chasing lasses and he's always been private about how he felt, so maybe he did feel something for Louisa. It's just like him to have stepped back as soon as he knew Mattie liked her.' She sighed. 'But even if he does have deeper feelings for her, it worries me that Louisa won't feel able to return his feelings because her love for Mattie was so strong. I'm afraid my brother could end up with his heart broken.'

Tom looked thoughtful. 'Have you told him what you're thinking?'

She nodded. 'He didn't say much. Just that I'm not to worry. He said he and Louisa have talked about it and they know what they're doing.'

'Then I think you need to trust your brother and your friend,' he said with a gentle smile. 'I know it's hard, but he's right. Try not to worry.' He offered her his arm. 'Come on, I'll walk you home.'

She blushed as she took his arm. She wished with all her heart that she could lean into his strong body and enjoy being close to him, but she didn't dare, so she kept herself stiff beside him, afraid of giving away how much his proximity affected her. When his free hand covered hers on his arm, she felt her blood heat. She wanted to close her eyes and savour the feeling for a moment, but she gave herself a silent talking to and pasted on a smile as they began to walk along the High Street towards West End.

Tom kept up a steady flow of conversation, talking about work, the Friends meetings, even the weather. Jeannie gradually relaxed and they were laughing as they approached her home. When they paused outside the gate, she smiled up at him. Tom squeezed her hand as he looked down at her.

'I wish...' He sighed.

'What do you wish, Tom?' she asked, knowing it was foolish to say it. If he was wishing the same things that she was, they were both setting themselves up for heartache.

'I wish I could kiss you again,' he said, his voice low so that only she could hear. 'But it wouldn't be fair on you. I've been trying to find a way for us to be together, but I can't see how. I won't disrespect you and I won't lie to you. If I were a better man, I'd leave you alone so that you can find someone who's free to love you like you deserve.'

She felt as though her heart stopped for a moment, before it began to race, leaving her breathless. 'You deserve love too, Tom,' she whispered.

'I'm not sure I do,' he said. 'All I can think about is you, when in the eyes of the law and God, I'm tied to another woman.'

She didn't know what to say about that. She thought about him far more than she ought to as well. She couldn't help herself. She closed her eyes and took a deep breath to give her the strength to step away from his warmth. Half of her was relieved when he let her go, while the other half – her wicked self – wished that he would cling onto her and convince her that they could overcome this barrier to their happiness.

'Please don't stay away,' she said. 'My brothers regard you as a friend and Ma thinks of you as another son. Don't deny them your presence just because of me. I'll stay out of your way if you like.'

'No, don't, please, I...' He reached a hand towards her but dropped it again when the door of Mr Baker's cottage creaked open.

His words were left unsaid as Cyril emerged from his grandfather's home. Tom gave the other man a brief nod.

'Tell Lucas I'll see him soon,' he told her. 'Take care, Jeannie.'

He was barely out of earshot before Cyril said, 'Is he your sweetheart?'

Jeannie frowned as she turned towards him, hoping that her flushed cheeks didn't give her away. 'No, of course not. He's a family friend.'

Cyril watched Tom walk along the road back towards the High Street. 'Is that limp genuine, d'you think? Or is he trying to get out of enlisting?'

Jeannie narrowed her eyes, feeling her anger build. She had to silently remind herself that Ma would not appreciate her screaming like a fishwife at the neighbour's grandson in broad daylight. 'Actually, he did enlist, back in 1914. That limp is on account of him having been injured in the trenches. He'll be getting a Services Rendered badge soon. He needs our gratitude for his sacrifice, not white feathers and questions about his honesty.'

He didn't look convinced, which fed Jeannie's outrage.

'Tom served his king and country willingly,' she went on, 'unlike your scheming cousin Douglas who lied and cheated to try and avoid it.' When Cyril shrugged and coughed, she took a step towards him. 'And how do we know you've really got asthma? For all I know, you could be pretending to have a bad chest. But, of course, you're a teacher now, so you're in a reserved occupation, aren't you? How lucky for you!'

'I am asthmatic,' he said, his face going red. 'I tried to enlist and they wouldn't have me.' He leaned over as he went into a coughing spasm.

Jeannie watched in horror as he gasped and choked, trying to pull enough air into his lungs. She wondered whether he was going to expire right there in front of her. She was about to hammer on his grandfather's door to get help when he finally managed some deep breaths and he was able to stand tall again and face her.

'I'm sorry,' she said, feeling deeply ashamed of her outburst. She had just been so worked up after that conversation with Tom, her emotions running so high, that Cyril's comment about Tom's limp had sparked her temper.

Cyril shrugged, looking away. 'I heard what Douglas did, but I'm not like him. I would've gone to fight if they'd have had me. I still get white feathers and questions, though, and I'm not eligible for any badge.' He scrubbed his hands down his face. 'I'm sorry I upset you, asking about your friend. It was because I was jealous.'

She gaped at him. 'Jealous? Why?'

He glanced back at her and away again. 'Because I was hoping to ask you if you'd like to walk out with me, and then I saw you with him and thought I'd missed my chance. But if he's just a friend, maybe you might consider letting me take you out?'

Jeannie's heart sank. She almost wished now she'd said Tom *was* her sweetheart. Now she had been nasty to Cyril and he was putting her on the spot. It occurred to her that he was more like Douglas than he thought. They were both happy to manipulate her to get what they wanted. But she'd learned her lesson from his cousin, so she took a deep breath and held her head high.

'Thank you for the kind offer,' she said. 'And I'm sorry that I got cross with you. But I'm afraid I'm not looking for a sweetheart and anyway, I've decided that I won't go out with someone who isn't a genuine Quaker. I'm sure you'd be happier with someone from your own church as well.'

His shoulders slumped and he nodded, still not looking at her. Compared to Tom's direct gaze, Jeannie found Cyril's reluctance to look at her rather rude.

Without another word, he turned and walked back into his grandfather's house, leaving Jeannie staring after him.

Shaking her head, she went into her own home. She didn't dare think about what had happened between her and Tom, and she wouldn't give Cyril another thought. But, her words about only going out with a Quaker gave her pause. If she couldn't have Tom, maybe she should put more effort into her correspondence with Michael and the other poor lads who'd been locked up as conscientious objectors. They all seemed nice and maybe she'd get to meet one through Mr and Mrs Clothier like Kate had with Gerald. If she didn't feel that anyone could make her feel the way Tom did, she would never admit it to another living soul.

* * *

In the meantime, Louisa and Lucas were in the back garden of the Musgrove family home. They were checking the vegetable garden, picking any ripe fruit and vegetables and pulling slugs and snails out from under the foliage and dropping them into a bucket.

'Ma drowns them in a pot of ale,' she said. 'Or sometimes she just pours salt over them and they dissolve.' She shuddered. 'Either way, it's a horrible way to die, isn't it? Can't we just take them out into a field and let them loose?'

He chuckled. 'Then the birds will feast on them. Either way, they're not long for this world. So long as they're not eating our produce, I don't care what happens to them.' He reached out to grasp some runner beans that were ready to harvest and grunted when he realised he was trying to use his injured right hand and it still wasn't always working right.

Louisa knocked his hand away and deftly picked them and

put them in the basket beside them. 'Don't fret,' she said softly. 'It's improving. But it's not been that long, has it?'

He sighed and scratched at his cheek with his good hand. 'I keep forgetting. Then I get annoyed.'

She nodded. 'I know. But remember, you held my hand firm enough when Ma confronted us at Pa's funeral tea.'

They worked side by side in silence for a bit before Lucas spoke again. 'I spoke to one the elders who deals with the registration of marriages. He would prefer it if your ma consented as you're not yet twenty-one.'

She had turned nineteen just last week. There hadn't been any celebrations, not so soon after her father's passing.

'But I think I've persuaded him that we can still go ahead if she withholds her approval,' Lucas continued. He grinned. 'Ma had already spoken to him and said how happy she was that you're willing to join the Friends now you're joining our family. I pointed out that, no matter what, you'll be moving in here when your ma leaves Street and it would break Ma's heart if we weren't properly wed before the Friends by then. Especially as we don't have much room. If you can't share my bed, you would have to share one with Ma and Jeannie. The elder said he'd do what he could.'

Louisa smiled, although not with her eyes. He sobered a little. 'I know we agreed it wouldn't be a real marriage,' he said softly. 'And you don't have to worry about that, but we need to make it look like it is. I promise you, Louisa, even though we have to sleep in the same room, you have nothing to fear from me. I'm not a monster. I know your heart lies with Mattie and I understand that because so does mine.'

She closed her eyes and nodded. 'I know. It's just so strange, thinking about it all.'

'We don't have to go through with it if you'd rather not,' he said. 'I just didn't want you to be forced to move away when I knew it was the last thing you wanted.'

She opened her eyes and looked at him curiously. 'How did you know that was how I felt? What made you say it?'

He shrugged. 'I don't know. Something inside me, I can't say what.' He could hardly tell her he'd heard Mattie in his head, urging him on, could he? 'It just felt like the right thing to do at the time, and when you didn't contradict me, I believed it was.'

She sighed. 'I think it was,' she agreed. 'I'm certainly not moving to Exeter, and I can't trust myself to live at Auntie Betty's without giving up my secret and ruining things for Peg and Will and little Mattie.'

'And your ma won't leave you in the house or help you find lodgings,' he concluded. 'So the only alternative is for us to get married. But I wouldn't want you to be unhappy, Louisa, and I won't force you to do something you don't want. You need to consider what it would mean if you fall in love again one day and you're tied to me.'

She shook her head. 'I've told you, that won't happen,' she said firmly. 'I've had my great love.' She gave him a sad smile. 'We both have, haven't we? And we both agree that we don't want another. No, I'll be content to be your wife... but... what if *you* fall in love again?' she asked. 'I regard you as one of my dearest friends, Lucas, and I'd hate to be the reason you can't find happiness with someone you really love.'

For a moment, they both paused. Lucas was sure she was thinking of Tom's situation and how he couldn't declare himself for Jeannie on account of his marriage vows to his faithless wife tying his hands. Then he reached out his good hand and touched her cheek.

'You know that won't happen, don't you? We've more in common than anyone else realises, haven't we?'

She covered his hand with her own, holding it against her cheek. 'We do.'

'That's why this makes so much sense. We'll be protecting each other, and stopping both of our mothers fretting about us being left on the shelf.'

She smiled. 'You're right. So if you're sure, I think we should get on with it. I'll speak to Ma when I get home.'

* * *

At the cottage in The Mead, Kate frowned as she looked at the envelope that had just been delivered to her. It was Gerald's hand-writing, but instead of the recently perfectly penned script in Indian ink, this was a small envelope and her name and address were written in pencil, like the letters she'd received from him when he was in prison. With a chill in her heart, she opened the letter and began to read. By the time Auntie Betty came in and found her, she was in tears.

'Whatever's the matter, lass?'

'It's Gerald,' she said, her voice scratchy. 'Oh Auntie, it's so cruel. He said the recruiting officer came to the house and told him he had to report for duty before he even had a chance to go before the tribunal to ask for exemption. When he refused, he was arrested again. He's at the guardhouse in his local barracks. They say he has to fight or face another prison sentence. But he's served his time, hasn't he? Why are they doing this to him again?'

Betty gathered her in her arms and let her sob out her distress. 'It's a terrible thing to do to a man,' she sighed. 'But Mr Clothier said it might happen. They've rounded up quite a few of the young men who've been released from prison. It seems they think that a few months in prison is going to change their whole moral compass and they'll be eager to enlist. Maybe some will, but I doubt if it will make a difference to our Gerald. He saw what's going on in the trenches when he was in the ambulance unit, trying to put men back together again when they've been torn apart by bombs and bullets. He'll not agree to go through that again.'

'So that's it? They send him back to prison? How can they do that? He's served his time.'

'I know, lass. But Mr Clothier says the authorities are regarding him as eligible for conscription again now he's free. If he refuses again, they see that as a new offence for which he can be prosecuted and incarcerated.'

Kate took out her handkerchief and wiped her eyes. 'That poor man. Hasn't he been through enough?'

'I know. And poor Ethel will be suffering. I expect I'll get a letter from her any day. I shall write to her now and let her know we're thinking of them both.'

Kate felt weary and so sad for the gentle young man she had become very fond of. 'I need to write to Gerald and tell him the same. He thinks that if he can hold out for a day or two and refuse to go on parade, they'll have to transfer him to the civilian police to be dealt with. Thank goodness the government decided to make it a civil offence now. I should hate it if he went through what they did to him last time – do you remember? They threatened to take him to France anyway and then shoot him for cowardice if he still wouldn't take up arms.'

Betty nodded and sighed. 'That's one of the cruellest things I ever heard.'

Kate thought about poor Stan Jackson, driven mad by what he'd witnessed in the trenches. Ted had told her that the army were considering executing him for desertion when he ran away from the trenches, unable to bear it any longer. That was why Ted agreed to enlist – to save his brother from the firing squad. 'It's all so wrong,' Kate declared. 'Gerald should be granted an exemption certificate on account of his faith and the fact that he's served for so many months on the ambulances. It's not as though he hasn't proved himself, is it? But it seems as though some of these tribunals considering applications for exemption are a law unto themselves.' She wondered whether their wives were stalwarts of the White Feather Association, like Mrs Jackson.

'It's a problem, that's for sure. We must ask Mr and Mrs Clothier whether there's anything else we can do. Perhaps if enough citizens express their outrage, someone will review the powers of the tribunals. If they're all making different decisions, well, that's not at all fair, is it?'

Kate gathered her letter-writing supplies and sat down to write back to Gerald. It broke her heart that he would likely be sent back to prison when his only crime was a faith in a peaceful god.

Life was so unfair, and she wished with all her heart that things were different.

25

For the next week or so, all three girls were subdued. Jeannie did her best to remain cheerful and to try to keep her friends' spirits up.

'I'm so excited that we're going to be sisters,' she said to Louisa as they sat in the canteen at dinner time. After her talk with Tom, she had decided that she was going to trust that Lucas and Louisa knew what they were doing. 'I just hope the twins don't drive you as barmy as they do me and Lucas.'

Louisa laughed. 'I don't mind if they do,' she said. 'It's such a relief that Ma has finally accepted I won't be leaving Street and has consented to me marrying Lucas.' She nudged Jeannie's shoulder. 'And you know I've always wanted a sister. If having a couple of daft brothers is the price I have to pay for that, that's fine by me.'

Kate rolled her eyes. 'You say that now. But these are the Musgrove twins we're talking about. There's still time to change your mind and move in with me and Auntie Betty.'

'Ah, you're just teasing,' she said. 'They're not that bad, are they, Jeannie?'

Jeannie raised her eyebrows. Lou would find out soon enough that they were sulky beasts when they were at home. 'Not in company, perhaps. But you'll be family,' she pointed out. 'They might be polite for a while until they get used to you. Just make sure they don't try and foist their chores off on you. Lucas has already told them they can't, but they're bound to try.'

Louisa shook her head. 'He's already said. I'm to help you and to leave the boys to their regular chores. I'd rather make your life easier than help them get out of doing their bit.'

Jeannie beamed at her. 'It will be good to have someone to share things with. I always feel like I'm neglecting Ma when she's poorly in bed and I'm busy with the laundry or the cooking.'

'Now you'll be able to spend more time with her,' said Louisa. A shadow crossed her face and Jeannie felt bad for her. Mrs Clements had all but cut herself off from her daughter and she knew that Louisa would have liked to have reconciled with her ma before she left Street, as her pa had wanted. But it didn't look like that was going to be possible.

'Are you going to give up work once you're married?' asked Kate.

Louisa shook her head. 'No. There's plenty of married women working here now, so I'll just carry on.'

'But what if you and Lucas have a baby?' asked Jeannie. She blushed at the thought of her brother and her friend doing *that*. She just hoped she didn't come across them kissing and canoodling in the house; it would be so embarrassing.

Kate frowned at her and shook her head slightly, as if to tell Jeannie to shut up, but it was too late, the words were out.

'Sorry,' she said quickly. 'It's none of my business. I shouldn't have asked.'

Louisa sighed, the familiar sadness wrapping itself around her. 'It's all right. Your ma has already said the same thing. I'll tell you the same as we told her. I'll carry on working for the time being and we'll see what happens.'

Jeannie nodded and patted her arm. 'I know it's hard for you to think about things like that. But people are bound to ask.'

'Mmm,' said Kate. 'Like they did with poor Peg. She got sick of people asking, as though any woman has any control over these things.'

Louisa was looking uncomfortable and Jeannie wished she hadn't brought up the subject. It must be so hard for Lou when people talked about her having a baby when she already had one and couldn't acknowledge him. She glanced across at Kate, sending her a pleading look.

'Anyway,' said Kate. 'The wedding's not for a couple of weeks yet, so we'll wait and see, eh?'

'Yes,' said Jeannie. 'Ma's so looking forward to it,' she said. 'I think you're going to be her favourite daughter.' She smiled at Louisa to let her know she was teasing.

She laughed and shook her head. 'I'll never be as good a daughter as you, Jeannie. But I'm glad she's excited about it.' The all-too-frequent shadow crossed her face. 'I'm not even sure if my ma is going to come to the wedding.'

'What?' Kate exclaimed. 'Surely she won't leave you on your own on your wedding day!'

Louisa shrugged, looking away. Jeannie's heart went out to her.

'She keeps muttering about it not being a proper marriage if we don't do it at Holy Trinity. But I pointed out that at least I won't have to get someone to walk me down the aisle.'

A Quaker wedding was very different from an Anglican one. There was no formal pomp and ceremony, no celebrant, but rather a gathering of Friends who would witness the couple stand and declare their intention to marry and promising, *through divine assistance, to be a loving and faithful spouse so long as they both on earth shall live.*

'I know,' said Kate, 'and I remember from Peg and Will's wedding, anyone who wanted to could stand and wish the couple well or offer them blessings or advice on being a loving and faithful spouse. Then all of us had to sign their marriage certificate. It's enormous!'

Jeannie smiled. 'It will be. Ma and Pa's certificate is up on the wall in our bedroom. I'll have to show it to you sometime. Pa made the frame for it himself. Ma says it reminds her of all the people who shared their special day with them.'

Louisa nodded. 'I've seen Peg and Will's one. I think it's a lovely tradition.' She pulled a face. 'Although it will look odd if there's not a single Clements signature on there, apart from my own. But, hey ho. If Ma doesn't want to come, I'll not force her.'

Kate and Jeannie shared a look as Louisa collected up her cup and plate and stood, ready to get back to work. Jeannie wondered whether Kate was thinking the same as she was – that they should try to speak to Mrs Clements. As they followed Louisa out of the canteen, she asked her, keeping her voice low so that Lou didn't hear her. It would only upset her if they tried to talk to her ma and she still refused.

'I think we should,' agreed Kate. 'Although I'm not sure it will make much difference.'

'We've got to try, though, don't we?'

* * *

When Jeannie mentioned their plan to Lucas that evening, he asked them to hold off for a day or two. 'I'm intending to go and see her myself,' he said. 'She's going to be my mother-in-law, whether she likes it or not. I know Louisa's being stoic about it, but I can't help thinking that if we can't get Mrs Clements there, both of them will regret it. I'd rather speak to her privately, appeal to her for her own sake as much as Louisa's. After all, it's her only child getting married.'

'If you're sure,' she said. 'It will probably be best coming from you. But let me know if you think it will help if me and Kate speak to her as well.'

'I will, thanks, sis. I'm going to pop out and see her in my dinner break tomorrow.'

* * *

If Mrs Clements was surprised to see him when he knocked at the house in Somerton Road, she showed no sign of it. Lucas thought she might slam the door in his face, but she clearly thought better of it when a neighbour walked past and called a greeting.

'You'd better come in,' she said, her tone not at all welcoming.

He didn't say anything until he was in the hallway and she had closed the door behind him.

'Thank you,' he said. 'I won't keep you long, but I thought we ought to talk.'

Mrs Clements gave him a cool look. 'I didn't think you wanted to hear anything I have to say. After all, you went ahead and publicly announced your intention to marry my daughter without so much as a by-your-leave.'

He had a feeling she was hoping he'd either be embarrassed or lose his temper. But he wasn't prepared to let her control their dialogue, not now he had her attention away from prying eyes. She might think he was a daft young lad, but the death of his father at an early age, plus the horrors of the past couple of years, had made him grow up fast. He wasn't some fickle boy who could be intimidated.

'I'm sorry about that, ma'am. But I wouldn't have felt the need if you'd bothered to tell your daughter that you were planning on uprooting her life whether she wanted it or not.'

She huffed. 'So, it's my fault, is it? She batted her eyelashes at you and you leapt to her defence?'

'I'm not blaming you, Mrs Clements,' he said calmly. 'I know you've had a terrible time of it with Mr Clements passing so suddenly.' She thinned her lips but didn't comment. 'You've had a lot on your mind,' he went on. 'But Louisa has lost her father, just as you have lost your husband, and she would have liked it if you had both been able to comfort each other in your grief.'

She turned away and walked into the parlour. Lucas followed. She turned as she reached the fireplace. On the mantelpiece behind her was a photograph of Mr Clements. It looked quite recent, probably taken at the local photographic studio. It still shocked Lucas to think that the man he'd worked for and looked up to since he was fourteen was no more.

'You'll forgive me if I find it hard to believe Louisa has any desire to nurture any kind of relationship with me now that her father is gone,' she said, her expression hard. 'After all, once she took up with that Searle boy, she changed into a defiant, deceitful girl. All we wanted for her was a decent marriage to one of our own kind.'

Lucas blinked but managed to refrain from wincing at her words. He knew she had been pushing Louisa towards lads at Holy Trinity and that, as far as she was concerned, both he and Mattie weren't ever going to be good enough for her daughter.

She wanted him to argue with her, he could see, but he knew there was no point. Whether she liked it or not, he and Louisa were getting married. If he worried about the wisdom of it, he'd tell no one. He was set on this path and he felt in his heart it was the right thing to do. Louisa said he didn't need to feel guilty, but he was sure that it was his actions that had sent Mattie to his death, and so it was his duty to protect Louisa with his name.

'I'm sorry that you're disappointed by her choices,' he said. 'But I swear to you I will be a good husband.'

She actually sneered at that. His heart sank.

'I know I'm not what you wanted for her, but I'm a hard worker and I'll give her a good life.'

'Oh you will, will you? You're happy to take on your friend's leavings, are you?'

This time, her words hit home and he did flinch. 'Mrs Clements,' he began, but she held up a hand to stop him.

'I don't suppose she's told you what that boy did to her, has she? That she's brought shame to this house?'

He stared at her. 'We have no secrets,' he said, maintaining eye contact with her so that she could see exactly what he meant. 'Nothing you can say will put me off marrying Louisa.'

'Does that mean she's shared her favours with you as well?' She shuddered and turned away. 'I tried to teach her right and wrong. I tried to show her how a good wife and mother should conduct herself. What did I ever do to deserve such a little trollop for a daughter?'

He stepped towards her at that. 'Stop it,' he said, his voice low and dangerous. 'Don't you ever call her that.'

Startled, Mrs Clements stepped away from him, almost tripping over the hearth. Lucas put out his hand and grasped her arm, saving her from falling. As soon as she regained her balance, she pulled her dignity around her like a cloak and shook him off.

'I'll speak as I find in my own house,' she snapped. 'You say you have no secrets. Does that mean you know about her bastard child?'

He closed his eyes, the full extent of Louisa's suffering becoming crystal clear in the face of her mother's disgust. 'I know,' he said. 'I also know that Mattie would have married her. He loved her.'

'Love? If he'd truly loved her, he'd have shown her some respect and not seduced her under our very noses.'

He saw no point in arguing with her. He'd been shocked that Mattie had anticipated the marriage bed as well, but Louisa had confessed that if anyone had been guilty of seduction, it had been her. She'd wanted him to know how much she loved him before he went off to fight. He didn't judge her for that, nor Mattie for accepting that love. But clearly, Mrs Clements had no intention of forgiving or forgetting it.

'I never thought she was so manipulative until she tricked her own friend's sister to conspire with her to defy me and her father.' She narrowed her eyes at him as she continued. He felt a chill run down his spine. 'Are you prepared to be here at her side when Will and Peg Searle come home to Street with the child?'

Lucas felt his stomach churn at the thought of how hard that would be for Louisa. 'Yes. I'll be at her side, supporting her,' he said. 'I want what's best for her.'

'Well, aren't you the saint, Lucas Musgrove?' Her sneer was back, but behind her aggression, he could see a woman in pain. 'Did it not occur to you that what's best for her is for her to leave this place and never have to see another woman being a mother to her child? Would you rather she was tortured, day after day, by the sight of him?'

He swallowed against a lump in his throat. He could imagine the pain that would cause her. But he also knew that the pain of never setting eyes on her child again, of never knowing whether he was loved and happy, would be even harder to bear. He looked at Mrs Clements and felt a wave of sympathy for her. She truly believed she was right about this and that she was doing what was best for her daughter. Yet, she knew so little about Louisa – not the strength of her love, nor her resolve to do the best for her own child.

'All she wants is to know that her child is loved,' he said softly. 'Every child needs to be loved, no matter what path they follow in life.'

She glared at him, understanding his meaning. 'I love my daughter,' she declared. 'How dare you question it.'

He nodded. 'I believe you do, Mrs Clements, just as she loves you. You've both become lost in the troubles of the past. That's why I'm here.'

She studied him for a long moment. 'Why *are* you here?' she asked eventually. 'Do you want money? A dowry for taking on damaged goods? Because I told Louisa that if she defies me on this, I'm cutting her off without a penny.'

He sighed. 'Mrs Clements, you don't know me well, but I can assure you that I do not want a penny from you, and nor does Louisa. I'm not a rich man, but I am a hard worker and I'll provide for my own family, thank you very much. No, I came here today to ask you to reconsider attending our wedding. I know it's not at your church, but a Quaker wedding is just as legal as an Anglican one, and it would mean a lot to Louisa if you were there to witness it.' He paused for a moment, hoping she would say something. But when she remained silent, he sighed again and ran a hand over his face, accepting that he had been on a fool's mission.

He turned towards the door, heartsore. He felt as though he'd let Louisa down. As he reached the hall, he paused, his heart pounding just as it had when he'd declared to the vicar's wife he intended to marry Louisa.

'Please, Mrs Clements. I'm not too proud to beg. I know you love your daughter, and she wants so much to make her peace with you, as she did with her pa before he passed. Don't let your pride keep you from your only child. Come to our wedding, please. Show her you still love her. Let her know that all isn't lost. If you go away without speaking, you'll never see her again, because I know you're both too proud to make the first move. Be there to see her wed. Wish her well and give her the chance to do the same to you. For she does wish you well, Mrs Clements, we both do. It's just that what is right for you isn't right for her. Not now. She needs to make her own way. But that doesn't mean she doesn't want and need her mother in her life.' He paused, gulping in air after the rush of words.

Mrs Clements stared at him, her eyes filled with tears. When he would have gone to her to offer some comfort, she blinked rapidly and looked away.

'I'll consider it,' she said.

He let out a slow breath. She would think about it. It was enough. No more than he could have hoped for. 'Thank you,' he said before he quietly let himself out of the house and headed towards the factory as the hooter sounded to call everyone back to work.

26

The wedding was going to take place in the first Sunday meeting for worship in October at the Friends' Meeting House but everyone still had to work their usual half-day shift on Saturday morning.

'Are you excited about tomorrow?' Jeannie asked Louisa as they arrived in the Machine Room. 'Ma's beside herself, she's so happy. She's driving Lucas potty with her fussing.'

Louisa smiled and nodded, although Kate was convinced she wasn't as excited about her marriage to Lucas as she had been about the prospect of marrying Mattie. It made her feel sad for her friend and for Lucas.

She knew why it made sense for the two of them to marry, but she still felt that it would have been better for Louisa to move into Auntie Betty's when her ma left Street rather than tie herself to a man that Kate was sure Louisa didn't think of as anything more than a friend. She just hoped they would grow to love each other as a man and wife should because otherwise, they could end up utterly miserable.

When she'd said as much to Louisa a few days ago, Lou had

gently pointed out that it was better to go into the marriage with their eyes open and in genuine friendship than blinded by love that could fade and die. It made Kate think about her own ma, who'd been dazzled by Reggie Davis, only to find out that he was a selfish monster who would neglect her when she needed him most. So maybe she shouldn't worry so about Louisa and Lucas. Maybe a union between friends was the best a lass could hope for. She sighed. She doubted she'd ever trust a man enough to make even a friendship match like Louisa and Lucas.

'I'm a bit nervous,' Louisa admitted. 'But I think that has more to do with the fact that I don't know whether Ma is coming.'

'Has she said anything?' asked Kate, surprised. She knew that Lucas had been to see her and he was hopeful she might be there for her daughter.

Louisa shrugged. 'Not really. She asked a few questions about the ceremony, and I still don't think she's happy about it. But it seems she's finally accepted I'm getting wed. But she hasn't said anything about being there.' She glanced around then leaned in closer to stop others reading her lips. 'She was horrible at first, saying he wouldn't marry me if he knew about the baby. But when I told her he already knew, she changed her tune and said he'd treat me like his...' She shook her head, her cheeks going red. 'I can't say it.'

Jeannie gasped and covered her mouth. 'Lucas isn't like that. He never would.'

'I know.' Louisa patted her shoulder. 'And I'm sure Ma knows it too. She was just being a dog in a manger. You wouldn't believe the arguments we've had these past weeks about this and whether I should give it up and go to Exeter with her.' She sighed. 'Anyway, she finally seems to have accepted it. I don't know what changed her mind, but that doesn't mean she'll come to the wedding.'

Kate frowned. 'She's not planning to try and stop it, is she?

You know – when the vicar asks, *If any person here present knows of any lawful impediment to this marriage, then they should declare it now*. Will she step forward?'

Louisa looked startled. 'I hadn't thought of that.'

Jeannie shook her head. 'It doesn't work like that at a Quaker wedding. The registrar elder will have established that you're free to wed beforehand, and anyway, there really isn't any *lawful impediment* to you two getting wed. No. Once you stand up and say your vows, you'll be wed. Although...' She frowned and bit her lip. 'Anyone at the meeting can stand up and speak from their heart, but that's *after* you've said your vows. Surely she wouldn't come just to ruin your day by saying something unkind, would she?'

Kate rolled her eyes. 'Stop it, the pair of you. This is Mrs Clements we're talking about. Do you honestly think she'll stand up in public and denounce her own daughter, especially in front of the Clark family?' She glared at both of them. 'Think about it. If your ma does come, Lou, she'll not do anything to embarrass herself or to change people's opinions of the family. It would tarnish your pa's memory, and she'd never do that.'

Jeannie looked relieved. 'You're right. I'm sure there's nothing to worry about.'

Louisa didn't look quite so convinced. 'I suppose so,' she said. 'Although... she's moving away. What if she doesn't care what she says?'

Kate turned, grasped Louisa by the shoulders and gave her a little shake. 'I said stop it, Lou. If you're worried, ask her outright if she's coming and if she says yes, tell her you want to know why. You know her well enough to work out if she's intending to do something to spoil your day.'

'Yes, but I can hardly tell her not to come, can I? I told her I want her there.'

'I know, love, and I'm sure it will be fine. But if she is planning to cause trouble, we'll just have to be on guard and make sure she doesn't get the chance.' She wasn't sure how they could, short of putting their hands over the woman's mouth to stop her speaking, but that would cause just as bad a scandal as Mrs Clements denouncing the marriage. But Kate wanted to reassure Louisa, not frighten her.

Louisa took a deep breath and blew it out, relaxing her shoulders. 'You're right. Ma won't shame us. And she's actually been a little nicer with me this past couple of days, so maybe she's coming round. I hope so. I didn't want her to leave still angry with me. It doesn't seem right to fall out with her completely. She's still my ma, after all, and she's got to get used to life without Pa, hasn't she? I know what it's like, losing the love of your life.'

Kate and Jeannie glanced at each other. Jeannie looked uncomfortable, as well she might. After all, it was her brother Louisa was now marrying. Kate sent her what she hoped was a sympathetic and understanding look. They all had to trust that both Louisa and Lucas knew what they were doing.

'I hope you part on better terms,' Kate told Louisa softly. 'Life's hard enough without having a family feud. Lord knows, I know what *that's* like.' She pulled a face. 'Anyway, I'm not going to think about my pa now – he doesn't deserve any consideration, the drunken old fool.' She sat down and switched on her machine. 'I've got better people to think about. I heard from Gerald this morning.'

'The conscientious objector you met?' asked Louisa, sitting next to her and doing the same.

'How is he?' asked Jeannie, reaching for her first pair of linings.

'Not good. Well, he says he's coping well and not to worry, but I'm not so sure he is. He got a six-month sentence – more than he had last time. So he's stuck in prison again until next spring.

They've sent him to Wormwood Scrubs in London, so it will be harder for his ma to visit him.' She shook her head. 'It's so unfair. He's told them he's prepared to work in a reserved occupation. He'd be happy to work in the market garden or on a farm growing food, or in a hospital, but they won't listen. His local tribunal seem intent on punishing everyone who tries to get exemption from fighting by denying them their certificates.'

'Oh no, that's so sad and unfair,' said Jeannie. 'But I expect your letters bring him a lot of comfort. Do you think he might ask you to be his sweetheart, Kate?'

'Watch out,' said Louisa. 'Mr Briars is coming.'

The three of them put their heads down and started work. Kate was glad she hadn't had to answer Jeannie's question. But as she worked steadily, her mind whirled with her thoughts.

She liked Gerald well enough. He was a fine lad – nice-looking, kind, polite and with a quiet strength that she admired. She already regarded him as a dear friend. Yet... the thought of him being her sweetheart simply didn't appeal.

It occurred to her, though, that if he asked her, she might feel obliged to say that she would be his sweetheart, if only to keep his spirits up while he was imprisoned. She knew from the other lads she'd written to, and from speaking to Mr and Mrs Clothier about it, that many young men sent to gaol for refusing to fight were finding it difficult to cope with life behind bars. One or two had had breakdowns. Others had given in when threatened with a second, longer term, and enlisted. She dreaded to think how they'd fare in the trenches. It surely wouldn't be any easier than being in prison, not from what Gerald had said about it. He was adamant that, even if it meant spending years being locked up, he would never go back to France and he would never take up arms against another man. But that didn't mean that being incarcerated for months again wouldn't affect him in the end.

He'd previously mentioned that, although some of the prison wardens were decent chaps, others were cruel and took delight in abusing the conscientious objectors. One of them had brought letters for Gerald to his cell and proceeded to tear them into little pieces in front of him before he had a chance to read them. Kate had been furious about that and even Mrs Clothier had been outraged enough to write a strong letter of protest to the prison governor. The incident had left Gerald shaken. He'd been helpless to stop the man, knowing that if he'd tried to wrest the letters from him, he'd be charged with assaulting a prison officer and have his sentence extended.

Mr Clothier had said that treatment like that could break a man's spirit, so Kate was careful to be encouraging and cheerful in her letters and prayed they didn't fall into the hands of someone like that horrible warden. She hoped that her correspondence would bring him a little sunshine to light the darkness of his existence. So yes, if he wrote to her from prison and asked her to be his sweetheart, she would feel obliged to agree.

She didn't see any harm in it, at least while he was locked up. Yet if he had asked her the same thing when they had met at the Clothiers' house a while back, she would have said no. Not that he did, so maybe she was fretting about nothing.

She knew her friends would urge her to accept him if he did ask her. Despite Kate telling them she didn't want a sweetheart, she knew they still wanted to see her with someone. But every time she thought about it, she would remember Ted, with his smile and strong arms that made her feel happy and safe. Then, swift on the heels of the warm feelings his memory gave her, she remembered the shock and hurt of his leaving and her resolve to rely on no one but herself returned.

27

It wasn't until Louisa was ready to leave for the Friends' Meeting House for her wedding that she realised her mother was intending to go with her.

She gave her a grateful smile. 'Thank you, Ma,' she said.

Her mother nodded, her expression unreadable. 'It will be expected,' she said.

Louisa closed her eyes briefly as disappointment swamped her at her cold tone. 'Please don't feel obliged,' she said. 'After all, you're moving away, so what does it matter whether you come or not? You'll not see these people again.' And Louisa could live with the fact that her surviving parent had refused to attend her wedding. She didn't care what people said, unlike Ma.

Her mother sighed. 'It matters to me. Your father would want me to be there, even if I am still in deep mourning.'

Louisa felt guilty now. 'I'm sorry, Ma.'

She nodded again, her tone softening. 'We've all got things we're sorry for, lass. But we can't change the past. We can only make the best of today. So, are we going, or not?'

* * *

Mrs Clements was shocked to see that Lucas and his family were waiting outside the Friends' Meeting House when she and Louisa arrived. Mr Roger Clark, the elder who was designated the registrar for the purposes of regarding the marriage, was also there.

'Why is the groom out here?' she whispered to her daughter. 'He shouldn't see you until you reach the altar. Maybe we should go away again until he's safely inside.'

Louisa touched her arm. 'No, Ma. It's not like that for Quakers, remember? I told you, me and Lucas will walk in together.'

Though it didn't sit well with Ma, Louisa was relieved that the presence of Mr Clark and the Musgrove family meant she wouldn't be able to protest any further. She would have hated to walk into the Meeting House with just her reluctant mother. She smiled as Lucas caught her eye and raised his chin in greeting.

Mrs Musgrove stepped forward, leaning on a cane. Louisa knew that her arthritis was getting worse, so she was probably in pain after walking the length of the village and then standing around waiting for them to arrive. She left her mother's side to greet her soon-to-be mother-in-law.

'Ah, Louisa, lass, you look beautiful. Doesn't she look lovely, Lucas?'

Louisa looked over at him and blushed as he nodded and agreed with his ma. She was wearing her nicest dress, a soft lilac velvet with a sweet matching hat. In deference to the recent loss of her father, she wore a black armband. Her mother wore her widow's black, having stated that it was far too soon for her to wear anything else. Louisa chose not to point out that if Ma hadn't declared her intention to uproot them to Exeter so swiftly after Pa's passing, there would be no need to rush into a wedding while they were both in mourning. Ma had however consented to wear a small corsage that matched the modest posy made of Michaelmas daisies Louisa had cut from the Clements' garden.

She felt such a mixture of emotions in that moment. She had never thought this day would happen after Mattie... but she wouldn't think about that now. It wouldn't be fair to Lucas.

'Mrs Clements.' His ma turned to Louisa's ma. 'We didn't want you to have to walk into the Meeting House on your own, my dear, not for your first visit. So we waited for you. Come now, John. Give Mrs Clements your arm. Peter, I'll take yours and we'll go in.'

Louisa tried to give Ma a reassuring smile, but she was trying not to laugh at the idea that her mother would ever make a second visit to this place that she held in such contempt. Of course, with Mr Clark standing there, Ma wouldn't say such a thing. Instead, she simply inclined her head, took John's proffered arm and let the lad escort her through the door.

When they had disappeared inside, Mr Clark turned to Lucas and Louisa. His usually solemn expression was firmly in place, but Louisa could see the kindness in his gaze as he faced them.

'Mr Musgrove, Miss Clements, marriage is a holy union, not to be undertaken lightly. Can you assure me that you are still free to marry each other and that you are content to proceed?'

Louisa glanced at Lucas, wondering what he was thinking. She couldn't read his expression, but his voice was firm when he responded, 'Yes, sir. I want to marry Miss Clements.'

They both turned to look at her. 'And you, Miss Clements?' asked Mr Clark.

She felt a moment of panic, an urge to flee. But then she looked into Lucas's eyes and she could swear she heard Mattie's voice, as clear as day, saying, *He's a good man, love, and he'll make you happy.* All her panic fled, to be replaced by a warm assurance. She nodded. 'Yes, sir. I want to marry Lucas.'

Mr Clark nodded, satisfied. 'Splendid.' He smiled briefly. 'I shall go inside now. I believe that a number of our guests are not familiar with the conduct of a Quaker wedding, so I will take a few moments to explain the proceedings to them. I suggest that you wait here while I do that. Then, when you're ready, come in and we shall begin.' He looked at Louisa. 'Miss Clements, you're aware of what will happen?'

She nodded. It had all been explained to her. 'Yes, I am. Thank you, sir.'

After he went inside, the two of them were silent for a moment. Louisa waited for the panic to set in again, but it didn't.

'Are you really sure about this?' Lucas asked her softly. 'It's not too late.'

She searched his face. 'I'm sure... so long as you are. It's not too late for you to change your mind, Lucas. I wouldn't blame you.'

He shook his head. 'I'd never do that to you, Louisa. So long as you're sure it's what you want, then I'll be proud to call you my wife.' He paused and took a deep breath as he grasped her hands in his. She was aware that the grip on his injured hand wasn't as strong as the other one, but she still felt his inner strength through his fingers where they touched her. 'I know I'm not your great love, but I understand and share your loss. I know we have vows to make in there' – he inclined his head towards the door – 'but I want to make you a solemn promise now that is just as sacred and sincere as what I'll say in front of everyone. I will do everything in my power to make you happy, Louisa. I'll never expect you to forget Mattie, just as I'll never forget him either. We're united in our love and grief for him, and in honour of him, I want us to make a good life together. I'll try to give you everything you need.'

She felt her eyes well with tears and blinked rapidly in an

effort to keep them at bay. 'Thank you, Lucas. And I promise the same to you. You've become such a dear friend to me these past months and I will make it my mission to make you happy and never regret the sacrifice you're making for me today.'

Lucas nodded. 'I feel his presence today.'

'So do I. But it doesn't make me so sad. Instead, it makes me feel that we're doing the right thing.'

He smiled. 'I know.' He let go of her hands and offered his arm. 'Let's go and get married, eh?'

* * *

Jeannie watched as Lucas and Louisa came into the silent Meeting House and took their seats in front of the table on which their marriage certificate rested. It was a large document, already inscribed with their names, the names of their parents, the date and the vows they would shortly take. Once they had been said, everyone present would sign the document as a pledge that each witness to this solemn occasion would continue to support and encourage the couple throughout their married lives. Like his pa before him, Lucas would make a frame for the certificate and it would hang on the wall in their home, a permanent reminder of the day.

Louisa laid her posy next to the certificate and took her seat next to Lucas, who smiled at her. Jeannie's heart filled with love for her brother as she noted his tenderness and consideration towards his bride. Louisa's shy answering smile eased Jeannie's worries and she sent up a prayer that a strong and steady love would grow between the two of them.

She let her gaze wander around the packed assembly. In addition to the Friends who attended here every Sunday, they were joined by others who wanted to come and wish the couple well.

Kate's sisters-in-law were there, their children sitting quietly beside them, perhaps intimidated by the silence that they weren't used to. Some of the workers from the Clicking Room and Machine Room had come along too. A few had been to Quaker weddings before, but those who hadn't were easy to spot because they fidgeted and looked uncomfortable in the silence. It made her heart ache that so many men were missing from the gathering – all away fighting to keep them safe. She hoped this horrible war would end soon and they would all come back safe to their loved ones.

If Mrs Clements was uncomfortable, she didn't show it. She sat, still as a statue, her head lowered as though in prayer. The thought reminded Jeannie that she should be looking inward, not ogling visitors to their sacred gathering and she closed her eyes, sending up a prayer of apology, before holding Lucas and Louisa in the light, praying that their marriage would be a long and happy one.

After a few minutes, she felt a movement in the air and opened her eyes to see that Lucas had stood and held out his hand to Louisa. Her friend took it and got up to stand at his side. Jeannie shivered in anticipation. She had witnessed many marriage vows in her life, but this was the first involving a member of her own family. The life-changing significance of what her brother was about to say seemed magnified a thousand times.

'Friends,' he said, raising his voice, clear and proud. 'I take this, my friend Louisa Elizabeth Clements, to be my wife, promising, through divine assistance, to be unto her a loving and faithful husband, so long as we both on earth shall live.'

Out of the corner of her eye, Jeannie was aware of Mrs Clements dabbing at her eyes with a handkerchief. Whether they were tears of happiness or despair, she didn't know for sure, although she suspected which they might be. She looked away, catching Kate's eye. They grinned at each other before they turned their attention back to the couple standing before them.

Louisa raised her chin and looked at no one but Lucas. 'Friends,' she declared, her voice as sure and true as his. 'I take this, my friend Lucas James Musgrove, to be my husband, promising, through divine assistance, to be unto him a loving and faithful wife, so long as we both on earth shall live.'

Ma didn't try to hide her tears as she put her hands over her heart and sighed. Unlike the bride's mother, Jeannie knew that Ma's were happy tears, a fact proven by the beatific smile on the older woman's face.

The couple resumed their seats. It was done. Her brother and her dear friend were wed. They might not have come together in a normal way, but Jeannie felt it in her bones that they were meant to be together and would make a good match. As the couple sat and the silence descended once again, Jeannie spared a thought for poor Mattie, sending love into the light, hoping that he could be happy for the two of them and that he was at peace, wherever he was.

Mrs Clements shifted slightly in her seat, glancing around swiftly, no doubt wondering what would happen now. Jeannie felt a little sorry for her. She looked lost and uncertain. Despite the heartache the woman had caused her daughter, Jeannie knew that she had sincerely believed her actions to be right. She felt sympathy for her, knowing that it was difficult for her to acknowledge the harm she had caused Louisa. She wished she could offer her some comfort, but now was not the time.

The silence was maintained for a few more moments before someone stood. It was a man who had been a friend to Jeannie's father, working alongside him at the factory until his untimely death. He had also known Louisa's father for many years.

'Friends,' he said. 'My heart fills with joy for this young couple today, yet at the same time it is filled with sadness that neither of their fathers is here in flesh to wish them well. I would therefore beg to presume and speak on their behalves. I knew both men and it was clear to me that they both loved their children very much. Lucas, you've grown into a fine young man, having been forced to take on the role of the head of your family all too soon. But you did it without complaint and have worked hard to support your dear mother and brothers and sister. You're a credit to your late father. I know he would be mighty proud of you.'

Jeannie didn't attempt to stop her tears overflowing at his words. He was right. The whole family looked up to Lucas and were proud of him. He'd taken on so much after Pa's death, when he'd been but a boy himself. He deserved to be happy, and if Louisa could help him with that, and he could help her in the same way, then all would be well.

'And little Louisa, you were the apple of your father's eye, and I'm sure he will rest easy, knowing that you've found a good man to share your life with. He knew Lucas to be a hard-working, dedicated lad and I'm sure he would be content, knowing you've found such a decent young man to guide you into the future. May God bless you both and may your dear departed fathers watch over you from Heaven. I wish you a long life, filled with much love and many children.'

Louisa sniffed. Lucas extracted a clean handkerchief from his pocket and handed it to her, even as he nodded his thanks to the man as he sat down.

One of the elders stood and spoke about the sanctity of marriage and how the love of God and shared faith would strengthen their union. He reminded them that everyone present today was charged with supporting and encouraging the couple as they negotiated their way through married life. Jeannie had heard something similar at most weddings she'd attended, but it seemed more important than ever now because this was her brother and her friend's union he was talking about.

Others stood and spoke about God's love and the joys of marriage. Someone had written a poem dedicated to the happy couple that made everyone smile. Even Mrs Clements managed a polite one. Others simply wished the bride and groom well.

Auntie Betty stood. Jeannie saw both Lucas and Louisa still. Jeannie held her breath. She knew that both of them had strong feelings that the sight of Mattie's ma brought forth. She saw Lucas take Louisa's hand as she began to speak.

'Friends,' she said. 'I give thanks to God that He has answered my prayers and held these two young people in the light and brought them together here today in holy matrimony. Both Lucas and Louisa were important to my beloved son Matthew. He loved them both and I know that his spirit will be singing with joy today to see them united in love, just as mine is. Lucas and Louisa, you bring such happiness to your friends and family and you have both given me much comfort in my darkest days. May God bless you with a long and happy marriage.'

As the older woman sat down, Jeannie felt as though she was going to faint. Next to her, Kate nudged her with her elbow. 'Breathe,' she whispered. Jeannie glanced at her, confused. She felt dizzy and there were spots before her eyes. 'I mean it, Jeannie, you've got to breathe!'

Kate nudged her again, in her ribs and a bit harder this time. It did the trick. In her heightened state of emotion, Jeannie had simply forgotten to do anything. With a shudder, she gulped in a lungful of fresh air. She didn't dare look at anyone, especially not the bride and groom. Mrs Searle's words had affected her deeply, so she could only imagine what it had done to them.

She glanced at Kate, who looked as emotional as she felt. Kate squeezed her hand. 'It's all right,' she whispered. 'Everything's going to be all right now.'

Jeannie nodded and looked down, contemplating her hands resting on her lap. Although a wedding band wasn't necessary in a Quaker marriage, her family maintained the tradition of a wife wearing a ring. Ma still wore her own one, even though the wedding vows said the marriage would last *so long as we both on earth shall live.* She had given Lucas her mother's ring for Louisa and she knew he would slip it on her finger when they had a moment alone together. Ma had assured Jeannie that she had their other grandmother's ring to pass on to her when she was wed, if her husband-to-be didn't have one for her. She had laughed at that, asking, 'What about the twins?'

Ma had shrugged. 'The first of them to marry can have my ring,' she'd said. 'We might have to find something for the other one.'

Lucas had laughed and said, 'I doubt any sensible lass would take on either of them, anyway. But if they do, a brass ring will do the trick.'

She was barely aware of the continuing silence, punctuated by the occasional ministry from people in the gathering, as she stared at her hands. She would love to wear a ring, to show the world that she was loved and a wife.

She looked up, her gaze landing on Tom as he sat in his usual place across the Meeting House. He was watching her. His lips twitched in a brief smile. In her emotional state, she was powerless to guard her fragile heart and she knew that all of her longing for him must be showing as she stared at him. She saw an answering longing for a moment, before his gaze became cloudy with regret and he looked down. Her heart felt as though it was breaking as she looked away, unable to bear the pain of the realisation that she probably wouldn't ever need her grandmother's ring because if she couldn't have Tom, she didn't think she wanted anyone else. One sweet, brief kiss from him had been all it had taken to ruin her for anyone else. He was the one she wanted, but he wasn't free, so it was hopeless.

At last, after no one else stood to minister or to wish the couple well, Mr Clark rose. He quietly directed Lucas and Louisa to sign the marriage certificate, and then Mr Clark himself signed and dated it. Then came the long process of everyone present lining up to take their turn in signing the document, before moving on to wish the happy couple well.

She didn't know how it happened, but she found herself standing next to Tom in the queue.

'Are you feeling all right, Jeannie?' he asked. 'I thought you looked a bit poorly there for a moment.'

He must have seen the moment when she'd had a funny turn and forgot to breathe. She was grateful that he spoke softly, so as not to draw attention to her. She nodded, not looking at him. 'Yes thank you. I just find weddings emotional, that's all.'

The person in front of her moved on and Jeannie picked up the fountain pen from the table and signed the certificate. She turned and handed the pen over to Tom. Their fingers brushed and she resisted the urge to linger and enjoy the feel of his skin against hers. Her eyes met his and she gasped at the passion in his gaze. She felt a jolt of electricity, as powerful as lightning, arc between them and she remembered the same feeling rushing through her on the night they'd met.

She had told herself then that the emotion she had seen in his eyes had been a lust for violence and it had frightened her as much as it had thrilled her. Now, she knew him better and she recognised the passion for what it was – a desire for love, not violence. She knew it without a doubt because she felt it too now. She felt as though she was going to burst into flames, so strong was the urge to touch this man, to have him claim her in another kiss.

This only took perhaps a second or two. But it rocked Jeannie to the core. She couldn't look away from him, until someone tapped him on the shoulder, asking him if he had signed yet and could he move on? It brought her back to reality, reminding her where they were and how many people stood within sight and sound of them. The blood drained from her face as shame flooded her. She turned and walked away, her heart shattering as she realised that the one man to draw these feelings from her was the one man she couldn't have.

28

Louisa had no idea what to expect on her wedding night, other than that it would be spent at the Musgroves' home in West End. It wasn't as though they could afford to go away on a honeymoon, and anyway, they would be back at work on Monday morning. She was only grateful that, with the labour shortages due to so many men being away in the trenches, she could carry on working even though she was now a married woman. She would have felt awkward, having to stay at home with her mother-in-law while the rest of the family went to the factory. Of course, once the war ended and the men came back, she might not be able to carry on working, but there seemed to be no end in sight, so she wouldn't worry about it until peace was finally declared.

The rest of their wedding day had been busy, with her and Lucas thanking people for coming and accepting their congratulations. She had blushed as she spoke to people, touched by their sincere good wishes. Even Ma had unwound a little, smiling her thanks to the ladies of the Meeting House who produced a wedding breakfast for everyone to share.

At long last, they were able to escape. They walked back to the cottage at West End. Lucas held her hand all the way, acknowledging greetings from people they passed along the High Street who had heard about their nuptials.

'We could have waited for your ma,' she told him. 'Will she be all right? Won't she be tired?'

Lucas smiled at her. 'She's fine. I haven't seen her this happy in a long time. And anyway, Jeannie and the twins are there to look after her.' He waved at someone else as they passed before glancing back at her. She noticed his cheeks were growing pink. 'She wanted us to have some time to ourselves at home before they all came back,' he said. 'You know... now that we're married.'

Now Louisa felt her own cheeks begin to glow. 'Oh my. She's expecting us to...? Now?'

He laughed. 'I don't know. Probably. We had the most embarrassing conversation last night after everyone else had gone to bed. She said as my pa wasn't around, she needed to tell me things about the private side of marriage, to make sure I could be a good husband.' He blew out a breath. 'I don't know who was more uncomfortable. It's not something I ever expected to discuss with my ma, I can tell you.'

Louisa gaped at him. 'I can imagine.' She giggled. 'I'm sorry. It must have been excruciating for you.'

He shrugged. 'I suppose I should've expected it. Ma takes these things very seriously.' He pulled a face. 'It was hard imagining her and Pa doing the things she talked about, though of course they did, otherwise me and Jeannie and the twins wouldn't be here, would we?'

She giggled again. 'I know what you mean. The thought of my ma and pa doing it... I just can't imagine. Yet, here I am, proof that they did it at least once.'

They laughed together. Louisa was grateful he was taking all this with such good humour. She sobered and slowed her steps. He matched her stride, patient as always as he waited for her to speak.

'Lucas, we've done the right thing, haven't we? I should hate to think you're trapped now because of your desire to help me.'

'Yes,' he said.

'Are you sure?'

He pulled her towards him before dropping her hand and putting his arm around her shoulders and hugging her close to his side. Right there in the middle of the High Street, he kissed her temple. 'I'm sure,' he said. 'You haven't trapped me, Louisa, and I hope I haven't trapped you. Rather, I feel like we've saved each other. We don't have to worry about match-making mothers and having to conform to anyone's expectations but our own now. We can enjoy our friendship and support each other without anyone else having reason to interfere in our lives. We'll have a good life together, I promise.'

Someone whistled and they turned to see a couple of lads from the football team grinning at them and making kissing noises. Louisa blushed and would have stepped away from him, but Lucas held her firm and laughed, calling out to the lads. 'Get on with you, daft lads. A man's entitled to kiss his bride on his wedding day, isn't he?'

'Lucas!' Louisa chided him, pulling on his arm as she started walking again. 'Can we please go before we acquire an even bigger audience?' But she wasn't really scolding him. In fact, she was trying hard not to laugh. He was right. He had saved her, and maybe, given that his true love had been of the forbidden kind in the eyes of the law, she had saved him, too.

A few minutes later, they reached the cottage in West End that would be Louisa's new home. It wasn't as smart as her parents' house on Somerton Road, but it was a happier place and she looked forward to living there with the Musgrove family. Lucas opened the front door, but stopped her as she went to enter.

'Hold on, Mrs Musgrove,' he said, a twinkle in his eye. He tilted his head towards the neighbouring cottages. 'Someone's bound to be watching. I can't let the bride cross the threshold on her own.'

'What are you doing—? Lucas! Put me down,' she squealed as he swung her into his arms. 'Your hand!'

'Hush now,' he said, close to her ear. 'If you're worried I'll drop you, stop fidgeting and let me carry you in quick before my wrist gives way.'

She immediately stopped moving, expecting his weak limb to fail at any moment. 'Well, get on with it then,' she said. 'Before I land on my bottom on the path.'

He stepped through the doorway and kicked the door closed behind him before he gently lowered her feet to the ground. 'Welcome to your new home, Mrs Musgrove.'

Louisa laughed and slapped at his chest. 'You daft so-and-so. You could've put your back out. You know you didn't need to do that.'

He grinned at her. 'Yes, I did. Someone was bound to have been peeking through their curtains, and didn't we agree that, as far as the rest of the world is concerned, this needs to look like a proper marriage?'

They both sobered at his words. 'Yes,' she said softly. 'Sorry, I keep forgetting.'

'I know,' he said, his voice gentle. 'It's not going to be easy for either of us. But people – especially Ma – will be expecting to see us acting like we're... you know...?'

'Doing all that stuff your ma told you about last night?' she suggested, wiggling her eyebrows. She was surprised by how light-hearted she felt about all this. It had worried her that the start of her marriage to Lucas might be overshadowed by the regret that he wasn't Mattie. But, although she still felt a bone-deep sadness that Mattie wasn't here any more, she also felt a strange contentment. Lucas was a good man. He knew all her secrets and didn't hold them against her like her parents had done, and because of his own feelings for Mattie, he possessed a unique understanding of her that no one else in this world ever could. What he'd said earlier about them saving each other seemed to have released something within her, truly setting her free to live the life she now wanted after months and months of hell. She felt comfortable with Lucas and wasn't about to spoil this day, or any other day to come, with regrets. What was done was done. She could only go forward and she wanted to do that with light in her heart, not darkness. She owed that much to Lucas and she knew that Mattie would approve.

He rolled his eyes. 'I should never have told you,' he groaned.

'Yes you should,' she said. 'We're married now and shouldn't have any secrets from each other.' She paused. 'But how are we going to keep the fact that we're not doing... you know... what your ma told you about, from her and the others while we're all living under the same roof?'

He shrugged. 'We'll figure it out. And if anyone is brazen enough to mention it, we can just smile and say nothing. If you can manage to blush at the same time, all the better.' He grinned. 'They can think what they like, can't they?'

* * *

Mrs Musgrove sat with Auntie Betty and some of the older Friends who remained at the Meeting House after most of the guests had gone home. They were no doubt gossiping about the wedding, while Kate and Jeannie helped the ladies from the refreshments committee with the clearing up. The twins were put to work by some of the men, glad to have some young blood with strong backs to help put away the extra chairs that had been brought out to accommodate the visitors who had come to witness Lucas and Louisa's marriage.

Kate grinned when she heard John grumbling as he came past her, a folded wooden chair under each arm.

'Didn't you enjoy your brother's wedding?' she asked, knowing full well he thought any lad paying attention to a lass was daft.

'Can't see why he bothered,' he muttered. 'Now there's another lass at home to nag us. He should've let her go. If I had the choice of staying round here or going to Exeter, I'd be off, I can tell you.'

She chuckled at his morose expression. 'I'll let you in on a secret,' she said. 'If you don't want to be nagged, do as you're told first time round. It makes life a lot easier, you know.'

He scowled at her. 'I'm never getting married,' he declared. 'I'm enlisting as soon as I'm eighteen. I want to see the world, not get tied to an interfering woman.'

Kate narrowed her eyes at him. 'Don't you let me hear you say that around your ma, your brother or your sister, John Musgrove, or I'll box your ears. You know what they've been through, Louisa, too. Don't you dare go upsetting them with talk like that. You promised you'd apply for exemption.'

'Won't make no difference,' he said. 'Hardly anyone like us who applies gets the certificate. Even if they issue it, you're sent to some dead-end job in a factory like your brother-in-law. I've already got a dead-end job in a factory, so why would I bother swapping one for another? I'd die of boredom quicker than any bullet would get me.'

'Well, you're too young to enlist yet, so why aren't you trying to get a better job for yourself like Peter is? You could get on the engineering apprenticeship like him.'

He pulled a face. 'It'll be years before he's earning decent money.'

'But eventually, he'll be one of the highest paid men in the factory.'

'Stuck in the factory forever,' he pointed out. 'That's not for me.' He gave her a sideways look. 'But if you really want to help me, you could get your George's missus to put in a good word for me with her pa. I'd rather be working on the lorries than stuck indoors all the time. George was going to ask for me, but he went away before he managed to get me a job.'

Kate frowned. She knew John had asked George for help, but she had a feeling that Lucas had asked him to hold off for a while in the hope that his brother would settle down at the factory. There was more opportunity for him there than in a small haulage company. But she could see that the lad wasn't inclined to accept that a job at Clarks, though hard, was a darned sight better than other jobs available in these parts.

'I'll see,' she said. 'If only to stop you from doing something stupid like enlisting.'

He nodded and walked away. She stared after him, shaking her head.

'What's he done now?' asked Jeannie, coming up to her.

'Ah, nothing. He's just being his usual self. He's never satisfied, is he?'

Jeannie sighed. 'No, he's not. Even Peter can't seem to get through to him these days. He's a miserable beggar. We're hoping it's just a phase he'll grow out of, because we're sick and tired of him moaning all the time.'

Kate looked around them. Apart from the small group of

Friends with Auntie Betty and Mrs Musgrove, the Meeting House was clear of people. 'We all done?'

Jeannie nodded and sat down on one of the long benches that ran around the sides of the large room. 'It was a lovely wedding, wasn't it?'

Kate smiled and joined her. 'It was. It reminded me of Peg and Will's. It seemed really strange then, but now I understand it a bit more, I think this was just right for Lou, don't you? She'd have hated all the pomp and ceremony of a wedding at Holy Trinity, wouldn't she?'

'I know. I'm not sure her ma appreciated it, though. But at least she came and didn't cause a fuss. Did I tell you, she's getting the train to Exeter tomorrow? The twins went round to her house this morning with a cart to pick up Louisa's things and they said the house is practically empty. There's just some boxes and the last bits of furniture that are being picked up by the movers in the morning, then she'll be gone.'

'That didn't take her long, did it? So that's that. Lou's your sister-in-law, and Mrs Clements is leaving for good.'

Jeannie nodded. 'Apparently, she's bought the house next to her sister's and they're going to take in lodgers. I suppose for women of their age who are widowed, it's as good a way as any to earn a living while keeping a roof over your head. I couldn't see Mrs Clements going back to work at Clarks like Ma and Auntie Betty did when they found themselves on their own, could you?'

'No. Not with all her airs and graces after being married to a foreman,' Kate laughed. 'She'd have hated it. I expect she'll be much better suited to being a landlady, lording it over her lodgers.'

'I'm glad for Louisa's sake that she came to her wedding, though.'

Kate was glad about that, too. She knew it had pleased Louisa that she'd had a family member there today. They might not have totally reconciled, but at least now there was a peace of sorts between them and they would keep in touch. It would have been hard for Lou if her ma had cut off all contact once she left Street.

The twins appeared.

'All done?' asked Jeannie.

They nodded. 'Can we go now?'

Jeannie frowned. 'You're to help me get Ma home, but she's not ready to go yet.'

'When will she be ready?' asked Peter. 'Only we said we'd meet our pals.'

'If you're thinking of going for a kickabout, you'd better not get mud and grass stains on your Sunday best,' she warned them.

'We can run home and get changed first,' said John.

'No!' she said. 'You mustn't go home yet.'

'Why not?' asked John.

Jeannie went red. 'Ma says we're to give the newly-weds some privacy.'

Kate laughed out loud as both lads went even more scarlet than their sister.

'Oh, yuck!' said John, looking disgusted. 'They better not be kissing around the house all the time. I might have to be sick.'

That made Kate laugh even harder and soon Jeannie was giggling beside her. 'One day, you'll want some private time with a lass, John Musgrove,' said Kate, 'and we'll remind you of what you just said.'

His habitual scowl appeared, as she expected it to, but he didn't bother saying anything. He just glared at them.

Peter rolled his eyes. 'So, when are we supposed to go home, then?' he said. 'It'll soon be supper time.'

Jeannie shook her head. 'How can you be hungry after the spread the ladies put on today?'

'I'm a growing lad.' He shrugged. 'I'm always hungry. But you didn't answer my question. How long have we got to wait?'

Jeannie shrugged. 'I don't know. You'd better ask Ma.' The twins turned and walked over to their mother. 'Truth be told,' Jeannie said to Kate under her breath, 'I'm ready to go home myself. We've been so busy thinking about today, I could do with a couple of hours to gather my thoughts and get ready for work tomorrow. I was hoping the twins would've eaten enough at the wedding breakfast that we wouldn't have to bother with supper.'

Kate put an arm around her shoulders and hugged her. 'Don't worry. Someone said they've put some leftovers in a basket for you to take home. You can make a picnic of it.'

'Thank goodness for that,' said Jeannie. 'Although how long Ma will want us to stay here, I've no idea.' She touched her warm cheeks. 'It's so strange, thinking about the two of them back at the cottage.'

'Man and wife?' Kate gave her an amused look.

'Exactly. I don't want to think about my brother and my best friend doing that sort of thing. Do you think John's right and they'll be kissing all around the house now?'

Kate shook her head. 'Of course not. I doubt they'll act any different. Not those two.' Not like when Louisa was with Mattie. It was clear that her relationship with Lucas was... not better or worse, just... different, and probably what she needed now.

Jeannie didn't look convinced. 'It's a strange feeling, you know? I'm delighted that Louisa is my sister-in-law now, but I really don't want to know what she gets up to with my brother.'

Kate tilted her head to one side. 'Mmm. I know what you mean. When my brothers' wives started having babies, and I realised what they had to do to *make* those babies, I was mortified. I could barely look at them for a while. But then Ma pointed out that that's the way of the world. If couples didn't fall in love and get married and have babies, none of us would be here. We have to accept that it's part of life.' She pulled a face. 'I still can't understand how any woman with an ounce of sense at all would want to do *that* with either of my brothers, though.'

This time it was Jeannie who laughed out loud. 'I know exactly what you mean.'

29

At the end of October, Kate's brothers were granted a few days' leave between finishing basic training and being shipped overseas to fight. The siblings, with the exception of Peg, who was still in Lincolnshire, gathered at their mother's grave to finally see her gravestone be installed to replace the wooden cross that had marked her final resting place up until now.

It was a simple memorial, stating her name, dates of birth and death, and the words *Beloved Mother*. Kate laid a small spray of chrysanthemums in front of it.

Kate gazed at the grave with satisfaction tinged with sadness, finally feeling as though Ma could rest in peace. 'I still miss her every single day,' she said quietly.

'We know, love,' said Fred. 'If only we'd known how that devil had been neglecting her... and you as well.'

'It's my fault,' she said. 'I should've told you. But Ma kept saying not to.'

'It's not your fault, lass,' said George. 'It was him. No one else. He held all the power then. But not any more. Ma's at peace, free from him and all the pain he caused her.'

'And you rescued me from him, as well,' she said, her smile sad. 'We might not have been able to save Ma, but you saved me, and I love you both for it. I just wish you didn't have to go off and fight now. Is this awful war ever going to end?'

George and Fred glanced at each other, their expressions grim. 'It looks like we'll be sent to the Somme. They're short on men because the French have had to move so many of theirs to defend Verdun,' said George. 'From what I hear, it's a stinking swamp of mud.'

'Those tanks that Will's been making have helped,' said Fred. 'Frightened the life out of the Hun to start with. But now they're getting bogged down in the mud, and if they're not in range of the German trenches, they're proving useless.'

'Oh, God,' said Kate. 'I can't bear it. I wish we'd been brought up Quakers. You could've both refused to fight and stayed safe.'

George shook his head. 'I can't stay here when there's still a war to fight. I'm not relishing the prospect, that's for sure. But I'll do my bit. Better that than end up in gaol like your man... what's his name?'

'Gerald,' she sighed. 'And he's not my man. He's a friend, that's all. He said it was bad in France, but it sounds like it's getting worse.' She noted their confused expressions. 'He might be refusing to fight, but he's no coward. He volunteered with an ambulance unit back in 1914 and was out there for over a year, caring for the wounded. But the tribunal don't care about that. They just want to force him to pick up a gun, even though it's against his faith. But because he won't give in, they keep locking him up. Mr Clothier says he'll likely be incarcerated for the whole of the war, for however long that lasts.'

'I'm sorry for your friend, Kate,' said Fred. 'But I hope that doesn't mean you're going to take against us for fighting.'

She blinked, surprised. 'Of course not. I know you're doing

what you think is right, just as Gerald is. I just want you both to be safe, that's all. Come home to your wives and babies in one piece.'

'Amen to that,' said George.

The church gate squeaked and they all turned towards it to see the rest of the family, plus Auntie Betty, Jeannie, Louisa and Lucas come through it.

'Don't say anything to Vi or Ada about what we've just said,' Fred told her in a low voice. 'We don't want to frighten them.'

Kate gave him a sideways look, her lips thinned. 'Yet you happily scared the living daylights out of me,' she pointed out.

His smile was a little lopsided as he gave her a one-armed hug. 'Ah, come on. You've taken on the Floozy and lived to tell the tale. Nothing frightens you, our Katie.'

'Hmm,' she huffed. 'I don't know about that. But, don't worry, I'll not say anything. Just promise me you'll both be careful and come home to us alive and kicking.'

'We'll do our best. Now hush and let's concentrate on Ma, eh?' He raised his voice and greeted the others. 'What do you think? A proper marker for Ma at last, God bless her.'

The newcomers gathered around, admiring the stone.

'Ah, that's lovely,' said Auntie Betty. 'She'd be so proud of you for doing this, despite Reggie's meanness.' She glanced around. 'He didn't come with you, then?'

'We didn't ask him, Auntie,' said Kate, raising her chin. 'He wanted nothing to do with it in the first place, so why would we bother with him now? Not that we thought he'd bother to come anyway. He's probably in the Street Inn. I hear he's there more than he's home these days.'

The others nodded in agreement. 'That man's the biggest fool in Somerset, if not the whole world,' said Auntie Betty, shaking her head. 'While you children are a credit to your ma.'

'I see you've put *Beloved Mother* but not mentioned her husband,' said Louisa, studying the stone.

'That's right,' said Kate, raising her chin. 'We agreed, we didn't want any mention of him on it because he doesn't deserve it. But she *was* our beloved mother, and that's how we want people to remember her, even after we're gone. That's why we had it carved into the stone.'

It had cost them extra because every letter and number that the stone mason carved had to be paid for, but it was the least they could do. Anyway, they'd saved money by not having any reference to her husband, so it was all good in the end.

'I'm so pleased you've managed to do this for your ma, Kate,' said Jeannie. 'I'm sure she's up in the light, smiling down on you all. It's just a shame that Peg couldn't be here as well.'

Kate nodded, wishing their sister could have been with them today. But she and Will were as much victims of the war as her brothers – forced to live far from home for as long as the fighting went on. 'I know. She wanted to see it.'

Louisa stepped forward. 'What if I sketch it and send it to her?' she suggested. 'I know it's not the same thing, but it will be a keepsake for her until she gets back to Street.'

'What a lovely idea,' said Ada.

'It is,' said Lucas. 'I remember that little watercolour you sent me of Glastonbury Tor. It reminded me of home the whole time I was away.' He smiled. 'Tom helped me frame it when I got home and it's hanging up at home.'

Louisa laughed. 'It's so small, no bigger than a postcard. I'm going to need to either paint a bigger version, or a lot of other little views so that we can have a gallery on the wall. That little one looks lost and lonely on its own.'

Kate laughed with her, happy that her friend seemed content after just a few weeks of married life. As she had

predicted, Louisa and Lucas didn't seem to act any differently –
there was certainly no kissing in public, although she did take
his arm when they were out walking, but she'd done that sometimes before, so it didn't seem strange. No, it was the way that
Louisa seemed less haunted, less weighed down since her
marriage that made Kate feel that it had been a good thing for
her friend. Of course, it might also be due to the absence of
Louisa's ma, who by all accounts was settling well into life in
Exeter.

'I think we'd better get back, Fred,' said Vi. 'This little man
will be ready for his supper any time.'

Kate saw her brother's stern features soften as he looked at the
baby in his wife's arms. She knew that he'd been disappointed he
hadn't been home when he'd been born a fortnight ago, and that
he was going to miss his growing family while he was away. He
stepped closer to his wife.

'Here, let me carry him,' he said, gently taking the child into
his arms. He kissed his son's forehead. 'Let's get you home, lad.
We don't want to wake up your grandma with your yelling when
you're hungry, do we?'

The others laughed, because the child was such placid baby,
never fussing. Which was just as well, with poor Vi having to cope
with a newborn and a toddler without her husband these days.

The others took their leave, but Louisa remained behind with
Lucas and Jeannie for a few minutes to visit her pa's grave. She
knew that Ma had ordered a gravestone for him before she left,
although it wouldn't be installed until the soil had had a chance
to settle. She didn't know what it would say on the stone; she
would have to wait until it arrived to see.

'I should have brought some flowers,' she said as she gazed at the bare earth.

'We can come back with some soon,' said Lucas.

She nodded, not taking her eyes off her father's final resting place. 'I wonder if the stone Ma ordered has erased me from his life like Kate and her brothers did with their pa.'

'She wouldn't, I'm sure,' said Jeannie. 'I mean, it's not the same thing, is it? Mr Davis is a horrible man who refused to even consider setting a gravestone for his wife.'

Louisa shrugged, feeling sad and weary. 'Ma thinks I'm the monster who killed Pa,' she said softly.

'But you didn't,' said Lucas, his hand on her arm. 'Your pa had a weak heart and worked too hard and too long. It was just bad luck it took him before they could operate on him. It's not your fault, Louisa.'

'He's right,' said Jeannie. 'We all knew your pa got to work before everyone and was the last to leave. He might have helped himself if he hadn't been so conscientious.'

Louisa glanced up, seeing the identical expressions of earnest concern on Lucas's and Jeannie's faces.

'Thank you,' she said, still feeling that lingering guilt, but appreciative of their support. 'He did work too hard, didn't he? Which is ironic really. He was a loyal employee to the Clarks while secretly despising them for not being Anglicans. I sometimes think he worked harder than he needed to, just to cover up his true feelings.' She shook her head. 'He should have moved away, gone to work for somebody else. But he never did, and he was never really happy.'

She shivered. Autumn was well established now. The churchyard was littered with the dried leaves that had fallen from the trees. She thought back to all those months ago, when she had come here in despair to light a candle for Mattie. Kate been at her ma's grave on that day as well and Louisa had confessed her terrible secret. It had been that conversation that had led her to Lincolnshire, where she had borne Mattie's child and given him over to the care of Mattie's brother and sister-in-law. Now she was back, standing at the edge of Pa's grave.

So much lost, she thought. *So much sadness. Yet...* She looked up at her husband and sister-in-law, who both waited patiently at her side. She knew that her marriage wasn't anything like a real one, or anything like she had expected it would have been had she been allowed to marry Mattie. Yet, even in the midst of her memories and her sadness, she felt hope... and even a measure of contentment.

'Let's go home,' she said, turning away from the grave and facing her future.

30

The Battle of the Somme had begun in July. By the end of November it was still raging and thousands upon thousands of men had fallen. The mood in the Machine Room was sombre as mothers, wives and sweethearts received news that their loved ones were wounded – or worse, would never come home.

Jeannie knew that Kate was worried sick about her brothers.

'We don't know that they're at the Somme,' Jeannie tried to reassure her as they warmed themselves with hearty bowls of soup at dinner time. 'They might be somewhere else where the fighting isn't so fierce.'

Kate rolled her eyes. 'It's fierce everywhere, Jeannie. Ask Lucas. Ask Tom. It's a hell of trenches and bomb craters and barbed wire all over Europe.'

'I'm sure the government is trying to negotiate a peace,' said Louisa. 'At least, I hope to God they are. This has gone on long enough. They can't let many more men die, otherwise we'll end up with none left.'

The three of them were silent for a moment. Jeannie shuddered to think what would happen if peace wasn't declared soon.

How many more lads like Mattie and Ted's brother Albert were going to be taken from those who loved them before this madness ended? And what if they lowered the conscription age? The twins would be sixteen in January. There would be no hope for Ma if they were sent off to fight. She would simply give up. She had barely survived the months that Lucas had been away. All Jeannie could do was pray that the war was over by the time they got to eighteen and that the government didn't decide to lower the age for conscription.

'I suppose we should be grateful that Lucas is home for good,' she said.

'And Tom,' said Louisa, nudging shoulders with her.

Jeannie looked away from her sister-in-law's teasing smile. 'Of course I'm glad he no longer has to fight. I'd feel the same about any lad we know and even those we don't. I still pray day and night that this awful war will end soon and the world can live in peace again.'

When both Louisa and Kate raised their eyebrows at her, she huffed. 'You know I can't think anything else as far as Tom's concerned. He's not free.'

Their expressions softened and she hated that she could see the pity they felt for her on their faces.

'Don't be feeling sorry for me,' she said, glaring at them.

'We feel sorry for both of you,' said Kate, blunt as ever. 'He's as sweet on you as you are on him.'

Jeannie sighed. 'It doesn't matter. We can't do anything about it. He's legally tied to another woman and I'll not live in sin like some folks do.' She was thinking of Kate's pa and the Floozy. That woman had a husband and had still had relations with Reggie Davis, a married man. She would never do something so wicked, even if Tom was the innocent party in all this. The hopelessness of the situation made her heart ache, but there was nothing to be done about it. She raised her chin. 'Anyway, someone else asked if I'd walk out with him.'

'What?' both girls cried at the same time. 'Who?' asked Kate.

She wished she hadn't said anything. Now she'd have to tell them. 'Cyril. You know – old Mr Baker's grandson who's teaching at the board school.'

Louisa's eyes widened. 'Not Douglas's cousin?'

She nodded. That was just one of the reasons why she was reluctant to say yes. 'He's not as sneaky as Douglas, though. He doesn't need to trick anyone to get his exemption. He's already got it on account of his asthma, as well as being a teacher. He tried to enlist, but they wouldn't have him.'

Kate pulled a face. 'He's a bit of a weed, though, isn't he? Do you really prefer him over Tom?'

Of course she didn't, but she didn't have a lot of choice, did she? She shrugged. 'It doesn't matter who I prefer if he's not free, does it?' The question came out sharper than usual, but she was tired of talking about something she couldn't change. 'And Cyril might not be as tall or well-built as Tom, but he seems nice and he's free to court me if that's what I want.'

Louisa touched her arm. 'But is it what you want, Jeannie?' she asked gently.

She sighed again. It wasn't, any more than she suspected Louisa wouldn't have chosen to marry Lucas if Mattie had still been alive. But her friend was making the best of her life and seemed content, as did Lucas, although he must know that he was second best. 'No, it isn't. I told him so. But maybe I should. After all, with so many lads away fighting, there's not a lot of choice, is there?'

Kate looked thoughtful. 'But he's not a Friend and we can see you don't fancy him. You don't have to settle, Jeannie. You'll be miserable, like you were with Douglas in the end. You knew you weren't going to fall in love with him but you didn't want to hurt him, did you? We don't want you to end up in the same boat with Cyril.'

Jeannie looked up at the ceiling, wishing she could argue with Kate. But she couldn't. Her friend was right. When Douglas had declared undying love, she'd felt trapped. When she'd caught him canoodling with Doris Lambert, she'd been relieved. 'You're right. I don't know what to do. I don't want to end up an old maid.'

'You won't,' said Louisa.

'Of course you won't,' said Kate. 'But you can do better than him.' She paused. 'Aren't you writing to some of the conscientious objectors, like I am?'

She nodded. 'They seem nice, but I don't really know any of them, do I?'

Kate shrugged. 'But you have your faith in common with them, and you admire their courage to stand by it. You're getting to know them through their letters. Who's to say one of them isn't the one for you? Perhaps the Clothiers will invite them to visit when they get out of gaol and you'll get to meet them like I did Gerald.'

Jeannie frowned. 'Are you telling me you've got feelings for Gerald?'

Kate looked startled, her gaze darting between Jeannie and Louisa, who was smiling and watching her with interest.

'He's my friend, that's all. I don't think of him like that,' she denied. 'Nor do I think he regards me as anything but a friend. How many times do I have to tell you? I don't want any man.' She stood up abruptly. 'Are you finished? I am. We should get back.' She picked up her bowl and spoon and walked away from the table.

'Have I upset her?' asked Jeannie, watching her go.

Louisa shook her head. 'No. But you know what she's like. She wants you to be happy with someone you love, but she'll fight until her last breath against the idea that she needs a man to make her own life complete.'

They rose and followed her. Kate had been stopped by Mrs Howard, the biggest gossip in the Machine Room, and the older woman was talking to her.

'Oh, lord,' said Louisa. 'What does she want with Kate?'

They hurried over, worried by the look on Kate's face. Mrs Howard wasn't a very nice person, always gossiping and picking on the younger women and girls. She'd been the only one who'd suggested that Louisa might be pregnant when she'd fainted at the factory and then disappeared to Lincolnshire for a few months. Of course, she hadn't been able to prove it, and as her husband worked in the Clicking Room where Louisa's pa had been his foreman, she hadn't dared spread the rumour for fear of making life difficult for her own family. These days, the three friends kept out of her way, which was why it was worrying that she had cornered Kate.

'Maybe it's something to do with Kate's pa,' Jeannie suggested before they reached them.

As they got closer, Mrs Howard's voice rang out loud and clear. 'I'm telling you, my lad had a couple of days' leave behind the lines and he swears he saw Ted Jackson, as clear as day, through the window of a house. He was with some lass.'

'Maybe it was someone who looked like Ted,' said Kate.

Mrs Howard shook her head, looking pleased with herself. 'It was him. He heard him laugh.'

Ted had a distinctive laugh – deep and rich and one of those sounds that made you smile.

Kate shrugged. 'That must have been nice for him, to see someone from home.'

Mrs Howard sneered. 'He was right cosy with that lass, I'm

told. And when my lad knocked to say hello, Ted pretended he didn't know him. Talked foreign, he did.'

'Well, there you are. It couldn't have been Ted. It was probably some local man who looked like him.'

She shook her head. 'You don't get it, do you? All the local lads in those parts are either dead or away fighting. No, it had to be Ted. But he was trying to hide, didn't want my lad to talk to him.'

'You said he was talking foreign?' asked Louisa.

'He was. Dressed like a local, too, mind.' She crossed her arms over her ample chest, her gaze never leaving Kate's. 'Must have deserted. That would explain why he didn't want my lad recognising him. If he's caught, he'll be shot like the coward he is.' She cackled. 'Ironic, ain't it? His ma handing out white feathers, while her own son's hiding behind some foreign woman's skirts.'

Jeannie gasped. 'I don't believe it,' she said. 'Not Ted.'

Kate glared back at Mrs Howard. 'That's a wicked thing to say, Mrs H. Imagine if someone said that about one of your lads? It was probably a case of mistaken identity. Some poor local, come home on leave to see his family, and you're spreading poison about one of our brave lads. What are Mr and Mrs Jackson going to say when they hear you've been telling lies about their son and condemning him without any proof? Because they'll know it was you – I'll make sure to tell them.'

Mrs Howard stepped back. Jeannie didn't know what the woman had expected when she'd caught up with Kate, but she should have known that the lass wouldn't appreciate what she had to say. She smiled behind her hand, seeing Mrs Howard go pale. The Jacksons were influential people. Ted's pa was another foreman, as well as a leading light at Holy Trinity and Mrs Jackson was a fierce woman.

It was Kate's turn to sneer. 'You haven't told them what you've heard, have you?' she said, loud and clear, making sure the growing crowd around them could hear her. 'You didn't have the decency to go round and talk to them when you heard from your lad that he thought he'd seen their son. You're happy to gossip and slander people, but you haven't got the guts to talk to the people whose kin you're speaking ill of, have you? You should be ashamed of yourself. Well, I'll go and tell them what you're saying and you can face the consequences. Maybe then you'll learn to keep your nasty opinions to yourself.'

At the back of the crowd, someone started clapping as Kate turned on her heel and marched out of the canteen with Jeannie and Louisa behind her. By the time they reached the door, others had joined in. Jeannie looked over her shoulder and saw people sneering at Mrs Howard, who looked furious.

As they made their way back to the Machine Room, Jeannie and Louisa linked arms with Kate. She was shaking.

'Well said, Katie girl,' said Louisa. 'I'm proud of you for standing up to that witch. Did you hear how people reacted? She's a laughing stock now and you're a heroine. She's made no friends with all her horrible gossip over the years.'

Kate shook her head but didn't say anything. Jeannie began to fret. The look on Mrs Howard's face didn't bode well.

'Are you going to see Mr and Mrs Jackson?' she asked Kate as they began to climb the stairs up to the Machine Room.

Kate sighed and nodded. 'I'll go on my way home, although I've a feeling Mr Jackson will hear about it before the end of our shift anyway, don't you?'

Sure enough, within the hour, Mr Jackson arrived and had words with Mr Briars before they both approached Mrs Howard. Every eye in the place watched as she was escorted out of the Machine Room.

* * *

Kate kept her head down, not wanting to get involved in the buzz of gossip going round. She didn't care whether the woman was going to get into trouble for her poisonous tongue. She certainly deserved to. Kate didn't care that she would probably blame her if she did and would do her best to make her life a misery from now on. No, what was occupying Kate's mind as she focused with fierce concentration on her work were thoughts of Ted.

Since he'd left Street eighteen months ago, she'd heard nothing of him, nobody had. She'd tried to ask his ma about him a couple of times, but she'd just sneered at her, as though a girl like Kate wasn't good enough for her son and wasn't entitled to any information about his well-being since he'd broken up with her before he'd gone away.

It had bothered Kate because, after all the shameful drama with Pa and the Floozy, she had been inclined to agree with the woman – maybe she *wasn't* good enough for a decent lad like Ted Jackson. But then she got angry, reminding herself of what Auntie Betty had said – that she was as good as any other lass, honest and hard-working, and didn't deserve to be treated that way by either Ted or his ma. And in the midst of her churning emotions, Kate couldn't deny the lingering hurt she felt at Ted's abrupt abandonment of her.

She had tried to forget him. She had focused on living a good life away from Pa and the Floozy; on corresponding with the poor lads who had been gaoled for their faith in a peaceful solution to conflict rather than causing more bloodshed; and on fulfilling her promise to her beloved ma to erect a proper gravestone to mark her final resting place. She had done all that. She hadn't needed a man. She had her friends and Auntie Betty, who was like a second ma to her. Yet... the moment she remembered Ted, all the good things in her life seemed insignificant against her feelings of rejection and hurt.

Even more surprising was the fact that, when Mrs Howard had first mentioned that her son had seen Ted with his own eyes, she had felt a welling up of hope inside her. After months and months with no news about him, someone was telling her that Ted was alive and well – and laughing.

Her heart skipped a beat as she remembered his laugh and how it had always made her feel happy. She knew as soon as Mrs H had mentioned it that she was right – it must have been Ted, even though she'd denied it loudly in the canteen. And what she said about him talking foreign struck a chord as well. Before he'd left, Ted had been learning Dutch and French from one of the Belgian refugees who had come to Street at the beginning of the war. Ted had a gift for mimicry and a sharp mind that meant he could learn things quickly.

But what did that mean? If he had been seen in a house, with a woman no less, and not in uniform... no. She refused to believe he would be a deserter. Not Ted. He might be daft sometimes, but he wasn't a complete fool. He'd enlisted in order to save his own brother from being shot as a deserter. He'd somehow managed to persuade the officer who came to visit his parents that his poor, broken brother Stan deserved to be treated with compassion and sent to an asylum rather than face a firing squad after witnessing their older brother Albert's death in the trenches. No, Ted wouldn't desert, not after all that, no matter what.

'Kate!' Louisa's voice broke through her dark thoughts, startling her. She yelped as she barely managed to avoid catching her fingers under the needle and her line of stitching went haywire.

'What?' she snapped, turning towards Louisa. 'Oh!' Behind her friend stood Mr Jackson.

'Can I have a word please, Miss Davis?' he asked. 'In private.'

Kate glanced at her friends, who both looked worried. She didn't dare glance around the Machine Room, knowing that every eye would be on her. Instead, she nodded and switched off her machine before she followed Mr Jackson to a small office off the main room which only managers and foremen used. As he closed the door behind her, Kate turned towards him, suddenly scared when she saw his solemn expression.

'Is everything all right, Mr Jackson?' she asked, not sure if she really wanted to know the answer.

He nodded. 'Nothing to worry about, lass. But also nothing I want anyone else to hear. I'd appreciate your word that nothing we discuss here will be repeated to anyone. Can you promise me that?'

She had no idea what this was all about, although it was reasonable to suspect that it was something to do with her altercation with Mrs Howard. But, whatever it was, she could see from his expression that he wouldn't say anything until she'd given her word. 'I promise,' she said.

He took a seat at the battered wooden desk and indicated she should take a seat opposite. 'Thank you. Right. I understand you had words with Mrs Howard this dinner time.'

'I did, sir. She was saying awful things about your Ted. I told her she shouldn't and that if she had any news of him, she should tell you and Mrs Jackson and not go spreading nasty lies about him. I was going to come round and tell you after work, but I suppose someone from your department must have told you.'

He sighed. 'They did. So I came right over here to find out what it was all about. I've heard two different versions of it so far. Would you tell me yours?'

Kate explained what had happened and how Mrs Howard had assumed that Ted was a deserter. 'I told her it was nonsense and it probably wasn't even Ted but rather some foreign man who looked like him and she shouldn't say such things because it was wicked and wrong. I know Ted wouldn't desert. He just wouldn't.'

Mr Jackson's stern face softened and he offered her a gentle smile. 'Thank you for that, Kate. I appreciate that you defended my son when he wasn't there to do it for himself. His ma will appreciate it as well.' He sighed. 'But she's not going to be best pleased when she hears what that woman has been saying.'

Kate didn't know what to say to that. She wouldn't blame Mrs Jackson if she blew her top. She knew she'd felt like slapping the woman, and she was only a lass who'd walked out with Ted for a few months. His own mother would be furious and, like Mrs Howard, she wasn't a woman you'd want to cross.

'Anyhow,' he went on. 'I've had words with Mrs Howard and if she persists in spreading untruths about my boy, she'll have to deal with the consequences.'

'I wouldn't say anything like that about Ted, Mr Jackson,' said Kate.

'I know, lass.' He held up a hand. 'I didn't bring you in here to reprimand you, but rather to thank you. I know you were upset when Ted ended it between you. You could have let that woman spread her poison and done nothing and I'd understand it. But instead, you stood up to her and I thank you for that. She's a difficult woman. It's common knowledge she picks on the younger women and girls and I appreciate you've put yourself in her path for Ted's sake.'

Kate shrugged, feeling embarrassed by his thanks. 'I just did what was right. She shouldn't have said what she did and I couldn't let her slander Ted.'

'Well, if you have trouble with her, you must let me know. I'll ask Mr Briars to keep an eye on her as well.'

She looked down at her clasped hands, grateful for his concern, but unconvinced that it would stop the woman from coming after her. 'I'll be fine,' she said, raising her chin. 'I won't let bullies win. I had enough of that in my own house after Ma died. I'll not take any more now I've escaped from that.'

'Ah, I heard. I'm sorry you went through that, lass. I know Ted admired your fortitude. He'd have liked to have helped you, but... well... events overtook him.'

She closed her eyes for a moment, remembering how hard the loss of his brothers, one to a bullet, the other to madness, had affected Ted. They'd comforted each other in their grief and after he'd gone, she'd never felt more alone in her whole life.

'Mr Jackson,' she said, her voice shaking a little. 'Can you tell me, please – is Ted all right? I mean, no one has heard from him all this time and we're all worried. I know he said he didn't want to keep in touch, but... I'd really like to know he's alive and well. All his friends would.'

He looked stern for a moment and she thought he was going to tell her to mind her own business, like his wife had when she'd asked. She bit her bottom lip to stop it from quivering. She wouldn't cry like some pathetic girl if he refused to tell her. But when he noticed her action, his stance softened again.

'He is, lass. At least, we haven't been told otherwise thus far, so we're putting our trust in God that he's safe and well. We get the odd message from him, but he's not the best correspondent. However, that's to be expected.' He studied her face for a moment, no doubt noting her reaction at his words.

'I'm glad,' she said, unable to stop her relieved smile.

'Thank you, lass,' he said. 'Look, I can't tell you much, but I will tell you this – and I trust you to keep it to yourself. Can you do that?'

She nodded, desperate for any news of Ted.

'I have no idea whether the man the Howard lad saw was our Ted or not. It might have been, but it probably wasn't. It could have been anyone, and I'd not rely on anything that daft lad has to say, any more than I'd believe his mother. No, all I know is that Ted is somewhere in Europe, and he's attached to a special unit, not a regular battalion. He most certainly *isn't* a deserter. He's like every other lad from around here, fighting for king and country, and if it pleases God, he'll be home one day, able to hold his head high and get on with his life in peace.'

Kate walked quickly back to her machine after Mr Jackson left, her heart singing with happiness at the knowledge that Ted was alive. She knew it was no guarantee he would remain safe, not while this horrible war raged across Europe. But she was content to know that, right now, as far as his pa knew, he was. Despite how he'd treated her at the end, she didn't wish him ill. She could understand that it would be easier for him to cut his ties and not look back, especially if he knew he was going into this *special unit* that Mr Jackson mentioned. She would continue to pray for Ted – for despite all her denials, she had never forgotten him – as well as her dear brothers. She wanted them all to be able to come home safe and well at the end of the war. Even if Ted chose not to, she would have to be content that he was living his life the way he wanted to.

31

November slipped into December. Mrs Howard kept her own counsel and, apart from glaring at Kate, she didn't bother her.

Kate's pa, however, had no such restraint. Every time he saw her, he hurled abuse at her, demanding money or that she move back into his house and do her duty as his daughter. She knew he didn't want her back because he had any fond feelings for her, but rather that the Floozy and their children were doing nothing other than wrecking the place and contributing nothing to the household. Kate soon learned to be vigilant and to run in the opposite direction the moment she spotted him.

But when he did finally catch her unawares on the High Street between the factory gates and the Friends' Meeting House one day, grabbing her by the scruff of her neck and hair from behind, she was helpless to stop him.

'Let me go!' she screamed, grabbing at her hair as he pulled her backwards, keeping her off balance.

There were few people around, but those that were – women and young lads mostly – moved out of their way. Despite Kate's obvious distress, none of them wanted to tackle Reggie Davis.

'Help me!' Kate cried.

'Let her go, man, you can't manhandle a lass like that,' said one old man, but he backed off as soon as Pa turned his rheumy-eyed gaze on him.

Satisfied that no one would challenge him, he pulled Kate's hair even harder, making her scream again. 'Shut up, you little mare,' he snarled. 'You're coming home with me. I've had enough of that witch and her whiny brats. You'll clean up their mess and cook me a decent meal.'

'I'll not be their skivvy,' she cried, fighting with all her strength to get away from him, but he had a tight grip on her and she couldn't escape.

'No, you'll be *mine*,' he told her, his mouth close to her face, his rancid breath making her gag. 'Now shut up and give me your purse.'

'No!' she shouted, turning her face away from him and clinging to her bag with one hand while trying to stop him pulling her hair out by the roots as he dragged her along. 'Get away from me! Someone call the constable!'

'I said shut up!' he roared, raising a fist to punch her.

She closed her eyes and flinched away from the expected blow, but it never came. There was a yell and a thud, then Pa's hands released her as he fell backwards onto his backside. Other hands caught her when she would have fallen too, pulling her away from him and against a solid chest.

'You're all right, Kate,' a voice reassured her. 'I've got you safe.'

She opened her eyes and looked up into Tom's grim face. He was looking over her head to where Pa was cussing and struggling with someone.

'Leave her alone, you monster! You're not fit to touch her. You hear me?' The shout was accompanied by another thud. 'See how you like it.'

Kate gasped as she recognised the voice. She twisted round to see Peter Musgrove straddling Pa's chest and arms, his fist raised to deliver another blow.

Through the gathering crowd, Auntie Betty rushed forward, grabbing Peter's hand before he could punch Pa again. 'That's enough, lad. You've made your point.'

He tried to shake her off, but she was having none of it, clinging to his arm with both of hers. 'He was hitting her and dragging her,' Peter told her, his voice shaking with the anger that seemed to give him super-human strength. 'He was hurting a girl and trying to rob her. He should be locked up.'

'Get off me, you little runt,' Pa snarled, arching his back and trying to dislodge him. Blood poured from his nose and his eye was swelling.

But, young though he was, Peter was tall for his age and no lightweight. Pa might have been heavier-built than the lad, but years of cider-drinking and tobacco-smoking had rendered him useless against the anger of a younger and fitter man.

Auntie Betty, still hanging onto Peter's arm, glared down at the older man. 'For once in your life, Reggie Davis, do as you're told and shut that foul mouth of yours. Someone's gone for the constable, so if you don't want to spend time behind bars, you'd better calm down right now. You too, Peter. I know you were defending Kate, but you've done your job. It's time to put your hackles down.'

Peter looked down at his captive. 'I won't hit him again, but I'm not letting him go until the constable arrives. He's not safe to be around his own daughter.' He looked up at Betty. 'He was dragging her by her hair, Auntie. I had to stop him.'

Those who had been witness to the attack agreed, telling others who were gathering to view the spectacle how Reggie Davis had mistreated his own flesh and blood.

Kate watched, shaken by the suddenness of the attack and her helplessness. She realised she was still clinging to Tom and took a step back. He released her immediately. 'Thank you,' she whispered.

He gave her a brief nod, watching carefully to make sure she wasn't going to collapse without his arms around her. But he seemed to have understood her need to stand on her own two feet and not lean on someone, and he let her be.

She walked over and stood next to Auntie Betty.

'Let me up!' shouted Pa. 'It's bloody cold on my back. You can't make an old man lie on the ground in this weather.'

Kate hadn't even noticed the December cold. It was probably because her heart was still beating nineteen to the dozen. Now, the bitter wind cut through her, making her shiver.

'No,' said Peter. He sounded so firm and no-nonsense that he seemed older than his years. 'You can't be trusted. You'll run off like the coward you are.'

Tom stepped forward. 'We can let him up, Peter. Between us, we can restrain him until the constable arrives.'

Peter looked unsure but Tom's steady gaze seemed to reassure him and he reluctantly got off the old man and jumped to his feet. Before Pa could make any moves, he and Tom hooked an arm under his and pulled him up between them. Tom grabbed the collar of his jacket, pulling it down his back, trapping Pa's arms. He cursed and struggled, but Tom had effectively put Pa into a straitjacket.

'Get off me,' he snarled at Tom, who looked unimpressed by the menace in Pa's voice. 'You'll regret this.'

Tom shrugged. 'I don't think it'll be me regretting this. You've attacked a young woman in front of all these witnesses.' He indicated the growing crowd. 'And been bested by a fifteen-year-old lad.'

'That's right,' said Auntie Betty. 'But then again, you always did pick on those weaker than you, didn't you Reggie? You're pathetic, nothing but a disgraceful bully, a coward and a thief.'

'Why you—' He made a lunge for her. Kate screamed, reaching out to protect Betty, but he didn't get anywhere near her. Tom yanked him back and away from the women.

Auntie Betty chuckled, not at all bothered by his attempted attack. 'They've got you good and proper, Reggie. You might as well give up.'

'You're the thief!' he yelled at her, spittle spraying from his mouth. Kate's stomach churned with revulsion. 'She's *mine!* She should be home with me, looking after *me* and handing over her wages! But you took her away and take the money from her now. You're robbing my daughter, don't deny it. I want you arrested!'

Rage filled Kate. She stepped forward, no longer afraid to get up close. She stood toe to toe and glared up at him. 'Betty looks after me and I pay her a fair rent,' she told him, her voice loud and clear. 'You're the only thief I know, Pa. You've taken more than your share of everything, including my own dear ma's life when you were too mean to let us get a doctor to her. You're the thief who stole our trust, carrying on with that floozy behind everyone's back, then moving her into Ma's home before she was barely cold in her grave. You wouldn't even give Ma a gravestone; her children had to see to that. If you'd have been a decent man, I'd have stayed and looked after you, but you weren't and that woman of yours is even worse because she's a liar and a cheat as well. And now you're stuck with her and the children you created with her and it's no more than you deserve.' Her voice rose as all her anger poured out of her. 'You're a horrible excuse of a man and I hope you rot in hell!'

Pa looked stunned as the crowd cheered and applauded before

they parted to let two constables through to where the little group stood. Kate turned away from her father, but not before she noted with satisfaction that Peter – little Peter who she'd known since he was a baby – had bestowed a splendid black eye on him and probably broken his nose. She stood quietly beside Auntie Betty while Tom calmly explained what had happened to the officers. No one took any notice of Reggie Davis's loud complaints, other than to tell him to shut up. Kate nodded to confirm that she agreed with Tom and Peter's version of events, as did a number of the onlookers. She also quietly mentioned to one of the officers that she had left home with the help of Mr Roger Clark when her brothers had confronted Pa about stealing all of her wages and letting his mistress and her children mistreat her. The mention of the Clark name, plus the fact that the younger officer knew her brothers through the football club, persuaded them to take Pa away to the station to prepare charges of assault, attempted theft and kidnapping against him. They assured her he would not be given his liberty before he'd been brought before the magistrate, if at all.

After he had been marched off, Kate sighed. As the crowd dispersed, no doubt in a hurry to spread the word of the Davises' latest humiliation, she turned to Tom and Peter.

'Thank you,' she said.

'You're heroes, both of you,' said Auntie Betty, hugging each of them. 'You saved our girl.'

Tom smiled. 'Glad to help. I can't abide men who treat women like that.'

Kate couldn't help the hysterical little giggle that escaped her. 'You're making a habit of it, Tom – first Jeannie, now me. And you were so brave, Peter. None of the others who were watching had the nerve to jump on Pa.'

Peter's chest puffed out, his expression earnest. 'I had to do something. I'm not sorry I hit him. He's got no call to go treating you like that.'

Kate smiled. 'You gave him a splendid black eye, did you notice? Only don't go acting too pleased about it around your ma and Jeannie. You know how they hate violence.'

His cheeks went bright red. 'But I didn't start it,' he said. 'I was defending you.'

'I know.' She put a hand on his arm and reached up to kiss his cheek, making his face glow even brighter. 'They'll understand. And I'll be forever grateful.'

'Now be off with you, Peter,' said Auntie Betty. 'Get on home, lad. Your ma will be wondering where you are. You don't want her to hear about this from anyone else.'

He nodded and took off running back up the High Street. They turned to Tom, who was chuckling quietly as he watched the lad disappear up the road. 'He spotted your pa sneaking after you and insisted we come and make sure you were safe. I'm glad we did. I've never seen him move so fast when Reggie grabbed you, not even on the football field. He didn't even hesitate.'

Auntie Betty beamed. 'Ah, bless him. I think he might be a little sweet on Kate.'

She gaped at them as Tom nodded. 'Don't be daft. He's just a boy.'

'A boy who's keen to grow up,' he said, sobering a little. 'He probably won't do anything about his feelings as he'll be too embarrassed. But if he does declare himself, let him down gently, won't you?'

Kate sighed. 'I will. He did a brave thing today. But if he hadn't caught Pa unawares, he'd have knocked seven bells out of him. You'd better warn him to watch his back from now on. Pa won't like to have been bested by a young lad.'

32

At the Musgrove home, Lucas told his brother he was proud of him when Peter related the events of Reggie Davis's attack. Jeannie rushed off to Betty Searle's cottage in The Mead to make sure Kate and her landlady really were all right and Ma and John sat Peter down to tell them again what had happened – his mother wanting to make sure he wasn't hurt or in trouble with the law, his twin keen to get every salacious detail so that he could share in the glory of his brother's triumph over a well-known drunkard and bully.

Lucas realised that in all the excitement, Louisa had slipped away to their room. He climbed the stairs. As he usually did, he knocked quietly before entering. Neither wanted to catch their spouse unawares or cause each other embarrassment. It had been hard enough getting used to having to share a room and a bed together.

'Louisa? Are you all right?' he asked when he found her curled up on the bed. 'Are you ill?'

'No,' she said, her voice muffled against the pillow. 'Can you get Jeannie for me?'

He sat on the edge of the mattress, concerned that she wasn't looking at him. 'She's gone to Kate's. Did you want to go with her?'

She shook her head. 'I can't... I...' She sighed. 'I need her to help with something.'

'Can I help?' he asked.

She shook her head again. 'It's a girl thing.'

'Shall I get Ma?'

'No!' She turned then and he was surprised to see the panic in her eyes. 'Please don't say anything to her.'

'I won't if you don't want me to,' he said, keeping his voice gentle, trying to calm her. 'Are you sure I can't help you? What's wrong?' He noticed that her cheeks were flushed even though her skin was generally paler than usual. Her eyes were dull with pain. He touched her forehead with the back of his hand. She didn't seem to have a fever, but she was clearly not herself. 'Do you need a doctor?'

She closed her eyes and shook her head. 'I'm not ill. I've just got my monthlies.'

'Ah.' He didn't know a lot about them, but he wasn't completely ignorant, having lived with two females all his life. She would be needing some rags. 'I'm sure Ma can help.'

She grabbed his arm when he would have stood up. 'Please don't tell her,' she said. 'You don't understand.'

He sat back down again and she gave a sigh of relief. 'Then will you explain it to me?' he asked. 'You get on with her, don't you?'

'Of course I do. Your ma is lovely. She's been nothing but kind to me. It's just... well, I think she's hoping I'll be expecting.'

It took him a moment to work out what she meant. He felt his cheeks flush with embarrassment as she went on.

'When she realised it was my time last month, she told me not to worry, that it might take a month or two and that I'd soon be with child. I'm sure if I tell her I'm bleeding again, she'll start giving me advice and being all sympathetic, and I'm not sure I can cope with it.'

Lucas scrubbed a hand down his face. 'Oh lord. I'm so sorry, Louisa. I should have realised she'd be thinking about grandchildren as soon as we were wed.' He paused. 'Maybe we should tell her the truth so she doesn't get her hopes up?'

Louisa closed her eyes. 'I hate to lie to her, but I'm not sure I can bear her disappointment if we confessed the truth.' She looked up at him. 'Can we wait a little longer? After all, it takes a while for some couples, doesn't it? Look at Peg and Will.'

'I know what you mean,' he said. 'I'm sorry, Louisa. I had no idea she would be so keen for us to...' He shrugged. 'Hopefully the news that our Peter is a hero will take her mind off it for a while.'

Louisa gave him a grateful smile. 'No doubt there'll be plenty of lasses showing an interest in him now he's shown his worth.'

He groaned. 'I suppose we should be grateful it wasn't John, although he'll no doubt try and jump on Peter's shirt-tails and grab some of the glory, especially if it attracts the lasses. If he'd been the one to get the better of Reggie Davis, we'd never hear the end of it.'

Louisa laughed softly, her expression clearing a little. 'Not that giving Kate's pa a black eye and a bloody nose is that much of an achievement. It was bound to happen sooner or later. If anyone deserves it, he does. I'm surprised no one has done it before now.'

Lucas smiled, relieved that she seemed to be perking up a little. 'We'll let Peter have his moment of glory, though, if only to distract Ma. Now, I won't say anything to her, but what can I do to help?'

She confirmed it was rags she needed. He nodded. 'I know where they keep them. I'll get you some without her seeing. But...'

He hesitated. 'You know she'll be keeping an eye on us, don't you? I'm sorry if it makes things awkward for you, Louisa. I didn't think. If it gets too much, you must say and I'll have a word with her.'

She nodded. 'Maybe we could hint that it's not happening as easily as she thinks it should. I mean, my ma struggled to have me. I think she lost a few babies before I was born.'

Lucas hadn't known that. He'd often wondered why Louisa was an only child. He'd assumed that, as Mrs Clements was a bit of a cold fish, they just hadn't been inclined to have marital relations after their first child was born. But what did he know about such things? He felt a pang of sympathy for his mother-in-law. It must have been hard for her. However, it was clear from the fact that Louisa had fallen pregnant with Mattie's child that she didn't suffer the same problems as her ma. He wanted to ask Louisa whether she thought her ma resented how easily her daughter had fallen, but he didn't want to remind her of what she'd had to give up. He felt a wave of sadness wash over him as he remembered the child.

'Lou,' he began, touching her shoulder. 'Do you regret it? Not being able to have another babe?'

She looked away. 'I don't know. Sometimes I don't. Sometimes I do. Another child would never replace little Mattie, and my heart aches when I think of him, I miss him so much.' She took a deep breath and straightened her spine. 'But I know he's in the best place with people who love him dearly, so I mustn't be selfish and wish it were otherwise.' She sighed and looked at him. 'And then again, I see women with their children and wish I could have at least one that would call me mother, who I can hold and love without any secrets or lies.'

'Aw, come here.' He lay next to her and pulled her into his arms and held her, wishing he could take away her pain. They remained like that for a long moment. It felt good to hold her. He'd noticed that, while they always went to sleep with their backs to each other, both of them clinging to the edge of the mattress so as not to encroach on the other's space, they more often than not awoke with their arms around each other, with Lou's head on his shoulder. It was as though they found comfort together in their dreams. They had both been horrified the first time it had happened, but they'd gradually got used to it and now they laughed about it, even though they still didn't cuddle as they went to sleep.

'I expect other people will start to comment when I don't end up expecting,' she said. 'I hope they don't make things awkward for you either.'

He shrugged. 'I'm not worried about that. But... if you ever feel like you *would* like a baby,' he said, his voice hesitant. 'Well, I wouldn't want to deny you the chance to be a ma again, so you must say.'

She leaned back and looked up at him, clearly surprised. 'You mean...?'

He felt his face begin to burn, but he held her gaze and nodded. 'If you need me to be a real husband, I'd be willing. But I'd never force you. That's not why I married you. I just want you to have the chance, if you're ever ready, to have another child. I can't bring your first-born back to you, but I won't see you denied.'

'But... I didn't think you'd want to, you know? You don't find lasses attractive, do you?'

He grimaced. 'I don't know. I like you well enough, and it's no hardship to give you little kisses and hold your hand when other folk are around. But neither have I ever felt drawn to another man apart from Mattie. He was it for me. No one else, man or woman.'

She sighed and nodded. 'It's the same for me. It's like he spoilt us for anyone else. Not that I regret loving him. It's just such a waste of all our lives, isn't it?'

'We can't think like that,' he said, stroking her cheek. 'I hate that he's gone, but we're not and we're still young. We've a lot of years ahead of us, and if you want to be a mother again, I'll do what I can to make it happen.'

Her eyes filled with tears. 'Thank you, Lucas. I... I'm not ready right now. I'm not sure if I'll ever be. But I appreciate that you're willing to grant me my wish if ever that day comes.'

'Then we'll be content with that.'

33

The resignation of Herbert Asquith, and the appointment of David Lloyd George as Prime Minister at the beginning of December sent a wave of optimism across the country that the new head of government would bring an end to the war. Mr Lloyd George was previously the war secretary and a well-known hawk. Many felt that he would ensure that the Allies would prosecute such a fierce campaign that the Hun would soon capitulate.

By the start of January 1917, Jeannie wasn't so sure. To her mind, all this warmongering could mean was more sons, brothers and sweethearts would be sent to their deaths. She wished they would call a halt to the fighting while the politicians and the generals had proper talks to find a way to end the war once and for all. But it was clear that that wasn't going to happen as the new year arrived. Every week, more lads marched off to war and more families received the news that they would never see their sons again.

In Street, life went on. The factory was as busy as ever, although she knew that Mr Roger Clark spent much of his time trying to find the raw materials needed to ensure that they could continue to make quality boots and shoes. Leather was in short supply, as was rubber. Clarks were making wooden heels and using alternative materials instead of leather for the soles of boots and shoes. The other major shortage was men for labour. For the first time in Clarks' history, over half of the four thousand odd workers at the factory were women.

'Some of the lads in the Clicking Room are complaining about lasses taking their jobs,' said Lucas at supper one evening.

'It's daft,' complained John. 'Why can't they do what I'm doing and let me do a proper man's job?'

'You could've applied, but you wouldn't,' Peter pointed out. While he had started his apprenticeship in the Mechanics Shop, John had stayed in the Carton Room, making shoe boxes, complaining that he hated it but doing nothing to change his circumstances.

'With the shortages, I doubt they'll be making cardboard shoeboxes much longer,' said Lucas. 'You need to talk to your foreman and see what else you can do.'

John scowled. 'He hates me. He won't give me a chance.'

Jeannie sighed. 'He might if you showed willing,' she said. 'But if you're as miserable at work as you are here, he's probably sick and tired of you.'

John looked ready to argue with her, but Louisa leaned forward, as ever the peace-maker, and changed the subject. 'Jeannie, did Lucas tell you that Mr Davis lost his job today?'

Jeannie nodded. 'He did.'

'Goodness!' said Ma. 'I'm sorry the man's lost his livelihood, but I can't say anyone is surprised.'

Lucas chuckled. 'We're more surprised he lasted this long. But he was in his cups again today and ruined a whole hide of leather before the foreman realised what he was doing.'

Louisa sighed. 'You'd think he'd have learned his lesson after he was locked up after he attacked Kate.'

Kate's father had been sentenced to a fortnight's hard labour.

'I know,' he said. 'He was warned then that he'd only kept his job because of the labour shortages, but he wouldn't be getting any more chances. I doubt anyone else in the village will employ him, so him and his floozy are probably heading for the workhouse.'

Ma frowned. 'Those poor children of theirs haven't got a chance, have they?'

Jeannie shook her head. 'Ma, I doubt they ever did. They've no manners; their mother hasn't shown them a decent example. She's never done a day's work in her life and doesn't lift a finger at home, so what does that tell them? I know we must look for the good in people, but I fear that woman has no redeeming qualities and she's ruined those little ones forever.' She shivered as she remembered that awful day when she'd witnessed the Floozy almost choking Kate to death in front of the children. They weren't distressed by the violence. If anything, they were encouraging their ma to carry on.

Louisa nodded. 'Maybe going to the workhouse will be the making of them,' she said. 'After all, they'll be separated from their parents. Maybe they'll find a better example there.'

'At least they'll have to do as they're told and do some work to earn their keep,' said Lucas.

John dropped his cutlery onto his plate with a clatter. 'Who cares about that old fool and those parasites?' he demanded. 'What I want to know is why some lass is going to get Reggie's job and not me. It's not fair!'

Peter rolled his eyes. 'Make up your mind. You've been saying for months you were going to leave Clarks.'

His twin scowled at him. 'Yeah, and you all gang up on me and tell me I can't.' He nodded his head towards Louisa. 'And now we've got another mouth to feed.'

Louisa raised her eyebrows. 'I pay my way,' she said, not intimidated by the lad's sulky demeanour.

'For how long?' he demanded. 'You'll be expecting any minute now and we'll have to listen to you chucking up and whining while you put your feet up and—'

'That's enough!' roared Lucas. He pointed a finger at John. 'You will not talk to my wife like that, d'you hear me? Louisa works hard and contributes more to this family than you do, John Musgrove, with her wages and the help she gives Ma and Jeannie around the house, so don't you take your frustrations out on her.'

John glared back at him but didn't say anything. Jeannie and the others remained silent, although she was glad that Lucas had spoken up. John was never satisfied and she for one was heartily sick of his moaning and groaning about every little thing.

'Now, if you're so dissatisfied with your life,' Lucas went on. 'Do something about it, like Peter says. Either put yourself forward like he did and see what happens, or find yourself something else. But if you keep doing the same thing, you'll get the same results. But we're all tired of listening to you. You're all talk.'

'You never support me,' John snapped. 'No one respects me in this house.'

'John, love,' Ma started to say. She looked distressed. But Lucas didn't give her a chance to say any more.

'You get back what you give out in life,' said Lucas. 'If you want our respect, you've got to earn it. So stop complaining and *do something.*' They glared at each other for a long moment before Lucas spoke again. 'And you can start by helping Peter clear the table and wash up.'

'And what are you going to do?' sneered John. 'Go upstairs and canoodle with your missus?'

Lucas stood up so suddenly, his chair tipped, clattering to the floor. Jeannie jumped up to stop him as Louisa grabbed his arm. The last thing they needed was for the brothers to have a fist fight over the kitchen table. She opened her mouth to remonstrate with John, but Ma spoke up first.

'Stop it!' she cried, putting her hands to her temples. 'I can't bear it! I will not have this ill-feeling in my house.'

They all subsided. Ma rarely lost her temper, but it was clear she had reached her limit.

'Sorry, Ma,' mumbled Lucas as he righted his chair and sat back down, looking shame-faced.

Jeannie nodded and sat. 'Me too,' she said.

They all looked at John, who went red and looked down at his hands, which were clenched into fists on the table. He didn't say anything, ignoring his siblings, who glared at him.

Ma put her hands on the table and regarded her family with sad eyes. 'If you don't mind, I'd like to speak to John on his own,' she said quietly, her voice resigned but firm. 'Will the rest of you go into the parlour or to your rooms?'

'I'll clear the table,' said Jeannie, getting up and stacking the plates.

'No,' said Ma, not taking her gaze off her son. 'Leave them, Jeannie. I want to talk to John.'

Jeannie hesitated, but gave in and followed when the others got up and walked into the parlour. She looked back and received a nod from Ma before she closed the door between the two rooms. Lucas grabbed the poker and stirred the embers in the fireplace before shovelling some more coal on.

'Blithering idiot,' muttered Peter as he sank onto the settee.

'Let Lucas sit there with Louisa,' she told him. There wasn't room for three people on there and they only had room for one other chair by the hearth.

Lucas straightened up and shook his head. 'Leave him be,' he said, sitting in the armchair and pulling Louisa onto his lap. His wife blinked with surprise before she relaxed into his arms with a small smile. Jeannie looked away, a little embarrassed by this display of affection between her brother and best friend. But she wouldn't complain. It was good to see them getting along so well. She still worried about the two of them, but she had resolved not to interfere. If anything, she was relieved. Maybe one day, Louisa might look at Lucas with as much love as when she'd gazed at Mattie. Her brother deserved no less.

Jeannie sat next to Peter, aware that he was growing broader as well as taller and, typically, was spreading his long legs and leaving her with less space to sit. She nudged his side with her shoulder. 'Budge up,' she said. Without a word, he shifted to give her more room.

She could hear Ma's soft voice, although she had no idea what she was saying. They all sat in silence, no doubt each of them wondering what was going on. Jeannie doubted John would change. He'd always been demanding, always followed his own path and did his best to do as little work as possible. She was only grateful that, thanks to Tom's influence, Peter had chosen to follow a different route these days. He was working hard on his apprenticeship and less likely to follow John's lead into mischief than he used to be.

'So,' said Louisa softly, looking around at the three siblings. 'What can we do to help John? It's obvious he's not happy.'

Peter shrugged. 'He's an idiot. Yesterday, he said he thinks he can earn a living playing football. He's good, but he's not *that* good. He'll never put the work in.'

Lucas rolled his eyes. 'God help us. Even if he managed to get onto a professional team, what's he going to do when he's too old to play? He'd be lucky to get a few years in before younger, fitter lads come along behind him and take his place on the team.'

'That's what I told him. Like I said, he's an idiot.'

Louisa looked thoughtful. 'If he likes his football so much, why doesn't he train to be a physical education teacher?' She turned to Jeannie. 'Didn't Cyril next door say something about the board school wanting him to teach PE now that most of the male teachers have enlisted?'

Jeannie nodded. 'He did. But he can't, on account of his asthma.' The two girls had seen him when they'd walked home the other day and he'd fallen into step with them and chatted about his job. He hadn't asked about theirs. She got the impression that he didn't think what they did was as important as his profession. It had irritated her. How would he get along if he didn't have a decent pair of shoes on his feet? She might not have his book learning, but it didn't mean that working at Clarks was any less useful to the community as teaching children how to use a slide rule or to recite their times tables. It wasn't as though most people used that sort of knowledge once they left school.

Peter laughed. 'Can you imagine John as a teacher? I'd like to see that.'

Lucas chuckled as well. 'Nice idea, love,' he said to Louisa. 'But it's not likely. He'd never do the book learning to get his teaching certificate, even if he was tempted by the idea of teaching football.'

'He doesn't even like listening to the team coach. Thinks he knows it all,' Peter muttered.

Louisa shrugged. 'It was just a thought,' she said.

They were silent again. Ma was still talking, but now John was responding. Jeannie couldn't make out what they were saying, but he didn't sound quite so sulky as he had before. She hoped Ma could convince him to pull his socks up and be a bit more cheerful around the house. They were all tired of his whining.

'Speaking of teachers,' said Louisa, looking straight at Jeannie, her eyebrows raised.

'What?' she asked, frowning.

'Is Cyril still asking you to walk out with him?'

She sighed and closed her eyes. 'No,' she said. 'I've told him I'm not looking for a sweetheart.'

Peter snorted and she glared at him. 'I'm not!' she said.

He held up his hands. 'I didn't say anything.'

'No,' she said. 'But you've clearly got an opinion. Come on, out with it.'

He shrugged. 'None of my business. But you can do better than him, sis.'

She hadn't expected that. Nor did she expect Lucas and Louisa to agree with him. 'Why d'you say that?' she asked.

Another shrug. 'He's a weedy know-it-all. Always looks down his nose at me and John.'

'What do you mean?' asked Lucas.

Peter scrunched up his nose. 'Me and John were talking to Mr Baker over the fence and he came out. His grandpa told him I was going to be an engineer and he said I'd probably not last the apprenticeship seeing as how I left school at fourteen, on account of me not having enough grounding in mathematics.'

'Well that was rude,' said Louisa.

'I know,' he said, looking fed up.

'But I asked him if he'd help you and he said he could,' said Jeannie, frowning.

'Yeah, well, he *could*,' Peter replied. 'But I don't think he's inclined to. He probably only said it to get in your good books.'

'I'm sure he would if you asked him politely. I think he's a bit shy,' she said. She didn't know why she was defending him. She agreed with Peter's assessment of him. She might have been tempted to go out with him at first, but after that time at the front door with Tom, she'd told him no. Much as she wanted to fall in love and get married, Cyril wasn't her idea of a potential husband. The image of Tom flashed into her mind, but she banished it quickly. She couldn't afford to let him take over her thoughts. He might make her heart race, he might even be just about as perfect as she imagined her future husband might be, but he wasn't free, so she had to stop thinking about him. That didn't mean she was prepared to settle for Cyril, though.

'Actually, I think he's a bit stand-offish,' said Louisa, wrinkling his nose. 'Like Peter said, you can do better than him, Jeannie.'

Jeannie sighed. 'Maybe,' she conceded. She hadn't admitted how she really felt about Cyril – or about Tom for that matter – to anyone. She couldn't see the point. There was also the depressing thought at the back of her mind that, if this war went on for much longer, the Cyrils of this world might the only option for a lass if she didn't want to end up a spinster. Not for the first time, she wished with all her heart that Tom hadn't married his childhood sweetheart, only to lose her to his treacherous cousin.

A chair scraped on the stone floor in the kitchen and they all turned their attention to the door, the vexed question of Jeannie's love life, or lack of it, forgotten.

Ma appeared in the doorway. Behind her, they heard water flowing into the sink. 'Peter, love,' she said. 'Can you help John with the washing up, please?'

He nodded and she stepped out of the way so that he could enter the kitchen. She came in and took his place on the settee next to Jeannie.

'Everything all right, Ma?' asked Lucas.

She nodded, relaxing back onto the cushions. 'Give them a few minutes, then maybe Jeannie can make us a hot drink before we go to bed.'

They waited, listening to the sounds of the twins clearing up and washing the dishes. The lads were talking in low tones. It didn't sound like they were arguing for a change.

'John's going to see George Davis's father-in-law tomorrow after work. He's still got a notion that he'll prefer working at the haulage company rather than the factory,' Ma told them quietly. 'I've said I'll give him my blessing so long as he works hard and he doesn't give up his job at Clarks without having another to go to.'

Lucas frowned. 'But there's not much of a future in it, Ma. It's not like he can take over the company like George will one day.'

'I know, son,' she said with a sigh. 'But he's not happy and if we don't let him at least try something different, there'll be no living with him. I've told him, if it doesn't work out, he must go back to Clarks and put a bit more effort into finding something there that will give him more satisfaction.'

'I don't care what he does, so long as he changes his attitude and pulls his weight around here without all his complaining,' said Lucas. 'He's getting us all down.'

'That's exactly what I've told him,' said Ma. 'I want all my children to be happy. If letting him leave Clarks makes him happier, then maybe we can look forward to a return to harmony in this house.'

Jeannie grinned. 'I think that's a good solution, Ma,' she said. 'At least he didn't talk you into letting him try out for a professional football team.'

Ma smiled. 'Oh, he tried, love. But I soon put a stop to that. I'll not have a son of mine kicking a ball for a living when there's important work to be done. No. He can carry on playing for the local team, but only so long as he's gainfully employed and he keeps the peace with the rest of you.'

'Well, that's a blessing, at least,' she said, getting up and kissing Ma's cheek. 'I'll go and make those drinks.'

34

On a cold evening in late January, Kate finished reading the latest letter from Gerald. She had sent him a small watercolour that Louisa had painted and he had asked her to pass on his thanks. She knew that he saw little of the outside world. The small window in his cell was too high to gaze out of and only looked out onto a tall brick wall. He could catch glimpses of the sky, but hadn't seen any grass, trees or flowers for months. He appreciated Louisa's depiction of a wildflower meadow, saying it brought a little of God's kingdom into his bleak existence.

The current prison guards seemed to be decent sorts, treating the conscientious objectors with respect. But she knew that if one of the warders was transferred or enlisted, his replacement might not be so kind. Over the months, they had come and gone and some had been beastly to the prisoners.

There was a knock at the door. Auntie Betty was visiting an elderly Friend this evening, so Kate got up to see who was calling. She was nervous about opening the door to a visitor until she saw that it was Jeannie and Louisa.

'Oh, it's you,' she said, peeking through the crack she'd

opened, breathing a sigh of relief that it wasn't her pa. If it had been, she'd have slammed it shut and locked it sharpish. She opened the door wide. 'Come in out of the cold. Do you think we'll get snow?'

Her friends followed her into the kitchen and she busied herself making a pot of tea. As they waited for it to brew, she passed on Gerald's thanks to Louisa.

'I'm glad he liked it,' she said. 'I can do some more. Do you want to send some local views to your brothers? I know Lucas liked the picture I sent him of Glastonbury Tor. He said it was like having a piece of home with him when he was away.'

Kate smiled. 'That would be lovely,' she said.

She was glad to see how well-suited Louisa and Lucas were, even though both she and Jeannie had been concerned by the speed of their marriage at first. She supposed it was because the love affair between Lou and Mattie was so intense that they couldn't imagine her considering another man in her life. But she seemed content now and Lucas made her smile. It wasn't the same as her love for Mattie, but just because it was different didn't mean it wasn't just as valuable.

'How are they?' asked Jeannie.

Kate shrugged. 'They're well, I think. They keep in touch with Vi and Ada, and they tell me when they hear. But neither of them are big correspondents. I suppose it's better that they write to their wives rather than their sisters.' She sighed. 'I would like to hear from them directly now and again, though. I write to them every week.'

'I'm sure they think of you,' said Jeannie. 'But from what I hear around the factory, a lot of lads are bad correspondents.'

'I know,' she agreed. 'And at least they mention me in their letters to their wives.'

'At least you hear from Gerald,' said Louisa. 'He'll be back soon enough, won't he? Didn't you say his sentence ends in March? He'll be back in time for Easter.'

Kate huffed. 'Until they arrest him again. Honestly, it's a cruel form of torture. They serve their sentences, don't cause any trouble, then as soon as they get a taste of freedom, they turn up and start the process all over again. Surely by now they can see that Gerald's sincere in his beliefs, but will they give him an exemption certificate? No, they won't. They're monsters.'

'At least he's safe,' said Louisa. 'We should be grateful for that, at least.'

Kate touched Louisa's arm as all three of them thought of Mattie. 'You're right. We should count our blessings, shouldn't we?'

Jeannie nodded. 'They say the Hun have been attacking American ships with their U-boats, and if they don't stop, President Wilson will be sure to bring his country into the war on our side.'

'Much as I hate the thought of more ships being sunk, I can't help hoping they do,' said Kate. 'With America on our side, we'll win for sure.'

Jeannie sighed. 'I just want it to be over. You know John started working at the haulage company on his sixteenth birthday?'

'I heard. How's he getting on?'

'He's loving it so far,' said Louisa.

'Which means he's not so grumpy at home, thank goodness,' laughed Jeannie. 'Mind you, he's keen to learn to drive the lorries like your George did, Kate, but he won't be able to for another year, so he'll have to be content with going out with the drivers and helping them with deliveries. I think he's trying to persuade one or two of them to let him have a go so he'll be ready to step up as soon as he's seventeen. He's got some notion that, if he can drive the lorries, they'll let him be a tank driver when he enlists.' She shuddered. 'Me and Ma are praying day and night that peace is declared before the twins are eighteen. I'm having nightmares about them being trapped in a burning metal box on tracks. I daren't tell Ma.'

Louisa pulled a face. 'Lucas still has nightmares. It's so awful over there. It's worse in the winter, what with the cold as well as the mud. And they say the gas attacks are getting worse.'

Kate poured the tea and pushed a tin of biscuits across the table. 'Enough of that. I can't bear to think about it. What else can we talk about?'

'They're having another dance at the Crispin Hall to raise money for the war effort,' said Louisa. 'Are you two going?'

Jeannie shook her head.

Louisa tilted her head to one side. 'Not even if Tom goes?'

Jeannie groaned. 'This has nothing to do with Tom.'

Kate and Louisa shared a look. 'Of course it does,' said Kate.

Jeannie shook her head. 'It *can't* have anything to do with him. It's impossible,' she said firmly.

'But you wish it wasn't, don't you?' Louisa pushed her gently.

Jeannie's eyes filled with tears. 'There's no point in wishing, so can we please talk about something else?'

'Sorry, love,' said Louisa, looking a bit shame-faced.

Kate took pity on them both. 'I hear Pa and the Floozy have sold just about every stick of furniture in the house,' she said. 'They've been trying to get relief from the parish.'

'He's still out of work, then?'

She nodded. 'He's had the odd day's work in one of the quarries, but as usual, the minute he had some money in his pocket, he spent it on cider. When they realised he was turning up to work drunk, they let him go. The last thing they need in a quarry is a man in his cups when they're working with explosives and pickaxes. It sounds like Pa's reached the point where he'll either have to move away to find work, or it'll be the workhouse for them.'

'He's not bothering you, though, is he?' asked Jeannie.

She shook her head. 'No. The magistrate bound him over and said if he heard he bothered me again, he'd put him back in jail for breaching the peace.' She didn't add that she was much more cautious these days, making sure she was aware of who was around her as she walked the roads and lanes. She never wanted to be taken unawares like that again. She'd spotted the Floozy and her brats a few times and managed to stay well out of their way. Pa had been nowhere to be seen. 'He did try and bother Ada and Vi, knowing my brothers were away. But Ada's pa paid him a visit and threatened him. He's keeping his distance now. You know Pa – he's a coward when it comes to real men.'

'He must be paying his rent, though,' said Louisa. 'Otherwise he'd have been evicted by now.'

Kate shrugged. 'Who knows? They might just be hiding when the rent man comes to call.' That was the more likely explanation. She'd seen how easily the Floozy and her children could slip away quietly when they needed to. 'Truth be told, I'm past caring. It would be a relief if they left Street and never came back.'

Jeannie sighed. 'Why is it that the people we want to see the back of hang around and make nuisances of themselves while the ones we want around are being sent off without a by-your-leave?'

'Life's not fair,' agreed Louisa. 'If it was, there'd be no war.'

'They promised it would be over within a few months,' said Jeannie. 'But it's been two and a half years now and there's no end in sight.'

Kate rolled her eyes. 'Listen to us. We're turning into moaning Minnies, aren't we? Life's been tough for everyone, but it's not all been bad, has it? I managed to escape from Pa and the Floozy, and

I'm standing on my own two feet. Lou's married, so her ma can't control her life any more. Lucas is home safe. And, even though you're not able to be with Tom, Jeannie, at least you've learned what's important to you and you won't settle for someone who doesn't deserve you.'

'You're right,' said Louisa. 'It's not the life we expected, but we've got a measure of control we didn't have two and a half years ago. I'm content – which is more than I could have hoped for.'

'So am I.' Kate nodded. 'Thanks to Auntie Betty, I'm learning to live life the best way I can. I thought after Ma died and Ted rushed off to war, I'd never be happy again. But I'm doing all right.' She would never admit how much she missed him and how much it had meant to get news of him, even though it was vague and might not be true.

Jeannie looked thoughtful. 'I suppose so,' she said. 'When you put it like that, I've learned that if I can't have what I want, I'll still survive. It doesn't mean I have to accept something I don't want.'

Kate nudged her shoulder against Jeannie's. 'Exactly. And you found your temper, didn't you? It was a joy to see, you tipping those drinks over Douglas and Doris.'

They all giggled as they remembered that night at the Crispin Hall.

'And don't forget how she brought Sid to his knees as well,' said Louisa.

Jeannie covered her face, but they knew she was laughing with them. 'No wonder I can't find a man. They all think I'm going to attack them!'

'Tom doesn't think that,' said Louisa with a smile. She held up a hand when Jeannie would have protested. 'No, it's obvious he thinks highly of you. We're all sorry that he's not free to declare himself for you, Jeannie. But if I've learned anything in my life, it's that we can't take anything for granted. You might think it's hopeless, but who knows what the future holds? I certainly never expected to marry after I lost Mattie. But Lucas came to my rescue when I needed it, and I'm sure we're going to have a good life together.' She paused as she studied Jeannie's expression. 'I know you've been worried, that I don't love him how he deserves to be loved. But I promise you, Jeannie, I think the world of Lucas and I'll be the best wife I can for him. God willing, he'll never regret taking me on.'

Jeannie nodded, too choked to speak. Kate put an arm around her shoulders.

'Lou's right,' she said. 'Who knows what the future holds? All we can do is make the best of it. Even after everything that's happened since this rotten war started, we've survived and we're together, aren't we? I doubt if I'd have managed it without you two.'

'Yes, you would,' said Jeannie, her voice scratchy. 'You're stronger than you think.'

'We all are,' agreed Louisa. 'We're the Three Musketeers, remember? *All for one and one for all...*'

The others smiled and joined in. *'United we stand, divided we fall.'*

ACKNOWLEDGEMENTS

Thank you for reading the third in my stories about the Clarks Factory Girls. Kate, Jeannie and Louisa have suffered a lot as the war continues, but their friendship and fortitude has helped them to survive and thrive.

Some of the things that have happened in this book are based on real events, the records of which are held in the archives of the Alfred Gillett Trust in Street, Somerset. For example, in the Clarks' Managers' Meeting Minutes, I found reference to a foreman who needed urgent treatment for a heart condition but didn't survive long enough to receive treatment from the specialist consultant that Clarks called in to see the man. That inspired Louisa's father's story. Also, I read heartbreaking letters from conscientious objectors, written to Mrs Esther Clothier from their prison cells, describing their treatment. Some of these incidents are included in the letters that Kate and Jeannie receive from the young men they write to. The gift of flowers picked by Master Peter Clothier is real, as is the wonderful response from the recipient, and I couldn't resist using it for Gerald's story. Such kindness from a young child is an inspiration to us all, especially in such dark times.

As ever, I would like to thank my wonderful editor at Boldwood Books, Rachel Faulkner-Willcocks, for helping me to make this book the best it can be; Colin Thomas for the superb cover design; the super marketing team led by Claire Fenby for spreading the word about it; and the family of Boldwood authors who continue to encourage and cheer me along. I'm also delighted and humbled by the wonderful responses I've received from readers. Thank you taking the trouble to get in touch.

The fourth and final book in the series will follow in a few months, when the friends will see the war end and loved ones return to Street. As peace returns to the country, Kate, Jeannie and Louisa will find their places in the new order of things and their enduring friendship will keep them strong.

ABOUT THE AUTHOR

May Ellis is the author of more than five contemporary romance and YA fiction novels. She lives in Somerset, within sight of Glastonbury Tor. Inspired by her move to the area and her love of social history, she is now writing saga fiction – based on the real-life stories of the Clarks factory girls.

Sign up to May Ellis' newsletter for EXCLUSIVE bonus content and see the wedding from the point of view of Beverley.

Visit May's website: www.alisonroseknight.com

Follow May on social media here:

 facebook.com/alison.knight.942

instagram.com/alisonroseknight

bookbub.com/authors/alison-knight

ALSO BY MAY ELLIS

The Clarks Factory Girls

The Clarks Factory Girls at War

Courage for the Clarks Factory Girls

Dark Times for the Clarks Factory Girls

Standalones

Lily's Choice

Sixpence Stories

Introducing Sixpence Stories!

Discover page-turning historical novels from your favourite authors, meet new friends and be transported back in time.

Join our book club
Facebook group

https://bit.ly/SixpenceGroup

Sign up to our
newsletter

https://bit.ly/SixpenceNews

Boldwœd

Boldwood Books is an award-winning fiction publishing company seeking out the best stories from around the world.

Find out more at www.boldwoodbooks.com

Join our reader community for brilliant books, competitions and offers!

Follow us
@BoldwoodBooks
@TheBoldBookClub

Sign up to our weekly
deals newsletter

https://bit.ly/BoldwoodBNewsletter

Printed in Great Britain
by Amazon